When Justice turned her gaze to him Sterling felt the full strength of her beauty. Yet he saw something else. Looking deeply into her eyes he drank in her soul. And it mesmerized him. It was something that couldn't be put into words. And he wanted her. He reached out to touch her cheek.

Justice turned her mouth to his hand and brushed her moist lips across it.

Sterling hissed his excitement. "Justice, I think you should know…"

"Shush," she said putting her forefinger to his lips. "I never knew what it felt like to be struck by lightning until I met you. I know it sounds like a cliché, but Sterling Hart, I've never acted like this before," she paused as she stared into his round, black pupils, "I would very much like for you to make love to me."

The silence was deafening. With deliberation Sterling placed his glass on the end table, stood, and in one swift motion lifted Justice into his arms.

Skeletons in the Closet

MICHELE CAMERON

ISBN: 13:978-0988950924
ISBN 10: 0988950928

DEDICATION

I dedicate Skeletons in the Closet to two very special men in my life: Philip Cameron, my brother, and his son, my only nephew, Philip James Cameron III.

ACKNOWLEDGMENTS

I would like to take this time to thank the following people: my editor, Sidney Rickman and my line editor Marguerite Lemons. I would be remiss not to include my graphic artist, Jeff Lancashire. website: http://www.adjacentdesign

CONTENTS

CHAPTER 1

Justice Fairchild heaved a long sigh. A truck carrying livestock rumbled past and she put her hand over her nose to ward off the stench of manure. Once the intersection cleared, she drove to the far end of town, commonly referred to as 'Skid Row.' She averted her eyes from the depressing sight of dilapidated houses, belonging to the poorest citizens of Eastman. Another quarter of a mile she made a sharp right turn onto the unpaved road that took her home.

Shutting off her car engine, she stared a critical eye at the blue tarp that had been covering the roof since the last hurricane, and the screen door on the front porch which was barely hanging on the hinges. Then she spied her mother at the clothesline. Brushing her discouraged feelings aside, she teasingly hollered out the window, "Mom, it's six o'clock and you still have that rag on your head?"

"I got more important things to think about than how I look. I got to get this house looking the best I can." Evelyn's southern drawl was laced with uneasiness.

The smile immediately left Justice's face. She went to her mother and after giving her a peck on the cheek lifted the straw basket full of clothes and walked towards the house. "I thought Aunt Minnie was coming over to help you today."

"She's at the church," Evelyn explained as she followed her. "One of the deaconesses from the mission department called an emergency meeting. Sister Templeton and her children are about to lose their house and the church needs to come up with the money to catch up their mortgage payments."

"Again?" The corners of Justice's mouth turned downward. "Last time she came to church she needed a new refrigerator. It's always something with them."

"Some people need more help than others, Justice."

"Some people depend on others to bail them out of their mistakes, Mother," she retorted.

"Everyone doesn't have the daughter that I do, Justice." Evelyn patted her on the arm. "I can always count on you."

"Mom," Justice said quietly.

"Yes?"

"Do you ever wish that you'd never met daddy?"

Evelyn stared at her daughter in absolute horror. "Of course not!

Why would you ask me such a thing?"

"It's just that," Justice said slowly, choosing her words carefully, "ever since Daddy passed you've been alone. Maybe if you'd married someone else you wouldn't be...," she said hesitantly, "so broke."

"I may not have money, but I have wealth in other ways. I have my memories."

"But is that enough? Are you being fair to yourself by not giving yourself a chance to let someone else make you happy?"

"I'm content, Justice. From the moment I set eyes on your father I wanted him. I won't settle for any other kind of love."

She searched her mother's face. "But don't you get lonely, Mom?"

"Only for your father, Justice. I think 'it's better to have loved and lost than never to have loved at all', as they say. I pray one day you'll find a man that you love as much as I did him. Then you'll know what I mean."

Justice, lying on her bed blocked the sunlight out with her arm. The faint musky smell of mold from the leaking roof drew her eyes to the ceiling. Unhappily, she focused on the stain that had widened even more during last few months. Justice closed her eyes and whispered, "Lord, when the county supervisor comes today to look at the property, please guide him to write a good report. We don't have the money to buy another house."

The sound of a bird chirping outside her window interrupted her prayer. A red-breasted robin sat on a limb in the oak tree she used to climb as a small child. Grinning, she pointed at the bird. "You wait right there."

Justice practically skipped to the kitchen. She opened a cabinet and grabbed a bag of bird seed and went outside. She scattered it in the patches of grass under the tree.

The bird looked at the seed, looked at her, and then flew away.

"Ahh!" she exclaimed. "Aren't you ungrateful?"

A chuckling sound made her turn around to face her mother.

"She's not ungrateful, Justice. She's just shy. She'll probably come back later when no one's around. You'll probably see the evidence of that on your car."

Justice made a grimace and pointed at the rusted out Focus in the sand pebbled driveway. "Bird crap on my car would be an improvement. Hopefully they'll deposit enough to camouflage the peeling red paint."

"They just might," Evelyn said as she eased herself into the weathered rocking chair on the front porch. "Birds love the color red."

Justice carefully scrutinized her mother's face. *She looks tired.* "Mom, are you feeling okay?"

"I'm fine," Evelyn replied. "I was on the way to your room to wake you, but I heard the screen door close and knew you was out here messing with them birds again."

"I just love this time of year in Eastman." Justice drew in a deep breath, drinking in the fresh air. She plopped down on the front porch step closest to her mother. "The sky is blue and the leaves are every shade of orange and red. Georgia in the fall is absolutely beautiful."

"And so are you," Evelyn said as she gazed at her daughter. "Every day you grow more and more striking. If I hadn't carried you myself and given birth to you at home I'd declare that you was someone else's child."

"I look just like you, even down to your large doe eyes. Everyone says so."

"Your face may look like mine but you possess a self-assurance that I never had," Evelyn commented. "And you get your height from your father, God rest his soul. You're six feet tall and you walk like you're floating on air."

"You make me sound like a giraffe," Justice protested. "I'm only five nine."

"The boys around here are so intimidated they won't even ask you out. You haven't had a real relationship since you and Miles Turner broke up."

Suddenly a shadow settled on Justice's delicate features. The memory of how Miles left town without saying goodbye still made her blood boil. "That was a blessing in disguise."

"So you never hear from Miles?"

"No." Justice averted her head, hiding her expression. "And I don't care to. I heard he's up north somewhere."

Her mother sent her a sharp look. "Don't let one bad relationship taint your opinion of all men, Justice."

"I don't think that I've done that," Justice replied defensively. "But he was my first, and he treated it like it was nothing… I won't make that mistake again."

"I'm sorry he hurt you so badly, Justice." Observing her daughters drooping shoulders Evelyn decided to let the matter drop.

"I just want to get started on my career," Justice said in a wistful voice.

"Someday you're going to be a great designer, Justice," Evelyn said with conviction. "You've been making your own clothes since you was in the sixth grade."

Justice made a face. "Yeah, and everyone knew they were homemade and laughed at me."

"They were just jealous. I'd get some material off the bargain table and you'd make a dress that was better than the stuff that they bought in the stores."

"They certainly were better than the clothes in the store where I work now," Justice admitted. "Mabel's clothes are ridiculously expensive and the seams rip apart. I know that because we have a lot of returns."She gave a snort of disgust. "They're an embarrassment to fashion. I can't wait to save enough money to enroll in design school and get away from that place."

"How much more you got to get?" Evelyn gave her a quizzical look.

"I have almost twenty-five hundred dollars. That's enough for half a semester."

"You'd have more saved if you wasn't always havin' to give me money to make ends meet." A guilty look stole across Evelyn's face. "I feel like I should go back to work."

"You know that you can't go to work so why fret about something out of your control?" Justice gave her mother a reproving look. "You are disabled from the fall you took at the school on that wet floor."

"I'm able to work." Her mother's lips pursed in anger. "They just don't want me suing them again."

"You can't sue them again," Justice gently reminded her. "That was part of the agreement for you to get disability checks."

"Well, now I wish that I hadn't signed that paper. The money they give me a month doesn't do much more than feed us with the rising costs everything."

"I do think that we should have gotten a better lawyer," Justice said with a scowl. "We should have gotten someone outside of Eastman and not off a commercial. I think ours was in the pocket of the insurance company."

"You might be right," Evelyn said in reflection. "But that guy was someone that one of the church members recommended."

"That was our first mistake. The minute I saw him I felt that he was a shyster. He probably took a cut under the table."

"If he did, one day he'll meet his Maker and have to explain to God what he did. You can't mess with God's children and get away with it forever. One day all of us will have to own up to the bad things we done and it doesn't always take forever. I'm seeing more and more people being punished right here on earth for their bad deeds."

"Amen, hallelujah," Justice chuckled as she clapped her hands.

"Don't play around like that, girl," Evelyn said, chastising her."God is omniscient. He sees and hears everything we do."

Justice couldn't help but give a fearful look behind her.

"I wish that things were different for you. If you had a brother or sister they could take some of the load off you."

"I love being an only child. I don't have to share your attention with anyone else," she laughed. "You've spoiled me ridiculously."

"I spoiled you?" Evelyn put her index finger to her chest. "You behave like the parent and I'm the child."

"Mom," she protested, "I'm twenty-five years-old and living at home. I'm an adult. I should help out."Justice added proudly, "Besides, I've worked a deal with the school. If I can come up with a year's fee they'll let me take out a promissory note for the second year. I should be in school this time next year."

"How did you manage to get the school to agree to that?"

"I told you, Mom." Justice gave her mother a confident look. "I'm an adult."

Justice stepped out of the shower. After drying off she hurried back into the bedroom. Planting her hands on her hips she eyed her closet. I'm so tired of looking the same way. Instead of reaching for the black trousers and white shirt she usually wore every Friday, she grabbed a black silk A-line dress that fell mid-thigh. I don't want to wear a thong with this dress. If I forget and bend over anyone in the vicinity will be able to see my business. Justice opened her dresser drawer and pulled out a pair of boy-shorts underpants and put them on. Then she began scrounging around for a strapless bra. Where is it? Deciding the search was futile she grabbed the dress and pulled it over her head. I'll have to wear a jacket in front of Mom or I'll hear her mouth. Grabbing a shrug she pulled it on. After brushing her black shoulder length hair and securing it into a ponytail she slid into a pair of black patent leather flats.

When she walked into the kitchen she saw her mother at the table with her head bent over a pile of bills. "Maybe I should stay home from work. I don't think that you should have to handle the inspection alone," she said with a worried look on her face.

"I'll be all right. Anyhow, I doubt if a decision will be made right away," she muttered. "They'll probably just take notes."

Justice placed her hands on her hips, her stance showing her annoyance. "I would have taken a vacation day if I'd known Minnie wasn't going to be here to support you."

"Now what could you do to change the outcome if you were here, Justice?" Evelyn smiled, the wrinkles around her eyes crinkling, "It is what it is," she finished softly.

There was a brooding silence in the room.

"Now go to work and don't worry about none of this," Evelyn said. "I'll be fine."

"I'm going to call you on my break and check on you," Justice said. She bent over and kissed her mother's smooth skin. "Try to have a good day, Mom."

"Drive safely and don't speed."

"Like I could even if I wanted to." Justice also smiled, trying to lighten the atmosphere and stave off the feeling of foreboding she felt as she walked out the door.

Outside, she stared at the spattered bird poop. She shook her head in amazement. Mom certainly has a way of knowing things.

"Justice."

"Yes, ma'am." Justice turned from the table of cowl neck shirts she was folding to face the store's owner, Mabel Flowers.

"Once you finish that table, I want you to redo the front window. Take those outfits off the mannequins." She pointed to a rack of clothes behind the counter. "And replace them with those."

"Yes, Miss Mabel."

The old white-haired woman gave her a smile. "You're such a good worker. I don't know what I'd do without you."

Justice carefully removed the pins from the back of the dress of one of the mannequins and placed them in a ceramic dish. Once the mannequin was bare, she pulled a bright yellow gauze dress over its head. Bending over, she lifted it and slid on different shoes. An ominous sensation that she was being watched sent a shiver down her spine.

Turning around, her eyes were drawn to a man who stood off to one side observing her. He was short, probably only about five feet six inches. He had shiny jet black hair and a small gold stud in one ear. His skin was swarthy and he was dressed in black from head to toe. When he realized that she'd caught him staring at her, instead of looking away, his penetrating, black eyes held her gaze. Then with his eyes he very deliberately perused Justice from head to toe.

Justice's body stiffened in response. She was used to men gawking at her but the demeanor of the stranger was unnerving. She shot him a look of censure before she deliberately turned her back to him. When Justice completed her task of dressing the remaining mannequins, surreptitiously looked over her shoulder. The man was gone. With the agility of a gazelle she stepped out of the window and walked over to the counter. She said to her coworker, "Nell, I'm going to break. See you in an hour."

"Take your time," Nell said. "Mabel's gone for the day and I'm not going on break until six o'clock."

"Why so late?"Justice asked.

"The fashion show at the hotel is at seven. I'm going to that and afterwards I'm going home." Nell gave Justice a look of astonishment. "I'm surprised you're not going since fashion is your thing."

"The fashion show!" Justice slammed the palm of her hand against her forehead in consternation. "I completely forgot about it."

"What time do you get off tonight?" Nell asked.

"I have to close," Justice answered in a disgruntled voice. She planted her elbows on the counter and cupped her face. "Not only do I have to miss the show, but I have to drive my wreck on those dark roads. I hate it. With my hour drive I won't get home until after midnight."

"If I were you, I'd stop by the club on the way home. Things don't start hopping until after midnight."

"You know I don't like the club scene. Besides, I didn't bring anything to change into."

"Change?" Nell repeated her words with wide eyes. "You're kidding me, right? Do you even see yourself, Justice? You can go as is and still pull more dudes than someone who's been in front of a mirror for hours."

"I've got a lot on my mind," she mumbled in a morose tone. "I don't have a lot of time for that sort of thing right now."

"Nothing's wrong at home, is it?" Nell asked, genuine concern reflected in her eyes.

"I don't know. I'm going to call my mother during my break and find out."

Justice sat at a small table in the mall courtyard. The plate of bourbon chicken with fried rice sat untouched. Crossing her fingers she opened her cell phone and hit number one on her call list. After a long series of rings the phone was picked up.

"Hello."

Justice heard tears in her mother's voice.

"What happened?" she demanded in a shrill voice, attracting the attention of the people at the next table. Then she whispered, "Mother, why are you crying?"

"The county inspector levied all kinds of fines on our property. We'll never be able pay them."

"Why did he do that?" Justice asked in a distressed voice.

"He said that the roof makes it unfit for us to live in the house."

"That's our problem, not his," Justice said in a harsh tone.

"Evidently not," she said. "He said that if we don't get the roof fixed in a month he's going to condemn the place."

"A month?" Justice echoed. "Did you tell him that our insurance company folded and that's why we haven't had the roof fixed?"

"I told him that there were so many claims in the county after the series of hurricanes that our company filed bankruptcy so they didn't have to pay its customers."

"Mom, did you show him the estimate? The lowest bid was twelve thousand dollars."

"He don't care nothin' about that," Evelyn whispered. "He levied even more fines besides the roof. We need about thirty-five thousand dollars to make this place habitable. We can never come up with that amount of money."

"What did Aunt Minnie say?"

"She said that we'll have to move."

Justice gave a snort of frustration.

"The banks aren't giving out loans for remodeling, only purchasing a home and you have to have good credit for that. Something we don't have," Evelyn ended in a forlorn voice.

"You can have the money I've saved."

"No," her mother stated emphatically. "Besides, that wouldn't solve the problem." After a small silence she said, "I'm going to start looking for an apartment for us in the morning. Do I need a one bedroom or a two?"

"What do you mean?" Justice responded, slowly, still overwhelmed with all the information she'd received.

"I thought that you might want to get a place of your own," her mother said in a forlorn voice. "You'd be better off."

"Don't you dare say that to me, Mother! I'm not going to move out when you need me."

"I'm not your responsibility, Justice," she said quietly.

"We're a family." Justice swallowed the lump in her throat. "We stick together." After Justice hung up the telephone, she stood and threw her untouched plate of food into the garbage can and lost in thought, went back to work. The store was devoid of customers, and she flipped through her latest fashion magazine. Once again she felt the sensation of being watched. She looked up and found herself face to face with the man she'd seen earlier and this time he was flanked by two people. They walked towards her.

The man with the swarthy complexion stuck his hand out and said with quiet authority, "My name is Caesar Brabantio." His Italian accent was so heavy she barely understood him.

"Hello," she offered hesitantly. "I'm Justice Fairchild."

The tallest of the trio said, "My name is Rossi." He possessed beautiful green eyes. His hair was cut into a black Mohawk and he wore a white barber's jacket. He too stuck his hand out.

Not knowing what else to do, Justice shook it and found his handshake oddly comforting. Then her attention was arrested by the last of the group. He said nothing yet his eyes spoke volumes as they stared at her breasts. The store was unusually warm so she'd taken off her jacket. Her breasts strained against the silk fabric and her nipples protruded. When she felt three pair of eyes on them she crossed her arms across the front of her shielding them from their sight.

Caesar gave a slight smile at her defensive gesture. He pointed to the remaining man who had not introduced himself. "This is my son, Cassius." He cleared his throat. "Let me get to the point. I am one of the designers from the show being held at the hotel."

"You are!" Justice exclaimed in astonishment, dropping her arms. Then when she saw Cassius's eyes staring at her breasts again, she defensively covered them.

"Do not hide your beauty," Caesar softly scolded her. "It is nothing to be ashamed of. I saw you earlier and meant to approach you so we could set up a possible meeting for tomorrow but I had an emergency phone call. One of my models has missed her plane and I would like you to take her place."

Stunned by his statement, Justice's mouth gaped open. "I'm no model," she gasped.

"But you could be," he replied quietly. "You strut like a gazelle."

Justice gave him a stern look. "Reputable designers do not walk up to total strangers in a mall and offer them a modeling job."

"They do when they're desperate."

Rossi turned to Caesar and spoke rapid words in Italian.

"What did he just say to you?" Justice demanded.

"He said that that your hair is natural and not a weave. He said because of that it will take more time to fix it for the show."

"He has a lot of nerve," Justice said in a curt tone.

"Rossi is a hairdresser. You must grow a, what do you Americans call it? Oh, yes, a thick skin if you are going to be a model. Always be open to criticism. It is the way you improve."

"Stop!" Justice held her hand up saying, "I'm not interested in being a model. I like to eat too much."

"You can eat. You are young. You will burn off your food intake." He did another quick perusal of her body. "How old are you?"

"I'm twenty-five years old," Justice replied.

"You look seventeen. Ethnic women do not age in the face as some others do. But if you desire to be a superstar in this business you must hurry because you would be considered old by many."

"I don't care if I'm considered old," Justice said, stung by the insinuation that she was over the hill. "I don't want to be a model."

Caesar made a sweeping gesture that encompassed the room. "This is what you desire out of life?"

"No," Justice stammered. "I want to be a designer. This job is just an ends to a means."

"I do not understand what that means. But if you are going to accommodate me we must hurry. You have to be at the hotel in twenty minutes so they can get started on your hair and makeup. They may only have to pin the waist of your gown because you have almost identical body measurements to Raven."

"Raven?" Justice asked.

Caesar stated with a hard inflection, "The model that did not make the show."

"I don't know the first thing about modeling," Justice protested.

"You are a natural. Just follow the other girls and you will make do for tonight."

"And I don't trust you," Justice said slowly. She pointed at Cassius. "And I certainly do not trust him."

Cassius' eyes hardened yet he said nothing.

"Cassius is harmless," Caesar said with a flash of his white teeth. "He has a wife and children. His bark is worse than his bite."

"But I don't want to be a model. I want to be a designer."

"I do not know if you have any talent in that field."

Justice bristled.

"What better way to find out if you do have talent than to work close in that field and make contacts? Everything in this world takes money. Even designers have to purchase material," Caesar said with a small smile.

"I'm the only person remaining to work the rest of the night." Justice hesitated. "I can't leave my job."

"Are they willing to pay you ten thousand dollars?" Caesar demanded in a harsh voice.

"Ten thousand dollars?" The memory of her mother bent over a table scattered with bills that morning as she left for work came to the forefront of her consciousness. "You're willing to pay me that?"

"Yes." He handed her a business card. "If you are at the suite in fifteen minutes and don't fall down on the runway."

"Why are you so desperate for me to model?" She held her hands out in bewilderment. "Can't one of your other models wear Raven's clothes?"

"All designers need to have at least four different models in the show. This is my first American show. My reputation is at stake," Caesar added quietly.

Justice studied the honest yet anxious look on Caesar's face. Then she looked at Rossi and he gave her a small nod of encouragement. Lastly, she focused on Cassius who appeared bored by the discussion.

"I," Justice stated in a calm voice, "want a cashier's check handed to me at the close of the show."

Justice noted that now Cassius' top lip curled with derision.

Justice anxiously skimmed the reference sheet for Mabel's home telephone number. Once she found it she quickly dialed the number. It went straight to voicemail. "Mrs. Flowers, this is Justice. I'm trying to reach you because something of an emergency has cropped up. I'm the only employee here so I have to close the store early. I'll explain better when I see you." Then she added as an afterthought, "I'm sorry."

Justice grabbed her purse and store keys. Quickly punching in the security code she locked the store. Once she got outside, clenching the business card in her hand, Justice sped to the elevator and pressed the button for the top floor. After glancing at her wristwatch she allowed herself to breath. Five minutes. Justice lifted her arms and smelled her armpits. Not great, but I'll do. She exited the elevator and spied the white floor sign with the words, House of Brabantio scrawled on it . Justice pressed the buzzer to the suite.

Immediately the door was flung open and she took a step backwards shocked by the mayhem. Half-naked models in heels walked freely around the room. Two chairs in front of large mirrors held models having their hair styled. The mixture of hair spray and perfume almost made her gag. The sight of the cart of cheese and crackers made Justice's stomach growl and she wished that earlier that day she hadn't thrown away her meal. With relief she spotted Rossi and he waved her over.

As Justice made her way across the room to him she felt the interest of every other occupant.

Someone whispered, "Who is that?"

"Where is Caesar?" Justice asked, giving him a tentative smile.

"He had to go and let the production team know of the changes. Usually Raven goes out first but we changed the order of things to give us time to get you ready. You'll be the last one of our models for each segment."

Justice gave a derogatory snort. "Since I don't know what I'm doing that makes sense."

"Don't put yourself down, darling." He wagged a finger in her face. "In the modeling world there are plenty of people more than willing to do that for you."

"I find that surprising. Every time I see models on television they look like the happiest women on earth."

"Ha!" Rossi replied. "That's for the benefit of the camera. Models can be the most insecure, self-involved, back-biting bitches on the planet. And you best remember that, or they'll eat you alive."

"It doesn't really matter to me. I'm only here for the night."

"We shall see," Rossi answered. "Since we have only a skeleton crew, Caesar has instructed me to take charge of you. We have to go to Raven's room and try on her wardrobe and make adjustments."

"Okay," Justice mumbled.

He turned and shouted, "Lucille, we're ready."

An elderly bespectacled woman who looked totally out of place next to the tall model she was talking to turned around. Quickly giving Justice an appraising look she nodded at Rossi. "I'm on my way."

"Follow me," Rossi said.

"Take that dress off," Lucille ordered as she turned to a rack of garments hung on a rolling clothing rack.

Justice slid a look at Rossi who stood watching with his arms folded in front of him.

Lucille turned to Justice and held an apple green martini dress towards her. "Why have you not done what I asked of you?" she demanded sharply.

"I'd like to change in the bathroom if you don't mind," Justice answered, trying not to show her nervousness at getting naked in front of strangers.

"Why?" Lucille asked, eyes wide open with astonishment.

Suddenly a burst of Italian flowed from Rossi.

As he spoke Lucille began to laugh and the crow's feet around her eyelids became more pronounced.

"What did you say to her?" She gave him a scathing look. "Haven't you heard that it's impolite to speak a foreign language when you know someone in the group doesn't understand what you're saying?"

"I'm sorry, darling. I was just explaining to Lucille that you are shy about disrobing in front of me because I am a man. She laughs because I am in a committed relationship with my male partner and have no interest whatsoever in the female body."

"Oh," Justice replied weakly and began disrobing. Once she was completely naked, Lucille gave Justice a thorough perusal. She looked at Rossi. "We will not have to tape her breasts." Lucille reached out and cupped one gently, making it jiggle.

A shock of surprise rocked Justice's body. Refusing to run and seek shelter, she slightly lifted her chin and locked eyes with Lucille.

"Raven has a problem on her hands." Lucille was practically giggling.

"Yes, she does," Rossi agreed with satisfaction.

Justice sat in a barber's chair and watched Rossi as he combed through her hair, piling it on top.

"It's very important that you do not look down as you walk the runway," he said. "Try to think mundane thoughts so the expression on your face does not detract from the beauty of your clothes."

"Do you mean sad?"

"No, because that would be reflected in your features. Try to think about something that gives you neither joy nor pain. Do not grin. That is the kiss of death on the runway."

"Oh my God! " Justice said nervously, placing her hand on her forehead. "I don't think that I'm up to this."

"Do not touch your face!" Rossi barked sharply. "I just spent thirty minutes on your make-up."

Justice dropped her hand and let it rest in her lap clenching the other.

With a look of intense concentration Rossi pulled, teased, and spritzed her hair until it stayed in place by itself.

Justice stared at her reflection in the mirror. Her only jewelry was yellow gold earrings that fell to her shoulders. Her large round eyes seemed to be sunken into her face. Different hues of green eye shadow looked like a rainbow on her lids. Her lips were painted a mauve gloss.

"Don't you think that this is too much makeup, Rossi? I don't even look like myself."

"No model does, darling. Don't worry," he said with certainty. "This is your coming out party and you'll most likely end up being the star."

"I hope I don't fall," she breathed.

"Models fall all the time," Rossi said, brushing that aside. "But if you do go down, get back up and continue your walk. That will make everyone looking think that you're a pro. Now we need to hurry to the runway. I'll be with you right before you go out for each segment."

When Justice stood in her six-inch heels she was taller than Rossi.

Lucille had been sitting on a settee on the other side of the room watching Rossi's creative process. Now she got up and walked over to them. She made a motion for Justice to turn around.

Justice slowly made a circle and then looked at Lucille.

"Walk to the other side of the room. Stop. Pivot from one foot to the other. Cross one foot over the other and turn around; then come back to the same spot."

Justice slowly walked the length of the room. She stopped, pivoted, crossed one foot over the other and turned. Then she sauntered back.

"Do it again and try not to walk as if you just got fucked," Lucille ordered.

"What?" Justice exclaimed.

"Stop swaying your hips so much." Lucille said in a musing tone, "I don't think you can help it, but you walk as if you just got some dick."

Justice tried to swallow the ball of angst that made her chest feel tight. Then she walked again. When she reached Lucille and Rossi again she looked at them questioningly.

Lucille turned to Rossi and spoke in Italian. He responded in Italian.

"What did she say?" she asked Rossi.

"She said that you will be the star of the show and I agree." A satisfied smirk hovered around his mouth. "Let's go."

CHAPTER 2

The bright red runway was centered in the middle of the hotel foyer. A large area makeshift dressing room walls sheltered the models from the view of any bystanders who happened to walk by or tried to get a peek at the models as they changed.

Justice followed Rossi and Lucille as they went to join the other Brabantio models on the side of the room delegated to them.

"Who is she?" a tall Asian model asked Rossi.

"This is Justice and she is replacing Raven in today's show since she was too stupid to make her plane."

The model stuck her lips out in a pout. "The plane left earlier than it was supposed to." She turned to Justice. "Who have you modeled for?" she asked.

"This is my first time," Justice replied in her husky voice.

"Well, you got lucky then, did you not? To model for Brabantio is something novices in modeling do not get to do." She looked at Lucille. "Who goes out first since Raven isn't here?"

"You do, Simone," Lucille replied.

"When does she go out?" She gave a curt nod in Justice's direction.

"Last," Lucille replied brusquely. "Now stop asking me questions. The show is starting."

Blaring music with an upbeat tempo filled the air. Strobe lights overhead flashed different colors as models lined up.

Rossi pointed at the floor. "I will be right here when you get back. The rest of your outfits are over to the left. You will need to change quickly so that I can rearrange your hair."

Justice studied the models from the other design houses on the small television that was placed by other electronic devices. When it was each model's turn, she strutted down the runway, arms hung down her side, and slightly moving alongside her body, never looking down. Then Justice took her place in line. When she was the last one left she heard Rossi whisper, "Go."

Justice hesitated, and then began to walk. With head held high, she strutted down the runway giving very little arm movement. She reached the end of the runway and stopped. Justice pivoted from one foot to the other, turned, and headed back. The sound of applause gave her confidence as she walked off the runway.

"Do that four more times and you will have made yourself ten thousand dollars." Rossi grinned at her.

Rossi unzipped the back of her gown and handed her an emerald mini-skirt and a black off-the-shoulder satin shirt. The collar of the shirt was the same emerald green as the mini-skirt. "Put those shoes on and sit down so that I can touch up your makeup and flatten your hair."

Without looking at the other naked models, camera men, publicists, or other people that were back there she quickly shed her clothes. Standing only in heels and a towel she quickly dressed into her second outfit.

"Sit in this chair," Rossi ordered.

Immediately he began raking a brush through her hair.

"Ouch, that hurts." Justice hunched her shoulders every time Rossi ran the brush through her hair.

"That is because it is your own hair. Weave is much easier to manage. That is why so many ethnic people wear it."

She muttered a little sarcastically, "I'm sorry that I have long hair, Rossi."

"I watched as you walked down the runway," he confided. "Caesar is very pleased with your performance."

"Good," she said. "Because I want my money tonight."

"You're talking thousands when you have to ability to make hundreds of thousands," Rossi scoffed. "Do you not understand what is unfolding right here, right now?"

Justice searched Rossi's eyes.

He stopped brushing her hair and twirled her chair around to face him. He bent down so that no one else could overhear him. "You are making your debut into the modeling world and are about to embark on a new life."

When Rossi's words finally sank in, Justice felt anticipation curl in the pit of her gut.

As Justice took her place behind the other three Brabantio models she felt coldness in the room despite the overheated temperature from the lights.

It was Justice's fourth time coming back from the runway. When she ran over to Rossi he handed her a metallic gold bikini. "There has been a change of plans," he said. "You have to wear this as your last outfit."

"I can't go down the runway in that," Justice protested.

"Where's the gown that you showed me?"

"Simone insists she wear it. It is the most awaited gown of our collection and since Raven is not here she is the next in line to wear the premier gown. It is only right," he acknowledged.

"I can't wear this," she wailed shaking the bikini at him.

"Stop whining," Rossi said in a brisk tone. "That is the quickest way in the modeling business to lose contracts. Learn to be flexible."

"My mother will kill me."

Rossi asked with raised brows, "Is she out there?"

"No," she said slowly. "But just because she isn't in sight doesn't mean that I should forget how she raised me."

"Do you go to the beach?" Rossi asked gently.

"It's not the same thing," Justice answered weakly.

"It is the same thing. You have no cellulite so you don't have to be worried."

"I just can't," she protested.

"Is it worth ten thousand dollars to not follow through on the deal that you made? You have come so far."

Justice hesitated for a moment. "I need a razor and shaving cream." She dropped her head in embarrassment. "I need to trim the forest."

As Justice strutted down the runway to Pharrell singing about how happy he was, she fantasized about her mother in a beautiful home. The image illuminated her face. She was shaken from her reverie by a standing ovation.

Exhausted, Justice lay back on the settee in Lucille's suite. After cleansing the heavy makeup that Rossi had so painstaking applied throughout the show, she'd changed back into her own clothes. She had a piercing headache from the lights, and had closed her eyes in an effort to merge back into her own self. The sound of the door opening roused her.

She opened her eyes to see a grinning Caesar standing there with an envelope.

She sat up.

"You were quite good, Justice. As I knew you would be. I have an eye for talent. You will be all the rage."

"All the rage?" she asked suspiciously. "What do you mean?"

"I mean that I want you to come to New York. I will pay for your plane fare, hotel, and another ten thousand dollars. Next week we are doing a small show in Bryant Park. But this time it will be only my designs. I have invited press and all the fashion magazine personnel, along with buyers for major stores."

Justice mentally calculated the money that he was offering. She asked quietly, "You would need me to stay a whole week?"

"Yes," Caesar replied, beaming as he handed her the envelope.

Justice opened it and looked at the cashier's check addressed to her for ten thousand dollars.

"Why would you offer me the same amount of money that you paid me for a night's work?" she asked in a respectful tone.

"I was in a bind tonight. Next week I am not."

"I see," she replied. "It's an amazing offer, but I would need to talk to my mother."

"I need your answer by twelve o'clock on Sunday. You have my cell number on your business card."

She nodded. "Where are Lucille and Rossi? I would like to personally thank them for everything they did for me tonight."

"They are handling things for our departure. They already know that you are grateful, Justice. Besides, I am quite confident that you will be seeing them again very soon."

###

The next morning Justice was met with a familiar sight. Her Aunt Minnie sat at the kitchen table reading the morning paper as she sipped a cup of coffee.

"Good morning, Justice," she said, looking over the rim of her Walgreen's reading glasses.

Justice bent over and kissed her on her cheek.

Then she went over to her mother. "Morning," she said, smiling gleefully. She put her arms around her mother's waist and hugged her close, breathing in her scent.

Evelyn kissed Justice on the cheek. "Good morning to you." Then she gave her a quizzical look. "What time did you get in last night? I got tired of waiting up for you and finally went to bed."

"Well, something unexpected happened at work yesterday. I'm glad to see you here also, Aunt Minnie, because I have something very important to talk to you two about."

"Nothing's wrong, is it?" Her mother looked anxious as she put a plate of grits, bacon, sausage, and eggs in front of her sister. Picking up a towel she wiped her hands.

"No, Mom," Justice replied, eager to replace her mother's

18

harried look with one of happiness. She reached into the pocket of the tee-shirt she wore, took out Caesar's check and handed it to her mother.

Shock made Evelyn drop it. "Justice," she said in a voice full of suspicion, "where did you get that money from?"

"Modeling," she said briefly.

"Modeling?" her mother exclaimed staring at her with a bewildered expression.

"It was so crazy," Justice said. She plopped down in a rickety chair at the table. "I was in the store and Caesar Brabantio..."

"Caesar Brabantio?" Minnie interrupted.

"He's an Italian designer," Justice said, rolling her eyes.

"Oh excuse me, but I haven't had a chance to watch the E channel lately," Minnie retorted dryly.

"Aunt Minnie!" Justice said.

"Go ahead, dear, tell your story," Evelyn said, giving Minnie a look of exasperation.

"One of his models didn't make the plane and he asked me to fill in for her."

"But you never said that you had an interest in modeling," her mother said in a confused voice.

"I didn't," Justice answered. "But Caesar said that he'd pay me ten thousand dollars. I'd just gotten off the phone from you telling me about all the fines on the house and it felt like a sign from heaven." Justice picked up the check and held it close to her bosom. "Mom, I want you to take this check with the money that I have saved in the bank and pay for the roof to be fixed."

"Justice, I can't take your money," her mother said.

"What?" she shrieked. "I can't believe that you would even hesitate."

"You should take this money and go to design school. I'll be fine. Isn't that right, Minnie?"

"Do as your mother says, Justice. She's already resigned to the fact that she's lost the house. Ten thousand dollars isn't going to change things."

"No, but twenty thousand will," Justice said.

"What do you mean?"

"Mr. Brabantio has asked me to go to New York next week and be in another show. He's going to pay me another ten thousand dollars."

"Justice, I can't let you do that," Evelyn whispered.

"What?" Her eyes bored into her mother's. "Go to New York? Or give you the money?"

"Neither one," she said.

Minnie said sullenly, "We don't know this Caesar Brabantio and I don't know nothing about New York."

"The two of you aren't thinking clearly. You're always talking about God making a way, and when you least expect it He comes through. Look at this as a blessing. We can save our house, and I can start working on being a designer earlier than I'd ever expected."

"How is that?" Evelyn asked.

"New York is the design capital of the world. I'll be meeting all kinds of designers and making contacts."

"In one week you expect to do all that?" Minnie asked suspiciously.

"Well, last night Rossi hinted that there would be more work down the road for me if I didn't fall down, and I didn't," she ended proudly.

"I have to meet this Borebantio before I allow you to go anywhere, young lady," Evelyn declared in an authoritative voice.

"Mom, his name is Caesar Brabantio," Justice said in exasperation.

"Whatever," Minnie interjected sarcastically.

Justice breathed in a deep sigh of acceptance. "He needs an answer from me by noon tomorrow," Justice said before leaving the room in search of Caesar's business card. "I'll see what I can arrange before he leaves town."

Justice anxiously peered out the curtains in the living room and saw a long black limousine pull into her driveway. She shouted, "Mom, Aunt Minnie, he's here."

Minnie said to Evelyn, "Let's go see why this guy wants Justice so much and what he wants to do with her when he gets her."

Justice sauntered down the driveway. She could see through the dark tint of the windows the watchful gaze of Caesar and the driver. Once she reached them Caesar exited the vehicle and held out his arms.

Justice hesitated for a minute and then walked over to him and gave him a brief hug. Justice said shyly, "Thank you, Caesar, for agreeing to this. I know that you meant to be gone already, but my mom is kind of old-fashioned. She wouldn't agree for me to go to New York without meeting you."

"I understand that they would be suspicious of my offer," he replied. "If I must set their minds at ease in order to pave the way for your journey, I am more than happy to do so."

Justice breathed a sigh of relief. "Good, then let's go inside."

As she climbed the stairs to the front porch, she felt Caesar behind her surveying the dilapidated condition of the house.

Once inside, he walked up to her mother and Aunt Minnie standing in the hallway. "I am the designer Caesar Brabantio." He stared pointedly at Evelyn, immediately noticing the resemblance. "I am very pleased to meet the mother of such a beautiful and graceful child."

Justice slid her mother a look. On hearing Caesar's words, her mother flushed with pleasure. But Minnie's eyes narrowed as she glared at him.

"Would you like a glass of lemonade, Mr. Brabantio?" Evelyn asked tentatively.

"No thank you, ma'am. I must admit that I am in a bit of a hurry. I sent my team ahead on our scheduled flight and I am slated to take the next one." He glanced at his wristwatch. "If I can make it to the Atlanta airport in time."

"We won't be rushed into making a decision about this," Minnie said in a tone filled with distrust.

"Let's take a seat in the parlor," Evelyn said.

Once they were seated in the room for the first time in a long time Justice really looked at everything, visualizing the way it must look to an outside observer. There was not a speckle of dust anywhere, but the outdated southwest sofa with its bright fabrics had faded and didn't match the worn carpet that had been covering the floor since she was a small child.

"In New York where would Justice be staying and who would she be staying with?" Minnie asked abruptly.

"She would be sharing an apartment with one of the other models."

"What exactly do you want her to model?" Minnie continued in a slightly hostile tone.

"She would model the clothes from my new line." Caesar gave Justice an approving smile. "She does my clothes justice," he quipped.

"What about Raven?" Justice felt compelled to ask. "What will she be wearing if I wear her clothes?"

"She is not in the next show," Caesar said shortly. "It is her punishment for not being a professional. She is always late to bookings. Maybe if she realizes that she is not the only size two with long legs she will take her job more seriously in the future."

"But won't she hate me?" Justice asked with trepidation.

"Raven hates everyone so that is not an issue." Caesar gave a slight shrug. "Modeling can be a, how do you people say it, 'dog eat dog world.'"

Minnie's eyes bulged out at the reference. "What people are you talking about?"

"Aunt Minnie," Justice hurriedly explained, "he means Americans."

"Are you willing to say that you'll pay for Justice's plane flight and accommodations besides the ten thousand dollars that she told me about?" Evelyn asked.

"Yes. I will have a contract for her when she gets to New York. She may sign it and fax it back to you if you like."

"What if she changes her mind and wants to come home?"

"She will not get the ten thousand dollars if she doesn't do the show," Caesar answered without hesitation.

"What if I fall down?" Justice asked nervously.

Caesar half-smiled. "If you get up and continue, this time I will pay you."

"How do I know that my daughter will be safe?" Evelyn asked in a tremulous voice.

Caesar leaned forward and looked her in the eye. "She did me a great favor last night and I appreciate it. I will look out for her."

Evelyn and Minnie looked at each other.

"Surely you want more of a future for her than working retail in a dress shop and living in," Caesar hesitated, obviously searching for the right words so as not to offend them, "this small town."

There was a heavy silence in the room. Finally Evelyn spoke and when she did it was with authority. "Justice may go to New York to do the show."

Minnie started to say something, but when she looked into Justice's hopeful eyes she said, "I guess that it'll be okay."

"Excellent!" Caesar Brabantio stood. "Now I'm afraid I must go." He shook the hand of Justice's mother and then her aunt. Then he turned to Justice. "You will have a plane ticket waiting for you in the morning at the Delta ticket counter. Your flight is at nine- thirty. Pack enough clothes for two weeks." He gave another half- smile. "Models change clothes a lot."

For the first time since Caesar had entered her home Justice relaxed. "You think?" She alone followed him outside to his limousine.

"I'll have a driver meet you at the airport and take you to the hotel."

"I promise that I won't miss the plane," she said jokingly.

"I know you won't, Justice," he replied without misgivings.

After she watched Caesar's limousine disappear out of sight she ran back into the house. She saw Aunt Minnie sitting at the kitchen table and she ran up and hugged her. "Thank you," she screamed.

"Thank your mother," she said gruffly.

"Where'd she go?" Justice asked in an excited voice.

"I think she's in her bedroom."

Justice tore out of the kitchen and ran down the long length of the hallway to her mother's bedroom. Without knocking she burst inside. Justice drew herself up short when she saw her wiping tears from her eyes with a tissue that she tried unsuccessfully to hide from Justice.

Justice got down on her knees and buried her head into her mother's lap. "Mama, why are you crying?"

"I'm crying because you're all grown up now, because I'm losing you, and because you are such a good daughter."

"Mom," Justice whispered, her words muffled because her head was still in her mother's lap. "I don't have to go."

"Yes, you do," she replied. "If you didn't I would never forgive myself for standing in your way."

"Mom, I'll only be gone a week."

"No you won't," Evelyn answered, her tears making her voice sound forlorn. "You will never come back to Eastman to live."

"How can you be so sure?" Justice whispered.

"That Caesar Brabantio is a good man," Evelyn said with a look of trust on her face. "He's decided to launch your career and apparently he's the person who can do it."

Justice looked up at her mother when the full enormity of what she was saying sank in.

Evelyn lifted her daughter's chin. "I just need you to do one thing for me, Justice."

"Anything, Mom."

"I've heard of so many young girls going to New York and losing themselves. Promise you won't lose yourself, Justice."

Justice buried her head in her mother's lap again. "I won't, Mom," she promised.

Justice walked into Mabel's Magnificent Creations.

When Nell saw her she ran up to her and threw her arms around her neck. "Oh my God, Justice! You were wonderful in the show."

Justice laughed. "How did you recognize me with all the junk on my face?"

"Those legs, girl. I'd know them anywhere. Why did you keep it a secret that you were going to model in the show?"

"I didn't know." Then she recounted blow by blow the events that had unfolded after Nell had left work the evening before ending with her upcoming trip to New York.

Nell clapped her hands excitedly. "That is freaking awesome. Promise when you become an internationally famous model you won't forget the little people you left behind," she joked.

"Please, girl," Justice protested. "Don't count on me being some high rollin' model." She looked around the half empty store early. "Where is Mabel? I need to talk to her about taking some vacation days."

"She's in the back and in a more than usual foul mood," Nell whispered.

"She's probably mad because I closed the store." Justice took a deep breath. "Let me see if I can smooth things over so you'll have a better day and not be punished for my behavior."

Justice knocked on the closed office door.

"Come in," Mabel barked from the other side.

Justice pushed open the door and when Mabel saw her she put the pen she was using to punch the keys of the calculator down. A mountain of invoices lay scattered on the desk. Justice surmised that they were unpaid bills to vendors. With a caustic look in her eye Mabel gave her a quick perusal.

Justice was dressed in a pair of black leggings, black patent leather flats, and turtleneck sweater. Her hair was fashioned in the same ponytail style that Rossi had groomed it in when she wore the bikini in the show.

Mabel sat back in the chair and it made a squeaking sound.

"I wanted to come in and apologize for closing the store early last night." Justice sat across from her. "I know that you depended on me, but something came up and no patrons had been in for over an hour. It was a slow night." Justice's voice trailed off.

Mabel's eyes narrowed in irritation. In a cold voice she replied, "Maybe they were coming in later and then found the store closed. But we'll never know how much money I lost because of your dereliction of duties, will we?"

Justice let that pass without comment.

"What was so important that you had to leave?"

Briefly Justice once again recounted the timeline that led to her being in the fashion show.

Once she was finished Mabel's mouth hung open as she stared at Justice. Once she recovered she said, "So are you trying to tell me that you left my job in order to do another? I could fire you for that."

Justice stiffened. Her body language showed what her tone disguised. "Today is my day off and I have a lot to do, but I took time to come in and apologize in person."

"So you think that makes up for what you did?"

"They offered to pay me very well and I needed the money." Now Justice's voice became hard. "I made a decision that I feel was right for me and my family."

Mabel looked taken aback by the severity of Justice's tone and decided to back down. "As long as you think that you did the right thing I'll let it go. Just don't let it happen again," she said with feigned bravado. "I would hate to lose you. You're usually a dependable employee."

"Thank you," Justice replied, softening her tone. "I also need to talk to you about something. I need to take some of my vacation time."

"When?" Mabel asked.

"I need off this week. I have to go to New York."

"That's impossible," Mabel said coldly.

"I have the vacation days," Justice said without giving away what she was thinking.

"Why are you going to New York?"

"The designer wants me to do another show."

"I can't give you the time off," she said forcefully. "The spring lines should be here any day now. You're supposed to give me a month's notice when you want to take your vacation."

"I would think that under the circumstances you would waive that rule. Besides, I've never seen it written anywhere."

"It's understood," Mabel replied stiffly.

"I have already committed to this show." Justice's jaw hardened and her lips were pressed together in anger.

"Justice, I'm an old woman and have seen a lot in my time. Don't throw away a good job for something you can't count on."

"I won't have a problem continuing to work here once I return from New York."Justice looked at Mabel wondering if her resolve was reflected in her eyes. "But this is something that I have to do, and I will not let you stand in my way."

"If you don't report to work on Tuesday you're fired," Mabel said resentfully.

"I'm thankful to have had a job but not grateful to have been employed here." Justice gave Mabel a frank look. "I need this money to help my family's finances. They come first."

A myriad of emotions crossed Mabel's face, jealousy being the most pronounced.

"You leave me no choice but to quit." Justice gracefully stood. "I can get a job that pays minimum elsewhere."

As she made her way out the door she spied Nell at a clothes rack showing a pantsuit to a customer and shouted over to her, not breaking her stride. "I quit." She added in a matter of fact tone, "You have my cell phone number, Nell. Call me if you need anything."

Justice took a minute to look at her father's picture. He'd been a handsome man and could have been a model himself. His features were prominent yet not overwhelming. She gulped at the faraway memory that she held so dear. Then she handed the large framed photograph to her mother.

Evelyn gave Justice a commiserating look, as she placed the photo glass down into the middle of the clothes so it wouldn't break. Evelyn closed the last full suitcase. "There," she said with satisfaction. "We got everything in."

"You got everything in, Mom. I don't know how I would have managed to get all of that stuff in three suitcases if it wasn't for you," Justice said gratefully.

"Working as a custodian at the high school taught me how to combine a lot of things. I'd have all my disinfectants, rags, broom, dustpan, and mop in one rolling cart. The older I got, the more I downsized."

"I thank God you don't have to put yourself through that sort of thing anymore." A determined glint came through Justice's eyes. She muttered to herself but her mother overheard her: "If I have anything to do with it, you'll never have to worry about money again."

"I don't want you doing anything up there in New York simply for the money, Justice," her mother said in a serious voice. "You have given me enough. Once we get the liens off this place we'll be fine."

"Mom." Justice looked at her. "If things go the way I'm praying for them to, you're going to get yourself a big, fine house in that new development on the other side of town."

Evelyn looked at her daughter and her eyes misted over. "Justice, I'm happy right here. I just need you to start looking out for yourself. I don't want you to forget your real dream of being a designer. This modeling thing is a sort of afterthought for you. It's like a bolt of lightning out of nowhere and I don't blame you for taking advantage of it." She gave her daughter a sheepish look. "As a matter of fact, I admire you. I never even graduated from high school and you're flying to New York to be in a fashion show. I've always wanted to get on a plane and jet off somewhere but I never had anywhere to go." She gave a self-deprecating shrug. "In my wildest dreams I never thought that someone that I brought into this world could go so far."

Justice took her mother's hand. "Mom, you're always putting yourself down because you don't have a high school diploma. What you do have is mother wit. Besides," she slid her a sidelong look, "I think that you're the one who is brave. The reason we've held on to this house for so long is because of your wisdom and determination. I only hope that if one day I'm faced with difficult choices that I make the right ones."

"You will, Justice," her mother said with pride. "The minute I had you and looked in your face I knew that I didn't need any more children because no other would compare to you."

Trying to still the tears that clouded her throat Justice asked, "Isn't Aunt Minnie going to see me off?"

"I'm right here," Minnie said quietly.

Justice and her mother whirled around to see her standing in the doorway.

"Oh," Justice said, laying her hand over her chest. "We didn't know you were there."

"I didn't want to interrupt the two of you." She coughed. "But I have something to say."

"What is it?" Justice and Evelyn asked in unison. If it weren't for Minnie's grave expression it might have been amusing.

"I don't think that Justice should go."

Evelyn sank slowly onto the bed. "Why, what happened?"

"I just got a phone call," Minnie said in a disapproving voice.

Justice's eyes opened wide. Then she weakly sat down next to her mother. "What happened?" she asked harshly. "Did Caesar Brabantio come to his senses and figure out what a rube I am?"

"I doubt that," Minnie said. "It was the pastor on the phone. It seems as if one of his nieces recognized you in the fashion show and told him about it."

"So..." Justice uttered blankly. "What does that have to do with anything?"

"You didn't tell your mother that you were strutting around half naked in a gold bikini." Minnie's eyes were full of displeasure.

"I didn't leave it out on purpose," Justice stammered. "I just didn't think about it." She added defensively, "I had everything important covered up."

"You mom is a deaconess in the church. Think of how embarrassing it is for you to be running around flaunting yourself like that in public."

"I think that you're more worried about the fact that I'm your niece than anything else. Have you noticed that Mom hasn't really said anything during your interrogation?"

"That's nothing new," Minnie retorted. "She's always let you do anything you wanted to," Minnie said. "It's obvious that you're hiding what's really going on with these out of the blue modeling jobs."

"There's nothing clandestine going on," Justice declared vehemently.

"I don't trust you to look out for yourself in New York." She glared at Justice. The next thing we know you'll be naked in Playboy. You're going to have to call this Caesar and tell him you're not going."

"I refuse," Justice said standing. She looked at Minnie. "You've always been a good aunt to me and I love you. But this is really not your decision." she said giving her a caustic look. "This house is in jeopardy, and this modeling job may fix it. I'm of age and I'll do what I want to. So I suggest as nicely as possible that you let me tend to my business."

Minnie's eyes practically bulged out of her head.

"Justice," Evelyn protested weakly.

"No," Justice interrupted her. "I'm not changing my mind. This whole conversation is ridiculous. I'm twenty-five years old. If I want to go to New York and model in a fashion show it's my decision. I don't need anyone's permission."

"You would embarrass your mother in front of her friends?" Minnie scowled ferociously. "You would prostitute yourself for money?"

There was a long, ominous silence in the room.

When Justice spoke her tone sounded foreign even to her own ears. "I've noticed that you haven't offered Mom any money to help keep things going around here."

Evelyn gasped in horror.

"We're about to lose everything. And I'm tired of my mother living like this."

"You're not even a model yet and you're already putting on airs," Minnie retorted in a critical voice.

"I want my mom to have a home that she's proud of," Justice said in a sharp voice. "Does it never occur to you why she never invites the church women over here?"

Evelyn gasped again.

"It's because she's embarrassed. So, if God has given me an opportunity to fix her home up for her, I'm going to take it. This discussion is closed."

CHAPTER 3

With a morose expression, Justice handed her luggage to the skycap at the Delta counter.

Her mother solemnly observed her movements. "Minnie would've come, Justice, but she had to work overtime today at Walmart."

"Oh," Justice said, quelling the deluge of tears she wanted to vent. Instead she turned and handed her license to the man at the ticket counter.

He punched in some numbers and handed her a ticket. "You're flying first class, Miss Fairchild. You need to hurry because your flight leaves in forty-five minutes."

"Okay," she replied. "Can I wait out here a little longer? I'm sort of waiting for someone."

"It's up to you, ma'am. But if you miss your flight you're in trouble because everything else going to New York is booked."

"All right, sir." She looked at her mother and held her arms out. The corner of her mouth drooped from sadness. "Come here to me, Mom. I'm going to give you two big hugs. One for you and the other for Auntie." Justice enveloped her mother in her arms. As she released her, she heard her cell phone ring. Looking at the caller I.D. she said excitedly, "It's Aunt Minnie. Hello," she said into the mouthpiece.

"Hey, gal. Are you ready for your big adventure?"

Minnie's voice sounded warm to her ears.

"Yes, I'm just telling mom goodbye." She sniffled, now feeling able to let the tears trickle down the sides of her cheeks. "I'm going to have to stop holding her hostage at the curb before security plasters a ticket on her car."

Minnie laughed.

Justice could visualize the dimples in Minnie's cheek that showed when she smiled.

"I'm sorry about what I said, Justice."

"Me too," she whispered.

"Knock 'em dead."

"I'll try," she whispered.

"Be careful up there, Justice."

"I will," she promised.

"Tell your mother not to cook tonight. I'm taking my sister out to dinner, so she doesn't cry all night because you're gone."

"I'll be back before you know it," Justice promised.

As the plane left the runway, Justice looked out the window. She couldn't see her mother but she knew that she was watching.

Out of the corner of her eye, Justice viewed each page of the fashion magazine the passenger seated next to her flipped through.

All of a sudden the man turned to her and his cologne wafted to her nostrils.

Without realizing it she inhaled as much of the aroma as she could.

"Were you finished with that page or am I going too quickly?"

Justice felt a rush of color flood her face. "I'm sorry," she said. "I didn't mean to be rude."

"You weren't." He smiled with a set of perfect teeth.

It disarmed her.

"I was just kidding around." He held it out to her. "Here, I'm done with it."

"Are you sure?" she said, unsure whether he was really done perusing the magazine.

"Yes," he said in a solemn voice. "That was pleasure reading. Now that I'm almost home, I've got to get back to business as usual." He reached down for a binder on the floor by his feet.

Justice took the magazine. "Thank you," she said.

"We will be landing at LaGuardia in thirty minutes," the now familiar voice of the captain announced over the intercom. "Please disengage all electronic devices and remain seated until the stewardesses indicate that it is safe to unbuckle your seatbelts."

The plane suddenly dipped and Justice anxiously peered out the window. When she saw the wide expanse of water as they flew over the Hudson River she felt a knot of anxiety tighten in her stomach. Gripping the arms of her seat she closed her eyes.

The man gave her a quick look. "Are you okay?" he asked, watching her carefully.

"Yes." She opened her eyes, smiling with false bravado. "It's just that it's my first time on a plane." She again darted a look out the window. "That's a lot of water down there."

"A lot of people don't like flying into LaGuardia because of it. I rather like it myself." The man chuckled lightly. "If a plane is going down I'd rather take my chances wearing a lifejacket in the water than the impact of hitting the ground at over a couple of hundred miles an hour." He gave her a soft smile. "So, I take it that this is your first trip to New York?"

"Yes," she replied. "I'm here to be in a fashion show."

"I'm not surprised." His eyes quickly skimmed her with an all encompassing look. "You look like a model."

"Well, I don't feel like one," she said.

"I was looking for a picture of you in my magazine," he said in a teasing voice.

"You won't find me in there. This is only my second time modeling and I'm scared to death about how I'm going to do."

"You'll be fine," he assured her. "I'm sure it won't be long before I see you featured on a billboard in Times Square."

"What on earth would make you say something like that?" she protested.

"I make it my habit to study beautiful women. I think every woman has something special about her but you have many things. I had to stick my face in a magazine throughout the entire flight to keep from staring at you."

Justice laughed and the dimples in her cheeks became more pronounced. "I think that you were able to manage that quite nicely. Until you spoke, I didn't think that you noticed me sitting next to you."

"Oh I noticed you all right," he replied in his deep, throaty voice.

Now Justice took time to really study him. He's so fine! He had a long, straight nose and black silky eyebrows. Her eyes moved to his full lips and wavy black hair that were the perfect complement to his chiseled cheekbones. "You don't model do you?" she blurted out.

"No."

"Well, you could," she stammered.

"I appreciate the compliment, Ms…?"

"Justice Fairchild," she answered.

"What an unusual name," he said.

"Justice is my mother's maiden name," she whispered.

"An unusual name for an unusually beautiful woman," he murmured.

The huskiness of his voice sent chills down her spine.

"My name is Sterling Hart."

"Hart?" she said breathlessly. "Does that mean that you have a big heart?"

"I try to," he murmured, continuing to hold her gaze.

"I see," she said almost drowning in his chocolate, brown eyes.

Sterling looked down at her hand. "So you're single?"

"Very," she said, her voice a dry whisper. "And you?"

Before he could answer there was another large bump and the plane seemed to nose dive.

She closed her eyes and braced herself against the back of her seat. Her hands clenched the armrest between her and Sterling Hart.

Suddenly she felt her right hand being pried from the armrest and enveloped in the warm, strong, comfortable one of Sterling.

The plane leveled off and she breathed a sigh of relief. Soon Justice felt the wheels of the airplane touch ground. But still, only when the plane had skidded to a complete stop did she reopen her eyes. When she did she found them locked with his. A fluttering in her stomach that had been a stranger for way too long filled her. She squirmed in her seat from the unaccustomed sensation. Unconsciously she opened her legs, seeking a more comfortable position.

With an unwavering stare, Sterling watched her movements. He squeezed her hand and began to lift it to his lips. But before his lips touched her skin he stopped and released it.

There was an unfathomable look in his eyes. "Until we meet again, Miss Justice Fairchild, I wish you safety on your adventure in New York." He placed his hand over his heart, and lightly tapped it two times, paused and then three more times.

Her throat was dry.

Abruptly, Sterling stood, grabbed his coat from the compartment above him, pushed past others, and after a quick wink at her disembarked.

Once Justice exited the plane, she cased the area for Sterling to no avail. An unusual feeling of loneliness enveloped her. *What the hell am I doing here? I miss my mother and Aunt Minnie already.* Then a feeling of resolution consumed here. *I'm here to do a job. And I have to be successful because so much depends on it.*

Justice breathed a sigh of relief when she saw a chauffeur with a sign bearing her name standing off to the side. She waved her hand at him. "I'm Justice Fairchild."

Relief flooded the man's face. "Hello, I am Jose. I'm sorry that I am late but there was a traffic jam on the bridge."

"That's okay," she said breathlessly. "We've only just arrived."

"Good. Your bags will be in baggage claim area 'B.' Let's go retrieve them."

"Lead the way," she said.

As she followed Jose's quick steps she located her cell phone in her purse. She viewed her missed calls list and realized that her mother had called three times while she was in flight. She hit her redial button.

Her mom immediately answered on the first ring

"Mom," she said. "I'm here."

"I've been scared to death. Did you get met by anyone?"

"Yes," she said. "We're going to get my luggage now."

"Good. You make sure that you call me every day."

"I will, Mom. By the way, I miss you two old women already."

Evelyn laughed at the joking tone in her daughter's voice.

"See you next week."

"If God says so," her mother said.

Startled, Justice asked, "What do you mean by that?"

"Nothing, darling," Evelyn said hastily. "See you next week."

Once her luggage was retrieved, she followed Jose as he wheeled her suitcases out the sliding glass doors. A blast of cold air stunned her and she bent her head, bracing against the wind.

Jose walked over to a black Hummer limousine and opened the trunk.

"Is someone else riding with us?"

"No," he said. "It is just you coming in today. Mr. Brabantio asked me to bring you to Bryant Park where the show is being held. The models have been rehearsing all morning."

The limousine inched its way through the bumper to bumper traffic. Justice craned her neck to view the sight. Building after building, all shapes, sizes, and colors lined the streets. She was pleasantly surprised to see clean sidewalks.

She knocked on the window that divided her and Jose.

The window immediately opened.

"This place looks nothing like it does on television. It's cleaner than I expected."

"Trash is collected every night. The mayor pays them well to keep the city clean so that tourists will want to come here," he said proudly. "It's working."

"How long will it take to get to our destination?"

"It is only fourteen miles but it can take an hour to get there, depending on the traffic." His exasperation was apparent. "No one in New York eats at home during the daytime." He made a motion to close the partition.

"Don't close it, please." Justice felt a little embarrassed. "I'm nervous."

"Now I know you are new to the world of modeling. Models never talk with the chauffer. They speak at him."

"I'm not a model," Justice denied. "I just got lucky because I was in the right place at the right time."

"You are a model, miss. Do you think that Mr. Caesar sends me to pick up all his protégées? He thinks that you are special and he wants you to be looked after."

"He does?"

"Yes. He is tired of the high maintenance demands of some. He will be replacing them one by one."

"Replacing who?"

"Now I cannot tell you that. I mean no disrespect to you. You are pleasant enough now, but people have a way of changing. I cannot afford to lose my job for being a gossip." He then closed the partition, ending their conversation.

Justice leaned back, respecting his wishes to end their discussion. She muttered, "I'm sure that I'll find out soon enough what Jose is talking about."

She sat back and took out her cell phone. She texted Nell the words, "I'm here. See you soon."

After forty-five minutes of bumper-to-bumper traffic Justice felt the limousine stop. She looked at Jose inquiringly.

"We're at your destination, ma'am. I am to escort you into the warehouse where you will join the others."

"What about my luggage?"

"It will be in your room when you get there."

Justice reached into her wallet.

"Tipping is not allowed." He gave a satisfied smile. "Mr. Brabantio pays me handsomely for my services. My son is enrolled at NYU thanks to his generosity."

"Wow," Justice said. "I would love to attend design school there."

"It is an excellent school. Mr. Brabantio looks out for every employee he feels is loyal. It would be good for you to remember that."

"I will," Justice said with a smile of gratitude. "Thank you for the advice, Jose."

His expression softened. "My pleasure. Come," he said, after exiting the front and quickly walking around the limousine to open her door.

Justice stuffed her hands into her jacket pockets and followed Jose down what appeared to be a back alley. Once they emerged from the middle of two tall buildings that blocked out a lot of the sun they were in an open area facing a brown building.

There were several black limousines in queue with the name Brabantio on the front license plates.

Jose opened the door, allowing her to enter the building.

As she did so he gave her a smile of encouragement.

She walked into a large room with a red runway that ran vertically between endless rows of chairs.

There were so many people scurrying about Justice didn't even attempt to count them. She spotted Caesar on the far side of the room. He sat at a desk, smoking a cigar. His thick eyebrows met at the bridge of his nose as he listened intently to what a model gesticulating widely was saying to him.

Justice hesitated.

"Why do you hesitate?" Jose said, "Brabantio is waiting for you."

"He seems kind of busy," she muttered uncomfortably.

"He is always busy," Jose replied dismissively. "Learn to stand up for yourself or you will be eaten alive." He strode off in the direction from which they'd come.

Justice surveyed the room and realized that her entrance had aroused the interest of a group of women sitting at a table. She walked towards Caesar and as she did she gave the women a closer inspection. She recognized that they were the three models that she'd met in Atlanta. They wore no makeup and were dressed casually in jeans but wore very high heels. As she strode past them she gave them a smile that was returned by all except Simone.

When she reached Caesar and the woman, he stood. "How was your flight?"

"It was good," Justice responded in her husky voice. Then she looked at the other woman. Even without makeup she was breathtakingly beautiful. Short black silky hair cut close to her head showed off her prominent features. A halter top and a pair of very short denim shorts showed off her long, graceful legs. She isn't cold? The woman wore a pair of heels that made her tall enough to look slightly down at Justice and she did so with a hostile look on her face.

"My name is Raven," the woman said in an accent Justice couldn't identify.

Justice gave a start of surprise. Uh-oh.

"I appreciate you stepping in for me in Atlanta."

Justice was a little surprised by the woman's kind words.

"You're welcome," she stammered. "I just got lucky."

"Yes, you did," she countered smoothly. Raven turned to Caesar. "Have you made a decision?"

"I have not changed my mind."

Raven's whole body stiffened. She opened her mouth and then closed it. Grabbing a handbag off the chair in front of Caesar's desk she stormed off, leaving through the exit behind Caesar's desk. The banging of the door as it hit the wall reverberated throughout the warehouse. There was a brief silence as everyone sat still.

Justice and Caesar's eyes met.

Then everything reverted to normal as everyone resumed what they were doing.

"You have really put me in an awkward position, Caesar," she said quietly.

His eyes pinned hers. "Do you not want the money?"

"I want the money," she said, swallowing the hard lump in her throat.

"Then do not complain." He pointed at the vacant chair. "Sit," he instructed in a commanding tone.

"I do not need five models for the show," Caesar said without preamble. "You are cheaper than Raven and have not yet acquired her tendency to cause confusion." He opened his desk drawer and handed her a folder. "Inside you will find a contract outlining what is expected of you. It is similar to the show in Atlanta. You will be paid ten thousand dollars. While in New York I will pay for all expenses. You will receive a stipend of one hundred dollars a day for food."

"That's a lot of money for food," Justice said as she skimmed the document.

"You do not know New York. You can spend that amount on lunch alone."

"Well, I'm going to eat cheap," Justice said. "I need to save all the money that I can."

"If you are what I think you are, and things work out the way I've planned, you will not have to worry about money for a very long time," Caesar said in a mysterious voice. "Now go and meet with Marcos. He's going to help you with your runway walk. It needs work."

Sterling slammed the door of the dark penthouse. After dropping his luggage he leaned back against the wall and exhaled. He opened his cell phone and pressed number three on his call log. His lawyer answered after the third ring.

"Hello, Sterling."

"You sound as if you've been expecting me to call."

"I knew that you were coming back from Miami today. I'm just a little surprised to hear from you so soon, though. Have you made your decision?" Chapman asked in a businesslike tone.

"Yes. I'm going through with the divorce. Start the paperwork."

"Are you sure that Harlow will agree to the terms?"

"Yes. After all, she's the one who broached the subject," Sterling answered in a derogatory voice. "I'm afraid I'm not enough of a social butterfly for her."

"No man is," Chapman said with disdain he didn't attempt to hide. "But still, be sure you're doing the right thing," Chapman advised. "Even though this is an amicable divorce you're going to have to settle a lot of money on her."

"Even if I gave her half of everything I own, I'll still have more money than we ever thought I would growing up on the poor side of Bedford-Stuyvesant. I'd rather be happy and financially comfortable that an unhappy millionaire."

"So a few days on the beach freed your mind?"

"Maybe," Sterling replied. "It was a combination of things. The flight home just sort of cemented my plans."

"Really?" Chapman said with obvious interest. "What could be so catalytic about a plane trip?"

"Nothing really," Sterling said in a noncommittal voice. "I just want my freedom. Besides, Harlow wants out and I don't want someone who doesn't want me."

"I know that you've always felt that divorce was the last recourse you'd take," Chapman said in a questioning voice.

The image of Justice Fairchild flashed before Sterling's eyes. He said quietly, "I decided today that instead of simply going through the motions of living I'm open to aggressively searching for something everlasting."

Harlow Hart sat in the upscale hotel room. One leg was crossed over the other and her foot nervously bobbed up and down. "Well," she said in a plaintive voice. "Aren't you going to say anything?"

The naked man who lay in the bed watched her with scorn. "What do you want me to say, Harlow? You're a married woman. Go tell your husband what you just told me and see what he says."

"Tell him what? That I'm pregnant by a friend of his."

"Sterling and I aren't friends," Lyle denied. "We just work at the same firm."

"If I tell him what you've done, you won't be working there," Harlow said in a threatening voice.

"Go and tell him how you pursued me," he said in a mocking

voice. "Tell him that you slept with a clerk at his firm because you're bored with your life. The only thing that will happen is that your husband will divorce you and you'll be raising this baby alone."

"I thought that I meant something to you," she whispered.

"I'm not going to marry you," he said with forthrightness. "We both went into this with eyes wide open. It was simply a sex thing."

"I thought that things had gotten beyond that," she whispered with downcast eyes. "I've grown to love you, Lyle."

"Think about this, Harlow." Lyle's thin lips curled insolently. "How could I ever trust you? A woman who cheats on her husband will also cheat on her boyfriend. How do I even know that the baby is mine?"

She swallowed hard. "It's yours. I'm certain."

"If you want your baby to have a daddy you'll go home to your husband and stop pretending that you're out of town."

Sterling was sitting in a leather chair nursing a glass of scotch when he heard the front door open. His eyes never wavered from the television.

"So you're back," Harlow said, placing her keys on a table in the foyer.

"Yes, I'm back." Now he looked at her. "I thought that you'd be in Chicago until the end of next week."

"I came back early because I'm not feeling well."

"I'm sorry to hear that, Harlow," Sterling said with sincerity. "What's the matter?"

"I'm just coming from the doctor. He ran some tests." She hesitated before adding, "He gave me some prescriptions to have filled and said that I need to get some rest."

"It's probably all the traveling you've been doing. I'm glad that you're here, though. I'd like to talk to you about the decision I've made. I, too, want a divorce." Sterling said in a voice devoid of emotion, "Our marriage hasn't been healthy or happy for years."

Harlow's eyes narrowed yet she said nothing as she closely watched Sterling.

"I'm not blaming you," he continued. "It's us. We have nothing in common. I've already called Chapman and he's going to start the proceedings immediately. Everything that we discussed before I went to Miami stands. I'm going to keep this residence and you can have the one in the Hamptons. How soon do you think you can get your things out of here?"

"I've changed my mind about the divorce," Harlow said in a clear voice. "I want us to work things out."

"No," Sterling said without hesitation.

"You can't say no like that." She sat down on the ottoman in front of him. "We need to discuss something."

Sterling gave Harlow a hard look. "I'm not surprised that you're saying this. Throughout our marriage you've always reacted the opposite way I expected. What happened in Chicago to make you suddenly change your mind? Before you left, you acted as if you couldn't wait to get rid of me."

Harlow searched Sterling's eyes with hers. "I'm pregnant."

A long, harsh silence filled the room.

Sterling swallowed the remains in his glass in one jerky movement. His eyes scanned Harlow's flat stomach. "I don't believe you."

"I knew you wouldn't." She took a small white paper out of her pocket and held it out to him.

Sterling took it. He read it three times.

"That's your son, Sterling. The child you've always wanted."

"What would make you think that it's a boy?" he asked in a frozen voice.

"I don't know what the baby is," she acknowledged. "I'm just happy to be having one."

"Your timing couldn't be worse," he said quietly.

"Our timing," she gently corrected him. "You were there, too."

"Not that much," he said in a hard tone. "What happened? I thought you said that you couldn't have children."

"The doctor said that I couldn't. I guess my lazy ovary got reenergized." She leaned forward and placed her hand on his knee. "There's a reason for this baby, Sterling."

"Yes," he said harshly. "It's called me getting drunk one night last month and you not taking the pill."

"That's a mean thing to say," Harlow whispered in a quavering voice.

"I'm sorry. But you've got to know that this is a lot to digest."

"Every marriage has its rough patches, Sterling. Maybe ours is over."

"I believe two healthy divorced parents are better than two unhealthy parents living in the same house, Harlow. I won't have my child raised in an unhealthy environment."

"When you were a teenager, your father walked out on you and you hated him until the day he died."

A pained look crossed Sterling's face at the mention of his father.

"Is that the behavior you want to emulate?"

"No." Sterling ground out the word.

"Let's put the divorce on hold," she said in a pleading voice. "Maybe the baby can make us close again."

"Children rarely fix marriages, Harlow. They merely prolong misery."

"What has happened to make you want a divorce so much? You went away for a few days to think about it. Now your mind seems to be made up and you act as if it's an emergency that we split."

He glared at her.

"Everything has changed, Sterling." Her eyes filled with tears and droplets hung on her long eyelashes. "We can't be selfish, and we can't think about just what we want anymore."

"I'll stay with you through the pregnancy," Sterling quietly agreed. "Then we'll see."

A triumphant look settled on Harlow's face. "When are you going to call Chapman and tell him that we've changed our minds about the divorce?"

"In the morning," Sterling said. "Right now I need another drink."

Sterling stood and without looking at Harlow walked past her and went into the kitchen.

Once Harlow was alone, she exhaled.

CHAPTER 4

Justice waited her turn.

"Go, Justice," Marcos barked at her over the microphone.

Justice strutted down the runway.

"Stop," Marcos ordered. "Go back and do it again and stop swinging your arms like you're a monkey."

Justice's spine stiffened angrily, but she bit back the retort that hovered on her lips. She heard snickers from the other models who stood behind the curtain. Justice turned around and went back to the runway.

"Go," he ordered again.

Justice strutted down the runway without moving her arms.

"Now you look like a fuckin' robot. Get your ass back there and do what I told you to do over an hour ago. And this time get it right. You're wasting everybody's time."

Justice forced back the tears that she felt building in her eye sockets.

She went back and stared down the long runway.

At the end sitting in a chair was Caesar. He carefully watched yet had said nothing for the last two hours the models had rehearsed.

Justice pivoted and stomped back to the entrance. She stood and waited.

"Go."

Drawing in a deep breath, she walked. She moved her arms gently by her side as she walked.

"Stop moving your head like that!" Marcos shouted. "You look like a damn giraffe. Get your ass back up there and start again."

With head bent, Justice walked back to the entrance. She turned and began her walk.

Stop looking down," Marcos ordered sharply. "Don't you know where the fuck your feet are?"

Startled, Justice looked up. Her ankle turned over, she stumbled, and then she went down. When she hit the floor all one hundred and fifteen pounds of her made a noise that sounded like a ton of bricks falling.

Now a burst of laughter erupted throughout the room.

Hearing this, Justice angrily got to her feet. Pasting a blank look on her face she almost limped back to the start of the runway. Justice stared down the long stretch of red that had become her walk of shame.

A svelte blonde had appeared out of nowhere and sat next to Caesar. She stared.

Justice recognized a look of pity in her eyes and inwardly flinched. Rossi was sitting on the other side of Caesar. He gave her an almost imperceptible nod of support. She yelled to Marcos, "I'm ready."

This time when she heard the duet of Alicia Keyes and Jay-Z welcoming her to New York City she picked up the rhythm. With head held high, she strutted to the end of the runway. She stopped. Then she pivoted from one foot to the other, turned and strutted back.

"Now you're getting it. Do it like that fifty more times and we'll call it a day. The rest of you can go and meet with Lucille upstairs. She wants to tell you what's on the agenda for tomorrow."

Two hours later Justice bolted to the ladies' room. Grabbing a handful of paper towels she ran into a stall. Sitting down on the seat she buried her face in the wad of towels and sobbed. After awhile she heard the bathroom door opening and buried her face in her arm trying to muffle her sounds. She heard three light taps on the stall door.

"Justice, are you okay?"

She recognized Rossi's voice.

"Come out," he said.

"I'm using the bathroom," she lied. "May I please have some privacy?"

"You've been in here for over fifteen minutes," Rossi said dryly. "Unless you're constipated you're in here hiding."

"Isn't it illegal for you to be in here?" she retorted, stung by his correct assessment of the situation.

"So come out and arrest me," he replied.

Justice couldn't help smiling when she heard the laughter in his voice.

Standing she flushed the soggy paper towels down the toilet.

When she came out, Rossi was leaning against the sink cabinet. His arms were folded and he stared at her red-rimmed eyes. "Tough day, huh?"

"You think?" she muttered sarcastically.

"Marcos is an Italian Hitler. He's an asshole, but he's good at what he does."

"Caesar pressed me to come up here and take him up on his offer. I didn't expect him to hang me out to dry."

"He's done nothing of the sort. It's just very important for you make a good impression at Saturday night's show."

"I kind of thought that Caesar would step in out there and tell Marcos that he didn't have to be so mean," she sniffled. "All that cursing was unnecessary."

"Wipe that line of snot hanging out of your nose."

Embarrassed, Justice turned on the water faucet and splashed cold water on her face.

She took the paper towel that Rossi handed her.

"You don't want Caesar to step in and save you. It would give you the reputation of being his favorite and make the other girls hate you."

"I think they hate me already," she said in a tiny voice. "Not one of them gave me an encouraging word today."

"You represent a loss of money for them." He shook his head from side to side. "They're not going to make it easy for you."

"What money? Everyone in the show is getting paid," she wailed.

"Stop whining," Rossi snapped, tired of her despondency. "And grow the hell up! Instead of caring about those bitches you need to be celebrating. Today you conquered the runway. You learned to walk like a million dollar model. Come on. Lucille is waiting for you."

They rode the elevator in silence. Once it stopped and they disembarked, Justice turned to Rossi and touched him on his arm. "Thanks," she said in a shamefaced whisper.

"Anytime, darling. Follow me."

Lucille was perusing a take-out menu when they entered. She scrutinized Justice's blotchy face. Reaching inside her desk drawer she handed her a box of Epsom salts and Bengay. "I heard that was quite a spill you took today. Soak in that," she pointed to the Epsom salts. "and rub the Bengay on your legs and thighs afterwards. I set you up for a massage tomorrow because we don't want you tightening up."

"Thank you," Justice said.

"I need to talk to you about some things."

"Yes, ma'am."

Justice looked at Rossi who had eased into a chair and looked on.

"Rossi and I have decided that we are going to work with you for the show. We have four hairdressers and stylists. Each model gets one of each. The show in Atlanta was a dummied down version as to what's going to happen Saturday night. You hair will be changed six times. So each time you come off the runway you are to haul your ass over to us. We will be waiting. I will help you dress. Here," she handed her a clear package.

Justice took the thin mesh hat with a zipper in it.

"Before you take off each outfit you put that over your face.

That way the makeup won't ruin the clothes."

"Okay," Justice said. "I had one of these at home."

"Do not apply any perfume the day of the show. We don't want stains on the clothes or a lingering scent."

"Yes," Justice answered quietly.

"Do not use a powder deodorant."

"Yes."

"After each runway walk you will need to go to Rossi. He will rearrange your hair and touch up your makeup. All the other models will be jealous because he is the best. But he chose you and Caesar agreed."

She gave Rossi a look of pure gratitude that included Lucille. "I want to thank the two of you so much. I realize what a big deal this is."

"Always remember, Justice," Lucille said succinctly. "The so-called little people can make or break a model. A lot of models don't realize that."

"That's right," Rossi drawled. "Now I'm going to take you to where you're staying. Caesar has leased a house not far from Madison Avenue. Try to make friends with Scarlett. She's pretty nice though dumb."

"She's pretty dumb all right," Lucille said, looking over her wire-rimmed glasses. "But she's harmless."

Justice stepped into the opulent foyer with its tiled floor and looked around in amazement. "Who would be willing to loan this out to strangers?" she asked Rossi. "If I had something like this I wouldn't want anyone in it when I wasn't around."

"A friend of Caesar's willed it to his son. Jayme spends the New York winters in the Caribbean so it sits empty. By leasing it to Caesar he has more money to blow on frivolous things. All he does is run around the world seeking pleasure."

"I guess that's okay for some people." She shrugged. "But I think that would be a boring way to live."

"It is the way of many. They depend on others and things to be happy. I have learned you must make your own happiness."

"So I take it that you're very happy?" she asked Rossi.

"Sometimes," he answered in a serious tone. "No one is happy all of the time."

"Where are the other models? This place seems deserted."

"They've gone shopping," a brash voice answered from behind.

Surprised to hear a noise, Justice and Rossi turned to find

Cassius standing there. He was looking at a pocket watch and slid it in his pocket.

"All but Scarlett," Cassius continued brusquely. "She's upstairs resting."

Rossi stared at Cassius with narrowed eyes. There was obvious tension between them.

Cassius looked at Justice. "Your things are upstairs in the last room to the right. I'm leaving now." He gave a curt nod to Rossi and said to Justice over his shoulder mockingly, "Don't fuck up the show."

Then he disappeared as quickly as he had appeared.

She and Rossi looked at each other.

"What's the deal with him?" Justice felt compelled to ask.

Rossi focused on some spot on the other side of the room. "He wants to be a designer but has no talent."

"Oh, so that's why he's the way he is."

"That's only part of it," Rossi said. "His soul is not at peace. Cassius is pretending to be something that he is not." He pinched her cheek. "I must leave now. Jose will be picking you up at nine o'clock in the morning and taking you to the spa. Caesar wants you to have a complete body treatment, including a facial. Get some rest. See you tomorrow."

Once she was alone, Justice gingerly climbed the stairs to the top floor. Walking down to the last room she opened it and spied her luggage. The worn out black suitcases looked threadbare in comparison to the furnishings in the room. A mahogany queen bedroom set contrasted nicely with the wheat shag carpeting and matching drapes. She touched the curtains admiringly. I would love to buy my mother some new furniture. But first I have to save the house so that we can have something to put it in.

"Hello," she heard a soft voice say behind her.

Justice whirled around. "You people sure have a way of sneaking up on me."

Scarlett gave her a genuine smile. "I'm sorry. I didn't mean to scare you. I'm Scarlett."

"You didn't scare me," Justice denied. "I just didn't expect to see you. Cassius said that you were resting."

"Oh," she said with an enigmatic look on her face. "If only that was possible."

"What's the matter?" Justice said, sinking down on the down comforter, grateful that finally a model seemed willing to have a conversation with her.

"Nothing," Scarlett quickly denied. "I'm just a little nervous. I always am before a show."

"You, nervous?"

"Of course," Scarlett replied. "That never goes away."

"I would think that modeling is a hard career to have."

"You'll soon find out."

Justice gave her a look of query.

"Everyone is aware that Caesar hopes to replace Raven with you in his future shows."

"But how often does he have a show?"

"Usually every six months in Italy. But I don't know what he plans to do in America. I'm just relieved that he's decided to enlarge his base here. There's a lot of work in New York."

"So you've been modeling a long time?"

"Since I was eighteen."

"How old are you now?"

"I'm twenty-nine." She threaded her hand through her long, blonde hair. "Almost one hundred and eighty-nine years old in the modeling world."

Justice scrutinized Scarlett's face closely. True, there were some lines on her forehead, but Justice surmised they could be from worry because it couldn't be from age. "I think modeling is the most bizarre career in the world. How can you be considered old?"

"I'm almost passé," she said seriously. "I'm hanging on by a thread."

"What are your plans when you retire?"

"I have none," she responded quietly. She said tentatively, "I'm hungry. Why don't we go and get something to eat? There's a restaurant not far from here. We can walk to it."

"That sounds like fun."

The cold air on the street blew right through Justice and she shivered in her leather coat.

Scarlett looked at her. "You need to wear a warmer coat. Leather looks good but its freezing."

"I don't have anything else." Justice grimaced. "It wasn't worth it to me to buy a coat for a couple of days."

"It's worth the investment. When you get sick in the modeling world and are unable to work, you don't get paid. The garbage men in town have better benefits than we do," she said bitterly.

Justice and Scarlett found a small table in the crowded restaurant. As they waited for their orders of broccoli and cheese soup Scarlett asked, "So what do you think of New York?"

"From what I've seen I like it. There's an energy that I feel here.

I can't explain what it is because I've never experienced it before."

"You've been bitten by the New York bug. Once you visit here you never want to leave," Scarlett said. "I come as much as possible."

"Where are you originally from?"

"I'm from a small town outside of Encino. I was working in a deli and Cassius came in and discovered me."

"Cassius discovered you?"

"Yes. He was scouting for models. I'll always be grateful for what he did. If it wasn't for him I'd probably still be working at that same deli. Unhappy and unattractive."

"I'm sure that you're grateful to him," Justice said carefully. "But Cassius didn't make you beautiful."

Scarlett dug into the bowl of soup the waitress placed in front of her.

When they returned to the house, Justice saw that the other models had returned. Clothes were strung out on the living room chairs and open cartons of Chinese food were on the counter. Simone lay on the floor in front of the television following the directions of some exercise guru while Raven lounged in a leather chair sipping from a Styrofoam cup. Laila was reading a textbook and briefly looked up at Justice's entrance. Then she refocused on what she was reading.

"Where have you been?" Raven said. She shot daggers at Scarlett.

Scarlett self-consciously inched away from Justice's side.

"We went to get something to eat," she explained.

A chill was in the air and it wasn't from the weather.

Justice stepped forward. She said brightly, "All of you have been so busy I haven't had the opportunity to say how happy I am to be with you for a few days."

There was no response. Finally, Laila put her book down. "Welcome. We hope that you enjoy your stay in New York. Right, Simone?"

Simone cast an anxious glance at Raven whose expression remained antagonistic. "Yeah," she said. "I didn't talk to you in Atlanta because everything was so hectic." Her voice trailed off lamely. "You really saved the show stepping in like that."

Raven made a hissing sound.

Hurriedly Simone added in a nasty tone, "I mean since Raven, the star of the show, was unable to make the plane I guess that you were better than nothing."

Justice drew in a sharp breath.

"I'm going to bed," Scarlett declared and bolted.

A steely look entered Justice's eyes. "I rather think that I was more than 'better than nothing'. As a matter of fact, I was a helluva lot better than you. Didn't you read the reviews in the Atlanta paper the next morning? I think the word they used for you was 'gauche' in comparison to me."

Laila burst into laughter.

"See you on the runway," Justice said and sashayed out the room. As she climbed the stairs two at a time Laila's continued laughter rang in her ears.

When she entered the room she shed her clothes and went into the bathroom to shower. She was so flushed with anger she didn't even notice the beautiful marble tile, double vanity, or sunken tub. Instead she quickly stuffed her hair under a shower cap, and climbed into the shower. She scrubbed her skin from head to toe and after thirty minutes of stinging heat, she felt relaxed enough to leave the shower. Justice dried herself in a large, fluffy white towel and emerged from the bathroom. She made a misstep when she saw Laila sitting on the bed reading her textbook. "What are you doing here?" Justice said, her lighter mood darkening again.

Laila slammed the book shut. "You should keep your door locked. Models steal from each other."

"They'd be sadly disappointed if they rifled through my things." Justice shrugged. "I have nothing of any value."

"I think that you handled yourself quite well down there."

"Aren't you afraid to be seen with me?" Justice said with a sardonic lift of her brow. "Scarlett certainly appears to be."

Laila admitted in a droll voice, "Raven does scare the shit out of her."

"But not you?" she said, only half believing her.

"Not so much," she responded.

"That Raven is a bully."

"Yeah, she is," Laila said. "And I prefer not to get involved with the petty bullshit. I only model because I'm saving money for college. I want to be a doctor and I don't want to work while I'm in school."

Thinking of Scarlett and her lack of ambition, Justice said, "At least you have a plan."

"Simone doesn't really like her, you know. She's just terrified of her."

"Then Simone is pathetic."

"So is Scarlett. She doesn't know that we know it, but she sleeps with Cassius."

"Shut up!" Justice said with a stunned look on her face.

"She thinks that he secures her position here." She added in a scathing tone, "Cassius makes no decisions as to who models the Brabantio clothes. Only Caesar decides that. Raven laughs at Scarlett behind her back."

"Why is she so mean? Raven is absolutely stunning to look at. I'm sure that she never has to go without modeling jobs."

"She has had to scratch her way throughout her whole life. Raven's from Russia and her parents died in a tragic mining accident. She was adopted by some people who turned out to not be very nice to her so she ran away. She got lucky and sort of fell into modeling. It has saved her life. This is all she has."

"That's a very sad story," Justice said.

"Yes, it is sad but that was many years ago." Laila got a faraway look in her eyes. "Everyone has a story, Justice. It's not my fault or your fault. Raven has a very strong mind and can easily make a weak person do what she wants."

"Well, she won't have to be bothered with me in a couple of days. After that I'll be gone."

"We'll see." Laila got up and gave a long languid stretch. "This should be very interesting."

"Your face needs a good buffing," Annabelle said. She took the palm of her hand and ran it down the length of Justice's arm. "Your skin is almost golden. I've not seen any quite like it. Your uniqueness will stand out on the runway."

"Thank you," Justice murmured, not quite sure that a response from her was needed or wanted.

"I will put you in the hands of my best girl. Lotus has not been in the states long and she still practices all of the talents that she was taught in Korea. She will have you looking like a well polished model when you leave here." Annabelle clapped her hands and out of nowhere a young Asian girl appeared. Annabelle spoke rapidly in Korean and Lotus, smiling enthusiastically, nodded her head.

Annabelle redirected her gaze to Justice. "Go with her. She will take good care of you."

Justice gracefully stood and extended her hand. "Thank you very much."

Annabelle smiled knowingly. "You will be a good advertisement for my services. If any reporter asks you how you got your skin to look so luminous, mention Annabelle's Spa and we will be even."

Justice chuckled. "I don't think that anyone will be interviewing me but if that were to happen I'd be very happy to give you a shout out."

As Justice followed Lotus down a long hallway she passed rooms on each side with closed doors. "What's behind those doors?" she asked Lotus.

Lotus simply grinned widely at her.

Lotus found an empty room and once they were inside she closed the door. Turning to her, she motioned for Justice to undress.

She did so leaving only her bra and panties on.

Lotus motioned for her to take off her undergarments.

Justice hesitated until she saw the questioning look on Lotus's face.

"Do you have a screen?" she asked.

Lotus stared blankly at her.

Breathing a deep sigh of resignation, Justice shed the rest of her clothes.

Lotus pointed to a table with a white sheet on it. Lifting the sheet Justice slid onto the table covering her body.

Lotus walked over to the other side of the room and scooped up a ball of wax. Walking back over to Justice she lifted one leg and with intense concentration smeared the hot wax on the inside of her thighs.

Justice gave a whelp of pain.

"You'll get used to it," Lotus said in perfect English.

Justice's eyes opened wide in astonishment. "I thought you didn't speak English."

"Sometimes I find it easier to pretend that I don't." Lotus shrugged again. She walked over to the tub of wax and scooped up another blob.

"No more," Justice protested. "I don't want to be hairless."

Lotus shrugged. "If that is what you wish. However, when you are walking down the runway what will you do if your bathing suit shifts in the front? Do you want people to see your hair?"

"No," Justice said, sick at the thought. Hesitantly she said, "I guess you better take it all off."

After Lotus balded her she examined herself with a hand mirror. Doubtfully she handed it back to Lotus.

Lotus stared at her handiwork with satisfaction. "Your man will go wild."

"I don't have a man," Justice responded quietly. Suddenly the image of Sterling Hart flashed before her eyes and heat invaded her lower extremities.

"You will," Lotus said with confidence. "These men in New York will pounce on you the minute they can. Now I must give you your facial and body treatments."

Hours later Justice stood naked in front of a long mirror. Her skin glistened in a way she'd never thought possible. Her eyebrows were perfectly waxed and her French manicure and pedicure accented the final result.

Lotus watched her. "You are pleased?"

Now she wasn't feeling self-conscious that she was naked and Lotus was fully dressed. She said, "For the first time, I feel worthy to walk the runway as a model."

"I will give you a sample of the products that are best suited for your skin."

"You've done enough. I think that I should purchase them from Annabelle."

"You have already paid for that. Did you not see that in the contract you signed with Brabantio?"

Justice gave Lotus a questioning look. "How do you know what I signed?"

"All the girls who come through here say that it is the standard of all modeling contracts. Out of their earnings models have to pay back the house what is paid out to get them ready."

"I do remember reading that but I didn't pay it much attention." Her brow was furrowed as she tried to remember the exact wording of the contract she'd signed.

"Annabelle is very expensive but worth it. You will get more work if you are refined looking."

"Well," she said, "I'll do whatever it takes." She picked up her panties and after donning them shrugged into her trousers. Reaching into her purse, she grabbed a wad of bills. "This is for you. I'm sure that Brabantio didn't include a tip."

Lotus looked at the money and counted it, handing back a couple of the bills.

"This is more than enough. Be careful with your money in New York," she warned. "I've only been here six months but have seen models that were once rich finding themselves out of work with barely enough money to purchase a bus ride home."

This time when Justice entered Bryant Park she felt and exuded the confidence of a runway model. Her eyes honed in on Rossi and saw him beckoning her. As she walked past the other models with head held high, she pretended not to notice the venomous stare of Raven as she sat with the other models that were in the show.

Once she reached Rossi's side he grinned.

"I have the sketches for your different hairstyles in my office. "Let's go."

As Justice followed him, she didn't notice the more than pleased look on Caesar's face as she floated by.

Hours later when Justice entered the house it was completely dark. Still unfamiliar with the layout, she took her hand and felt along the wall for the light switch. Suddenly the room was illuminated and the harsh glare made her blink.

Raven was sitting at the bottom of the stairs.

Warily Justice looked at her, waiting.

"I think that we got off on the wrong foot, Justice," she said with a small smile. "I would like us to be friends or at least pleasant to each other."

Justice breathed a sigh of relief that Raven was extending her hand in friendship. She said earnestly, "I would like that too, Raven."

"If you really mean that you will bow out of the show."

"I can't do that," she stammered. "Caesar is depending on me."

"Don't think that you're more important than you are," Raven scoffed. "He is using you to punish me. How does it feel to be used as a pawn, Justice?"

"I don't look at it like that," Justice replied with candor. "For some reason Caesar saw something in me that I didn't see myself. Now that I've done that one show and the rehearsals for this next one I feel that I've earned the right to walk the runway."

"One show doesn't make you a runway model," Raven sneered. "You'll see that."

Justice stared at Raven. "I don't think that I have to explain to you but I really need the money. I can't bow out."

"I really need the money also," Raven countered. "I send most of it home to relatives in Russia. They depend on me."

"I thought that you were adopted and didn't have any contact with them or even know your real parents," Justice blurted out.

"Who has been discussing my personal business with you?" she demanded harshly.

"No one," Justice stammered, realizing the huge gaffe she'd made by disclosing what Laila had told her.

Raven's slanted eyes narrowed to the point that they almost looked like slits. "Once I find out…"

Justice was appalled at how Raven had lied and her lips protruded in disapproval. "So you were making up the sob story about your family." She looked at Raven whose stance was defiant. "That's so sad it's pitiful. You should be ashamed of yourself. You aren't the only person who has had a rough time. It would be good of you to remember that."

"Quit the show," Raven said in a tone full of warning. "Tell Caesar that you are sick and can't do it. That way he won't sue you."

"I refuse," Justice said in a tired voice. She turned and began to climb the stairs. "Now I'm going to bed. It's been a long day."

"I'll find a way to make you sorry," Raven hurled at Justice's retreating back.

"I'm sure you'll try," Justice replied.

Once Justice reached her room she closed the door and leaned back on it for support. Her heart was beating rapidly from the altercation and she had a sudden feeling of homesickness. Reaching into the pocket of her jacket she grabbed her cell phone and called home.

"Hello," her mother said sleepily.

"Hi, Mom. I'm sorry to wake you. I thought that you'd still be up."

"No, I went to bed early tonight. I'm just sort of feeling rundown."

"What do you mean?" Justice asked, worry creeping into her voice.

"It's nothing," Evelyn said hurriedly, brushing her daughter's fears aside. "How are you enjoying yourself up there?"

"Everything's great," Justice lied. "It's just a lot colder than I expected."

"It's cold here so it's got to be cold up there. The weather won't start to warm up until April. Maybe you should go and buy yourself a new coat. You certainly deserve it."

"I might just go and do that. But if I'm going shopping I'll have to hurry. I'll be coming home in a couple of days." She paused, "Did you get the money that I wired you?"

"I sure did," Evelyn said, her voice laced with appreciation. "Right away I went down and paid the county clerk. We're almost done with the liens the city levied on us. I think that now I can maybe get a loan to cover the rest."

"How can you do that?"

"Well, maybe borrow against the house. Since our financial picture is so much brighter than it was last time I tried they might not turn us down."

"I don't like that idea, Mom. That means that we're only getting into more debt because we'll have to pay interest on that money."

"I'm going to look around for a loan that would charge us less interest than the penalty fees of the liens. It's only another ten thousand dollars, give or take a few cents."

Justice had a sudden premonition. "Don't do anything until I get back."

"Justice," her mother said.

Justice said in a no nonsense tone, "Mom. Promise me that you'll sit tight."

"Okay, dear," she slowly agreed.

Then Justice heard a lot of screeching in the hallway.

"What's all that commotion?" Evelyn asked. "I can hear those girls you live with all the way down here in Eastman."

"I don't know, Mom," she mumbled uneasily. "I think that they're just having fun."

All of a sudden Justice's bedroom door was kicked open and Laila stood on the threshold. Her hands were planted on her hips and fire shot out of her pupils.

"Mom, let me talk to you later," Justice said hurriedly.

"Is everything all right?" Evelyn asked, worry evident in her voice.

"Sure, mom," Justice said in a sort of strangled voice. "I just need to talk to Laila for a minute."

After she disconnected Justice held up her hand. "Let me explain," she said.

"I told you that I didn't want to be dragged into any of this bullshit around here. Why the fuck did you tell Raven what I told you?"

"I didn't," Justice said. "It just sort of came out and I never said that it came from you."

"Now she's bitchin' at me. I don't have time for this craziness. Your ass ain't got to worry," Laila said in an icy voice, "I won't tell you anything else." She stormed out, slamming the door behind her.

Feeling lonelier than ever, Justice grabbed her coat and crept down the stairs. Seeing that the den was empty she bolted to the front door and quietly closed it behind her. She looked down the dark street trying to get her bearings. I think I saw a coffee shop a couple of blocks away. Justice walked the dark street for thirty minutes. Looking at a street sign she realized that she had no idea where she was. Panic filled her heart, and digging into her coat pocket, she realized that her cell phone wasn't in it. Suddenly, her attention was arrested by a man across the street. She warily watched him watch her.

His body shook and he babbled incoherently. Then he began to stumble towards her.

Justice whipped around and ran in the opposite direction. Not waiting for the sign for pedestrian crossing she ran out into the street. From behind, she heard tires screeching, brakes being slammed, and someone shouting, "Get the fuck out of the street before you get yourself killed." Dazed from the dangerous encounter, Justice shakily clung to a street pole. She never saw the man in the blue Bentley pull into a nearby parking space and head towards her.

"Justice!" he said in a wondering voice.

She turned and threw herself into the arms of Sterling Hart.

They closed around her.

She felt safe.

Sterling held her tight for an interminable time. Finally he pushed her from him, yet he didn't let her go. "Why are you wandering around this time of night?" He shook her gently. "You don't know the city well enough for that."

At once Justice began to pour her heart out to him: the hard time she'd had at Bryant Park, the meanness of Cassius, the animosity of her roommates, and the final straw, the fight she'd had with Laila. Then she burst into tears.

Sterling listened, and when she began to cry reached into his pocket, took out a white handkerchief, and mopped her tears. Once she'd stopped sobbing, he put the handkerchief to her nose and said with a soft smile, "Blow."

Justice did and the noise was so deafening that she had to smile.

"I'm sorry that you're not enjoying New York, Justice."

"I'm just lonely," she said, her tears now a mere sniffle.

"I wish that I could do something about that, Justice."

"You're doing something right now. This is the most fun I've had since you got off the plane."

"Crying to a stranger on a street corner is fun? That must be the saddest thing I've heard of in a long time." He looked at his watch. "It's getting late. Let me take you home so you can get there safely."

"It's not home," she said hoarsely, emotion clouding her voice.

"You know you have to go back sooner or later," he said gently.

"I'd rather make it later than sooner," she said. "I can't bear the thought of dealing with those people just yet."

Drizzle began to mist the air. It clung to their clothes and dampened their skin.

Justice looked at Sterling from under her long eyelashes. "Where were you going when I ran into the street, if you don't mind me asking?"

"I was going to the Waldorf. My corporation has a suite. Sometimes I stay there," he hesitated, "when I need to think about things."

"That sounds wonderful," Justice breathed. "I wish I had a place to go."

A long, heavy silence filled the air between them.

"You can join me, if you like." He gave her a small smile. "I promise that I'm not an ax murderer or anything."

Justice felt her breath constrict. But she managed to say, "I already know that. And being with you is safer than the streets, and preferable to going back there."

They rode to the Waldorf in silence. As Charlie Wilson belted out the lyrics to his latest hit, Justice slid Sterling a sidelong look. *I wish I could call Sterling my baby.* She observed Sterling absently chew his bottom lip. *He appears nervous. Of me?*

Inside the suite Justice swung her head appreciatively at the taupe and mahogany furnishings. "This is really nice, Sterling. Some getaway." Then she sneezed.

Sterling watched her and his expression was indecipherable. "You're going to catch your death of cold if you stay in those wet things. There should be a white robe on the hook of the bathroom door."

"Can I take a shower?"

"Certainly." Crossing over to the mini bar he opened a bottle of bourbon, filled a shot glass, and downed it. Easing himself onto the soft leather couch he said, "I'll take my turn in the bathroom after you finish."

Once Sterling was alone he wrestled with the thoughts of lust that encompassed him. *I have to tell her I'm married. She's so innocent. For all she knows I could be an ax murderer. But technically, I'm not a stranger.* Sterling poured himself another shot of Bourbon. And then he poured Justice a glass of red wine.

In the bathroom Justice savored every moment of the hot, pelting spray that seemed to wash away every miserable minute she'd had since Sterling had disembarked from the airplane. *I feel something that I've never felt before. Now I know what my mother meant. I want him.*

Justice sipped her wine and wandered around the master suite as Sterling took his turn in the shower. Finding herself in the bedroom, she eyed the California bed with white down comforter and feather pillows. She smoothed her hand wonderingly over it. She heard a large cough behind her and startled turned around. "Sterling," she stammered. "I'm sorry if I'm in your space."

Sterling was clad only in a huge bath towel. Long, silky black hair fanned his chest, and a line of it tapered down his flat stomach and disappeared underneath the towel. His eyes were hooded and once again she couldn't get a read on what he was thinking. When he spoke his voice sounded thick. "This is your space, Justice. I'll sleep in the adjoining bedroom."

"I don't want to put you out. I mean, I didn't ask if I could stay the night."

"You don't have to ask, Justice. I'm going to put something on and then join you in the sitting room."

Don't..."Okay," she murmured.

Minutes later Sterling stood at the bar. "Would you like a refill?"

"Yes," she murmured from the sofa. "That would be nice."

They quietly watched the flames flicker in the fireplace. They sat close but not quite touching on the brown leather couch.

Justice felt heat throughout her body, but it wasn't from the fire. When Sterling left the plane, I doubted that I'd ever see him again. Running into him is a gift from God. I don't want to waste it.

Sterling cleared his throat. "Justice," he said and his voice rumbled.

"Yes, Sterling," she murmured, remembering the vision of him clad only in a towel that hit him mid-thigh. I'd like to see all that is concealed. She looked down. Thank God he's as excited as I am.

When Justice turned her gaze to him Sterling felt the full strength of her beauty. Yet he saw something else. Looking deeply into her eyes he drank in her soul. And it mesmerized him. It was something that couldn't be put into words. And he wanted her. He reached out to touch her cheek.

Justice turned her mouth to his hand and brushed her moist lips across it.

Sterling hissed his excitement. "Justice, I think you should know..."

"Shush," she said putting her forefinger to his lips. "I never knew what it felt like to be struck by lightning until I met you. I know it sounds like a cliché, but Sterling Hart, I've never acted like this before," she paused as she stared into his round, black pupils, "I would very much like for you to make love to me."

The silence was deafening. With deliberation Sterling placed his glass on the end table, stood, and in one swift motion lifted Justice into his arms.

Justice slid her arms around his neck, clasped her hands behind his head, and buried her face into his chest. She felt as light as a feather as Sterling carried her into the bedroom.

He only paused his purposeful stride to kick the door shut with one foot before he gently placed her on the bed. Leaning over, he peered at her in the darkness. Emotion welled in his body. *I love her. I don't know how it happened so quickly, but I want her in my life forever.* Sterling took his time undressing giving Justice her time to change her mind. But inwardly he prayed she wouldn't.

She lay there patiently, and impatiently, wanting him.

When he joined her, naked, he pulled her into his deep embrace.

Justice felt the heat emanating from his body. His hard manhood was the only wedge between them.

"I don't want to hurt you, Justice," he groaned.

"Then don't wait any longer to make me yours," she whispered.

Sterling kissed her. It was the kind of kiss that a man gives to a woman he wants in his life for eternity.

Justice returned it with a passion that she'd never felt before and realized this was the kind of love that she'd never felt for another human being. Justice trailed her fingers down Sterling's back and clung to him, never wanting to let him go. She felt the muscles in his back, the tautness of his buttocks, as he gathered her even closer. She felt a rush of fluid inside her as he ran his hands down her smooth body. Suddenly Sterling stopped, feeling nakedness where he was used to hair. Pulling slightly away he looked down. "Hmm," he said wonderingly. "This is new."

"It's not new," she replied.

"It is to me."

"Do you like it?" she asked breathlessly.

"I absolutely adore it," he murmured. He pressed his full lips to her hairless vagina. "And I adore you." Then he began to lick every hairless inch of her.

Justice moaned, arching her hips upwards, clasping the wavy hair on his head.

He lifted her hips, drinking in as much of her as he could. And when his tip found her she couldn't help releasing her excitement. Only then did Sterling enter her wet womanhood.

Every time Sterling pushed inside her she clenched her walls tightening herself around him, drawing him deeper.

Their moans of pleasure filled the room endlessly before he suddenly lost control, as did she.

Rolling onto his side, Sterling pulled her into the crook of his arms and stroked her hair. The only sound she heard before she drifted off to sleep was Sterling's drowsy voice. "You have my heart, Justice."

The next morning Justice rolled over to see an empty bed. On the pillow was a handwritten note.

Justice, last night was so very special. Making love to you was the greatest joy I've ever had. But when I woke up this morning and watched you sleep, I realized that you're too perfect to be drawn into my world of problems. As you know, timing is everything. Yours is perfect, but mine is not. I'm sorry to leave you like this but there are things about me that you don't know. The bottom line is that you're too good for me. Learn to love New York and it will love you. That's such an easy thing to do. I understand if you hate me.

Sterling.

Justice sank to the floor, and in despair let out a wail like that of a wounded animal.

CHAPTER 5

Sterling walked stiffly over to the bar, poured himself a shot glass of bourbon, and downed it.

Harlow warily watched him from the couch.

He turned around to face her. "I want to move out. The baby will be born before our divorce will be started."

"You said that you'd try!"

His eyebrows furrowed. "I'm miserable with you, Harlow."

"Once the baby comes, you'll feel…" she said with a catch in her voice.

"Nothing for you."

She gulped. "He didn't raise you, but you're just like him."

Sterling stared out the window. The sky looked as bleak as he felt.

"Are you going to break your promise? What's six months, Sterling?"

"A death sentence."

"If you force this separation on me in my condition, I promise you won't be a part of the baby's life."

Feeling like a caged animal desperate for freedom, Sterling slammed out of the penthouse.

"Ouch," Justice gasped as Rossi raked a comb through her hair.

"I cannot believe that Raven is getting to be in the show tonight," he said irritably as he put the brush down and began dousing her coiffure withholding spray.

"She is?" Justice asked. "I thought that Caesar wanted only four models."

"He does," Rossi replied irritably. "Simone is sick and can't be in the show. "

"What's wrong with Simone?" she asked suspiciously. "She seemed all right last night."

"It's food poisoning. She sent word to Caesar that she could not get out of bed. When questioned, Scarlett confirmed her illness."

"Did anyone call a doctor?" Justice asked, staring almost unbelievingly at the mirror because of the transformation Rossi had worked.

"I don't know," he shrugged. "But because of this he had to send for Raven. She will take Simone's place."

"I know that Raven's happy," Justice said dryly. "Simone needs to do some hard thinking and figure out who gave her what food and when."

Rossi laughed. "I see that you have finally begun to understand the high jinks that are part of the modeling world."

"I've certainly figured out that people can be ruthless and you better look out for yourself. Unfortunately, I think that's the way it is in most jobs nowadays so why should modeling be any different?"

After she was finished with hair and makeup, Justice found a quiet corner. She clasped her hands in front of her and bent her head. "My sweet Lord, please keep me from making a fool of myself tonight." The minute the words were out of her mouth an inner peace flowed through her. It started at the top of her head and settled in her feet.

When she lifted her head, Justice found herself meeting the eyes of Cassius. Dressed in all black, he was standing in the semidarkness. Giving him a brief nod, to acknowledge his presence, she turned and walked to the other models as they stood together and waited for the show to start. Strobe lights and blaring music flooded the darkened warehouse.

Justice watched Raven as she strutted back towards them. The triumphant look she shot her as she walked past gave Justice a small feeling of disquiet.

She then watched Scarlett as she headed back towards them. Once she was out of sight of the audience she gave Justice a look that begged for forgiveness. "You look gorgeous."

Justice gave her a small smile, but shifted her attention to Laila who was now coming towards her. Their eyes met and the distant look on Laila's face let Justice know that she'd not forgiven her for her indiscretion.

Brushing aside these dismal thoughts, Justice readied herself for her last solo walk down the runway. This time she wore a black net bikini which hugged her like a second skin. With a confidence she hadn't felt the last time she'd been so scantily dressed, she stared straight ahead. As the tempo of the music changed to her signature debut song she broke through curtain that had hidden her from eager eyes. As she strode down the runway a feeling of exhilaration soared throughout her making her knees tremble. She sensed a presence in the arena that made her insides quiver and had to fight down the urge to swing her head around and scan the crowd.

At the close of the show, Justice stood on the runway with the other models. They all turned and clapped in unison as Caesar proudly walked up the steps, turned towards the audience, and took a deep bow to the resounding applause.

In the dimness of the room, a smoldering man watched Justice. Very slowly, his eyes hungrily ran up and down the length of her nearly naked body as she disappeared from view.

Justice didn't see Sterling Hart before he slipped out as noiselessly as he'd entered.

"You did it," Lucille said with an exultant look on her face.

Feeling as if all her strength had been sapped out of her, Justice sat on a stool and leaned the back of her head on the wall for support.

"I couldn't have done it without your help." Justice reached out and grabbed Lucille's hands. "Two times I would have put on the wrong dress if it weren't for you."

"You got confused because of the adrenalin rush. Models get mixed up all the time," Lucille replied. "Here comes Caesar and the official verdict of your performance. I won't hang around because I already know what it is. I need to go and get the models' wardrobes together. Sometimes things have a way of disappearing after a show."

Caesar headed towards her, followed by Rossi. But she felt herself focusing on the blonde who accompanied them. It was the same woman she'd seen with Caesar the day she'd fallen on stage. Justice stood to greet them.

"Justice, I would like to introduce you to Ursula Klein. She owns Catwalk Modeling Agency."

Justice stuck her hand out. "I'm very pleased to meet you."

Instead of shaking her hand, Ursula placed a small business card in her palm. "I watched you during rehearsals for the show. You've come a long way in four days, young lady. Come to the office tomorrow morning at ten. I'm interested in signing you with my agency."

"You are?" Justice placed her hand on her chest trying to soothe the rapid beating of her heart.

"And you are surprised? Why?" Ursula stared at her. "You stole the show."

"I did?" Justice replied, stunned by the turn of events.

"Good. You are humble. Don't lose that." She said to Caesar, "Thank you very much for inviting me to your show. Catwalk Agency models have some upcoming photo shoots for some high fashion magazines including Elle and Marie Claire. I would be very pleased for my models to wear some of your designs."

Caesar flashed a smile. "I think that can be arranged."

"Good," Ursula replied. She pulled her iPhone out of her jacket pocket. "I'm available tomorrow in the early evening. How would you like to meet me around seven for a meal at Cipriani Dolci?"

"It would be my pleasure," Caesar agreed.

"Good," Ursula said with satisfaction. "We can work out the details then."

Caesar nodded his head in assent.

Ursula turned to Justice. "Don't be late."

Justice swallowed hard. "I won't be, ma'am."

After Ursula was out of sight, Justice turned to Caesar and flung her arms around his neck. She gave him a big, sloppy kiss on his cheek.

"I thought that you didn't want to be a model," Caesar said playfully.

"That was before I knew that I could."She scampered over to Rossi, slid her arms around his waist and hugged him tightly."I owe you guys so much. Thank you, Rossi." Tears began to trickle down her cheeks. "I don't know how I can ever repay you."

"One thing you can do is buy me a new shirt," Rossi joked."You just smeared makeup all over this one."

"After I get paid from my first modeling job, I'll not only buy you a new shirt, but I'll buy you dinner too," she promised. She blinked away her tears. "I don't know why you guys have done so much for me, but I'll never forget it."

"Models come and go, Justice," Caesar said quietly. "But you have a raw, natural grace that can't be manufactured. You made my clothes come alive. You helped my debut in America be the best that it could be." He gently touched her cheek. "Tomorrow, I will have the car take you to your meeting with Ursula. But you have to learn your way around New York since it appears that you'll be spending a lot of time here."

"I'll learn how to use the GPS on my cell phone."

"That should help," Rossi piped in.

That night Justice whispered into the darkness, "Thank you, Lord, for answering at least one of my prayers."

At nine thirty the next morning, Justice sat in the office of Catwalk Modeling Agency. As she thumbed through the latest issue of

Vogue she heard in the deep recess of her mind a familiar voice. She looked up in search of its owner. Suddenly she felt the hairs on the back of her neck rise. The back of a tall, lean, man was in her line of vision.

He leaned over the receptionist's desk engaged in conversation.

Startled, she dropped the magazine and it slid off her lap onto the floor. Then she slid down into her seat in vain trying to hide her presence.

The man turned.

Justice was trapped by the gawking eyes of Miles Turner.

Miles stared at her. His Adam's apple seemed to gorge through his neck and he swallowed. Then he hesitantly walked over to her. "I can't believe that it's you, Justice. What on earth are you doing here?" Miles was dressed in a pair of stretch Levi jeans, black suede boots, and a turtleneck peeked out from under his coat.

Justice didn't respond as she stared dumbly at him.

Miles picked up her magazine and handed it to her.

"What are you doing here?" she stammered. Her tongue felt heavy and her mouth was dry.

"I'm trying to sign with Catwalk as one of their models."

"Have you graduated from college?"

Miles gave an awkward shrug. "I flunked out of school. I graduated with honors in high school, yet I was still unprepared for the college courses."

"So now you want to be a model?"

"Why not? I'm not going back home as a failure. I work as a waiter in the village and this guy came in and gave me his card. So here I am. What about you?"

"I've already modeled two shows for Caesar Brabantio," Justice said with a proud tilt of her head.

Miles gave a high-pitched whistle. "That's a big deal. How did you get discovered?"

"It's a long story that I don't want to share with you." Justice gave Miles a look that spoke volumes.

Miles coughed. "I don't blame you for being mad at me, Justice."

"I'm not mad," she replied in an aloof voice. "I'm just not interested in discussing my personal business with you. Why on earth would I?"

"I deserve this because I didn't end things the right way between us," he murmured softly.

"End things?" she spoke in a cutting tone. "You mean that I'm not your girlfriend anymore?" Now her look was scornful. "Funny.

Since you never called me and said that it was over I thought we were still together."

Mile's eyes devoured Justice. "Where are you staying?"

"None of your business," she replied coldly.

"Let me take you to lunch," Miles said.

There was a pleading look in his eyes but Justice was immune. "I think not."

"Please," he whispered, moving closer to her.

"I don't have any interest in spending time with you, Miles."

"Justice Fairchild," the receptionist shouted.

"Yes," Justice answered, bounding to her feet.

"Ms. Klein is ready for you."

"Justice," Miles said. He placed his hand on her arm.

She shook it off. "Get lost," she said before going to the young woman who stood in a doorway holding a clipboard.

Only when Justice knew she was out of Miles sight did she feel as if she could breathe freely.

"What are you wearing?" Ursula asked bluntly.

Justice looked down at the denim skirt, tights, and cardigan. "I thought that I looked nice," she replied self-consciously.

"That outfit is last season's rage," Ursula said. "You're a model so you need to dress like one."

"I haven't had any time or money to go shopping," Justice retorted defensively.

"What about your earnings from the two shows?"

"I had some personal business to take care of with it."

"So you sent it to your family in Eastman?"

"How do you know about them?"

"Caesar has apprised me of the financial straits your mother is in," Ursula said with a look of sympathy in her eyes.

"We're fine," Justice retorted. "There's no need for you to feel sorry for us."

"As a model you always need to look your best. We have a wardrobe room here at Catwalk. You may borrow three outfits. That will give you time to purchase something suitable."

"Thank you," Justice mumbled.

"Don't mutter! Also hold your head up," Ursula said sharply. "You have nothing to be ashamed of. Millions of girls would like to be in your shoes."

Justice gave Ursula a frank look. "Modeling is not my lifelong dream. I want to be a designer."

"Caesar mentioned that to me. If that is the case you are in a good position to get noticed. You will have access to many important people in the business. But first you have to be a successful model and must learn how to make the camera love you. You need a book."

"A book?" Justice asked.

"Yes. I have to be able to send your picture out to different magazines so that they will know about you."

"How much will that cost?"

"Around four to five thousand dollars, depending on which photographer we can book for you. We use several. The one who is available will get the job."

"I don't have the money," Justice admitted with a look of mortification.

"I will front it for you and take the money out of your wages."

"But I don't want to owe you any money," Justice protested. "What if I can't get a job and pay you back?"

"You would not be in my office if I weren't confident that I will make back my money and then some." She handed her a contract. "This is for a year. You may take this with you and bring it back signed tomorrow if you wish to work for me."

Justice felt compelled to say, "This is happening so fast, but I'm grateful for this opportunity."

"Good," Ursula said with satisfaction. "Now go to wardrobe and ask for Grant. He will help you pick out a few outfits. Be back here the day after tomorrow at nine with a, scrubbed face. We will have you work on your book."

"See you then," Justice said with an ecstatic smile.

Once Justice walked out on the street, she drew her coat closer around her.

"How did it go?" a low voice rumbled behind her.

"Yipes!" Justice screeched. Turning around she found herself face to face with Miles. "Don't stalk me," she spat out.

"We've known each other for too long for us to pretend to be we're strangers, Justice. I've missed you."

"You did not," she countered.

"I did so," he replied. "Did you ever stop to wonder why I took off the way I did?"

"No," Justice lied, looking away avoiding the intensity of his eyes.

"It was because I was afraid."

"Afraid?" she said suspiciously.

"I was only twenty years old and crazy in love with you. But I had nothing to offer you. So I felt that if I went away and made something of myself I could come back for you." He added softly, "Have a life with you."

"Give me a break," she said contemptuously. "What made you think that I would still be available after you finished finding yourself?"

Miles shrugged his shoulders. "I just always felt that if we were meant to be we'd end up together. And I was right. What are the chances of the two of us ending up in New York City and running into each other? Working for the same modeling agency? There must be a reason, Justice."

She stuffed her cold hands into her pockets. "So you did get signed?"

Miles hesitated. "Not yet. I think that Ursula is mulling it over."

"Humph," Justice said, patting a bag that held the three outfits that she'd chosen. "She offered me a year's contract to model for Catwalk. All I have to do is sign it. I'm coming back soon to do my book."

Now Miles looked away. "Let's go and get something, a glass of wine. I remember your favorite is Riesling."

"I've changed, Miles," she said. "I don't have a yen for the things I used to." With a slight curl of her lip she added, "And I'm not going anywhere with you."

"The fact that you're so angry must mean that you still care for me." He stared deeply into her eyes.

"Not really," Justice denied. "Maybe it just means that I'm appalled that you think that you can walk back into my life. Had you ended things differently, maybe we could be friends. But you just took off." Justice swallowed the lump in her throat. "It took me a long time to get over you. And now that I have I don't want you back in my life. So leave me alone," she finished in a hard tone.

As Miles watched Justice stalk off, his erection subsided from the continuous hard on he'd had since he'd seen her.

When Justice got home, she spied a set of plaid luggage in the foyer.

Laila was descending the stairs but stopped when she saw Justice. She put her hands to her lips and beckoned Justice to her.

Glancing into the den she stifled a feeling of annoyance.

Cassius had his back to her and was standing in the middle of the room. His hands were stuffed in his pockets and he was speaking in clipped tones to the other housemates.

68

Noiselessly Justice climbed the stairs and followed Laila to her room. Once inside she saw no personal objects at all. Justice looked at Laila questioningly.

"I'm leaving," Laila said bluntly.

"Why?"

"Because the show is over and the House of Brabantio is no longer paying for our room and board."

"What?" Justice uttered in surprise.

"Caesar had to tend to his business in Italy so Cassius is here delivering the news."

"Cassius is evicting us?" Justice asked fearfully.

"Not exactly," Laila said wryly. "You may continue to stay here but it will cost you."

"How much?"

"Six thousand dollars a month."

"Six thousand dollars a month! That's a ridiculous price," Justice exclaimed.

"Not for the New York fashion district. And certainly not for this."

"Even though Catwalk Modeling Agency signed me I don't have any money."

Laila's eyes opened wide. You got signed by Catwalk?"

Justice watched Laila closely. "Yes, that's where I'm coming from."

"Let me see the contract," Laila demanded.

Justice hesitated.

Laila gave her a shrewd look. "You think because I have been distant to you that I'm not to be trusted. I was angry about Raven, but I'm over that. You can trust me. But the others in the house, I think not."

Justice reached into her shoulder bag and took out the contract. She handed it to Laila.

Laila sat on the bed, motioning for Justice to do the same. She read the contract two times. Handing it back to Justice she said, "It's a fair contract. Sign it."

"Are you sure?"

"Yes. It's quite good for a beginner."

"But I don't have a place to stay now."

"You are settled here so I would stay here. It is extremely difficult to find apartments in New York. Besides, this is a safe area and since you are a newbie this is where you should reside. In the long run you will be better off."

"But I don't have any money," Justice half whispered.

"It states in your contract that they will pay for your housing until you get a surplus from modeling jobs. Let Catwalk pay your rent."

"I'm getting into a lot of debt," Justice said doubtfully.

"That's the way of the modeling world. It took me two years to become solvent and start saving money for college."

Justice gave Laila an inquisitive look. "Where are you going?"

"Since I was only on loan from Ford Modeling Agency I am flying out this evening. I have a photo shoot in Miami Beach. That will be a welcome change from this freezing cold weather."

"That sounds like a crème job."

Laila shrugged. "Being a doctor is the crème job for me. Modeling is only a stepping stone and that's all it should be for everyone. It doesn't last forever and you should remember that."

"I will," Justice promised.

"Let's go and join the others. I want to be present when you deliver the news to them that you will be remaining in New York and working for Ursula Klein." Laila chuckled, "That can be my going away present from you."

When they entered the den all eyes focused on them.

Cassius stared at Justice before shifting his eyes to Laila. "I'm guessing that Laila has informed you of the situation."

"Yes," Justice answered. "I would like to remain here at the house. I think that it will be convenient for me."

"Caesar apprised me that would probably be the situation with you."

"You're staying in New York?" Simone asked, shifting an uneasy look toward Raven.

Raven sat up and leaned forward. Her hazel eyes were as hard as diamonds.

Justice gave an encompassing look to everyone in the room. "Yes. I'm going to work for Catwalk Modeling Agency."

Scarlett offered after a slight hesitation, "Congratulations, Justice, though I'm not surprised you were offered a contract after your performance in the shows."

"Are you going to continue to live here?" Justice asked.

"Yes." Scarlett dropped her head and stared at nothing noticeable on the floor.

"Anyone else staying?" Justice gave Simone a pointed look.

"Yes, but I don't know for how long," she replied. "If I don't get booked with an agency, I won't be able to hang here much longer."

"I'm staying," Raven said.

Cassius looked at her. "Make up your mind," he snapped. "You just said that you were going to look for an apartment."

"I've changed my mind. I'm too busy modeling to look around."

"If you change your mind again, you'll lose your residence. Plenty of other people would like to live here. Do you understand me, Raven?"

"Yes, Cassius," Raven answered averting her gaze from the others.

"Good," he replied. "Now that that's settled, the rent is due on the first of the month. Do not be late on your payments or you will be asked to leave." Then Cassius gave everyone a brief nod and walked out.

There was a thickness in the air once the women were alone.

Justice scrutinized everyone's demeanor. Scarlett looked uncomfortable and after muttering, 'Goodnight,' scrambled out of the room. With a closed look on her face, Simone turned towards the television and began channel surfing, avoiding everyone's eyes. Raven stood and gave a long, exaggerated stretch before striding out the room without speaking to anyone.

Justice walked outside with Laila.

Laila turned to her and said, "Good job." Then the blaring of a car horn got their attention. "That must be my taxi." Laila leaned over and gave Justice a brief hug. "See you on the runway."

As Justice watched the taxi spirit Laila away, the familiar feeling of loneliness she'd felt since she arriving in New York flooded her. Then she sensed she was being watched. Justice looked to the left.

Across the street, Miles was standing in the doorway of the Wyndham watching her.

Justice stared at him. She stood her ground, refusing to run and seek shelter in the house.

He purposefully strode towards her.

"How did you know where to find me?" she spat out angrily.

"I called your mother. Please hear me out."

"Don't bother my mother," she snapped through gritted teeth.

"I explained the situation and she gave me your address," he said doggedly.

Justice glared at him. "What situation?"

A steady stream of words erupted from him. "That I'm here alone in New York. That you're here alone in New York. That it can be a very dangerous and lonely place for someone from the small town of Eastman, Georgia."

"I don't want you scaring my mother, Miles," she said harshly.

"I didn't mean to do that," he said. Miles wore a sincere look of apology. "Was that a friend of yours that just left?"

"She could have been," Justice answered in a despondent voice.

"Look," Miles said. "It's really cold out here. They have a really nice café across the street in the Wyndham. Let's go and have a cup of something hot."

Justice gave him a wary look.

"Please, Justice. Ursula called and offered me some work. We're going to be seeing a lot of each other and I don't want you to stiffen up every time I'm around you. I'd like to clear the air."

Justice mentally counted to twenty. Finally she said quietly, "Okay."

The atmosphere in the lounge was one of camaraderie among patrons as they consumed steaming cups of coffee, glasses of wine, and hor d'oeuvres. After her second glass of wine Justice leaned back against the booth, fully relaxed for the first time since she'd left Eastman.

"So you too got signed with Catwalk."

"By the skin of my teeth," Miles grimaced. "I think it was just because I was in the right place at the right time."

"What do you mean?"

"Ursula didn't give me a contact," he explained. "But I'm going to be commissioned to work certain jobs. I'm sure if there's a shoot where the model needs some guy just to stand there and look adoringly at her they'll call me."

"Oh."

"That's better than nothing," Miles said in resigned tone. "Most male models don't make half the money of their female counterparts anyway."

"You seem to have a good attitude about it."

"Whenever the agency calls me, I'm going to work my butt off and make all the contacts I can. A lot of male models start this way."

"Really?"

"A good example of that is Ashton Kutcher. He started off modeling for extra money and look where it's taken him. He's managed to branch out into all kinds of avenues in the entertainment world, from acting to producing."

"I've never heard you talk like this before, Miles, you appear to have so much more ambition than…" she trailed off lamely.

"Than before?" He gave her a quirky smile. "I guess I did grow up. I realize what's important now, Justice. I can't undo the damage that

I've done by leaving you the way I did. I did it because I was so insecure. I always thought that you were too good for me, Justice."

"I was," she replied in an only half-teasing manner.

"You are too good for me, Justice." He placed his hand on hers as it rested on the table. "But we've been thrown together by some force that's bigger than us. I still have love in my heart for you, Justice. Let's be here for each other." He gave her a soulful look. "This could be our second chance."

Much of Justice's anger for Miles melted and a fear of loneliness made her say, "I'm going to kill my mother."

"Really? Miles whispered. "When I see her I'm going to hug her neck and thank her. Now I'm hungry," Miles said. "Let's order something to eat."

As Justice and Miles feasted on chicken fingers, fries, and wings she studied his face. Miles looked the same way he had the first time she'd seen him when she was in the ninth grade.

"Remember when we skipped school and went to Six Flags amusement park?" Miles grinned as he munched on a French fry. "That was the best school day ever."

"It was a lot of fun," she agreed. "But I know you. I think you enjoyed yourself because we were getting away with something. Anything we weren't supposed to do excited you."

"Our parents never found out," he replied smugly. "I had connections in the front office."

"Is that why the school didn't call my house that night about my absence? I never figured that out."

"Remember my cousin Paul? He was a student assistant. I paid him ten dollars and he took our names off the absent list."

She laughed. "That sounds like something you would do."

"I didn't want you to get in trouble and be made to stop seeing me."

"Oh."

"Do you regret us, Justice?"

"I did after you left. But now," she admitted, "I don't know."

"You have a right to feel the way you do. I've thought about you every day. Once when I was in Atlanta, I stood outside and watched you work at Mabel's Magnificent Creations."

"You did?" she said in surprise. "Why didn't you let me know you were there?"

"Because of what I'd done to you." His voice was full of regret. "I knew how much you'd cared for me and I let you down. I was embarrassed."

"Had you come in and apologized I would feel better about things now. How do I know that you've honestly changed?"

"I give you my word," he replied. "Give me a chance to make it up to you," he asked in a beseeching voice.

"I'm confused as to what to do about you."

"I'm not. It's all I can do not to beg you to let me make love to you tonight."

Justice averted her gaze from his searing one.

"I won't rush you," Miles promised. "Take all the time you need."

CHAPTER 6

They stood on the front stoop. It was dark outside and the only illumination was a lamp post farther down the street.

Miles cupped her face in his hands and planted his lips on hers. He gently explored her mouth as if it was the first time they'd ever kissed. It evoked feelings in her of a time gone by. After he freed her mouth, he stepped back.

Justice grabbed the lapels of his coat, with her hands pulling him back towards her. This time she took her hands and cupped the back of his head pulling his mouth down to hers. The second time she tasted him she felt she was back in Eastman. Once she let him go she smiled tremulously.

"I thank you, Justice."

"For what?" she whispered.

"I think for giving me another chance."

Sterling's face flashed in front of her. With supreme will power she pushed it away. She gave no response.

"I guess that I need to get going," Miles said slowly. "I'm still not comfortable on the subway at night. They even mugged Kevin Bacon."

"He was probably mugged because they recognized him and figured he had money on him."

"Then I should be safe," Miles said in a self-deprecating manner. "You even had to pay for our meal because I don't have a dime."

Justice gave Miles a reassuring smile. She looked over her shoulder at the dark, cold, place she now called home. Then she looked back at Miles who reminded her of home. "That may be true, but at this time, in this place, I'm more than happy to see you," she said honestly.

"Really?" Miles said with a pleased look.

"Really," she murmured. "And you don't have to go." She took Miles by the hand and led them into the dark house. She whispered, "Be very quiet so we don't wake anyone."

"I promise I'll be a good boy," he teased.

"You better be," she lightly replied to his banter.

Justice turned to Miles. "I'm going to light a candle." Crossing over to the dresser she picked up a BIC lighter, withdrew a small candle, and lit the wick. Making sure it was secure, she turned around.

Miles had divested himself of his clothing and stood naked. "See how much I've missed you?" he said.

Justice stared at his hard shaft that pointed at her. "Yes, I do," she answered in a pleased voice.

Miles drew her close to his body. He took her hand and placed it on his penis. Its warmness pulsed inside her hand.

The loneliness she'd felt since Sterling Hart had abandoned her eased just a little bit. The familiar scent of Mile's body combined with the memory of what it had felt like with him inside her made her desire him.

As Miles lifted the hem of her sweater, she lifted her arms so he could disrobe her.

Miles hooked his fingers in the belt loops of her skirt and pulled it down. Next he freed her of the leggings and pushed her gently onto the bed. Justice lay back, closed her eyes and waited. She felt the front closure of her bra unclasped and tugged off her. Then she felt her panties slide down her body.

Miles kissed the middle of her stomach before feathering light kisses across her stomach. She felt his mouth close on one of her breasts. He licked the darkness around her nipple before he lightly bit her nub. Justice let out a small gasp of pleasure.

Miles took her fully into his mouth. With one hand he stroked the inside of her thighs and the other he entered her with his fingers.

She felt as if his fingers were inside her chest.

"It's you and me against the world," he muttered.

She felt safe.

Then he planted a long kiss on her mouth before letting his lips trail down the middle of her body past her stomach. He lifted her thighs so they fell over his shoulders. She stiffened in surprise at this unexpected move from him. "Don't be afraid," he said. "Just relax and let me love you."

Miles licked her from top to bottom and she felt dizzy. But then he covered her body with his and spread her legs.

"Not without a condom," she gasped.

Miles stopped. He begged hoarsely, "Please let me go bareback."

"No." She took the flat of her hand and planted it on his chest. "We've been apart too long."

After what seemed to be an eternity, Justice felt him lift off the mattress. After a slight noise, Miles rejoined her in the bed. "I keep a couple of condoms in my wallet just in case I get lucky," he murmured.

Then he entered Justice's wet body.

"This is good," she breathed as he thrust inside her. All of a sudden Sterling Hart's image came to her consciousness and she didn't try to push it away. Instead she lost herself in the memories. Justice lost track of how long they rocked together. Only after she heard Miles scream, "Justice!" did she release her desire.

Completely spent, Miles lay on top of her, his breathing labored. Then she felt his fingers wiggling inside her once again. As he took them out, he said, "My rubber slipped off in the end. You are just that damn good." Miles turned over on his stomach and soon she heard his light snore.

Justice stared at the ceiling.

The next morning, she sat on the side of the bed and watched Miles as he dressed. "I guess I can't get out of here without being seen," he said.

"I don't care who sees you," she said. "I'm grown."

"This is some setup you have here. You should see the dump I share with Billie."

"Who is Billy?"

Miles didn't answer for one long minute. Then he said, "An actor that I share an apartment with who's surviving off one commercial made three years ago."

"That's pretty good that he's been able to make his money stretch that far."

"Residual checks are the bomb." All of a sudden Miles leaned down and planted a possessive kiss on Justice's mouth. Leaning back he asked, "What are you going to do today?"

"I have to go shopping." She grimaced. "Ursula doesn't like my choice of attire."

"If you want purchase a nice pocketbook, I suggest you go down to Canal Street."

"I don't know how to get there." She admitted in a sheepish voice, "I'm deathly afraid of the subway system."

"Then I'll go with you."

"Don't you have to work today?"

"Today's my day off," he said. "But I want to go home and change clothes. I'll be back in a couple of hours."

"That's a lot of going back and forth. Why don't I just go with you and we'll take it from there?"

Again Miles hesitated before speaking. "My apartment isn't fit for you."

"Don't be embarrassed by where you live. I know that you've been having a hard time financially." She gave him a commiserating look. "I think almost everyone is."

"Yeah, it's been tough. But my house is dirty because I haven't had a chance to clean up. I don't want you to see how big a slob I am or you'll never marry me."

"Marry you?" Justice exclaimed in a shocked voice.

"Not now," Miles hastily added. "You know we used to talk about it when we were teenagers and now... Well, first I need to get a career."

"So do I," she said diplomatically.

"Walk me downstairs." With one hand Miles held out her robe and the other hoisted her to her feet.

As Justice and Miles descended the staircase hand in hand she felt a sudden hush fall over the conversation that was being bandied about in the den. Not looking in that direction Justice pulled Miles to the front door and opened it.

Miles looked curiously over Justice's shoulder before gathering her in his arms. She closed her eyes and lost herself in his kiss. "I'll be back around one o'clock for you."

"I'll be ready," she promised.

After Justice closed the door on Miles she turned around and headed back upstairs.

"Justice!"

She stiffened her shoulders and went to join her housemates. "What do you want, Raven?"

"I just wanted to say that I got you all wrong," she said in a snide voice. "I thought that you were some shy rube from a small town but instead you come up here and score yourself some dick."

"You know, Raven," Justice said in a sharp tone, "I'm so sick and tired of your mouth and assumptions about me. Not that it's any of your business but Miles and I have known each other for years. As a matter of fact, he was my high school sweetheart."

"He was!" Scarlett exclaimed in an astonished voice. "He's so cute, Justice."

"Is he up for a visit?" Simone asked, sneaking a look at Raven.

"No," Justice explained. "He lives in Greenwich and he's just breaking into modeling."

"What a coincidence," Raven sneered. "It seems as if New York is being invaded by a bunch of wanna be models or what is commonly referred to as 'flashes in the pan.'"

"Don't be too quick to write us off," Justice stated with smugness. "I've already been offered an excellent contract and Miles is the kind of man who will do anything he can to get what he wants. That's why he was here last night." She added confidently, "He wants me."

"Maybe," Raven retorted, her voice laced with innuendo.

"There's no maybe to it. I'm going to say this one time and one time only. I don't want you talking to me unless you have something nice to say. You seem to live your life with a lot of drama. All I want is to be happy and you're a real downer."

Justice was lying on the bed thumbing through the pages of a clothes design manual when she heard a tentative knock on her door. "Who is it?" she called.

"It's Scarlett. May I come in?"

"Yes." Justice threw her book aside and sat up, her body flush against the headboard. "Aren't you afraid to be seen talking to me?" she said sarcastically. "Raven might get mad at you."

"I want to apologize for my behavior."

"What behavior are you referring to?" Justice asked with a bland look on her face.

"Acting as if I don't want us to be friends when that's the exact opposite of how I feel," Scarlett said with a sheepish look on her face. "You seem like you're a really cool person. Besides I need to work on standing up for myself."

"How on earth have you managed to survive so long in the modeling industry?"

"Cassius looks out for me."Scarlett sat down on the bed.

A scowl immediately appeared on Justice's face.

"You don't like him?"

"No."

"Why not?"

"Why do you like him?" Justice countered.

"He's all I've ever known."

The air hung heavy.

"He's taking advantage of you," Justice said quietly.

"I guess that you heard that we're lovers."

Justice shot her an inquisitive look.

"I know that the others know about us. I've just chosen not to explain it to them."

"Then why explain it to me?" Justice asked.

"Because I like you." Scarlett explained in a halting voice, "Cassius doesn't sleep with his wife. The only reason he doesn't divorce her is because of his children."

"I'm from a tiny town and even I don't believe that shit."

"It's true," Scarlett declared hotly.

"Has his wife ever told you that?"

"Obviously she couldn't have since she knows nothing about us."

"I'm just saying that if the wife herself hasn't told you that there's nothing between them, I wouldn't believe that they don't sleep together."

"Cassius looks out for me," she whispered.

"Aren't you uncomfortable sleeping with a married man? How would you like it if your positions were reversed and Cassius was your husband?"

Scarlett averted her gaze. "Cassius loves me, not Nina."

"How do you feel when she comes to the shows?"

"She never does. Cassius makes sure of that. I told you that they don't really have a relationship."

Justice gave a snort of derision.

"He's paying my part of the rent here."

"He does that because he has nothing else to offer you. All he's doing is taking up your youth and one day you'll wake up and wonder where all the years have gone."

"I want us to hang out, Justice," she whispered. "But if you're going to badmouth my lover all the time I don't see how that can happen."

With her index finger Justice pointed at Scarlett. "You came in here." She looked at Scarlett's crestfallen face. With reservation she said, "But you're right. It's none of my business so I won't say anything else."

Scarlett drew in a deep sigh of relief. "Thank you, Justice, because I would really like us to be friends." She stood. "Oh, I almost forgot to tell you. Your boyfriend woke all of us up three times screaming your name. We were extremely jealous."

Justice's mother answered the phone on the first ring. "I was getting worried about you. You haven't called me in two days."

"You were getting worried because you gave Miles my address without my permission," Justice said in a dry tone.

"Oh," Evelyn said, apprehension apparent in her voice. "So he's already gotten in touch with you?"

"Yes, Mother," Justice said dryly.

"Are you two okay?" Evelyn asked.

"I think so," Justice replied.

Her mother's guffaw resounded through the connection.

"Don't get too happy, Mom. I don't know what I want."

"What do you mean?"

"I mean that we spent time together and it was," Justice hesitated, not wanting to disclose too much information or her mother would be purchasing wedding books for her to look at, "it was nice."

"Oh?"

"Yes, but it was different. I mean that there was a time that Miles really rang my bell. Even though I'm not sorry that we hooked up it wasn't the way it used to be."

"Give it time. The two of you have been separated a long time."

"Almost seven years. He left me on a 'supposed' vacation and never came back."

"He explained to me why he did that. That was the only way he was able to convince me to give him your address." Evelyn's voice grew pensive. "Men do a lot of stupid things because of insecurity. It's a natural part of their DNA."

"I don't like it when you make excuses for men, Mom," Justice said in a caustic voice.

"I'm not making excuses," Evelyn denied. "I was very unhappy with the way he broke your heart. But I do believe in fate, and the way the two of you ended up in the same place at the same time, I think that means something."

"Fate or a run of bad luck," Justice said in a flippant voice.

"Tell me this, Justice, when you and he were together, do you think that Miles felt about you the way he used to?"

Remembering what Scarlett said, she answered in a wry voice, "Yes, he was pretty much as excited as he was when we were in high school."

Evelyn chuckled again. "I rest my case, Justice."

"We'll see how it goes. It is kind of nice for Miles to be the one off kilter about us instead of me. Anyway, he's not the most important thing in my life. I have some really good news."

"What is it?"

"I got signed for a year with Catwalk Modeling Agency."

"I knew that was coming," Evelyn said with acceptance. "So that means that I'm definitely losing my baby."

"It's only definite for a year."

"That's what you say. What about your dream of being a designer?"

"There appears to be a lot of downtime between modeling jobs. I'm going to work on sketches and I might get lucky and meet someone willing to look at them." Sterling's face flashed in front of her eyes. "Sometimes timing is everything."

"Sometimes it is," Evelyn agreed.

"Come on," the man behind Justice said.

Flustered, she pushed her subway transfer into the slot for the third time. She tried to push the turnstile and still it wouldn't budge.

"It says that you don't have any more passes on your card," he shouted angrily at her. "Do you mind getting out of my way?"

She looked at the man's beet red face and stammered, "That can't be right. We just bought it."

"Well it's not letting you through and I'm not missing my train because of you."

From the other side Miles yelled through the iron turnstile, "Justice, move to the side and let that crowd through."

She dutifully got out of the way and once the crowd thinned Justice tentatively approached the turnstile again.

"Look at the direction of the arrows on the card," Miles advised patiently. "Follow the diagram."

In her hand, Justice turned the card around four different ways. Then taking a deep breath she slid the card into the slot. A green light appeared on the panel on the turnstile and she slammed her hand against the iron poles and rushed through to the other side. She practically fell into Mile's arms.

"Oh my God," she gasped. "That was harder than graduating from high school."

Miles laughed out loud, giving an okay to the interested New Yorkers who had been watching the scene.

Justice bristled, not enjoying being the butt of the joke. "Why did you go in front of me?" she asked crossly. "I told you that I didn't know what the hell that I was doing."

"I'm sorry, honey. From now on I'll let you go first." Miles grabbed her hand and Justice clutched it fearful of being lost in the throng of people as they ascended the stairs.

Once they surfaced, Justice handed Miles her subway card. "Here. You can have it."

"You have to learn the subway system here," Miles protested.

"I'll take a taxi."

"That's too expensive."

"I'll cut back on something else," she said. "I'd rather do that than lose my life because of a disgruntled native New Yorker."

They strolled through Canal Street mitten to mitten and the biting cold turned Justice's golden skin a deep ruddy hue.

Miles turned and pulling his scarf from around his neck, wrapped it around her throat. "You have to get a warmer coat." He pointed behind her. "There's Filene's Basement. That's about as reasonable as you're going to get around here."

Justice swung her head in search of the department store. Suddenly she found herself mesmerized by the stare of Sterling Hart. He stood several feet away from her and Miles.

Sterling was clad in a black, three-quarter length coat and a black hat. He wore a red scarf and his hands were stuffed into his coat pockets.

Trance like Justice stared back at him. Without realizing it, she withdrew her hand from Miles.

"What are you staring at?" Miles asked.

Justice didn't answer. Then her attention was dragged away from Sterling and she focused on the woman next to him. When she turned to Sterling and said something, her profile was breathtakingly beautiful. She too was dressed in a black coat, teamed with a red scarf and black hat. Sterling bent his head and she stood on her tiptoes in order to whisper in his ear. Then she possessively began to drag Sterling along the busy street.

Sterling stopped, turned, and through the crowd his eyes hungrily snaked down the length of her body.

The woman at his side swung her head around in an effort to find out what had Sterling's rapt attention.

Then Sterling stalked off, pushing his way through the throng on the street.

Justice watched the woman follow him, practically running in an effort to catch up with his long strides.

"Who is that?" Miles asked. He had a scowl on his face and his eyes glittered with obvious jealousy.

"No one," she answered in a tight voice. Her breathing was ragged and she felt her heart beating rapidly as she unsuccessfully tried to quell the feeling of agony at seeing Sterling in the company of another woman.

"You sure were staring at nothing for a long time," he said curtly. "I felt invisible."

"You're questioning me?" she snapped. "After what you did?"

"I've already apologized for that," Miles retorted with attitude.

"Do you think that because of last night you're off the hook?"

"I thought that you were at least going to let me try to make things right," Miles said in a low voice.

"I thought so too," she replied with an enigmatic look on her face.

"Well, it appears that I can't count on you to be with me forever."

"That's right. You can't." Then Justice felt a small tug of guilt at the hurt look that crossed Mile's face. "Come on Miles, let's see if we can find me a coat before I catch pneumonia."

In Filene's Basement they examined rows of garments. Miles dutifully followed her from rack to rack and held each item she planned to purchase. Justice managed to find a coat, five pairs of designer jeans with sweaters to match, black leather knee boots, and two pairs of eel skin gloves with soft fur on the inside. Once she felt satisfied that she had enough clothes to start her life in New York she went to the cash register.

"That will be twelve hundred fifty two dollars and seven cents, ma'am," the clerk said.

"That's quite a load you have there, Justice." He gave her an envious look. "I wish that I could help you pay the bill, but I'm broke."

"I wouldn't let you pay it even if you did have the money." Justice handed the clerk a credit card. "I don't want to owe you anything."

In an effort to erase the tense atmosphere of the heated exchange they'd had earlier, Miles said in a teasing manner, "How about last night? Don't you owe me something for that?"

Justice retorted swiftly, "Dude, you're the one who owes me."

In silence they continued their walk down the avenue until they reached Justice's place. Once they let themselves inside, Justice turned to Miles.

Putting down her purchases, he pulled her into his arms, lowered his mouth to hers and gave her a long, ardent kiss. When he released her he said, "It was almost like the old days, wasn't it?"

"It sort of was," she murmured.

Suddenly Miles' attention was taken away from her. He stared over her shoulder.

Justice turned around.

Raven was descending the staircase clad only in a push up bra and a pair of thong underwear. Her hair was tousled as if she'd just gotten out of bed. Her face was lightly made up except for her eyes. They had charcoal rings of eye shadow around them giving them, a smoldering look. Her skin glistened as if she'd just rubbed body oil on it. She was barefoot but a shiny gold bracelet adorned her ankle.

Miles' mouth fell open and he didn't look away.

"I didn't know that we had a man in the house," Raven drawled. Walking over to them she said, "You must be Miles. Excuse my appearance. I'm just so used to walking around naked in front of people I don't even think about it anymore."

Miles continued to stare at the mounds of Raven's breasts that practically fell out of her bra that was two sizes too small.

"That's okay," Miles finally stammered.

"Excuse us," Justice said curtly. Grabbing Miles by the hand she dragged him upstairs to her room. Once inside she said fiercely, "Don't talk to her."

"What did you expect me to do, Justice? Not speak when spoken to?"

"She hates me." Justice planted her hands on her hips, staring at Miles with an incensed look on her face.

"She seemed friendly enough." He took his hand and rubbed his chin thoughtfully. "Though I might add she appears to be a bit of an exhibitionist."

"She's never walked around half naked like that before," Justice said in a derogatory voice. "She staged that whole little act in order to get your attention."

"I've seen her somewhere before," he said musingly.

"Of course you've seen her before. Raven's a big deal in the modeling world. But she's a total bitch and out to get me because Caesar replaced her in the last two shows with me."

"She can't be jealous of you, can she?" Miles exclaimed in amazement. "She's gorgeous."

"Are you trying to say that I'm not?" Justice's eyes bulged in anger.

"Of course not," he said hastily. "It's just that you're Justice Fairchild and she is… I think I've seen her on a billboard in Times Square."

"Don't write me off as second to her, Miles." Justice took her index finger and pointed to her chest. "Just because she's been modeling for a while that doesn't mean that she's better at it than I am."

"This is a 360 degree change in you, Justice," Miles said in a confused voice. "I thought that you were just sort of pulled into this and it was only a way to come up with some quick cash for your mom."

Justice subsided on her bed. "It started out like that," she admitted. "But the more I model, the more I like it. It's a real high to have people clapping for you, envying you, praising you, and telling you that you're beautiful. I never got that type of adoration from anyone but my parents."

"I understand," Miles said quietly. "I too want to shed my past and start all over. I need to be a success at something."

Once Justice was alone in the room, she opened her cell phone, clicked on the Internet icon and searched the white pages. No Sterling Hart is listed. Damn!

Sterling sat on the couch watching the Miami Heat pummel Philadelphia.

"Sterling," Harlow said tentatively as she entered the room, "I've been putting so many baby things in my bedroom I can barely turn around. "Can I move back into the bedroom with you?"

He walked over to the bar and poured himself a shot of bourbon.

"Surely you jest," he retorted. Sterling slammed his glass down on the bar. "I'm going to take a shower."

CHAPTER 7

In a white dress made of feathers, Justice stood on a plastic rock formation. A fountain flowing in a pool of water served as backdrop.

"Turn your head to the left," Maximilian ordered.

Justice dutifully turned her head to the left.

"Now part your lips and give me the sexiest look you can."

"That's great, Justice. Turn towards the camera and find a comfortable position."

Maximilian's camera clicked and flashed.

"Now sit down and think about something that you'd like to have."

Sterling Hart's swarthy countenance surfaced in her mind. Justice sat down, faced Maximilian and spread her legs.

"Damn, girl, you're a natural," he said in an excited voice. "I think that's the last shot we need for your portfolio."

Justice breathed a sigh that was a combination of relief and exhaustion. She gingerly climbed down the slick plastic rocks, not wanting to end up in the pool of blue water.

Once she was steady on her feet, she took the hand Maximilian extended to her and allowed herself be escorted over to where Ursula and Jean Paul had sat for most of the afternoon.

"She was magnificent, wasn't she?"

"I'm very pleased with her performance," Ursula acknowledged. "Now we have to see if her sexuality transfers well in photos."

"If you are willing to pay me overtime I can develop the pictures tonight and have them for you tomorrow."

"That depends on how badly Justice wishes to see the finished product," Ursula said. "After all, it is her book."

Jean Paul interjected, "As Catwalk's publicist I need them as soon as possible so I can start sending them out to magazines. Designers' spring lines are getting ready to be shot."

"I too would like to see them as soon as possible," Justice replied earnestly. "Naturally I'm curious to find out how they look."

"It seems as if we're all on the same page," Ursula said, beaming.

Maximilian began to gather his equipment. "I'll meet you at Catwalk tomorrow around twelve with the pictures."

"Excellent," Ursula said. "Go and take off that dress and give it to Grant so he can have it cleaned."

"Yes, Ursula," Justice said.

After she was out of earshot, Maximilian said, "There's not any cellulite on that girl's bootie. She's a rare find."

"I think so," Ursula said, leaning back in her studio chair with a satisfied look on her face.

"We'll see," Jean Paul said in a more reserved tone.

When Justice reached the street she stuck out her hand for a taxi. With relief she saw the car halt in front of her. "Please take me to 6037 Madison," she told the driver.

The driver nodded his head and she climbed in.

Even before she was fully settled the driver pulled out into traffic. Pangs of hunger gripped her body. She leaned forward and tapped on the window. "I'm starving. Do you know where I can get some good old fashioned barbeque?"

"Dallas Barbeque on 42nd Street has the best in town."

"Please take me there."

"Certainly," he said, making a U-turn in the middle of the street.

"Aren't you afraid of a ticket?" she gasped.

"No," he answered.

At the restaurant Justice found herself a small table in a corner. She dug into a plate of ribs, corn on the cob, cornbread, and macaroni and cheese. Once her hunger was satisfied, she wiped her mouth with a napkin.

Immediately a waitress appeared. "Is there anything else you would like to order?"

"What is that?" She pointed to a huge glass with different layers of liquors in it.

"It's a blue martini. It's one of our specialties and I heartily recommend it."

"I'll take one of those, along with the check."

"Yes ma'am," the waitress said and disappeared.

An hour later, Justice stumbled out of a taxi in front of her house. Through her inebriated haze, she caught sight of Cassius' car parked out front and with disgust her lip curled. Once she let herself inside, she struggled up the stairs. Sliding her hand along the wall as a guide she reached the landing and found herself under the scrutiny of Cassius.

"Well," he said and his accent seemed more pronounced than

usual. "I see that you're learning to enjoy New York. Maybe you and I can go sightseeing one night." Cassius reached out and fondled Justice's breast.

She stumbled back against the wall. "If you do that again, I'll slap the shit out of you," she said in a serious tone.

"Don't think more of yourself than you should," Cassius replied caustically. "I can make or break you."

"I don't work for you," she shot back.

"Get a better fuckin' attitude or you won't work for anyone," he said in a threatening voice. Then he brushed down the stairs past her and slammed out the door.

Inside the safety of her room, exhausted, she crawled into bed fully dressed and fell into a dead sleep.

Ursula, Jean Paul, and Maximilian were pouring over the spread of photographs. Maximilian held a magnifying glass over one of the glossies.

Justice tentatively knocked on the door.

All their heads popped up.

"Come in," Ursula said enthusiastically. "We were just trying to decide which photos to send out to the design houses and magazines. Each photo seems more stunning than the previous."

Justice clasped her hands excitedly in front of her. "You mean that you like them?" she asked.

"The camera loves you, darling," Maximilian quipped.

"I've already sent some photos by courier to Elle," Jean Paul broke in. "They have a shoot coming up tomorrow and the model they hired had to drop out."

"Oh?" Ursula asked.

"Yes. Her mother died so she can't make it. It seems as if everyone else is booked at the moment or passé so they're kind of up the creek. It works for us."

"I'm sorry about her family tragedy, though," Justice said quietly. "It's kind of eerie the way I get jobs."

"Well, unless you killed her, don't give it another thought." Ursula advised, "Take the opportunities when you can."

Jean Paul's phone rang. "I need to take this call. I'll go outside in the quiet."

"Come and sit," Maximilian ordered. "Now tell me what you think."

"I like this one," Justice said and pointed to a pose with her lying in a hammock.

"Yes, that's pretty good. But in the future you need to elongate your leg. You're tall, but as a model you need to look the tallest that you can in photographs."

Elongate my body. I need to remember that.

"I'm impressed." Ursula sat back in her chair. "I've never seen such a natural."

Jean Paul reentered the room. "I just booked you for Elle. The job pays over fifteen thousand."

"Thank God," Justice exclaimed.

"You'll be the centerfold." Jean Paul put his cell phone back into his pocket and looked at Ursula. "But we have to also provide a male model who's taller than she is."

"I'll go through my books and find out who's available," Ursula said.

"How about that new guy that was here the other day?"Jean Paul asked.

"I don't know about that, Jean Paul," Ursula answered. "He seems a little too slick to be teamed up with Justice."

"What do you mean by that?" Maximilian asked.

"He seemed kind of full of himself. I hadn't locked him into a contract, yet when I called, he acted as if he expected it."

"Had you offered him any work?" Maximilian asked with a raised eyebrow.

"No. I only made up my mind this morning," Ursula said.

"This morning!" Justice exclaimed before she could stop herself.

"Uh-huh," Ursula said, giving her an inquisitive look.

"But he'll work for cheap," Jean Paul said. "Besides it's only a one day shoot."

Should I say that he's my ex?

"Let me see a picture of him," Maximilian said.

Ursula stood as she said, "I'll be right back," and dashed out the room.

In less than a minute, she came back with a large book and flipped to the back pages. "Let me see. We have another picture of him."

"He's certainly handsome enough."

Justice mentally crossed her fingers.

"We'll try him for this shoot," Ursula said.

"What are you going to pay him?" Jean Paul asked.

"I'll give him one of the suits that he has to wear for the shoot as a payment."

"That doesn't seem quite fair," Justice protested. "I mean, look what you're paying me."

All eyes turned on her.

"Don't tell me how to run my business," Ursula said sharply.

A tense silence invaded the room.

"Exposure in a major magazine for a newcomer in modeling is worth thousands of dollars." She glared at Justice. "Anyone in the shoot should keep that in mind and be grateful to be a part of it."

Justice dropped her head. When she looked up she caught Maximilian watching her carefully.

Seeing her discomfiture, he adroitly changed the subject. "I happen to be the photographer on that shoot. Since Justice and I have already worked together, I think that things should go rather smoothly."

"See that it does, Max, and I'll make sure you get even more work."

"It sounds like a plan." He grinned. "My goal is to become Catwalk Modeling Agency's number one photographer."

"We'll see," Ursula stated without commitment.

Justice stood in the doorway and viewed the scene with distaste. Miles and Raven sat close on the couch, whispering. Justice reached behind her and opened the door and slammed it, announcing her presence. Their heads popped up.

A guilty look stole across Miles' face.

Raven's countenance was watchful as she tried to gauge from Justice's expressionless face what she was thinking.

Without giving them a second look, Justice bounded up the stairs. Inside her room she sat on the bed and with arms folded, she waited.

"Hey, honey. What's going on?" Miles asked in an attempt to sound jovial. He stood in front of her and shifted from one foot to the other.

"I thought that I told you not to socialize with Raven," she spat out. Her eyes stared menacingly into his.

"I was just trying to be nice," he stammered. "I can't sit in her house and ignore her. Besides, I might be working with these ladies one day, and I'm not in any position to be a prick."

She gave him a look that spoke volumes.

"Besides, I was just waiting for you."

"And who told you to come here without my permission?"

"You didn't answer your cell phone so I figured that you'd show up here eventually. I have some really good news and couldn't wait to tell you."

"I was in a meeting."

"I got a modeling job. I'm going to be in a spread for Elle Magazine tomorrow."

"I know," Justice said, the coldness in her voice not melting. "I was there when Ursula decided to give you the job. We're going to be working together."

Miles leaned over and gave Justice a smacking kiss on her lips. "I should have known you were behind it. Thanks for having my back, girlfriend."

"First of all, I'm not your girlfriend." She ticked off fingers one by one. "Second of all, I had nothing to do with it. No one at Catwalk has an idea that we even know each other and I'd like to keep it that way. Thirdly, why did you lie to me?"

With each piece of Justice's tirade, Miles eyes had gotten rounder. After a long hesitation he asked, "What did I lie about?"

"You said that you were put on commission for Catwalk the same day I was offered my contract, yet I found out that Ursula just called you this morning."

Miles got a sheepish look on his face. "I was just trying to think positively." He shrugged his shoulders in an effort to appear nonchalant. "I knew that given the opportunity you would speak up for me, Justice. Help me sort of get my foot in the door. We're cut from the same cloth."

"What do you mean by that?" she asked in a suspicious voice.

"We have the same family background. We attended the same high school. We're alike, you and I." He reached out to caress her cheek.

She slapped his hand away before he could make contact. "You lie way too easily. I mean, did it even bother you that you misled me about the real deal with Catwalk?"

"Of course it did," he said, swallowing hard. "But I had to come up with a reason for you to let me back into your life. So I said that Ursula had already signed me." He lifted her chin. "The bottom line is that I'll do anything to be with you, Justice. Take a minute to think about it. There's nothing wrong with a man loving you to distraction, so that he'll do anything to be with you." Miles sat down on the bed next to her. "The lie was worth it. For me, the added bonus is that I get to take a picture with you tomorrow and we'll be in a spread in Elle. All the people in Eastman who thought that I was going end up back home with my tail between my legs are going to be so jealous, because I have the beautiful Justice Fairchild, model, and designer extraordinaire, hangin' on my arm." Miles wrapped his arms around her and pulled her close. "Now can I please take you to bed?"

Justice sat at the breakfast bar, sipping a cup of coffee. She smiled at Scarlett when she padded into the room in Scooby Do pajamas.

"Where did you get those from?"

"Don't laugh," she replied. "These are real warm and cozy. Besides, they're real cheap."

"Then I think that I'll go and get some," she said. "The word cheap fits into my vocabulary."

"I finally got a financial advisor. He looked at my credit cards and said that I'm spending too much money on crap and I need to cut back."

"Money doesn't go very far."

Scarlett said, "I don't have to pay any bills here but I'm trying to boost my nest egg. It's kind of hard because the last shows I did were the first ones in a long time; but I did manage to save some of it."

"Hmm," Justice mused. "That sounds like a good idea. Once I get my mom's finances straightened out I need to do the same."

"Don't wait as long as I did. The fresher your face is the more jobs you usually get."

"Who's your investment adviser?"

"His name is Frederic Missoni from Italy and he has a lot of high profile clients. I looked at his portfolio and Googled him on the Internet."

"When I'm ready I'll check him out." Justice gave her a cautious look. "What are you going to do today?"

"Get the hell out of here," Scarlett answered in a meaningful tone.

"Why?"

"Have you noticed that Simone hasn't been around that much?"

"Not really," Justice said. "Where is she?"

"She moved out yesterday."

"Good," Justice said, taking a sip from her cup.

"She couldn't pay the rent. Those two last fashion shows were the only jobs she's had in a year."

"That's too bad. But I'm not going to pretend that I'll miss her."

"Well," Scarlett said slowly, "without her lapdog around making her feel superior, Raven has way too much time for mischief."

Justice put her cup down and looked at Scarlett. "What are you trying to tell me?"

"Before you got here last night I overheard Raven coming on to Miles."

Justice pursed her lips in displeasure. "I figured as much. What did she say?"

"She asked him if he wanted to escort her to an event." Scarlett gave a wide grin. "He told her no because you were his girlfriend and wouldn't like it."

A feeling of satisfaction warmed Justice's belly. "Then what did she say?"

"She told him that you couldn't help him get where he wanted to go but that she could because she has connections. Then she kissed him."

Justice's eyes narrowed into angrily slits. "Did he kiss her back?"

"I don't think so. I could hear but not see them because I was listening from the other side of the laundry room door." She screwed up her face, trying to remember the sequence of things. "But on second thought he couldn't have because the next thing I heard was her angrily calling him a country boy."

"Raven has some real issues," Justice said in utter disgust. "Miles didn't tell me any of this last night."

"He probably didn't want to upset you or cause any more tension in the house. I just thought that I'd warn you what Raven was up to and let you know that your man is a keeper."

Justice walked into the studio at Elle and sauntered over to the receptionist. Smiling warmly at her she said, "I'm from Catwalk Modeling Agency and I'm here for a photo shoot."

"May I see some identification, please?" the receptionist asked in a haughty voice. "I don't recognize you and we get a lot of people pretending to be models so they can get upstairs and waylay the executives."

Justice handed the receptionist her driver's license.

She looked at a list and crossed through Justice's name with a yellow highlighter. "You're all clear. Take the elevator to the top floor. That's where the shoot is being held."

The first thing she spied was Miles standing in a black suit and white shirt talking with wild gestures to Maximilian. He eagerly nodded his head as Maximilian pointed to different pieces of scenery that would be used as backdrops for the photo shoot.

Justice walked over to them. "Good morning, gentlemen."

Maximilian gave her a bright smile. "Good morning," he said with an approving look. "I'm glad to see your face bare because hair and makeup are waiting down the hall for you." He turned to Miles and pointed. "This is Miles Turner. He's the model working with you today."

Justice held her hand out. "It's nice to meet you, Mr. Turner."

"Please call me Miles," he replied with a twinkle in his eyes as he shook her hand.

Maximilian studied them carefully. "This should work out just fine. Miles is not much taller than you so we won't have to change the height of the floor camera in order to get both of you in the shots." He looked at Justice. "Hurry up and get ready." Maximilian turned his back to her and began fiddling with his equipment.

Justice knocked three times on the door that was labeled hair and makeup.

"Come in," was shouted from the other side.

Justice pushed it open and Lucille and Rossi stood on the other side.

"Oh my God," Justice squealed, rushing to them and throwing her arms around them, hugging one and then the other. "I thought you guys were in Italy," she exclaimed.

"We were," Rossi laughed. "But Caesar sent us back to start getting things ready."

"What do you mean?" Justice asked.

"He's setting up a permanent base in New York. Lucille and I have volunteered to help him get his studio started. We're also doing freelance work for magazine shoots so when we were offered the opportunity to work with Catwalk's latest protégé we jumped at the chance."

"It's so good to see you guys," she said. "I've missed you. It's been kind of a bummer without you."

"But Catwalk signed you," Lucille beamed. "That is good."

"I have a feeling that the two of you helped me get that. I know that Caesar did."

"Caesar is a class act," Rossi said. "He's all about fashion and beauty with no hidden agenda."

"I hate to sound mundane," Lucille said, "but are they paying you well?"

"This job is going to pay my rent for a month and I can also finish paying off the liens on my mother's house in Eastman."

"I told you that you were going to make a lot of money," Rossi

said with a touch of smugness. "I'm never wrong about things like that."
He wagged his finger at her. "Follow my advice and you'll go far."

"But enough of the chit chat," Lucille said. "We have to get you ready for your shoot."

Hours later, Justice was dressed in a white Grecian style gown that swirled around her feet.

"That's perfect, Justice. Now I want you to give me the look of a confident woman who's not afraid to use her sexuality to get what she wants."

"What!" Justice exclaimed.

"There's nothing wrong with using your beauty to get what you want from a man, Justice. Look at Miles as if he is completely under your spell and later that night the two of you are going to fully satisfy each other."

Justice shifted slightly from one foot to another while at the same time folding her body slightly into Mile's.

Miles placed his hand possessively on Justice's waist and stared down into her eyes.

"That's all wrong, Miles," Maximilian screamed. "Who told you to touch her? How many times do I have to tell you not to move unless I tell you to do so? You've ruined the shot. Now I have to take the picture again. Justice," he said in a raspy voice, "try to recreate the exact expression that you just gave Miles."

Justice tried to block out the angry look in Miles' pupils as he stared down at her. She refocused by drawing to her mind the same face she'd been using all afternoon. When she visualized Sterling's smoldering countenance she heard the flash of the camera.

"That's it for today," Maximilian said in a worn-out voice. "I think that I have enough pictures."

Without speaking to anyone Miles stormed out of the room, slamming the door.

Maximilian looked at Justice. "I don't like him." As he gathered up his equipment he said, "You did an excellent job today, Justice. You're a real pro. I'm in a hurry to see the finished product. See you at Catwalk." Then he too disappeared out the door Miles had just slammed.

With tired steps, Justice shuffled down the hallway to the hair and makeup room. Once there she found only Rossi. "Where's Lucille?" she asked in an exhausted voice.

"She had to leave right after she fitted you in your last outfit. Why the glum look on your face?"

"I feel sorry for Miles. Max was kind of hard on him."

"I saw some of that." Rossi closed the laptop he had been using when she entered the room. "But Maximilian was right. That Miles was stiff as a board. His clumsy ass trod on the bottom of your gown and even bumped into the scenery. Most of all there was absolutely no chemistry between the two of you."

"Maybe that's both of our faults," she mumbled. "Maybe there's nothing there."

"But it's a model's job to make it appear as if something is there. You managed to accomplish that, Justice. It's not your fault that this Miles person doesn't know what the hell he's doing."

That evening Justice was grateful for the solitude of her room. She picked up her phone and called Miles for the third time. Once again his phone went straight to voice mail. "Miles, I'm sorry things didn't go well for you today. Don't be too discouraged. It was your first time. I'm home now if you want to come by and talk."

Maximilian showed Ursula and Jean Paul the stills from the afternoon's photo shoot.

"You were right not to sign Miles with Catwalk," Maximilian said in exasperation. "He doesn't have it."

Jean Paul looked at the photo and in disgust handed it to Ursula. "They're worthless. What's Elle going to say when we send them those photos?"

"Nothing bad because we're only going to send the ones with Justice posing alone," Ursula flatly stated.

"But that's not the assignment," Jean Paul exclaimed. "They wanted some duets."

"That's only until they see Justice alone. Her pictures are fantastic."

"I agree with Ursula," Maximilian interjected. "Don't forget my reputation is on the line too. I don't want to send any of that out with my name attached to them." He pointed to the stack of pictures that Miles was in.

"You don't have to worry about that," Ursula said soothingly. "I won't be using him again."

Justice called Miles' cell. Again it went straight to voicemail. "Miles, I'm not going to call you again. I know that you're upset about the photo shoot, but it was your first time. Call me or better yet come over so we can talk." Justice wearily sank onto her bed. That pasta I ate before I came home made me sleepy. I'll just close my eyes for a minute. A few seconds later Justice fell into a fitful sleep. Later that night in the dark recesses of her mind she thought that she heard a doorbell. But then she didn't hear anything thing else and drifted back to sleep. Hours later she awoke. Glancing at the clock on her nightstand she saw that it was almost midnight. Opening her mouth, the bad taste of the day combined with the fact that she hadn't brushed her teeth before she'd fallen asleep was more than she could bear.

She stumbled into her adjoining bathroom and after brushing her teeth and gargling stepped into the shower and under hot, stinging water. Justice thoroughly scrubbed every inch of her body and after she used the facial cleanser that Lotus had given her she felt like a new woman. She quickly dried herself, wrapped the towel around her and went back into the bedroom.

She found Miles leaning against her dresser. His arms were folded and the ruthless expression in his eyes was one she'd never seen before.

"How'd you get in here?" Justice stammered in surprise.

"Raven let me in," he answered in an expressionless voice.

"Oh," she said. "I'm glad that you're here, Miles. I wanted to talk to you about today."

"What about it?" he muttered harshly.

Justice walked over to Miles and touched him gently on his cheek. "So you had a bad day."

"Don't blame me for what happened at the studio," he said in a hard voice. "My job is to make you look good and I did that."

Justice stiffened in shock. "Are you trying to say that you made all of those mistakes at the photo shoot to help me out?"

"Are you saying that I didn't?" he answered shortly.

"Well, if that's the reason I wouldn't do it again," she offered in an unconvinced tone. "Sometimes you have only one chance and that can make or break you."

"You had more than one chance."

"But they came looking for me, Miles," she said gently. "You're trying to impress them."

"You blew it on your modeling shoot in Atlanta. They had to train you to get you where you are."

"First of all, I didn't blow it in Atlanta. What would make you think something like that?"

"Raven told me."

"She lied to you. You need to think about what you're saying.

How the hell would she know that? She wasn't even there because she was too stupid to make the plane. And I thought that I told you not to talk to her," she said angrily.

"You're not the boss of me, Justice. No one talks to me in any derogatory way." Miles said in a spiteful voice, "I guess I showed that Maximilian that."

"What did you show him, Miles?" she asked in derision. "That you can't take directions and you're childish by stomping off, not even acknowledging him, saying thank you, or being gracious. The people who work with models can make or break them. It's not the other way around."

"I'd had enough," he said coldly. "But you're right," he finally said in a softer voice. "I shouldn't have let him know that he got to me."

Justice saw the look of false bravado in Miles' eyes. Her heartstrings tugged with memories of the good times they'd shared in Eastman when they'd both been so young, and carefree. She wanted to pacify him. "Let's not fight, Miles. Let's just say that what happened today was out of the control of either of us. We had a bad day, but we can have a better night."

Miles peered into Justice's eyes. For a split second she thought she recognized a flicker of regret in his. But then a shutter seemed to close over his expression. "I have an early appointment in the morning. I'll call you when I get a chance."

After Miles departed Justice fell into a deep sleep.

Justice was turning over sausage in a frying pan when Scarlett entered the room.

"Hey, Scarlett. What you been up to?"

"I went to the market." Scarlett placed a plastic bag of fruit down on the counter. "How's everything with you?"

"Okay, I guess. I don't have anything to do today except go to Catwalk and see how my pictures came out. I'm not really looking forward to that. Yesterday was not a good day."

"That's good," she mumbled, shifting her eyes from Justice's.

"You are totally distracted and didn't hear a word I said. What's going on with you?"Justice asked, putting the cooked sausage on a plate and soaking the grease off it with a paper towel. "Is there something on your mind?"

"I have something to tell you and I don't know how you're going to take it."

"What?" she said.

"I saw Miles coming out of Raven's room. He was in there for hours."

"What? When?" Justice asked in a disbelieving voice.

"Last night," she said, her face full of misery. "I'm sorry, Justice, but I thought that you should know."

"I don't believe you," Justice said heatedly. "Miles was with me last night!"

"I know," she said. "When he saw me he went into your room."

"You're wrong." Justice shouted angrily, "I'm so sick and tired of you instigating bitches. If it's not one thing it's another. How dare you tell me about my man when you're going with someone else's husband?"

"At least Cassius's wife and I don't live in the same house," Scarlett retorted, stung by Justice's words. "Besides, what does my situation have to do with anything?"

"It means that you don't see things clearly."

"I don't hallucinate, Justice," she said in a defensive voice. "I hoped that I wouldn't have to say anything else, but right now they're at the corner Starbucks having coffee. I saw them when I left the fruit stand."

Justice glared at her. "My mother always says to watch the dog that brings you a bone."

"Well, I don't know what the hell that means, but if you're not afraid and so sure that I'm not telling the truth, go and see for yourself. I was just trying to be a friend to you," Scarlett finished in a hurt voice, as she turned on her heels and slowly climbed the stairs to her room.

Justice bowed her head in shame for what she said to her friend.

"So you're going to be a father?" Chapman said. "You always wanted that."

"I'm warming to the idea of fatherhood."

"How are things between you and Harlow? Are they any better?"

"Of course not," he answered without hesitation. "We know that we're only together for the baby."

"You were almost free and you got pulled right back in," Chapman said in a frustrated voice.

"It's not all Harlow's fault that we're unhappy," Sterling said. "I've changed. The things that I enjoyed when we first got together just got boring for me."

Chapman grimaced. "Maturity has a way of doing that."

"It wasn't just that. In the beginning it was a kind of high being a Wall Street stockbroker analyst. I was invited to and catered to at all the important parties. Harlow and I really enjoyed attending those functions together, and I felt as if I was on top of the world. But then it got to be so vicious that I began to feel like a lobbyist. The more I sucked up, the better chances you had of getting tips from people as to what should they buy stock in that day."

"Yeah," Chapman said with a teasing laugh. "I think that's called insider trading. You're lucky that you're not in jail."

"I've never gotten information from disreputable sources, but I think that some of my coworkers have crossed the line."

"I wouldn't be surprised. You said that they made a lot of money even in a recession."

"We made a lot of money. I really don't have to work if I don't want to. And I want out. It hurts me to see small businesses go under and people losing what they've worked their whole lives for."

"So are you going to quit Wall Street and follow your dream of becoming a clothes designer?"

"I checked out several institutes while I was in Miami because I still have my house there. I showed them my sketches and they seemed really interested. But now since I have to stay in the area because of the baby, I'm going to apply here in New York. The only reason I was going to relocate to Miami was to put as much distance as possible between me and Harlow and my old life."

"I take issue with that, man," Chapman protested. "I'm a part of your old life."

"I don't mean you or Constance," Sterling explained. "But hell, I don't even get to see the two of you guys that much because Constance can't stand Harlow."

"I'm not even going to pretend to deny that," Chapman said. "Constance has never forgiven Harlow for snubbing her in front of her high society friends. The morning of the wedding I had to practically force Constance into the bridesmaid's dress. The only reason she finally agreed to go through with it was because she has love in her heart for you."

"I wish you'd told me about that. I would have straightened Harlow out from the beginning."

Chapman shrugged his shoulders. "It was too late and the damage was done. Besides, Constance should have never said anything."

"I sort of forced it out of her. After declining three party invitations because she was sick, tired, or too late getting off at work to make an appearance, I felt the need to get to the bottom of things."

"Constance can't get past our poor roots of Bedford-Stuyvesant. Even though we two now have all the money that we need she looks for people who think that they're better than she is so she can put them in their place."

"But you two are happy, right? You've grown in the same direction."

"We're very happy," Chapman affirmed. "Not that we don't have our fights. But we did that when we dated so it's kind of expected."

"You know it's funny." Sterling said, "Harlow and I never had one argument before the wedding."

"That's probably because she was pretending to be something that she's not. I knew the moment I met her that she wasn't the right woman for you."

"You should have told me," Sterling said with some censure in his voice.

"You wouldn't have listened. A man in love never listens to what his friends say about his woman. Besides, the minute you saw Harlow posing naked in your art class you were a goner."

"That wasn't what attracted me to her," Sterling protested.

Chapman made a derogatory snort.

"She approached me, man, and you know it. When I started talking to her she seemed so exciting and passionate about life."

"That's because she thought that she was going to be a famous model. The minute things didn't work out the way she wanted them to she turned into this person you're married to now."

"Well, in the future if you know anything else that I need to know, tell me."

"Promise." Chapman held his hand up and Sterling slapped it.

"All she seems to care about is her position in The Inner Circle."

"That social group is an outlet for rich women with not enough to do. How about the baby? Is she excited about the thought of being a mother?"

"I don't know about that. But I do know she wants the baby to have two parents. I just don't see how we can live the way we do year after year."

"Raising a child in a hostile environment is a no win situation for everyone."

"You know it's weird. Harlow and I still don't argue. We just talk at each other or ignore each other's existence."

"That's such a bad sign. It means that you're not passionate enough about each other to argue. It sounds kind of boring to me."

"It is," Sterling said. "But then I got thrown for a loop. I've never felt what I'm feeling before and I can't figure it out."

"The girl on the plane," Chapman said.

Sterling looked at Chapman. "How'd you know?"

"The last three telephone conversations I had with you Justice Fairchild's name came up. If she's still here in New York, why don't you try to find her?"

Sterling looked down and mumbled, "I have something to tell you."

"What is it?"

"I ran into Justice after meeting her on the plane. She'd had a rough day and wanted to go somewhere quiet."

"Uh-oh, you didn't!"

"Yeah, I did."

"Why are you just telling me this, man?"

"Because I'm ashamed of what I did; I feel like such a user."

"So you didn't tell her about your wife or the baby?"

"No," he said slowly, "because I wanted to spend time with her and I knew if she knew the truth... So the next morning I bolted, and I kind of left her a Dear John letter on her pillow."

"The great escape!"

Sterling dropped his head.

"What did the letter say?"

"About how I have too many problems and can't drag her into my baggage."

"Damn, man," Chapman's eyes were round from astonishment, "you ran out on her."

"I couldn't stand the thought of what I'd see in her eyes once I told her the truth."

"But, dude..."

"Justice deserves more than a married man with a pregnant wife."

"But if she has one tenth of the feeling for you that you have for her, maybe she'll be patient until you extricate yourself from your present situation."

"Until Harlow has the baby I have a responsibility to her and my child."

"I was shocked when you called me and told me that she was pregnant," Chapman said, shaking his head at the memory.

"It was a huge surprise. We've been kind of hit and miss sexually. But there was one night we seemed to be in tune. The Hangover was on television and she'd never seen it."

"The first one is the best of the series. But it still doesn't seem like anything she'd like."

"She'd been at a luncheon with one of her sorority sisters and it came up that the actor who plays Alan is a Kappa."

"Get the hell out of here!"

"Yeah, and she went to college with him in North Carolina so she wanted to see it."

"He is freaking hilarious."

"Tell me about it. We watched it together and really enjoyed each other's company so after a couple of beers one thing led to another." Sterling said in a frank voice, "It had been a while. But then things got back to business as usual with Harlow never at home and out doing all of her society stuff for charities. That's the reason why when Harlow asked me for a divorce I first said no."

"I don't get it," Chapman's brow creasing in confusion.

"I just figured that if we could maybe find some things that we could enjoy together again things would get better. But by the time I got off that plane, I knew that there was something better for me out there. Living your life is more than just existing. I know that a happy marriage isn't in the cards for me and Harlow."

"But this girl," Chapman said. "It sounds as if she really is the one."

"I know that she is the true love of my life...." Sterling said quietly. He drained the last of his cold coffee. "If I can ever fix this mess I will," Sterling promised with conviction.

CHAPTER 8

Justice stomped over to the hall closet and threw on a light sweater. She let herself out of the house and quickly walked the short distance to Starbucks. She looked through the window and saw neither Miles nor Raven seated in the coffee shop. Still, she threw open the door and stormed inside.

She looked like ready to attack as she stood in the doorway. Her warlike stance and ferocious expression attracted the attention of several people seated by the door and they gave each other uneasy looks, as if they feared she was getting ready to go postal.

Chapman gave a low whistle and then said, "Aw, suki, suki, now."

"What is it?"

"Look what beauty the wind just blew in."

Sterling turned around to see who Chapman was looking at. "Oh my God," he breathed. "It's her."

"Her who?" Chapman's eyes widened in amazement. "You mean that's Justice?"

"Yes."

"Damn, man. She's fine as wine. But she looks upset." Chapman urged, "You should go and see what's wrong."

Sterling sat there indecisively.

"This may be your only chance. New York is a huge place and you might not run into her again." He paused. "At least find out if she's okay."

These words spurred Sterling into action and he slid out of his seat, attracting Justice's attention.

The sight of Sterling advancing towards her almost buckled her knees. She placed the palm of her hand over her heart trying to calm its erratic beat.

He stopped in front of her. "Hello, Justice." His low voice almost took her breath away.

She barely eked out, "Hello, Sterling."

"I'm here with a friend. And I know that I don't have the right to approach you." He asked in a humble voice, "But will you please join us so that we can talk?"

Justice dumbly nodded yes.

Sterling cupped her elbow, and led her over to the corner booth where Chapman sat quite amused by the turn of events his morning coffee had brought.

"This is my best friend, Chapman Keen," Sterling said.

Justice smiled at him. "Hello," she murmured softly.

Chapman nodded his head and said, "And hello to you, too."

Once she was situated Sterling asked, "How do you like your coffee?"

"I drink hazelnut with extra cream and sugar."

Sterling lightly touched her on the shoulder. "I'll be right back, Justice." Then he gave Chapman a stern look of warning.

Once Sterling left, Justice felt Chapman watching her with extreme interest.

"Sterling talks about you all the time," he said mysteriously.

"He does?" Justice said, taken aback by Chapman's statement.

"Yes. I know about the night the night you two spent together."

Justice felt color flood her face.

Chapman continued, "He's beating himself up emotionally about that dumb stunt he pulled. Give him a chance to explain. He really cares for you."

Justice felt hope ignite within her.

"Sterling is a good man. Don't judge him by the baggage he's carrying. Give him a chance to get his act together and don't tell him what I told you." Then Chapman folded his arms in front of him and settled back against his seat with a satisfied look on his face.

When Sterling rejoined them, he held a saucer with a muffin and put it in front of her with the coffee. "I didn't know what kind you liked so I guessed blueberry."

"You guessed right." She took a huge sip of her coffee, the hot liquid burning her throat.

"The weather has turned unusually warm, hasn't it?" Sterling said as he gave Justice a soulful look.

"I'm done," Chapman muttered in a teasing voice.

"Excuse me?" Sterling murmured, not taking his gaze from Justice.

"I hate to leave this scintillating conversation," Chapman quipped, "but I'm due at court in an hour." He stood. "It was very nice to meet you, Miss Justice Fairchild. Words do not do you justice." He cocked an eyebrow at Sterling. "See you soon."

"Yeah, man," Sterling said eyes never leaving Justice's face. "I'll see you soon."

Once they were alone Justice picked up her muffin, and took a huge bite out of it. As she munched on it, she rolled her eyes as if it were the best muffin she'd ever tasted.

Sterling watched her antics and had his first genuine smile since leaving her at the hotel.

Feeling as if there were crumbs on her mouth she took the tip of her tongue and ran it around the rim her lips.

Sterling gulped. Then he circumspectly slid his hand under the table and adjusted his privates that steadily rose since he'd seen her again.

"Thank you for breakfast, Sterling."

"You call that breakfast?" he teased. "I can buy you more than that."

"Unfortunately, I can eat a lot more than that."

Sterling drank in her beauty. "You don't have to worry about your weight. You're perfect."

"I don't know about that," she said, dropping her eyes from his obvious admiration. "But I'm what they seem to want; a stick with breasts and a butt hanging off it."

"Justice, I felt like a bolt of lightning hit me when I turned around and saw you standing there. I want to right a wrong."

"I understand, Sterling. It was the right place but the wrong time," she said with a small smile.

"There's more to it than that, Justice."

She interrupted him with obvious jealousy in her voice. "On Canal Street, was that your girlfriend you were with?"

There was a long, tense silence. "I don't have a girlfriend," he said tersely. "Was that your boyfriend?"

A diamond hard look entered Justice's eyes. "Not anymore."

"Well, he really lost out," he said. A rush of guilt at his continued deception made him quickly change the subject. "Do you live in the area?"

"Yes," she replied. "I'm renting a place right down the street at 6037 Madison Avenue."

"So the modeling world is treating you right?"

"So far so good. I didn't expect to get work so quickly."

"I knew that after one look at you all the agencies would be clamoring to hire you." Suddenly Sterling asked in an anxious voice, "What are your plans for today?"

"Nothing much. I have to take care of something but that won't take long. I mean, that's why I actually came into Starbucks, but my mission didn't pan out the way I expected."

"Oh," Sterling said obvious interest in his voice.

"Without going into details a friend told me something that I didn't want to believe. But I have that gut instinct that she's telling me the truth." Justice bowed her head. "I feel badly about the way I talked to her. I need to right that wrong."

"I hope it's not bad news."

"It's not good. But then I shouldn't be surprised. I just feel so stupid."

"I'm angry?" Sterling stated in a hard voice.

"You're angry, why?"

"Because someone stole that beautiful smile of yours," Sterling said with a ferocious expression. "Is there anything that I can do to help?"

"You already have. But if you do want to spend some more time with me, I have a request."

"Anything."

"I've never been through Central Park."

"You want to walk the park?"

"I feel as if I don't get enough fresh air."

"Welcome to New York," he said with a smile. "I have a great idea. Come on."

Once outside, Sterling swung his head around looking in all directions.

"Who are you looking for?"

"It should happen in just a minute," he said with a hopeful look on his face.

Suddenly Sterling let out a high, pitched whistle. A man with a horse drawn carriage had just rounded the corner and when Sterling saw him he started waving his arm frantically.

Immediately the horse's speed accelerated and in a moment the carriage shuddered to a stop in front of them.

"We want to go to Central Park," Sterling told the driver.

The driver nodded his head in agreement.

They sat in companionable silence listening to the rhythm of the horse's hooves as they hit the pavement. Finally, Justice said, "I've been here for months, but haven't really seen the city. This is wonderful, Sterling."

"It's fun seeing it through your eyes. People from the city don't always appreciate it."

"We're lucky we're able to hail a carriage. I heard that the city is doing away with them."

"I saw that on the news," Justice said.

"The city has other things to offer. If you stroll through Times Square it sounds like a U.N. convention."

"I know," she said. "I was down there observing a modeling shoot and I felt drab because I don't have an accent."

"We just passed the Smithsonian. I'd like to take you there one day if you'll let me."

Justice gave him a small nudge with her shoulder. "I'll let you."

"We'll see," he said. Suddenly Sterling's expression dimmed. "We're at the park." He climbed out of the carriage and handed the driver some bills.

Once again the driver simply nodded.

"Does he speak English?" Justice whispered as they walked off.

"Probably. Most of them do because they need to understand where people want to go. He probably didn't answer because silence makes him seem more exotic."

Justice and Sterling strolled through the park. After an hour she said, "Let's sit on the bench and rest. I really haven't had any exercise since I came up from Eastman."

"Do you miss Eastman?"

"Yes and no. It's really tiny, and country, but its home."

"There's nothing wrong with small towns, Justice. People from there have values."

"Some," she said, thinking of Miles. "But not all. You know, Sterling, I don't really know anything about you but I feel as if I've known you forever."

"I know what you mean. I hadn't realized until lately how lonely my life is."

"What do you do?" she asked. "I can tell from the cut of your clothes that you're not poor."

"I'm a stockbroker," he replied.

"Ohh," she said, impressed. "You're a money man. You have the power to change the world."

"Being a stockbroker isn't what it's cracked up to be. My lifelong dream is to be a fashion designer."

"Oh my God!" she exclaimed. "That's what I want to do."

"It is?"

"Ever since I was a little girl I've made my own clothes. One of the reasons I decided to give modeling a shot was to make contacts with designers. On my days off I make sketches, hoping for the chance to show them to someone."

"Are they any good?" he asked teasingly.

"Yes, they're good," she said, replying seriously to his banter. "How about you? What do you know about designing clothes?"

"I took some classes while I was at NYU."

"But I don't understand. Why are you working on Wall Street? Fashion and Wall Street are totally different worlds."

"When I went to college Finance was my major. Junior year, Chapman and I partied real hard."

"So you guys have known each other for a long time?"

"We grew up together in Bedford-Stuyvesant. But anyhow, I missed the deadline to sign up for my classes. I hadn't taken any electives and I needed them to get my degree. Clothing design was the only thing left."

"Oh my God," Justice said, laughing.

Sterling shook his head at the memory. "I was so pissed. But if I didn't carry a full course load and maintain at least a 3.5 GPA, I'd lose my scholarship and I didn't have any money."

"So you took the class and liked it?"

"I loved it. It turned out that I was a natural," he said proudly. "I like creating things, and I love beautiful women. I felt as if I'd finally found my niche. But I couldn't switch my major so late in the game. Instead, I filled up my remaining electives doing what I enjoyed."

"So you graduated as a stockbroker but wanted to be a designer. Why didn't you pursue it when you graduated?"

"Money is the only reason I made the choice that I did. I'm an only child and my mother was a single parent. I was able to retire her to Miami and she enjoyed the last years of her life in financial comfort."

"So your mother's gone?" Justice asked softly.

"Yes. She died a couple of years ago after a long illness."

"What about your father?"

"He's dead and I don't talk about him," he said abruptly. "The last time I saw my mom she told me that she knew that I was unhappy with my life and I needed to make some changes. That's what I'm trying to do," he finished in a somber tone.

Respecting his need for privacy she slid her hand into his. "My dad is gone too, but I have vivid memories of him. You remind me of him because you have mannerisms like him. You tilt your head the same way when you're listening to me."

Sterling gave a start of surprise. He leaned over and placed his free hand over Justice's and said with heartfelt meaning. "I'm so glad that I'm not."

Justice's tinkling laughter filled the air. Once it subsided she continued, "My mom has struggled financially also. We've always been poor. But I think that modeling will be our financial savior. I must admit I enjoy being admired, but I too want to make other people feel beautiful."

"I knew that you were something special the moment I set eyes on you, Miss Justice Fairchild."

"It seems as if you and I have a lot in common, Mr. Sterling Hart."

He swallowed hard. "Justice, let me take you to dinner tonight. I have something that I'd like to talk to you about."

"What is it?" she asked.

Sterling hesitated. "It's kind of involved, and long."

"Does it involve me?" she asked, remembering what Chapman had said.

"Sort of. At least I'd like it to."

They stood on the sidewalk. With his fingers Sterling traced her delicate features.

Her heart palpitated.

Sterling tilted her chin.

Justice closed her eyes in readiness for his kiss.

When his lips touched hers, she melted into the warmth of his body. Her arms crept up around his neck and she leaned into the folds of his body. His lips were tender yet firm. Then his tongue entered her mouth. Very slowly he explored every inch, finally finding her tongue. Justice had no concept of how long they kissed. Once he released her, he cradled her close to him, breathing in the fragrance of her hair. Then he leaned his head on top of hers, his arms secure around her waist. "Seven o'clock, right?" he murmured.

"Right," she choked out with her eyes still closed.

Sterling continued to hold her close. He only broke their embrace when he heard obvious coughing by a spectator. Mustering up all the will he could, he pushed her gently away from him and looked for the source.

A very elderly lady sat on a bench observing them. "That's enough, young man."

"Yes, ma'am." He whispered in Justice's ear, "My cell is 212 597-4312.You can call me anytime day or night." Sterling hailed her a cab. Once she was seated comfortably he handed the driver some money, "See that she safely gets where she wants to go," he said. "That's some precious cargo you're carrying."

Justice gave him a tremulous smile.

Sterling took his hand and tapped his heart two times, paused and then three times. Then he crossed the street and hailed another cab.

Justice watched him until he was out of sight. The sound of her cell phone shook her out of her reverie. "Hello," she said.

"Justice, this is Ursula."

"Hello," she said cautiously. "How are you doing?"

"I'm great," she said enthusiastically. "Maximilian brought me your shots for Elle and they are magnificent."

Justice felt as if a huge burden was lifted from her shoulders. "Thank goodness," she breathed. "I was so nervous that I was going to come over this afternoon and talk to you about them. I'm glad that things worked out."

"They worked out for you all right," Ursula said dryly. "For Miles, not so much."

"What do you mean?" Justice asked.

"We cut him out of the campaign for Elle. He has what we call dead eyes. Catwalk will no longer be using him."

"Oh," Justice said in an evasive voice.

"Does that bother you?" Ursula asked.

"No, why would you think that?"

"Max seems to think that Miles was too familiar with you and that maybe the two of you have some sort of history."

"I knew him from Georgia," Justice admitted. "But I hadn't seen him in years and by chance ran into him at Catwalk."

"Well, you won't be seeing him here again." Ursula paused. "Will that bother you?"

"No," Justice answered truthfully. "It doesn't bother me at all."

"Good. I do need you to come by this afternoon. I have some really fantastic news for you, and I don't have time to go into it right now because I'm late for another meeting."

"What time?" Justice asked.

"Four o'clock is good."

Less than thirty minutes later Justice stared doubtfully at the brown, broken down apartment building. She gripped Miles' business card. Miles Turner, Actor, Model. "Humph!" she said, "he should add User, and Loser." Then with determination, she climbed the stairs of the apartment house and banged on the door.

A sleepy Miles opened it.

If she weren't in such a hurry to get this over with she would have laughed at the look of alarm on his face. He looked fearfully down the street in both directions as if he thought that he was on a bad reality show and there was a hidden camera. "Justice," he said warily. "This isn't a good time. I have to get ready for work."

"Too bad," she said pushing past him. Once inside she surveyed the room and was surprised to see it decorated so tastefully. Giving Miles a derogatory look she said, "This must be Billy's stuff because I know you don't have any taste."

"I don't know what's going on with you," he said with a resentful glower, "but I've already told you that now is not a good time to talk."

"Did Scarlett see you leaving Raven's room last night and having coffee with her at Starbucks?"

After a long pause he answered in a surly voice, "Yes, so what?"

"Why?" she demanded.

"I'm so tired of this same old shit, Justice. I'm sorry that you don't like her but I think that she's real cool. She's going to try and hook me up with some modeling jobs and maybe an agent."

"Are you too stupid to see that you don't have what it takes to be a model?"

"Maybe it was my prop that ruined the shoot!" he yelled. "You have done nothing to help my career!" he shouted.

"I'm just starting out myself, Miles." She glared at him. "How the hell am I going to help you? Obviously the only reason you got back with me is because you knew Catwalk signed me and you want to hang on my coat tails."

Miles' mouth pursed with annoyance.

"Did you sleep with Raven?" she asked demandingly.

"We didn't sleep," Miles replied in a nasty voice.

"You suck, Miles," she said in a voice full of repulsion.

"I didn't suck," he said before he paused. "She did."

"You're disgusting. I think that the two of you deserve each other. Raven is a has been," she paused, "and you're a never was."

"That's what you say," he said. "You'll see." His chest seemed to puff up right before her eyes. "I'm going to be a leading male model."

"You blew your only chance, Miles." Justice started laughing so hard that she had to bend over and hold her stomach.

"What's so funny?" he said suspiciously.

"Ursula isn't going to use any of the photos that you were a part of. She said they were so bad that your face won't be seen in Elle representing Catwalk. As a matter of fact, I've got a feeling that you won't get another chance anywhere. News travels fast in the modeling world." Justice put a deliberately haughty look on her face. "Now I have to go because I have plans later this evening." She waited for Miles' reaction.

The myriad of emotions that crossed his face were interesting. First he looked angry, then scared, and finally contemplative. "I didn't sleep with Raven," he said hoarsely.

"I don't believe you," she countered. "But it doesn't matter to me if you did. I want someone else."

"What?" Miles shouted angrily, "Already?" Then he grew very still, looking past her.

Justice turned around and found herself staring at a woman.

The woman held two bags of groceries that she slammed onto the kitchen counter.

"What are you doing in my house?" she snarled.

"Your house?" Justice asked startled. "You're Billy?"

"Yes, I'm Billie." She went over and stood defiantly next to Miles. "And what are you doing here with my man?"

"Nothing important," Justice answered, sadly shaking her head. "By the way," she leaned in and said in a conspiratorial tone, "he's cheating on you. First it was with me and now it is with a model named Raven Sugalsky. Her address is 6037 Madison Ave."

Miles' mouth dropped open from dismay.

Billie turned to Miles and started screaming at him in fluent French.

Justice closed the door behind her and it still didn't block out the virulent tirade. Without looking back she strolled down the street.

Three hours later, Justice sat across from Ursula and Jean Paul.

Ursula assessed her appearance. "I like what you're wearing. You're beginning to dress like a model."

"Thank you," Justice said.

"That coral shirt is amazing with your complexion," Jean Paul complimented her. "Where did you get it?"

"Because I don't know where to find the best bargains in New York, I've been doing a lot of Internet shopping. I pretty much bought a whole new wardrobe through the Internet. Bluefly.com and Gilt are amazing."

"That's a smart thing to do," Ursula said. "Your schedule is about to be very hectic so you need to find a way to condense things. I brought your here today to tell you that I have some awesome news for you." She smiled at Jean Paul. "Since it was your idea, you can tell her."

"Justice," Jean Paul said, "I flooded the market with your pictures and Nile Cosmetics bit."

"What do you mean?" Justice asked.

"Nile Cosmetics is a subsidiary of Max Factor. They're launching a new line of cosmetics for African-American women and they want you to be the face."

"Me?" Justice explained. "I'm a nobody. Don't these

companies usually use a star or somebody well known to push their product?"

"Usually they do," Ursula said smugly. "But actresses demand millions of dollars. The economy is better but businesses are still cutting back."

Justice asked, "Ursula, will I make enough money to pay you what I owe you?"

"And then some," she crowed. Ursula opened her desk drawer and handed Justice a check. "They want you to show up tomorrow morning so they can start working on their campaign. Here's your signing bonus."

Justice gasped at the amount.

"I've already deducted what you owe me, plus the administrative fees that I've incurred advertising you," Ursula said. "This is what's left over."

"I've never seen a check with four zeroes," she said in awe.

"This is just the beginning," Ursula said. "Just keep looking the way you do and you'll be fine."

"What do you mean keep looking the way I do?" asked with a perplexed look on her face. "What would change?"

Ursula handed her a contract that had Nile Cosmetics boldly printed across the front page. "A lot of times models get drawn into the fast lane. They start partying too hard and begin to look haggard. Make sure that you take care of your appearance. The clause in this contract is the same as in the one you have with me. We can break our contracts if you can't fulfill your duties to our satisfaction."

Justice brushed that aside. "I won't ruin this, Ursula. I never thought that I'd get paid this much money for something that I don't have to work for."

"Modeling is hard work, Justice."

"I know that," Justice said. "But everyone has looked out for me. You even paid my rent until I could get on my feet."

"That's standard practice, Justice."

"Well," she said in a musing voice, "you won't have to worry about paying it anymore. I'm moving anyhow. I hate where I live and with this check I can start looking for a place right away."

"Why do you hate living there?" Jean Paul asked. "I've heard that it's absolutely beautiful."

Justice decided to be diplomatic. "I want my own place. I'm an only child and used to having my own space."

"That's probably a smart move," Ursula agreed.

###

The minute Justice got outside she called home. "Mom," she said in an excited voice. "Guess what?"

"What?" Evelyn said.

"I got a cosmetics contract with Nile Cosmetics. I'm going to be on television."

"Are you going to be an actress?" Evelyn asked, stunned by the latest accomplishment of her daughter.

"Not exactly," Justice chuckled. "There will be pictures in magazines of me wearing the makeup and one commercial to go along with it. Ursula handed me a script. I only have one line."

"I can't wait to tell it," Evelyn laughed.

"Mom, I want you to remodel the house. Now that all the liens are paid and the taxes are up to date we can afford to splurge a little."

"It would cost too much to do that," Evelyn protested. "I can't take any more of your money. You earned it, so spend it on yourself."

"Mom, that's my house too. I want you to be comfortable. I'm on my way to Chase Manhattan to deposit my check. You can withdraw money from your branch because you're listed on my account."

"Are you sure about this, Justice?"

"Mom, you've been living in that house forever. Those bathrooms need to be remodeled and the carpet is threadbare. Every room needs to be painted. You fix it up the way you've always dreamed. When I come home for Mother's Day, I want to see a big improvement. Is Aunt Minnie around? I want to tell her my good news."

"She was here for lunch but went home."

"Shoot," she said. "You know how she hates getting news secondhand."

"Justice," Evelyn said with a catch in her voice. "I hope you know how much I appreciate you."

"I hope you know how much I love you and Aunt Minnie," she said before she hung up.

###

Justice stood and turned around, staring at her body from all angles. Her long black hair was pinned and combed into a pony tail at the top of her head. Ringlets of curls cascaded to the nape of her neck. Her skintight black dress from Bergdorf's with black tights and four inch stilettos made her look ready for a fashion shoot. Large gold-hooped earrings and dramatic make-up gave her face a sultry and mysterious look. Satisfied, she grabbed a bottle of Calvin Klein perfume, applied it sparingly on all her pressure points, then sprayed some into the air and quickly walked through it so that it would cling to her body. Nervously, she wiped her hands on a small washcloth and after grabbing her small clutch went to meet Sterling.

As Justice stood outside in the dusk she spied Scarlett walking towards her.

Scarlett slightly stumbled when she saw Justice.

Justice went to her, closing the distance between them. "I'm sorry that I went off on you this morning, Scarlett," Justice said. "You were right about Miles. I confronted him and he didn't even try to deny it."

"That's okay," Scarlett said with a nervous quiver in her voice. "I just hated to be the one to have to tell you something like that."

"I'm glad that you did." She touched Scarlett on the arm. "You are a good friend to tell me and I called you a bitch. I don't want to be that kind of woman."

"What do you mean?" Scarlett asked.

"The kind who won't face the truth about the man she's sleeping with. Women like that walk around with blinders on and turn on all their friends. The bottom line is I'm really angry at myself for giving him a second chance when I wasn't really feeling it. I was just so lonely and he was convenient... but to be deceived like that... It's one thing to know your man is a cheat and to accept it, but..." Her voice trailed off.

Scarlett dropped her gaze.

An uncomfortable silence ensued.

Deciding to change the subject Justice said, "I even found out that Miles is living with a woman. I didn't suspect anything."

"He is!" Scarlett exclaimed. "How did he manage to pull that off?"

"He never invited me to his place, using the excuse that it wasn't fit for me to see. I went over there to confront him and surprise, surprise," she added bitterly.

"Oh my goodness," Scarlett said in an appalled voice. "What did you do when you found out?"

"I told Billie that he was cheating on her with me and Raven." Justice gave a smile of intense satisfaction. "I also gave her our address so that she can confront Raven if she doubts me."

"Miles must be livid."

"I think he was more flabbergasted that I would tell her. I think men that cheat always think the woman is going to be so broken-hearted and embarrassed that she'll just run away from the situation. I'm running," Justice said softly, "but I won't be part of a cover-up for his sexual infidelity. It's not my shame. It's his."

"Raven is going to really go after you now."

"I'm not afraid of Raven," Justice stated with confidence. "Besides, I had already decided to move out the minute I made enough money and could find a place."

"I hate for you to leave. Now with Simone gone, I'll be stuck alone with Raven until someone else moves in and I might not like them."

"Don't sweat it, Scarlett. You can get along with anybody."

All of a sudden Scarlett gave Justice a long appraisal. "Where are you going all dolled up?"

"I have a date with Sterling."

"Sterling," Scarlett mused. "Where have I heard that name before?"

"I might have mentioned him to you. I met him on the plane ride here." She hesitated not wanting to go into details of all of their history. "Thank you for sending me to Starbucks. He was in there having coffee with a friend and asked me to join them." Unbeknownst to Justice a dreamy look settled on her face. "After coffee he rented a horse-drawn carriage and we went to Central Park."

"In all the time that I've been here I've never gotten to do that," Scarlett said in a wistful voice.

"You should," Justice said. "Today was a good day. It's as if that nasty diversion with Miles never existed."

"But why are you standing out here waiting for him? Your mother would never approve." She grinned. "You're supposed to make your date come to the door."

"Raven's home and I don't feel like dealing with her," Justice answered in a rough voice. "If she came downstairs in a bra and thong in front of him I think I'd slap the taste out of her mouth. With Miles, I didn't care enough to confront her. But Sterling is different."

"Oh," Scarlett teased. "I'm going to wait right here so I can get a look at this man that can stir such passionate emotions in you."

Suddenly a soft blue Bentley pulled to a stop in front of them. The door opened and with agility Sterling stepped out. He was dressed in a black suit, and white shirt.

"Oh my God," Scarlett whispered in awe.

Sterling flashed his million dollar smile at them. "You must be Scarlett."

She nodded at him in a sort of stupefied trance.

"It's nice to meet you." He said smoothly to Justice, "I hope that

I'm not late."

"No, Sterling," Justice answered, barely breathing, "you're right on time."

Sterling walked around to the passenger side and opened the door for Justice. "We have to hurry. Our reservation at Sardi's is at seven." He gave Scarlett a look of concern. "It's getting dark. Maybe you should go inside."

"Yes, Sterling," Scarlett eked out.

As the Bentley pulled away, Justice couldn't help looking in the side view mirror. Scarlett still stood on the sidewalk, mouth gaped open, watching them drive away.

CHAPTER 9

They were quiet on the drive to Sardis's. Stevie Wonder's greatest hits played on the Bose system. Eerie feelings slithered down her spine as she listened to Stevie warn people about having skeletons. She pushed her nervousness aside and slid a sideways look at Sterling. She placed her hand on his knee. "Before we get to the restaurant, I want to say how much I enjoyed our date tonight. The food was scrumptious and the conversation entertaining."

"I couldn't agree more," Sterling said, smiling at her in the dark confines of the car. He took one hand off the steering wheel and placed it on her knee. Currents of electrical energy riveted through her body at his touch. And he knew. I love this woman. I really, really love her. Outside the restaurant, Sterling pulled up behind a queue of cars waiting for valet service.

A young man bounded towards the driver's side of the Bentley and another one opened Justice's door.

"I'll let you know when I want it brought around," Sterling said.

"Yes, sir," the valet said sliding into the driver's seat.

When Sterling reached her side, she whispered, "I didn't see you give him the car key."

"There isn't one. I have a remote in my pocket, so I can start it from a different location."

"I can't imagine what a car like that costs."

"It's only a material thing and they don't necessarily go hand in hand with happiness," he said. Suddenly a worried frown furrowed his brow.

"Is something wrong?" she asked him.

"No," he answered quietly. "I just don't want this night to end."

"Maybe it doesn't have to," she said, slipping her hand into his.

He gently squeezed it and led her into the restaurant.

Once inside, Justice was struck by the old world décor. The foyer was reminiscent of the ones in black and white movies and if she closed her eyes she could visualize the late Marlon Brando smoking a cigar in the corner while he conversed with one of his leading ladies.

"I have a reservation for Sterling Hart," he told the formally dressed maître d'.

"Your table is ready," he said. "Please follow me."

As the maître d' led them to a table in the middle of the

restaurant, Justice had to physically stop herself from swinging her head from side to side in curiosity. From the corner of her eye she spotted a couple of well-known actors huddled together in a corner booth.

When they reached their table, Sterling held her chair out and she sank into it.

"I just have to say, Sterling, your mother was a really wonderful woman."

"I agree. But what made you say something like that?"

"She obviously raised you right. You open my car door for me; you pull out my chair. You even match your stride with mine as we walk. Those are the small niceties women don't always get."

"My mother was big on manners," Sterling chuckled. "I used to do whatever I could to keep her from nagging at me about things."

"Well it seems to have worked."

"She would have liked you," Sterling said quietly.

"I'm sure that I would have liked her too." She added shyly, "I certainly like her son."

Sterling grew very still. "I hope that you always feel that way, Justice."

A waiter appeared at their side. "My name is Dominic and I am your waiter for tonight. "Would you like to order something to drink?" he asked.

Sterling looked at Justice. "Do you like wine?"

"Yes," she said.

"What kind do you prefer?" Sterling asked.

"Red," she said.

He turned to the waiter. "I'll take a bottle of Jordan Cabernet Sauvignon Sonoma County, 2003."

"Yes, Sir." He gave a light bow. "I will return shortly," he said and disappeared as quickly as he'd appeared.

"The food here is delicious," Sterling said.

"Then you order for me," she said, putting the menu aside. "I don't recognize half the names of the dishes served here, but I'm sure that I'll like whatever you choose."

"One of my favorites is cannelloni au gratin."

"That sounds interesting. I guess the fancier the name the better the food."

"Not always," he said. "But this dish is one of Sardi's traditions. It's a combination of beef, veal, and sweet pork sausage rolled into a French crepe."

"That sounds great," she said. "I love sausage."

The minutes the words were out of her mouth Sterling's eyes

twinkled.

Justice felt her blood rush to her face and her whole body got hot. "I meant," she stammered.

"I know what you meant, Justice," Sterling interrupted her. Obviously deciding to refrain from commenting on her unintended sexual innuendo he said, "I'm adventurous when it comes to food. I never order at a restaurant what I can cook at home. But sometimes when my plate is set before me, I'm hesitant to try it because it looks so odd. But most of the time, I get lucky."

Dominic returned with a bottle of wine and two glasses that he placed in front of them. He filled each three quarters full before placing the bottle in a holder. Picking up the discarded menus he asked, "Are you ready to order?"

"Yes," Sterling said. "We'll have the smoked cannelloni au gratin and for dessert the baked Alaska."

"Very good choice, sir," he said.

Once they were alone again, Sterling raised his glass, motioning for her to do the same. Sterling said, staring into Justice's eyes, "I know that it's not champagne, but I still feel like making a toast. I'm very happy that I sat next to you on the plane, Miss Justice Fairchild," Sterling said in his deep voice. "The night you spent in my arms is forever seared into my memory as a magical time. And I couldn't believe my luck when I ran into you at Starbuck's today. It's my fervent wish to spend many days of happiness in your company."

"Ditto," she said, taking a sip from her glass.

"Ditto," Sterling said after he swallowed. "That's from Ghost."

"That's still one of my favorite movies. The love that Demi Moore and Patrick Swayze had for each other was amazing. I'd like to have that one day," she said in a wistful voice.

"But their love was cut short," Sterling said. "It turned tragic."

"I know," Justice said thinking of her mother. "But I think that I'd rather have an all-consuming love that was short lived than to remain in a bad relationship forever."

Sterling swallowed hard. "I agree."

"It's funny," she said. "I don't know very much about you, yet I feel as if I've known you for years."

There was a heavy silence that filled the air. "And I feel as if I've searched for you my whole life yet I didn't know what was missing."

"If you feel that way, why did you run off the plane and away from the hotel the way you did?"

"Timing," he answered in a brusque voice. "I apologize for that,

Justice. If I could turn back the hands of time, I would."

"You can't," she said lightly. "So let's not talk about it anymore."

"But I think that now is the time I should explain."

"I know all about timing, Sterling. But for tonight, the timing is perfect and I don't want anything to spoil our evening." She gave him a soft smile. "Can't we talk about something other than mistakes that should be forgotten?"

"We can," Sterling replied quietly. "Tell me about Justice Fairchild."

"I already did that when we were at Central Park."

"I know that you want to be a designer but got dragged into being a model. But those are career choices. Tell me what makes you happy," he said.

"Taking long walks and watching a good movie makes my day. I take pleasure in simple things."

"That's a wonderful characteristic to have. Some people are always looking for excitement and that incites drama." Sterling propped his chin on his hand. "Tell me about your childhood."

"My dad had a brain aneurysm when I was nine," she said. "After he passed, my Aunt Minnie sort of took his role. She's never been married and doesn't have any children." Justice laughed. "I argue with her more than my mother. My mother is a strong woman but she also has a tenderness about her that my aunt lacks. Sometimes it's hard to tell that they're sisters."

"So you never missed having a brother or sister?"

"Nope," she said without hesitation.

"Did you feel lonely because you were an only child?"

"No," Justice said. "I had friends that I played with. But once I got home I felt as if I didn't need anyone else. I've never had to share attention and I'm fine with that."

"I agree that being an only child isn't the end of the world," Sterling said in a somewhat mysterious voice.

"Are you an only child? You haven't mentioned any siblings."

"I don't know what I have out there," Sterling said with a bitter inflection in his voice, "since my father took off when I was in elementary school. When he died he was living right there in New Jersey and didn't bother to try to have a relationship with me."

"You dislike him."

"I don't care enough to dislike him," Sterling denied roughly. "I don't like what he did to my mother. After he left she seemed different."

"Did she ever meet anyone else?"

"Lots of men came on to her. But she wasn't interested. I became her total focus. I think that she felt discarded by my father and didn't want to put herself through that again."

"How about you? Did you feel the same loss that she did?"

"I have memories of him from childhood and none of them are pleasant. But I'm grateful to him," Sterling said quietly.

"Grateful," Justice said. "That's an odd way at looking at being abandoned as a child."

"That man taught me not to be like him," he said in an even voice. "He taught me not to abandon a child and showed me what not to do to women."

Dominic returned with their food. He placed the plates in front of them and a wonderful scent wafted to her nostrils.

Justice picked up her fork and cautiously dug into the crepe.

Sterling watched and waited.

The minute the delicious food entered her mouth she gave Sterling a nod of approval.

With relish, he then dug into his food.

During dinner, conversation was limited because of their enjoyment of their meal. After Justice's second glass of wine she said, "Thank you so much, Sterling."

"I'm just grateful for your company, Justice"

"Do you think about me, Sterling? About us?"

"Every day," he said. It's been a long time…"

"A long time for what?" she asked quietly.

"It's been a very long time since I've been happy. And the truth is, I've never felt this before." Sterling placed his hand over his heart lightly tapping as was his custom.

"Meaning?" she asked breathlessly.

"You make my heart race," he whispered. "I want to make it up to you. For before."

Justice's lips parted in anticipation. She felt desire ooze from her thong underwear. At that moment she wished that they were not in a public place but alone and able to shut the rest of the world out. "I want to be alone with you," she whispered. " I don't want to take you back to where I live. There's drama there."

Sterling wiped the corners of his mouth in a nervous gesture. He said quietly, "We could go back to the scene of my infamous crime. I need to talk to you about something and I want privacy to do so."

Ina sort of bemused state of mind she said, "I think that sounds like a plan."

After Sterling paid the bill, he walked around to her and helped her to her feet with one possessive hand. Then he cupped her elbow and led her outside into the brisk night air.

As Justice and Sterling rode the elevator to the suite at the Waldorf Astoria she cuddled closer to his side.

He kissed her cheek.

Once inside, Sterling pushed a button on the wall and subdued lighting cast a sensual shadow throughout the suite. Then the sensual voice of Melaney Fiona filtered throughout the room.

"I have something that I need to say to you."

Justice stared at Sterling's brooding countenance. An urge that she couldn't control overcame her and she went to him. Justice put her fingers to his lips and silenced him. Then she replaced her fingers with her lips taking his breath away. Finally breaking away she whispered, "And your face appears before my eyes morning, noon, and night."

The desire of the two filled the room.

Sterling growled and held her tight. He slid his hands down the length of her body as if trying to memorize every curve. "I've never felt so drawn to a woman in all my life." He murmured, "I want you, Justice."

"For now and for always?"

"Of course."

"Then have me, Sterling,"

"But…" he protested.

She leaned in. Justice asked in a beseeching voice, "Can't it wait?"

"It's going to have to," Sterling groaned. He sounded like a wounded animal in pain. He stepped back.

Immediately Justice's eyes fell to his fly and a thrill ran through her to see the imprint of his shaft poking out the soft material of his trousers.

The memory of the last time they were together made her suck in her breath sharply.

Sterling unzipped his pants. He quickly shed his clothes and stared at her with unabashed longing.

Justice couldn't look away from his chocolate six pack and the smooth wavy hair that spread across his chest.

With deliberate steps, Sterling advanced towards her and then easily scooped her into his arms. He turned to the dark, adjoining bedroom and once again, kicked the door shut with his foot.

Sterling took his time undressing her on the large bed. As he pulled each article of clothing off her, he planted warm kisses on the bare skin.

Once she was naked, Sterling stepped back and viewed the vision she made.

Free from its ponytail Justice's hair cascaded across the pillow. Her long legs were spread invitingly, and her breasts rose and fell in anticipation of his caresses.

Sterling admired the black toenail polish that matched her fingernails. "I have never wanted anyone as much as I want you," he said.

"Ditto," she replied in a soft voice.

When Sterling lay on the bed next to her, he pulled her into the curve of his body and held her close. His words were muffled in her hair. "I hope that you don't regret tonight," he said.

"I won't," she said her voice cloudy with anticipation.

Sterling kissed her long and hard. His hands firmly but not roughly roamed the length of her body from top to bottom.

The pleasure of his touch made Justice moan and she clasped her hands around the back of his head, pulling him to her.

As his head lowered, he brushed a trail of kisses across her collarbone. "You smell good from the top of your head to the tip of your toes," he murmured. Then he licked her from head to toe.

"Oh my God," she gasped when he found her center.

His tongue wreaked havoc inside her for an eternity. Then he raised his tongue upward and held it still up against her clit.

Justice arched her back, giving him as much freedom as she could. She trembled right before she unloaded into his mouth. After he swallowed her femininity, Sterling groaned, "You're as sweet as candy."

Justice lay weakly on the bed as Sterling's tongue licked the valley between her breasts. Then his mouth closed in on the fullness of one, as his other hand kneaded the other. Then he dropped a hand between her legs, parting them.

"Are you ready?" he asked.

"Please fill me, Sterling," she moaned. "I can't wait anymore."

Sterling eased on top of her and entered her in one fluid moment.

Once his rod was tucked inside her, he waited giving her the opportunity to adjust to his girth. Knowing that he was waiting for a sign from her she gasped, "Come on, baby. I want you now."

"Not more than I want you," he whispered with deep sincerity. Sterling began to move inside Justice.

She clung to him, moving her arms up around her neck.

Sterling murmured in her ear, "You have my heart. I love you, Justice."

Joy coursed throughout her body. She barely managed to say, "I love you too, Sterling," before he began to move harder inside her.

His long, even, strokes made Justice feel as if he were reaching up to her throat. She kept her eyes open, watching his every movement, wanting to savor every moment. Wanting him to be as fulfilled as she was each time he drove deep she clenched, holding him inside her, and each time she did he moaned.

Justice lost count as to how long they rocked in unison, but she did know that when they exploded, it was simultaneous.

Later that night, their passion resurfaced and Sterling rocked her world again.

When she opened her eyes the next morning, Sterling was staring at her.

The expression in his eyes was indecipherable.

"We need to talk," he said. Then his cell phone rang. "Yes," he barked into the receiver. "I'll be there as soon as I can." He hung up with a look of displeasure. "I'm sorry, Justice but I have to go. It's sort of an emergency."

Justice snuggled deeper under the covers. "I understand," she said and her voice was laced with contentment.

"Can I take you out to dinner tonight?"

"You're going to make me fat," she protested.

"I doubt it," he said. He got out of bed and started dressing. "Is seven o'clock okay?"

"That sounds great," she said in a dreamy voice.

"Are you okay getting home by yourself?" With an upset look he said, "I hate leaving you like this."

"I'll be fine, Sterling," she assured him. "What time do I need to be out of here?"

"You don't. The company owns this and there's no one on the calendar using it any time soon."

"Oh?" she asked.

"Yes, so take as long as you like." Sterling took his hand and placed it over his heart. He quickly tapped it three times.

A warm glow coursed throughout Justice's body and she squirmed under the Egyptian sheets.

"See you tonight," he promised.

"I can't wait," she countered, burying her face in the pillow where the smell of him lingered.

###

Sterling slammed his fist down on Chapman's desk. "I'm so fucked!" Sterling shouted. "Is there no way around it?"

"Not that I know of. I asked some of the most creative lawyers in the field and they all say that Harlow basically has to agree to a divorce. New York is the last state in the country to change it. You have to live apart a year."

"What if I buy a house in California? Will having a residence there change the rules?"

"No," Chapman said in a voice filled with compassion. "Sterling, I hate to say it, but you have to go through the motions of the court system," Chapman said.

"Explain." Sterling sat completely motionless and waited for his lifeline.

"You can sue Harlow for divorce but you have to cite her as an adulterer."

"I don't have any proof of that, and I won't slander the mother of my child."

"If the two of maintain separate residences for a year and if she agrees then to a divorce, it's yours. But even with that one person has to take the blame for the dissolution of the marriage. There is no such thing as irreconcilable differences in New York."

That evening, when Sterling entered his penthouse, he walked down the long hallway and knocked on Harlow's bedroom door.

"Come in," she said.

When he entered, she was lounging in bed, reading a magazine.

Sterling stared at her with determination. "I want a divorce," he said.

Harlow pulled the covers up around her as if they could protect her from Sterling's hostile demeanor. "Why now?" she screeched. "We had an agreement to stay together at least until the baby is born."

"I want to be free," Sterling said in a clipped voice. "Chapman is drawing up the separation papers." He heaved a heavy sigh. "Sign them. For once do the right thing." Then he went to the bathroom to ready himself for his date with Justice.

###

This time they sat at a corner table. Soft candles cast a subtle shadow over their faces. Sterling had been quiet throughout most of the meal, only picking at the succulent pieces of escargot in front of him.

"What is the cologne that you wear every time that we're together?" Justice asked.

"It's oil that I have specially made." He gave her an inscrutable look. "Are you already tired of smelling it?"

"Of course not," Justice hastened to clarify what she meant. "It's simply that because I've been in the modeling industry I thought that I'd smelled every cologne or oil, yet I've never come across that scent before. You smell scrumptious," she lightly.

Sterling said quietly, "Thank you for that, Justice."

"Is everything okay?" Justice ventured in a tentative voice.

"I'm sitting here with you so everything has to be okay," he responded.

"You seem different tonight," she said in a quivering voice. "Aren't you enjoying your meal?"

"The food here is always delicious," Sterling answered with a closed expression. "What do you think of your dinner?" he asked.

"The grilled salmon is delicious," she replied.

"I'm sorry if I haven't been a good date," Sterling said, wiping his hands on a cloth napkin. "I don't mean to be off-putting."

"Is it because of what happened between us?"

"Sort of," Sterling said and stared deeply into her eyes.

"Do you regret it?"

"Yes and no."

Humiliation filled her. "I'm sorry if I disappointed you," she mumbled.

"You've got to be kidding me," Sterling said with an astonished look on his face. "You are the best thing that has happened to me in like forever. I'm just afraid that I took advantage of you." He looked down at the white tablecloth. "I think that I may have dragged you into something that you aren't ready for."

"You didn't drag me into anything, Sterling," Justice said in an intense voice. "If you remember, I asked you if we could go somewhere alone. It wasn't the other way around."

"I booked the suite at the Waldorf again for another night. I would greatly appreciate it if you would join me," Sterling said in a disquieting tone. "This time we really will talk."

An uneasy feeling settled on Justice. "Okay," she murmured.

Their waitress Tonee reappeared and this time she held their check.

Sterling paid by roughly throwing down a wad of bills on the table. "Keep the change," he said. "Are you ready?"

"Of course," Justice answered.

As they waited for his car to be brought around she moved her body to stand flush at his side.

Sterling turned to her. He encircled her body, drawing her into his embrace. He leaned over and kissed her upturned mouth.

Justice closed her eyes and fell into his kiss.

"Hello, Sterling."

The sharp, caustic words broke their embrace.

In sort of a daze, Justice looked for the strident voice that had interrupted their passionate embrace.

"Hello, Andrea," he said in a harsh tone.

"Who is this? I know that she's not a kissing cousin!"

"None of your damn business," he replied coldly.

The woman planted her hands on her hips. "I couldn't believe it when I stepped out of my car and saw Harlow's man kissing another woman in front of Triomphe," she said with a sardonic look on her face. "This is New York, Sterling, not Europe. You really should be more discreet."

"And you should mind your own damn business." He spat out the words.

"I just think that your behavior is pretty tacky, Sterling. What about your wife?"

"Wife?" Justice interjected weakly and suddenly clutched her stomach.

Andrea looked amused. "Yes, his wife, whoever you are. Sterling is married. Didn't he tell you?" She said tauntingly, "How do you think Harlow would feel if someone told her about your indiscretions?"

"Why the hell do you care about Harlow's feelings?" he sneered. "The two of you don't even like each other."

"You're right," Andrea said with a tinkling laugh. "We don't." She flung those last words over her shoulder as she sauntered into Triomphe.

Sterling looked at Justice and tears brimmed in his eyes. "I'm not sleeping with my wife," he said in a distraught voice.

Justice's hand snaked out and the slap that she delivered to Sterling's cheek would have flattened a smaller man, but he only flinched. Her insides churned from rage. She screamed, "No wonder you only gave me your cell phone number and took me to a hotel."

Interested onlookers pretended to avert their eyes from the drama unfolding before them.

"I was going to tell you," he said quietly.

"When?" she choked out. "After you got me into bed again? Or maybe that was your intention after I fell in love with a person who doesn't exist."

"No." His breathing was labored. "I was going to tell you tonight. Before things got out of hand."

"It's too late for that." She said in a biting voice, "How dare you do this to me and your wife?"

"Let me explain."

"I thought that you were different," she choked out with a pained look on her face.

"You don't understand," Sterling said and now the tears streamed down his face. "I love you! I don't want to lose you!" Not caring about the tears he didn't even attempt to brush them away.

"What is wrong with you men?" She cried out, "Is there not a decent one among you?" Justice turned to walk away and Sterling grabbed her arm. Once he turned her back to him, she slapped him on his other cheek with all the force she could muster. "You made me love you," she choked out, her vision blurred from tears. "Don't you dare ever come near me again!" Ignoring the open door on the passenger side of Sterling's Bentley, she ran across the middle of 49 West 44th Street dodging cars. She stuck her hand out, and pushing an elderly man out of the way she jumped into the taxi that was rightfully his.

"Hey!" the man yelled.

Reaching inside her wallet she handed him a fifty dollar bill. "I'm sorry to take your taxi, sir," she said in a quivering voice. Justice pointed to Sterling as he watched her from across the street. Her voice trembled, "The guy over there is a married man and he's trying to take me to a hotel. I'm afraid."

Rage flooded the man's face. "I'm sorry to hear that, young lady. Of course you can take the cab," he said and handed her back her money. "Do you want me to call the police for you?"

"No," she said weakly, leaning back into the safety of the vehicle. "I don't think that he'll be bothering me again."

Once the taxi pulled out into traffic, Justice said to the driver, "Take me to 6037 Madison Avenue."

The driver gave her a sympathetic look. "Yes, ma'am."

Throughout the slow ride, Justice clutched her stomach. The combination of the wine, rich food, and disappointment made it hard to keep her meal down. With relief, she caught sight of her home. Handing the driver a twenty dollar bill she said, "Keep the change." Once the taxi was out of sight, Justice slowly walked over to a drain on the side of the road. She stared down at the iron grail. Oh, my God, I slept with another woman's husband. She emptied her guts. When she lifted her head, she spied Sterling standing by his car observing her.

Their eyes met across the street and there was enough light to show a look of torture on his face

Justice turned and ran up the stairs to the sanctuary of her bedroom. She stormed over to her window and peeked through the blinds.

Sterling waited until he saw a light illuminate a top floor window and then knowing that she was safe he got into his car and sped off, tires screeching.

After his taillights were out of sight, she collapsed onto her bed and stuffing her head into her pillow she wailed, drenching the pillow with her tears.

CHAPTER 10

As Harlow sat drinking a cup of coffee, the phone rang. She gave a start of surprise. Who is calling me at eight o'clock in the morning? Looking at the caller I.D. in a sighed in annoyance. "What the hell does she want?" she muttered. "Hello," she said curtly.

"Hello, Harlow, this is Andrea."

"I know who it is," Harlow said in a brusque tone. "What do you want?"

There was a sullen silence. "So I guess by your cold reception that Sterling told you."

"Told me what?" Harlow demanded.

"That I saw him last night at Triomphe."

So that's where he was. "No he didn't mention it, Andrea. He and I only talk about interesting things," Harlow snapped.

"Interesting things?" Andrea drawled. "I think that it's pretty interesting that he was with a woman."

Harlow had been absently stirring her coffee but when she heard these words she put her spoon down. "Sterling has business dinners quite often," she retorted with false bravado. "Triomphe is one of his favorite restaurants, so it makes sense that he would go there."

"Some business dinner. When I got there, Sterling was mauling this woman on the sidewalk. They were kissing so hard they were oblivious to the world around them. I thought that they were going to fuck right then and there."

"I don't believe you," Harlow denied halfheartedly.

"Ask him," Andrea retorted with confidence. "And she was absolutely beautiful slim and voluptuous in just the right places," Andrea said in a gleeful voice. "Girl, you better watch out. I think that she's a good ten years younger than you."

Harlow slammed down the phone. Staring at the receiver, she dared Andrea to call her back. Jealous rage consumed her. So that's what he's up to. Be calm. Come up with a plan.

When Sterling entered the kitchen he was fully dressed. Harlow sat at the table in front of a cold cup of coffee.

"You shouldn't be drinking that," he said bleakly. "Caffeine isn't good for the baby."

"You don't care about me or the baby, Sterling," she said in a pitiful voice. "Why pretend?"

Sterling reached for a cup and poured himself the remaining coffee. "Why pretend that we have something when we don't? That's the real issue here, Harlow." He turned to walk away. "You can take everything in the apartment."

She said to his retreating back, "I thought that you didn't want to be like him."

Sterling stopped but didn't turn around.

"You weren't raised by him, but you may as well have been. I hope that our baby doesn't take after you."

Sterling didn't turn around.

"You gave me your word." Harlow forced tears to trickle down her cheeks. "You made a commitment to me and the baby, and now you want out. Why is it so important that we end our marriage at this time?"

Sterling turned to Harlow and agony was written all over his face. "I don't want to be with you."

Harlow dropped her head and tears gathered at the base of her chin. "I can't believe that you're abandoning us."

"I'm not going to be like my father," he stated harshly. "I will be involved with the raising of the baby."

"That's going to be hard to do with me living in Chicago," she said quietly.

Sterling's nostrils flared angrily. "Chicago? I don't want my child raised there!"

"I can't raise this baby alone, Sterling," she whimpered. "I'm not strong enough."

"So you plan on moving far away with the baby because you can't have your way?" he said with loathing.

"Since my mother is there it might be a smart thing to do."

"I'll sue for partial custody."

"And you'll lose. I'm the mother, and I'm not unfit."

"That's a matter of opinion, Harlow," he retorted cruelly.

"How about you, Sterling? She retaliated, "Are you an honest man? Do you deserve fifty-fifty custody of an infant? Maybe you have a few skeletons in your closet. I think," she paused, letting her words sink in, "that you're hiding something from me."

Guilt made Sterling look away.

"Where were you last night?"

"None of your business, Harlow," he answered with a closed look on his face. "We don't have that kind of relationship."

"You're right." Harlow did some quick thinking. "Sterling," she said softly, "I don't want someone who doesn't want me. But I want my child to be born in wedlock. Stay with me until after the baby is born," she pleaded. "After that I give you my word that I'll sign the divorce papers."

Sterling said nothing.

"I know that you want your firstborn to bear your last name. He won't if you pressure me into a divorce. I'll see to that."

Sterling's shoulders drooped dejectedly. "All right," he finally agreed in a shaky voice. "We'll stay together until the baby is born." Then leaving his coffee on the counter he slammed out of the apartment.

Later that morning Harlow stared at the latest issue of Marie Claire. Violently she tossed the magazine aside before shattering Sterling's coffee cup against the wall. Rivulets of liquid made lines as the coffee streamed down the white wall. He's trying to cast me aside for a younger woman? I'll be damned. Then, very calmly, she picked up the telephone and called her maid service.

"This is your fault," Sterling said crossly as he glared at his friend.

"My fault," Chapman exclaimed. "Why are you blaming me?"

"Because you pushed me into something that I wasn't ready for."

"What?"

"To have her again and lose her is worse than not having had her at all," Sterling said in distressed voice.

"What do you mean 'have her again'?" He planted the palms of his hand on his mahogany desk. "Did you…?"

"I didn't mean to," he said with sorrow.

"Didn't mean to?" Chapman said dryly. "Don't even try it, Sterling. You either meant to sleep with her or you didn't."

"She said that she wanted to go somewhere to be alone. I only agreed because I wanted a chance to explain things to her. But after we got there," he paused, "I smelled her hair."

"You smelled her hair," Chapman echoed.

"Justice is like no other woman I know. I lose my head when I'm around her. I feel something that I can't put into words."

"Man, you are really sprung," Chapman said, staring at the frazzled look on Sterling's face.

"Every time I'm with her I can't think straight. All rational thought flies out the window. And now I've blown it by listening to your advice."

"My advice," Chapman said defensively.

"If you hadn't coerced me into talking to her at Starbucks this wouldn't have happened."

"I told you to straighten out the mess you created when you did your disappearing act. I didn't tell you to ride in an open carriage with her through New York City," Chapman protested.

"You're right," he said, burying his head in his hands. He muttered, "This is my fault. I hurt her. You should have seen the look in her eyes when she found out that I'm married. What a mess I've made."

"You should have had dinner at the hotel, dude."

"What do you mean by that?" Sterling said, shooting him a hard look.

"Then you wouldn't have run into big mouth Andrea. I mean," Chapman replied in an even tone, "you know your situation."

"Justice's not a cheap woman," Sterling growled. "And I'm not ashamed of her. I want to take her out and treat her the way she deserves to be treated."

"But you are married." Chapman shook his head, feeling pity for his friend.

"I just had to have another taste," Sterling groaned hoarsely. "I wasn't thinking clearly."

"I understand that. But you should have known that you would be spotted sooner or later. Sardi's and Triomphe are places where our crowd hangs out."

"I'm sorry, Chapman." His eyebrows were drawn together in a frown. "For the fact that I don't know how to cheat on my wife."

"Well neither do I," Chapman said vehemently. "But if you'd handled the situation better maybe Justice would have been more understanding when confronted by someone like Andrea."

Sterling said morosely, "Justice thinks that I was trying to get her to fall in love with me so that she'd be in too deep to make a rational decision as to whether or not to let me stay into her life."

"So she slapped the hell out of you?" Chapman looked compassionately at his friend.

"Twice. And that girl packs one hell of a wallop." Sterling touched one of his bruised cheeks. "But I know I deserve it."

Chapman leaned back in his leather chair and gave Sterling an appraising stare. "What's your next move?"

"What do you mean?"

"I mean, how long are you going to give her to calm down before you explain to her what's going on?"

"I'm not going to approach Justice or try to talk to her. I can't bother her anymore with my dysfunctional life," Sterling said fiercely. "I'll abide by her wishes and leave her the hell alone." Then he said after a long pause, "At least until I'm worthy of touching her."

###

When she got home Justice curiously stared at three worn suitcases in the foyer. Then she saw Miles sitting on the loveseat in the den watching television.

Storming into the room, she planted her body in front of him. Her eyes flashed fire and her lip was curled in derision. Pinning Miles' eyes with hers, she demanded in a nasty tone, "What the hell are you doing here?"

"I have no place to stay," he said quietly.

"So why the fuck are you telling me?" She crossed her arms in front of her and tapped her foot.

"I'm moving in," Miles said as his eyes slid away from hers.

"What!" Justice said. "No, you're not. What would make you think that I would agree to that? You must be out of your mind."

"It's only temporary," he said in a small voice.

"You are insane if you think that I'm going to let you stay here."

"You can't do anything about it," Raven sneered. She had walked into the room and stood behind Justice.

"Shut up, Raven!" Justice said. "I'm not talking to you."

"Miles and I want to be together." She wore a superior look on her face.

"Give me a break," Justice uttered in revulsion.

"It's not my fault that Miles was content for you to be his woman on the side. Now that he and I are together it's only natural that he'd move out from Billie." Raven crowed, "I'm sorry that he didn't do it for you."

"Miles, she's just using you to try and hurt me," Justice said in a tone full of warning.

"It's your fault that Billie kicked me out," he stated in a stone cold voice.

"Don't blame me," Justice shouted. "You're a man whore. But you know, it's fitting that you should hook up with Raven," Justice said before she stalked out of the room. Over her shoulder she said, "You'll get yours because after the newness wears off she's going to throw you away like the trash that you are."

From her bedroom, Justice called Rossi.

"Hey, Justice," Rossi chortled. "Lucille and I already heard. Congratulations."

"Thank you, Rossi," she said quickly. "But that's not why I

called." Quickly she apprised him of the antics going on in the house.

"She's one nasty stick of ass, that Raven," Rossi said in his heavy Italian accent.

"Tell me about it," Justice said.

"I'm going to tell Caesar. He's already sick of her shit."

"Don't bother. Raven can have Miles. I'm really calling because I'm looking for a place. Do you know of any decent apartments available?"

"I know that one just went up for sale. But it's even more expensive than where you're staying. Do you think that you can afford it?"

"Is that the only place around?" she asked. "Because I don't know if Nile Cosmetics will resign me after my contract is up," she said in a worried voice. "I hate to be locked into a mortgage payment that I can't pay."

"Don't you get commercials with that contract?" Rossi asked.

"There's at least one because it's a national campaign."

"Then the residual checks from that should help you in your lean times."

"I have to get out of here, Rossi," she said. "When can I see the place?"

"Meet me at the Jerry Orbach Theatre at the corner of 50th Street and Broadway. It's walking distance from there."

"I'll be there in an hour," she said and hung up.

When Justice saw Rossi she ran to him, flinging her arms around his waist. She burst into tears.

"Why are you crying, Justice?" he said, smoothing her hair. "You're going to be a star."

"But sometimes I wish that I'd never left Eastman. I don't get the people up here."

Rossi pushed her away. He took a black and white polka dot handkerchief from his pocket and wiped Justice's tears. "Then go home," he said quietly.

"I can't," she wailed. "I already signed the contract and besides," she said with fortitude, "I won't be run out of town."

"I don't get it," he said and turned her east, heading her in the direction she needed to go. "I thought that you didn't care about this Miles. How can he and Raven bring you to tears?"

"It's not them," she gulped. "It's Sterling Hart."

"Who's that?" Rossi asked.

"A man that I thought was the one," she said in a pained voice. "But he's a liar. Sterling Hart is a married man who used me to cheat on his wife."

There was a long silence as they walked. Finally Rossi spoke, "I know that right now you think that it's the end of the world, but it's not."

"I feel so stupid, Rossi."

"It's not your fault," he whispered.

"It is, sort of. I'll never sleep with another man without thoroughly checking him out."

"I'm going to tell you something that you have to promise not to tell another living soul."

"What is it?" Her tears subsided as she looked at Rossi's sad expression.

"Promise me that you won't tell anyone."

"I won't tell a living soul, Rossi," she promised.

"What you're going through happened to me too. A man broke my heart. I almost ran, but I didn't because I couldn't let him win."

"You're such a good person, Rossi, I hate that happened to you."

"You don't know it, Justice, but you're blessed in a lot of ways."

"I know," she whispered. "I feel awful complaining about anything. There are people who can't feed their children and are losing everything. And I'm crying about another woman's husband."

"Those aren't things of the heart, Justice, so you can't measure it the same way. What I mean is, I have to see my ex all the time."

"You do?" Justice asked. "Who is it?"

Rossi stared at her. "Think about it, Justice. Who is hostile to me and vice versa?"

"I know him?" She screwed her face up. "Oh my God, you can't mean…" she gasped.

"Yes, it's Cassius. He married Nina while we were together. I too thought it was the end of the world, but I survived."

Justice stammered in disgust, "How can you work around him, Rossi?"

"I don't care about him anymore and it pleases me."

"Why?"

"He hates looking at me because I remind him of who he really is."

"I'm surprised that he doesn't fire you."

"Only Caesar can do that."

"That's a very dangerous situation with his wife and Scarlett. Their health could be compromised."

"I know. Cassius is definitely an undercover lover. But if they choose to not see him for what he is, that is their choice."

Justice and Rossi walked arm and arm down the street.

"A couple of weeks ago I was over at your place." Rossi gave her a peculiar look. "Didn't Scarlett mention it?"

"No," Justice responded surprise on her face. "Were you looking for me?"

"No, I needed to talk to Scarlett and I just wondered if she'd mentioned it to you."

"No," Justice said, her brow furrowed with concentration. "I wonder why she didn't mention it."

"Please don't tell her that I mentioned it." A pensive look was on Rossi's face.

"Is something going on that I need to know about?"

"No."

Justice searched Rossi's face for clues and was met by a bland look.

"She'll probably say something to you about it eventually."

Justice decided not to pry anymore and let the matter drop.

Justice stared in amazement at the vaulted ceilings and the hardwood floors. She walked from room to room. In the bedrooms, her feet sank into thick carpet. "It's so spacious and well maintained," she said admiringly.

"Fifteen hundred square feet is hard to find in this area."

Once they reached the master bedroom suite with its separate tub and shower she said, "I absolutely love it."

"I knew that you would," Rossi beamed.

"How did you even know about it?"

"Word of mouth is how you find the best places in New York," Rossi said. "Caesar was asked if he was interested in purchasing it and he declined."

"How is Caesar? It seems forever since I've seen him."

Rossi shrugged. "Overwhelmingly busy I guess. I saw him last weekend and he looked exhausted. His color seemed off the whole time he was here."

"I wish that I'd had a chance to see him," she said wistfully.

"It was a quick trip. He only flew over last weekend to meet with Cassius."

"He flew all the way from Italy for a meeting? It must have been important."

"Yes," Rossi explained. "He didn't want to do it via telephone."

"Maybe he's going to fire him." Justice chuckled at the thought.

"He would if he weren't his only son."

"That name thing. I mean, why would Caesar name his son Cassius? In history Cassius helped Brutus kill Caesar."

"It was out of Caesar's hands. He wasn't married to Cassius' mother. While she was pregnant Caesar married another woman. She was so upset she hoped that one day Cassius would betray his father the way she felt betrayed. Her naming Cassius what she did was her way of marking him. It was only after her death that Cassius and Caesar began spending time together."

"Oh, now I know why they interact so oddly."

"They have never had a decent relationship. I just hope that Cassius' mother's plan of son betraying father doesn't come true."

Once they were back outside, the clean crisp air lightened Justice's mood. "I'm going home and pack my things. I want out of there as soon as possible."

"How about furniture?"

"I'm going to just start off with the basics. A couch, television, a bedroom set and barstools for the kitchen counter."

"That's smart," Rossi agreed.

"I don't want to overextend myself. I'm refurbishing my mother's house and she's my first priority at this time."

"When do you shoot your commercial?"

"On Wednesday. I'm so nervous."

"You'll do fine," Rossi answered. Rossi reached into his pocket and handed her a card. "This is where you need to go to finalize the paperwork for the apartment. They are expecting a cashier's check for thirty thousand dollars."

"Thank God for my signing bonus," Justice breathed.

When they reached the corner where they'd go their separate ways they embraced.

"Rossi, you've been a rock in my life since I met you. I don't know what I'd do without you to depend on."

"You won't have to worry about that, Justice." Rossi waved his arm. "I'm going to catch this cab. Now you be sure to call me if you need anything else."

"Why are you so good to me?"

Rossi said as he climbed into the taxi cab, "You're a good person, Justice. And you deserve the best."

As Justice strolled home she felt as if a huge weight had been lifted from her shoulders. Then the image of Sterling's face surfaced and in her despair stumbled. Righting herself before falling she brushed away fresh tears knowing that it was useless to think about a future with him.

This time when she arrived at the townhouse the Brabantio limousine was parked outside. "Hmm, Cassius is here to see Scarlett in the daytime. That's a switch," she muttered sarcastically.

Once inside Justice's steps again faltered. Scarlett and a very pregnant woman were standing in the foyer. Tears streamed down Scarlett's face. "Stay away from my husband," the woman said before she stormed past Justice, slamming out the door.

Scarlett stumbled into the den and sat down with a dazed look.

Justice followed her. She took her hand and gently smoothed Scarlett's hair.

"That's Cassius's wife."

"So I figured," Justice said quietly.

"He's told me that she doesn't care what he does and that they're just together for their children. That's obviously not true." A gut wrenching burst of anger, Scarlett screamed, "How could I have been so stupid?"

"Don't be too hard on yourself, Scarlett. We all believe what we want to when our heart if involved. How did she find out about the two of you?"

"She found a birthday card that I gave him. She said that I'm not the first whore that Cassius has cheated on her with. He'd left the others and he'd leave me because I'm not even pretty."

"Give me a break," Justice said. "If she's so great why does he keep stepping out on her?"

"She is gorgeous though, Justice."

"So what? She's clearly unhappy. Do you think that as a wife I would lower myself the way she just did? "

"She was so mean," Scarlett whined.

"She's being mean to the wrong person. She should do something with him. You didn't make Cassius have an affair with you and neither did any of the other women he's been with."

"I didn't know that she was coming," Scarlett whispered. "And I sure didn't know she was pregnant. Cassius should have warned me."

"He's probably somewhere hiding until things cool down. Nina looked like a real hellcat, for sure."

"I'm so embarrassed," Scarlett said. "She said that she called Caesar and told him. Nina said that she'll make sure that I'll never work for him again."

So that's why he was in town. "So what are you going to do? Are you going to confront Cassius with his lies?"

"What's the point?" she said tearfully. "He'd just lie to me the way he has been all along."

"I know that you may feel like crap right now, Scarlett. But this is the best thing that could have happened to you."

"I knew that my relationship with Cassius wasn't what it should be. But I thought I was the only one he was cheating on his wife with," Scarlett said. "I feel so stupid. I don't know if I want to go on."

Justice grabbed Scarlett by the shoulders. She gently shook her. In a meaningful voice she said, "I can't explain how, but I'm sure this will turn out to be a blessing from God. Now that you've been cast out of Cassius' life you can live a very long and healthy one."

"I'll have to move." Scarlett sat up and wiped away tears with the back of her hand. "I haven't had a modeling job in such a long time and I can't count on anything coming up soon. Cassius isn't going to continue to pay my bills," she added hastily, "not that I would let him."

"Well, I just happen to know of a beautiful brownstone that has opened up. It has two spare bedrooms and you could take one."

"How much is the rent?" Scarlett sniffed.

"How much do you have?" Justice teased, trying to make Scarlett smile.

"I don't know. I'll have to call Frederic and have him wire me some of my money. I can probably do three thousand dollars a month."

"Then three thousand a month it is."

"What?"

"I'm going to finalize the paperwork tomorrow."

"Are you offering me a place to stay?" Scarlett asked in a grateful voice.

"Yes."

"Does three thousand split the rent?"

"Not quite," she said. "But I'm buying it so I should pay more."

"Justice, why are you being so good to me?" Scarlett whispered.

"You're a good person, Scarlett. And you deserve the best," she said, echoing Rossi's words to her.

"Smile as if your life depends on you selling this product," Max shouted at her.

"It does," she laughed. Justice placed her hands on her hips. The fan behind her blew her hair into swirls around her face. She leaned forward and parted her lips. A whimsical expression settled on her features and she heard the click of the camera. Then she folded her arms across her front. She heard another click. Next, she leaned down, placing them on her knees, adroitly balancing; she leaned forward slightly, staring at the lenses.

Click! Click! Click!

"You rock!" Max chortled. "You're done, sweetheart. These pictures will be in all the major fashion magazines next month."

"You make it so easy, Max. Thank you for being here."

"Don't thank me,' he said. "Thank Ursula. She got Max Factor to allow me to photograph you."

"When do you think the commercial will start airing?"

"Probably next week sometime."

"How soon can I expect a residual check?" Justice asked.

"Darling, don't tell me that you're broke already," he drawled.

"No," she smiled. "But I'm cutting it close. When I went to sign the papers on the place I'm buying it cost more than I expected."

"Then why didn't you back out and stay put?"

"I can't stay where I am. I've been miserable the last two weeks and so has Scarlett."

"Scarlett?'

"Yeah, she's moving in with me."

Max shot Justice a look. "That's good for her."

"By the look on your face I take it that you know."

"Everyone knows about her and Cassius. When Nina showed up I knew all hell had broken loose. She's still in town, by the way."

"So that's why I haven't seen Cassius. I kind of expected him to come over and try to lie to Scarlett. Why does Nina put up with him?"

"I don't know her. I just know of her. She kicked up a fuss in London about a model a couple of years ago. She attacked the poor girl. Caesar had to soothe some ruffled feathers over the chaos."

"That's too bad. I really like Caesar."

"And I really like you." Max's voice changed to a sexy one. "Do you have a man in your life, Justice?"

"Nope," she answered without hesitation.

"Well, I'm really attracted to you. If I asked you out sometime, would you go?"

"No," she replied. "Max, I think that you are amazing, but I don't want to mix business with pleasure. I want to keep you as my friend and if we started dating it could ruin things."

"Things could work out and we could live happily ever after," he said with a quirky smile.

"I don't want to take the chance. Besides, I don't want to be involved with anyone right now."

"Who broke your heart?" Max felt pity for her because the beauty of her eyes seemed to dim right before him.

"I can't handle a discussion about it right now," she replied morosely.

Justice walked out of the bathroom.

Miles was sitting in a chair.

A flush of anger coursed through her. "Get the hell out of my room!"

"Please, Justice. May I talk to you?" he said in a mournful voice.

"I give you three seconds to get your ass out of here."

"I want to apologize for what's been going on."

Justice glared at him and her eyes looked like slits.

"I never meant to hurt you."

"Sure you didn't," she stated in a flat voice. "Where the hell is Raven?"

Miles fidgeted in the chair. "This thing with Raven is nothing."

"I know," Justice said. "Nothing you're involved in is ever anything, Miles."

He looked away and then back at her again. "I heard that you're moving tomorrow. I hate that I forced you out of here."

"You just don't get it, do you, Miles? I'm not moving because of some raging jealousy I have seeing you and Raven together. I just despise the two of you and I don't see why I should have to see your faces."

"I'm looking for a place, too, Justice. Apartments are hard to find in New York."

"No modeling jobs lately, Miles?" Her words deliberately dripped honey.

There was silence.

"I just finished a commercial for Nile Cosmetics."

"Congratulations," he mumbled.

"Yes, I bought my new place with some of the advance money," Justice said in a nonchalant voice. "Never in my wildest dreams did I ever think that I'd ever be able to afford to purchase a place like that."

"So where are you moving?" he asked.

"None of your business," she said. "And if you do find out

where I live and show up there," she said in voice of serious promise, "I'll call the police. Now get out!"

Miles slowly stood. "I'm really sorry for everything that has happened ,Justice."

"You should be," Justice snapped.

All of a sudden they heard his name being called.

"You're being paged," Justice said in derision. "Don't tell her that you were in here talking to me. It's not worth the argument because there's nothing to argue about. I don't want you."

Once she was alone, Justice picked up her sketchbook and started working on some designs.

CHAPTER 11

"I just love it! When is the new furniture being delivered?" Scarlett spun around the spacious foyer.

"This afternoon," Justice grimaced. "Even if they couldn't get it here today, I wasn't going back to Madison Avenue. I'd sleep on the floor before I did that."

"I hear ya," Scarlett echoed.

"Thanks for your part of the rent. It really helped me out. I was able to buy more than I'd anticipated."

"Frederic is usually pretty prompt and I can always reach him. He must sleep with his cell phone under his pillow."

"So you trust him."

"Yes, even though Cassius gave me his name," Scarlett answered with some amusement. "Frederic has a lot of high profile clients. My last quarterly reports showed he'd made me twenty thousand dollars from investments."

"The minute I finish getting my mom straightened out and have some money to fall back on, I'm going to contact him." They heard a loud rumbling sound coming from outside. "Our furniture is here," Justice said excitedly and ran to the door.

Two hefty men jumped out to the cab of the truck. "Is this the residence of Justice Fairchild?"

"Yes, it is," she smiled.

"We have a kitchen set, couch and love seat, and two bedroom sets."

Once everything was all set up and the moving men were gone, Justice sat on the couch with a glass of white wine and looked around admiringly. "I'm so blessed. I can't believe how much has happened for me since I left Georgia. It's like a whirlwind and I can barely catch my breath."

"Well if anyone deserves it you do. The minute you walked down the runway; I knew that Raven's days were numbered."

"Who's Raven?" Justice replied.

"I hear ya," Scarlett reiterated.

"I'll have to sleep in the guest room tonight but my bedroom set will be delivered tomorrow."

"That's cool. Where did you end up buying it from?"

"I went to AKEA."

"Ooh, trendy," Justice laughed.

"Yes, and functional. These rooms are so large I was able to buy a matching desk for me to sit at and do my schoolwork."

"Schoolwork?"

"Yes, Scarlett is going back to school."

"That's fantastic!"

"I've finally accepted the fact that I won't be getting any more modeling jobs. And now that I've broken things off with Cassius I know that I won't be doing any runway shows for the House of Brabantio. I couldn't get into NYU. I've been out of school for too long; I took an entrance test and failed miserably. But I did get accepted into a community college in Brooklyn. If I really watch my pennies, I won't have to work until I get my degree. I want to carry a full course load and be done in four years."

"I'm so proud of you, Scarlett. You're back on track to doing what's right for you. Have you decided on a major?"

"I think physical therapy. I've seen so many models with injuries from being on their feet for long periods of time, one day I'd like to be the person that they come to for relief."

"And I want to be the person whose clothes they're wearing," Justice said wistfully.

"You will be," Scarlett said. "Are you working on anything?"

"Sure. I have six sketch books of designs. I think that I'm going to set up a sewing room in the small room off the kitchen. On my lulls between modeling, I might start trying to put things together. Then if I meet the right person..."

"You're going to zing them."

"Yep," she said, draining her glass. "Before they know it, I'm going to have some of their models wearing my clothes while I pitch my line."

"You know, now that I don't have to starve myself anymore, I'd love to have a pizza."

"Let's have one delivered with wings."

"No black olives or anchovies."

"One large pizza coming up," she said and opened her cell phone to place the order.

After they polished off a large pizza and some wings, Justice said with a yawn, "Now I'm going to go and put my new sheets on my bed and turn in."

"It's only nine o'clock," Scarlett protested.

"I don't know why I'm so tired," Justice said in a weary voice.

"It's probably the excitement of moving into your own place,"

Scarlett said. "I'm going to be lonely sitting here all by myself with no TV."

"The television is being delivered tomorrow. You should get used to early nights since you're starting school."

"Okay," Scarlett said with a small pout. "I'll see you in the morning."

"Bet," Justice said and slowly walked to her room.

Harlow stood in front of Sterling who stared blankly into space. "I want to know if you're going to go with me to the doctor tomorrow."

"I can't get off from work during the middle of the day." He said in a flat tone, "Next time try to schedule your appointment after three o'clock so that I can make it."

"Okay," she acquiesced. "Sterling, we're still sleeping in separate rooms. I thought that we were going to try and work things out."

"What on earth would make you think that? You keep me here out of guilt."

"Then go ahead, Sterling. Leave if you want," Harlow shrieked. "No one's holding a gun to your head."

"Are you sure?" he asked with a sardonic lift of his brow.

Harlow stormed out the room slamming the door behind her.

Sterling raised his eyes to the heavens. Four more months of this.

"Mr. Hart."

"Yes, Ada," he said into the intercom on his desk phone.

"Cousin Chapman is here to see you."

"Send him in," Sterling replied.

Chapman gave Sterling along, appraising look. "You look like shit," he said.

"I've been up a lot at night. Harlow's morning sickness starts at night and runs through the morning. When I hear her vomiting, I get up and sit with her."

"That is tough," Chapman said in a sympathetic voice.

"How would you know?" Sterling said in an exhausted voice. "By the way, when are you and Constance going to make me a godfather?"

"I don't know, man," Chapman said dryly. "But since you make pregnancy sound so inviting maybe Constance and I should get started on it right away."

Sterling couldn't help laughing at the look on his friend's face.

Chapman joined in and once the laughter subsided he said, "I came by to show you something that Constance had. I was unsure about whether or not you'd want to see it, but here you go." He handed Sterling a copy of Elle magazine. Justice was featured on pages three thru six.

"Damn, she looks good," Sterling said, flipping through the fashion spread.

"She really does. I stared at it for so long Constance caught me. Then she got mad and we had a huge argument. Finally I fessed up and told her how I know Justice."

Sterling groaned. "Chapman, you have the biggest mouth. You tell your wife every damn thing."

"I didn't feel like seeing Constance's lips stuck out for no good reason. I'd rather save that for something that I'm really guilty of. But you don't have to worry. You know that Constance won't say anything to Harlow. As much as she dislikes her, she loves you."

"It's just that Harlow can be so vindictive. If she finds out that I want another woman she'll never sign the divorce papers."

"She's not going to sign them no damn how," Chapman retorted, angry on his friend's behalf.

"She'll sign them," Sterling said with a hard glint in his eyes. "After the baby is born I'm going to leave her."

"But you have to be content to be separated a year before you can take her to court."

"Harlow is only with me for appearances. If I start going out with another woman in public she'll divorce me just to save face."

"You think Justice would go for that?"

"I wouldn't think of even asking her." Sterling rubbed his chin in a thoughtful manner. "But I'm desperate enough to hire someone to pretend to be my girlfriend. The embarrassment of her friends seeing me in public with another woman will make Harlow see that there's nothing left for us."

"That would do it for my wife. Speaking of Constance, she wants to know how Ada's working out."

"She's fantastic," Chapman said.

"Thank God," Chapman said. "I was worried about you hiring her just because she's Constance's cousin but she really needed a job and she's good people."

"It's unfortunate that she doesn't have a degree, but she's a fast learner."

"She is?"

"Ada has already reorganized the filing system to where it's manageable and her typing has picked up."

"She told Constance that she purchased that Mavis Beacon computer program. The lawyers at my firm wouldn't hear of my bringing her in."

"Well, they really lost out. She's an asset even without the paperwork that gives her the credentials."

"Ada's not too presumptuous, is she? Sometimes when people have personal connections outside the workplace the two don't mix."

"She is busy mothering me," Sterling admitted dryly. "She feeds me meatloaf, collard greens, turkey necks, and even chitlins' and rice sometimes. I haven't eaten this good since my mother passed."

"Ada does have a way in the kitchen."

"Every day she brings me leftovers from her dinner. Who eats like that during the week?"

"I don't know," Chapman chuckled.

"I protested in the beginning and then I decided, why the hell not?" Sterling said with a sheepish smile. "I don't get anything decent to eat at home since cooking has never been Harlow's forte."

"Come on and spill it, Sterling." Chapman asked half jokingly. "You two never do it? I mean, it's not as if you've never done it before. She is pregnant with your child."

Sterling's brow creased in concentration. He looked at his friend and said with forthright honesty, "I have absolutely no desire for Harlow."

"Mom," Justice said excitedly. "They started running my television commercial today. I just saw it."

"I think that's great," Evelyn said in a tired voice.

"What's the matter? Are you sick or something?"

"I got caught in the rain and got wet all the way through. It's just a little cold, that's all."

"Why were you out in the rain?"

"The car broke down and I was only a half mile from home. So I started walking and a thundercloud came out of nowhere."

"That's Georgia for you," Justice said in a resigned tone. "Where was Aunt Minnie?"

"At church," they said in unison.

"What's wrong with the car?" Justice asked.

"It needs a new motor so I'm driving yours."

"My car doesn't have an air conditioner or heat," she said in a frustrated voice.

"But it beats walking. I don't go that many places, Justice. Church and Walmart are just about it."

"But you still need decent transportation," Justice exclaimed.

"Don't worry about it. I'll be fine with a little more Nyquil," she said, sniffing.

"I'm coming home next weekend."

"You are?" Evelyn's voice brightened. "I prayed that you'd come home for Mother's Day, but I didn't want to pressure you. I know how busy you are up there in New York."

"I'm never too busy for you, Mom."

"Do you need me to have someone meet you at the airport?"

After a long minute, Justice said. "No, mom. I don't know what flight I'm taking. I'll take a limousine to the house."

"Well, la di da," Evelyn teased in a weak voice.

"Go back to sleep, Mom. I'll see you next weekend. Love ya."

"Me too, honey," Evelyn said before she hung up.

Justice lay in bed and sleepily she looked at the clock. Ten o'clock. Oh well, I don't have anything to do today except go visit Lotus and have the works done.

Her phone rang and she knew from the special ringtone it was Ursula.

"I have a casting call for you down on Fashion Avenue," she said without preamble. "If you get the job it pays very well. It's a billboard of you with two other models. It will be all around the city, including Times Square."

"What kind of ad is it?"

"It's a jeans ad. Can you be there at one o'clock?"

"Of course I can," Justice said enthusiastically.

"You have to audition, but I heard on the down low that's just a formality."

"I'll be there with fresh scrubbed face at twelve-thirty."

"Make it twelve forty-five. You don't want to look too eager."

Justice stopped by the mailbox on her way to her photo shoot. Pulling out several envelopes which held her monthly bills she tore one open with trembling fingers. Once she looked at the check she clutched it to her bosom. "Thank you, God," she said aloud. Stepping out onto the side of the street she stuck her hand out. "Please take me to 1519 Fashion Ave."

"Yes, ma'am," the driver said.

Justice settled into the back of the taxi with a feeling of resolve.

The marquee for Shrek the Musical combined with billboards for Wicked illuminated the skyline behind the models. Because she was the tallest, Justice was positioned in the middle of the other two models.

"Position your hands in the loops of your jeans and smile into the camera."

Like robots they all did what they were instructed to do.

Mikael ordered, "Now everyone turn to the left, thrust one leg out in front of the other and bend slightly at the knees."

They complied.

"Okay," Mikael said. "I need all of you to bare yourselves to the waist."

Paula muttered, "I knew this was coming."

Simone whispered, "I wouldn't care at this point if I was buck naked with the jeans lying in a pool around my feet. I really need this ad. Come on, Justice, we can put our clothes on the table behind the curtain."

Justice followed her and once she was out of earshot of Mikael she grumbled, "Why must we be half naked? I wasn't told this when I signed the contract. I don't want my breasts exposed all over Times Square."

"They won't be," Paula said. "The focus of the ad is the jeans so they don't want anything else to take away from that."

"I have a feeling the sight of my swinging breasts might do just that," Justice commented dryly.

"He'll have you cover them with your hands," Simone said. "The idea is for women to think that if they buy these jeans their breasts will look like ours."

"And for a man to buy them for his woman so she'll walk around the house like that," Paula scoffed.

"I find it uncomfortable to go braless," Justice said.

"That's because yours are so big. I've never known a size four model to have such large breasts."

Paula stared at Justice's naked breasts in admiration. "Are you telling me that you don't have implants?"

"No," Justice said with a touch of pride.

"Hurry up," Mikael barked from the stage.

"He has no bedside manner at all," Paula said with a small chuckle.

The girls emerged from behind the screen.

"Strike a pose," Mikael said.

All the models returned to the same position they'd been photographed in for the last few hours.

"Now spread your legs and place the palms of your hands over your nipples."

Once they were in place there were several flashes of the camera.

"Paula and Simone, for the next shot keep your hands in place but turn your heads to look at Justice. Justice, you look seductively into the camera."

Justice leaned in and once again the countenance of Sterling surfaced in her mind.

"That's perfect, Justice," Mikael said in admiration. "And you're done."

Justice drew in a deep sigh of relief.

Simone said to Paula and Justice, "Would you like to go and get some lunch or something? I skipped breakfast."

"Sure, since I'm done for the day," Paula agreed.

Justice looked into Simone's earnest expression and acquiesced. "Okay," she said. "Just let me get my purse."

They sat outside at a corner bistro. "I'll have the chicken ravioli, with a diet coke," Justice told the waiter.

"I'll just have the salad with fat free dressing," Paula said. "And Perrier water."

"And I'll have the same," Simone said.

"Hey," Justice protested after the waiter disappeared. "I thought that you guys said that you're hungry."

"I am," Paula chuckled. "But I can't afford to put on any more weight. Those jeans I just peeled out of probably gave me a yeast infection because they were too tight."

"The only way I got that job is because I lost eight pounds," Simone said with a grimace. "I can't afford to put them back on."

"Have you never had to diet?" Paula asked.

"No," Justice said. "I've just been blessed with a high metabolism. I feel guilty eating ravioli in front of you."

"Don't worry about it," Paula smiled. "I'm used to people eating in front of me. My husband does it all the time."

"And I'm used to smelling good food and not eating it," Simone said. "Now let's change the subject from something that I can't do anything about to something that I can. Justice, I'm glad that you agreed to come eat with me. I want to apologize to you for the way I acted when we lived together."

"You two lived together?" Paula said after she took a swallow from the bottle of Perrier that had just been placed in front of her.

"Yes, and I wasn't very nice to her," Simone said. "I went over to Madison to see you and apologize, but found out that you'd moved out."

"Yes, Scarlett and I are sharing a place uptown."

"Who was that good looking guy that answered the door?"

"My ex, if you can even call him that."

"Your ex?" Simone asked in a confused voice. "Then why is he still there and you're living somewhere else."

"He's a casualty from my war with Raven."

"Raven Sugalsky?" Paula asked.

"Yep. Sleeping with Miles was Raven's revenge for my taking some modeling jobs from her."

"She's notorious for being a bitch," Paula said. "It's too bad that you made an enemy of her."

"I'm not afraid of Raven," Justice said in an emphatic voice. "If the worse thing she can do to me is sleep with a boyfriend that I didn't really want, then I'm doing pretty damn good. It did make me move out earlier than I was financially prepared for but somehow I've managed to have a lot of luck and the right people looking out for me."

"That's great," Simone said. In only a half joking manner, she asked, "Would you like another roommate?"

There was a thoughtful pause before Justice said, "I'm afraid not. I only have one empty room and that's reserved for my mom when she visits."

"I understand. Besides, with work so sketchy for me, it's better for me to stay with family."

The waitress placed their meals in front of them and Justice dug in.

Paula and Simone stared enviously at her plate. Then with resigned looks they began to eat their salads.

When Sterling let himself into his penthouse, there was an unfamiliar smell coming from the kitchen. He placed his briefcase on the floor and walked down the long corridor, he leaned on the doorjamb to the kitchen with his arms folded across his chest.

Harlow stood in front of the stove. An apron hung around the middle of her swollen belly and she was turning over a piece of chicken in the frying pan. A blob of grease sparked out and struck her on the neck.

"Dammit," she said, covering her burnt neck with her hand.

Sterling chuckled. "So you're teaching our son to curse already, huh?"

Harlow spun around. "I didn't hear you come in," she said.

"I guess not," Sterling said dryly. "You need to turn the heat down on that chicken. You're frying it too fast."

Harlow gave Sterling a frustrated look. "I knew that I should have baked it instead of frying it." She turned the knob on the stove down to a lower temperature.

"I'm surprised that you're even cooking fried chicken," he admitted.

"I had a taste for it," she said, "and I didn't feel like going out."

"Take a seat at the table and I'll finish it for you."

"But, Sterling," she protested. "I wanted to cook dinner for you tonight."

Sterling pulled out a chair and Harlow gratefully sank into it.

He washed his hands at the sink and wiped them dry on a paper towel.

"Here," Harlow said. "You need this more than I do." She took off her apron and walked over to Sterling. Harlow securely tied it around his waist and then wrapped her arms around his middle.

Sterling let her hold her position for a few seconds before he moved away. "I think that I'm okay now."

Harlow stared down at the kitchen floor as she went back to her chair.

"My committee is having its annual charity fundraising next Saturday night. Will you go with me?"

Sterling groaned. "You know how I hate all black tie functions, Harlow. Can't I just make a sizeable donation and be done with it?"

"I really want you to be there with me, Sterling. The event won't be ending until two o'clock in the morning. I'd think that you wouldn't want you pregnant wife traveling alone at night."

"Maybe you shouldn't go at all," Sterling said.

"I have to put in appearance. You know that I'm usually the chairwoman but I gave it up because of how difficult my pregnancy has been."

Sterling just looked at her.

"We don't have to stay until the end."

He looked at her again.

"You don't want me to lose the baby, do you?" she blurted out in a disheartened voice. When no answer was forthcoming, Harlow asked,

SKELETONS IN THE CLOSET

trying to inject enthusiasm, "How was your day at work?"

"Just like the rest," Sterling said. "I can't wait to get out of there."

"What do you mean?"

"I've made a decision and I guess that I should tell you about it. After the baby is born I'm going to take an indefinite leave of absence from the company."

"You are?" she exclaimed.

"Yes," he said, taking the pieces of chicken out of the pan and placing them on a platter that had a paper towel on it to soak up the grease.

"I want to keep the insurance that we have until the baby is born. If I take a leave of absence I can still maintain coverage, albeit the premium will be much higher."

"How long a leave of absence are you planning on taking?"

"As long as it takes me to complete fashion design school."

"Sterling!"

"Don't waste your breath, Harlow. We're not going to be together after the baby is born anyhow so it's really none of your business. This conversation is merely a courtesy."

"You're too young to be going through a midlife crisis," Harlow said with a sour look.

He gave her a penetrating look. "I told you when we got married that was my dream."

"I didn't think that you meant it," she replied shortly.

"I feel that I need to do this for myself."

"Do you know how many men would love your career and all that goes along with it?"

"I know that you've always enjoyed it, Harlow. But I feel emptiness. I don't want to wake up an old man regretting the way that I've lived my life."

"You have responsibilities, Sterling."

"I have more than enough money for you and the baby," he said cynically.

"What if you're wrong?" she said with scorn. "There are so many people trying to break into fashion. What if you have no talent? How can you be sure?"

"I'm willing to step out on faith. It's better to have tried and lost than not to have tried at all."

"That quote refers to love, Sterling," Harlow said bitterly.

"I know," Sterling retorted.

###

Instead of driving her rental car to her mother's house, Justice checked into the Days Inn in Atlanta.

"How long will you be with us, ma'am?" the young clerk asked with a happy smile.

She handed her American Express card to her. "I'll be leaving in the morning," Justice answered.

Justice drove to the Buick dealership she and her mother frequently passed on shopping trips. She browsed rows and rows of cars until she found exactly what she wanted. Patiently, Justice waited in a cool breeze as a salesman hurried over.

He stuck his hand out, "My name is Ernest Pittman. But you can just call me Ernest."

Justice shook the salesman's moist hand.

"Is there any way that I can be of assistance?" he said in a hopeful voice.

"I don't have a lot of money," Justice hedged. "I was just sort of browsing."

"But young lady, your timing couldn't be better. We have a lot of inventory that we need to get rid of before July and we have some excellent deals."

"This price on this car is thirty-three thousand dollars. I don't want to pay that much."

"That's because it's fully loaded."

"Let me be honest," she said. "I want to purchase a car for my mother. Because it's a gift I want something nice for her, fully loaded with conveniences, and not out of the world expensive because I will also have to pay the insurance premiums for her."

"I see," he said. "Your mother is lucky to have such a generous daughter."

"I haven't bought her anything yet," Justice said in an ironic voice. "And I'm not going to unless the price is right."

"Well, you're the first customer to come to the lot all day," Ernest said in a conspiratorial voice. "I think that today might be your lucky day."

"We'll see," she said, not giving anything away. "Let's take it for a test drive. I want to see how it handles."

As they drove the route that Ernest had programmed in to the GPS, Justice felt exhilarated at the thought of her mother driving this car. Her mind was made up once they were back at the dealership. She cut off the engine of the car and said without preamble, "I'll give you a twenty five thousand dollar check for this car."

Ernest shook his head. "I don't think that I can go that low."

"Then I'll have to go to the Toyota dealership down the road," she said with a no nonsense inflection in her voice. "I'm sure they'll be grateful for the business."

A heavy silence filled the car. "I'll have to check with the manager."

"Please do," she said. In just a few minutes she learned that she had bought the car.

As Justice waited for the detail men to finish with the black onyx car, she dialed Nell's number.

"Hello?" Nell answered.

"Hey, girl, it's Justice."

Nell screamed into the phone. "Girl, I saw you on television."

"Do you like the commercial?"

"I sure do. 'If you want a face like this, buy Nile Cosmetics,'" Nell mimicked Justice's line in the commercial. "You were marvelous."

She laughed at her friend's on cue imitation of her. "Thank you, Nell. I'm here in town and I need a huge favor. Are you busy?"

"No, I just got out of class."

"You're going to school?"

"I sure am. When I saw all the great things that you were doing I felt that I needed to get my act together."

"You always had your act together, Nell. Listen, I need you to drive a rental car back to the airport for me."

"Okay, but how am I going to get to the car? I was getting ready to buy a token for the bus when you called me."

"I'll come and pick you up. Then we'll have to come back to the Buick dealership and get another car and I'll follow you."

"Why are you at the Buick dealership?"

"I bought Mom a car."

"Girl, you really got it going on," Nell said with a touch of envy.

"Believe me, it was a necessity. I called home and Mom was in bed sick from walking in the rain because my car broke down."

"Yeah, having experienced that myself I know how much that sucks," Nell said.

"Where are you?"

"I'm on Peachtree at the Dunkin Donuts."

"Sit tight and I'll come get you. By the time we get back my mom's car should be ready."

Nell and Justice sat at a table at the Chili's. Nell stared out the window at the car. "Your mom is going to be so excited. I can't think of a better Mother's Day gift for her."

"We were watching television one day, and I remember the look she got on her face when they ran the commercial for that car. But I never thought that I'd ever be in a position to buy her one. God has really blessed me."

"And you're blessing others. Does she know that she's getting it?"

"No," Justice said in a sleepy voice and yawned. "I must have jet lag or something because I can barely keep my eyes open. I called Mom and told her that I'm going to meet her at the church tomorrow."

"I'd be thankful for any car," Nell said in a mournful voice. "I hate taking the bus."

"I don't want to insult you but you can have my old car if you want. I mean..."

"Do you really mean that?" Nell asked in a buoyant voice.

"Don't forget how raggedy it is," Justice warned.

"But my cousin Jimmy has a little mechanic shop. I can get him to fix what's wrong with it real cheap."

Justice mused, "Then I'll pay for it."

"No," Nell protested in a weak voice.

"I insist or you can't have the car at all," Justice said firmly. There was silence. "I mean it, Nell. I wouldn't give that car to my worst enemy the shape that it's in."Justice quipped, "Well, maybe my worst enemy."

"It sure as hell beats the bus," Nell mumbled gratefully.

CHAPTER 12

Justice slid into the pew behind her mother and Aunt Minnie, and tapped each lightly on their shoulder. They both turned their heads and seeing her smiles beamed across their faces. Then they turned their attention back to the podium.

Pastor McClellan stood in the front of the church flailing his arms around. Justice knew that meant that he was almost finished with his sermon. She settled back against the pew. Feeling stared at Justice surveyed the church and met the eyes of Frances Turner, Miles mother. She gave her a quick nod of acknowledgement.

Frances didn't return the gesture, but instead put a fan in front of her face.

Justice bristled. She has a nerve.

After church, Justice stood patiently in the churchyard waiting for her mother to finish her goodbyes. She stiffened when she saw Frances coming towards her.

"How are you doing today, Mrs. Turner?" she said once Frances reached her.

"I'm fine, Justice. I almost didn't recognize you all gussied up like that."

"New York has a way of following you even when you're not there," Justice said quietly. She looked over at her mother, hoping she would come and rescue her, but she was busy chatting with Aunt Minnie and Sister Rawlins.

"Miles told me that you two were spending a lot of time together up there in New York," Frances said.

Justice chose her words carefully. "Things didn't work out. We don't keep in touch anymore."

"Why is that?" Frances' narrowed eyes squinted.

"What did he tell you?" Justice countered.

"I'd rather not say, us being on church property and all. I just hope that you know what you're doing."

"I think that's the advice that you should be giving your own child," Evelyn said from behind.

"Excuse me?" Frances said in a curt voice.

"Justice is too polite to tell you but your son will do anything he can for a dollar." Then Evelyn gave Frances a dismissive look before turning to Justice. "Your Aunt Minnie has to stay behind for a meeting."

She looked with an approving smile at the Lacrosse. "Is this your rental car?"

"No, Mom, it's your Mother's Day gift."

Evelyn put her hands to her cheeks and her lips trembled. "Oh, good Lord, Justice. You shouldn't have. It's too much."

"Nonsense, Mom." She gave her a hug. "You're the best mother a person could have and you deserve it."

"Ill gotten gains," Frances said, clucking her tongue in disapproval. "Are you trying to tell me that you got this expensive car with Godly money?"

"I sure did," Justice retorted. "I paid for this with a jeans ad that is being placed in Times Square. If you see your son in any magazine, you can best believe it's because he slept with someone to get the job. Now go away, you're spoiling our Mother's Day."

Frances stormed off in a huff, ignoring the other church members who hid smiles as she jumped into her beat up Ford pickup and drove off, kicking up sand in the church makeshift driveway.

Justice handed her mother the keys.

Evelyn backed away, "I can't drive it now. I'm too jumpy."

"Okay," Justice said in an understanding voice. "Once I get you away from the crowd, I'll let you take over."

Evelyn's eyes never left the road. Her hands gripped the steering wheel so hard that the skin on her fingers looked stretched.

"Relax, Mom," Justice said softly. "It's only a car."

"It's not only a car. This is my dream car and you know it."

"I got a really good deal on it. It's not as if I bought you a Lexus or anything."

"I didn't want a Lexus," Evelyn said. Tears of gratitude hung on her eyelashes. "But Justice, I need you to promise me something."

"Anything, Mom, what is it?"

"Don't buy me anything this expensive again without asking me first."

"Okay, mom. I promise," Justice said.

Once they were home Evelyn gave Justice the grand tour.

"I love what you did with the place, Mom. It looks great."

"It does," Evelyn said with satisfaction. "I couldn't decide whether to have the cabinets in the kitchen redone in walnut or cherry. I finally settled on the cherry because the furniture that I liked was the same."

As Justice perused the house satisfaction enveloped her body.

"Your Aunt Minnie is a little jealous," Evelyn whispered as if Minnie were somewhere in the house. "I told her that you couldn't afford to redo both our homes but she could move in here if she liked. I certainly have enough room."

"What did she say to your offer?" Justice asked with a raised eyebrow.

She said, "'No thanks, I get on her nerves too much.'"

"You should have said ditto," Justice said.

"I heard about it but I had to see it for myself," Minnie said when she walked into the kitchen.

"After y'all left they came and told me that you'd bought your momma a fine car," Minnie explained.

"Who told you?" Evelyn said, her eyes crinkling up from mirth.

"Sister Sinclair told me right before the pastor started the meeting."

A sober look settled on Evelyn's face. "How'd that go?"

"Not too good," Minnie said, sitting down at the kitchen table. "Yvette doesn't want to do it but she's going to have to or get out of the church choir."

"Whatever are you two talking about?" Justice asked.

Evelyn busied herself by pouring all of them a glass of lemonade.

"Yvette Smith has been going with another woman's husband. It's a shame before God."

"But she gave him up, didn't she?" Evelyn said. "Shouldn't that be the end of it?"

"No, siree, she has to beg that woman's pardon in front of the church or she can't be a part of any of its functions."

"Good Lord," Justice said in a heated voice. "Do you really think that it's necessary to embarrass her in front of everyone in the church? Her absolution should be between her and God."

"I agree, Minnie," Evelyn said in a soft voice. "I feel sorry for Yvette."

Minnie slammed her hand hard down on the table. "You don't need to feel sorry for that adulteress. She's grown," she said, taking a large gulp of her lemonade. "She knew what she was doing."

"What if Yvette didn't know the man was married?" Justice asked in a passionate voice. "Is that her fault?"

"Then it serves her right for being so dumb. This is a small area. Everyone knows everyone else's business."

"How about the man?" Justice asked fiercely. "Does he have to stand in front of the church and beg everyone's pardon?"

"He don't go to church so there ain't nothin' we can do about him," Minnie retorted sharply. "That's the way it's done, Justice. Yvette can't serve on any church committee until she begs Debra's pardon in front of the church congregation. And it's only fittin'. I think a woman who sleeps with a married man should be horsewhipped. I don't believe she didn't know that Eddie was Debra's husband." Minnie drained her glass of the rest of her liquid.

"Maybe he hid it from her," Justice retorted sharply.

"Then she was too stupid to find out," Minnie countered.

"I think sometimes that church people are a little too judgmental about others," Justice said in a careful voice.

"The bible says that's the way to settle things so that's the way we do it," Minnie said. "Now forget that mess. Let's talk about whether or not you gonna buy your aunt a car like you done your momma? Mine ain't got to be that fancy."

Justice unsuccessfully tried to suppress the ball of anger that arose as a result of their conversation. "I'm out of money," she said, swiftly standing. "Maybe if you're lucky mom will let you ride in hers." She stormed out the house letting the screen door bang to a close behind her.

Minnie stared in astonishment at Evelyn who had a pondering look.

###

On the way to the airport Evelyn drove the Lacrosse with ease. She glanced at Justice. "Are you feeling all right?"

"I'm fine, Mom. Why do you ask?"

"You've just seemed kind of quiet while you were visiting."

"I'm okay, Mom," she said in a low voice. "I just found out something about someone that I thought was a friend. It turned out that he isn't."

"Are you talking about Miles?"

"No, not him," she said. "I already knew he wasn't any good."

"Then who is it?"

"I don't really want to talk about it." Justice said evasively. Then, in an effort to ease the creases in her mother's forehead," she said in a deliberately offhand voice, "I'm over it."

"That's good," Evelyn said. She added in her quiet manner, "Justice, keep your values while you're up there."

"I try, Mom. I mean, I really try."

"I know that you do, Justice."

"I'm finally adjusting to the fact that for some reason I've been blessed. I'm going to see how big a model I can become." She said with a huge grin, "It's really kind of neat."

"It's real neat," her mother countered.

Justice found Scarlett sitting at the kitchen table. Papers and books were strewn all over the table and she wore a harried look on her face.

"Hey, Scarlett," Justice said, bending to give her a warm hug.

"Hey to you too." Scarlett smiled in return. She took the pencil that was tucked behind her ear and scribbled something on a pad. "I missed you the last couple of days."

"It seems more like weeks to me since I've seen you. You're at school during the day."

"And you're in bed by the time I get home. Do you think that you can stay up past nine o'clock on Sunday night?"

"What, whatcha got planned?"

"My science professor had two tickets to a charity wine tasting that he couldn't attend and I took them off his hands."

"Why cause is the charity supporting?"

"AIDS awareness."

"Oh?" Justice said, surprised.

"I think that people should be more aware of the dangers. But I don't want to go alone," Scarlett finished in a subdued voice.

"Okay," Justice said. "I'll go with you. It's certainly a worthwhile cause."

"Mom, where have you been? I've been calling you all day."

"You don't want to know."

Justice could hear the strained tone in her mother's voice. "Yes I do. What's wrong?" she asked sharply.

"I just left a town hall meeting because Eastman is in an uproar. Now I need to take some Tylenol because I have a blistering headache. I'll call you tomorrow."

"No, Mom," she said firmly. You go take the Tylenol and I'll call you right back. Answer the phone, okay?"

"Yes, Justice," her mother said weakly.

Justice sat on the couch and nervously drummed her fingers on the table. She counted to ten, then called her mother again.

Evelyn picked up the phone.

"Now what's going on?" she demanded.

"The city is taking our land and giving us practically nothing for it."

"What on earth are you talking about?" she exclaimed in a shrill voice. "We paid all the liens."

"It's something called eminent domain. Everyone in the neighborhood is losing their property."

"I'm flying down this weekend to find out what I can do to stop it."

"You can come and I'd love to see you. But there's nothing you can do. The state needs the land to run a highway through it. Over thirty families are being uprooted. We tried to start a class action lawsuit, but they shut it down. I didn't say anything, hoping that things would work out but they didn't."

"All that money fixing up the house down the drain," Justice shouted angrily.

"I'm sick about it, Justice."

"How is Minnie taking it?" Justice asked.

"She cut up so much down at the county office they threatened to arrest her."

"Oh my goodness." Intuitively she said, "That's why they added all those liens to the property, hoping we'd lose it."

"I reckon so," Evelyn agreed in a tired voice.

"They may be cheats, Mom, but they can't beat us. I want you to go over to the new Riverside Estates development and pick out a house. I'll deposit the money in the bank, but have the bank fax me the paperwork before you sign anything," she warned.

"Justice, I can't let you do that. All this beautiful furniture will look good in those apartments by the church."

"Mom," she groaned, "you wouldn't know how to live in an apartment or any place without a garden and a place for your flowers. Get a two or three bedroom. Tell Aunt Minnie to move in with you."

"I don't know that she'll do it. You know how independent she is."

"She doesn't have a choice. Aunt Minnie doesn't have any money and I can't afford to buy two houses. Besides, I don't like either one of you living alone. You're too old for that."

Once Justice hung up the phone, she lay on the bed with a cool washcloth across her forehead. On the nightstand next to her lay the residual check that she'd taken from the mailbox that afternoon.

Harlow stood in front of the mirror massaging wrinkle cream around her eyes. Then she turned to the side. The sight of her protruding belly made her feel older than her thirty-five-years. She pushed her feet into a pair of stilettos. Then she turned around in front of the mirror. Her red dress swirled around her knees and her short cropped hair was sleek making her features even more striking than unusual. But she leaned forward towards the mirror in despair. No matter what I use on my face I'm still aging. Picking up her makeup compact she used a heavy amount of powder. Then she outlined her lips with red lipstick that was a stark contrast to the black eyeliner she'd rimmed her eyes with. Taking a deep breath, she went to meet Sterling.

Sterling stood in the foyer in his black tux. His brooding countenance looked sexy and dangerous all at the same time.

Harlow gave him a sweet smile. "You look so handsome, Sterling."

"Thank you, Harlow. As usual you look beautiful."

"I'm too fat," she protested.

"You're pregnant. You're supposed to put on weight," Sterling responded. He looked down at her feet. "Do you think it's wise for you to wear those heels? Won't they be uncomfortable?"

"They make my back hurt. But if I wore flats it would ruin the whole effect."

"The things you women do for fashion," Sterling said, shaking his head in a fatherly gesture.

She said in a conspiratorial whisper, "After we sit down, I'll slide them off under the table."

"It's up to you," Sterling said and held the front door open for Harlow.

They were silent for most of the drive. In order to break the ice Harlow said, "I'm surprised that you managed to get Constance and Chapman to not only buy tickets but agree to come."

"You know that Chapman tries to support me in everything that I do and Constance supports him."

"I remember when I first met the two of you I thought that you were brothers."

"I've heard that when people hang out together too much they start to look alike."

"I hope our baby looks like you. Have you decided whether or

167

not you want to make him a junior?"

"I think Sterling Junior works."

"Good," she said then, "It's been a long time since we went somewhere together, Sterling."

"Until you got pregnant you were quite content to travel without me," Sterling responded in an expressionless voice.

Harlow stared out the dark window pretending to have an immense interest in the traffic as they traveled down Broadway.

Once they arrived at the hotel, Sterling spotted Chapman's silver Mercedes with the license plate Keen printed on it. "I see that Chapman and Constance have arrived."

"We're running a bit late," Harlow said. "Thank God there's assigned seating at the tables, or we might end up sitting with no name people."

As Sterling turned his car over to the valet, Harlow slid her arm in the crook of his.

He looked down questioningly at her.

"My swollen ankles are throbbing," she complained in a plaintive voice. "Do you mind if I lean on you for support?"

Sterling's expression was indecipherable. "Of course, Harlow. I certainly don't want you to fall and injure yourself or the baby."

As they made their way through the crowded foyer, Sterling spied Chapman and Constance as they stood to one side obviously searching the crowd for a glimpse of them.

"I see that the two of you waited for us before going to your seats," Sterling said, leaning over to give Constance a kiss on the cheek.

Constance's eyes twinkled in amusement. "I can't believe that you invited us and you're late."

"I'm afraid that's my fault," Harlow chimed in. "It takes me a little longer than it used to get dressed."

"I think that you get a pass on that. And by the way, congratulations, Harlow. I haven't seen you since I heard the news."

"Thank you," Harlow responded. "It was quite a shock."

"I bet it was," Constance blurted out. When she saw the look of anger cross Harlow's face she swiftly added, "What I mean is that nowadays so many women seem to have babies in their forties it seems almost unusual for a woman in her thirties to get pregnant."

"Well, I hate to admit it, but I'm pushing thirty-five. So I'm glad to get it over with now."

"You only want one baby?" Constance asked in a seemingly innocent voice, avoiding the pointed stare Chapman gave her.

Harlow's eyes darted to Sterling's bland face and she said

nonchalantly, "I don't know. We'll just have to wait and see."

"Let's go inside," Chapman said.

As they made their way to the front tables, Harlow clung possessively to Sterling. She smiled broadly and nodded her head at people she knew. When her eyes fell on Andrea seated with several other women she deliberately lifted her chin, shooting her a look of triumph.

Once they sat down Constance admired the table setting. "The table decorations are beautiful, Harlow," she said in a sincere voice. "Did you have anything to with them?"

"Yes I did," Harlow cooed. "I was able to order most everything via the Internet and I met the workers here and told them how I wanted everything set up."

"Well you certainly did a good job for a worthwhile cause."

"We only have a couple of hundred people in attendance but we have a lot of pledges from corporations already on the books," Harlow explained.

"What's being offered besides wine?" Sterling asked, picking up a menu.

"There will be trays of appetizers as accompaniment to the wines."

"What's this card for?" Constance asked.

"It's a trivia game. All the bottles and glasses are listed with numbers and you're supposed to guess which wine it is on the list. The winners get door prizes."

"That leaves me out," Chapman said. "I'm a beer drinker myself."

"It wouldn't hurt you to switch up," Constance teased, pointedly staring at Chapman's belly that had recently begun to protrude.

Harlow took her hand and lovingly smoothed it across Sterling's stomach. "I hate it for you," she said. "My husband's belly is flat as a board."

Sterling's body stiffened at the unaccustomed feel of Harlow's manicured hand.

"Yes," Constance snapped at the hint of criticism of Chapman. "Sterling is certainly bored. I mean his stomach is."

An elderly gentleman walked to the mike at the front stage and cleared his throat. "Welcome, welcome, welcome," he said.

A hush fell over the room. "I am more than thrilled to see such a huge turnout tonight to support our annual wine tasting benefit. As a physician at the Metropolitan Research Center for Diseases I know how important funding is and how difficult with the economy the way it is to get people to pay five hundred dollars for sipping wine."

Laughter erupted throughout the room, followed by applause.

"But your heart is in the right place. In a few minutes, the waiters will circulate with trays. Please enjoy and choose a designated driver." There was another burst of laughter accompanied by applause as he walked off the stage.

Harlow looked at the two empty seats at their table. "I wonder where they are?" she said.

"I don't know," Chapman replied. "But I certainly can't see losing out on these tickets."

Harlow shrugged her shoulders in an indifferent gesture. "The tickets were bought ahead of time so The Inner Circle won't lose any money."

"A waiter is showing two women over. I guess that's them."

Constance coughed and said, "Boys."

They turned around and did a double take as did every other man who watched Justice and Scarlett traipse down the aisle towards the front of the room.

Justice wore a yellow dress that stopped mid thigh. Her hair was piled high on her head and was adorned by a matching yellow ornament that secured a bun at the top of her hair. She wore no stockings and her legs glistened. Open toed, black stilettos contrasted nicely with the brightness of her dress.

Not to be outdone, Scarlett wore an off the shoulder black halter dress that had a red belt cinched around her waist. She too wore high heels, which made her only half an inch shorter than Justice. Her hair was also piled on top of her head and ringlets cascaded along the sides of her face.

"Why is every man in the room staring at them? They don't look that good," Harlow said, glaring at Sterling whose eyes appeared mesmerized as the women made their way over to them.

Constance said, "Maybe because that black girl is a model and was featured in Elle." Then she said, "Ouch!" and glared at Chapman.

Once they stood in front of the table everyone was motionless.

Justice stared at Sterling with a frozen look on her face.

Scarlett was the first to recover. She turned to the waiter that was holding a chair out for Justice. "Are there no other available seats?"

The waiter looked nonplussed. "I'm sorry, ma'am, but the seats are numbered according to the tickets."

Justice gave Scarlett a dazed look before she practically fell into her chair.

Another waiter brought a tray of glasses. Before he began

explaining the origins of the liquids, Sterling, Chapman and Constance grabbed one simultaneously.

"Cheers," Constance said to no one in particular before slurping the contents of her glass.

The tension at the table was palpable. Harlow said to the waiter, "There's a bottle of non alcoholic wine in the kitchen reserved for me. "Will you please bring it?"

"Yes, ma'am," he said, disappearing at once.

Harlow looked at Justice and Scarlett. "As you can see, I'm very pregnant. But I had to come and support my charity tonight."

Justice stared at her full glass of white wine for a long minute. "Congratulations on your pregnancy," she said quietly. Then she squared her shoulders and turned to Scarlett who watched her with a pained look on her face. "Thank you so much for asking me to join you tonight. This is just what I needed for my moment of clarity."

Scarlett drank from her glass but couldn't avoid a look of concern she felt as she looked at Justice.

"I heard that you're a model," Harlow said to Justice.

"Yes."

"Who do you model for?" she asked.

"Do you think it's polite to start quizzing someone you just met, Harlow?" Sterling asked severely.

"I'm just curious because I was in the business," Harlow asked. She said to Justice, "I used to model myself."

"Really," Scarlett interjected. "For who?"

There was an uncomfortable silence.

"I modeled for artists and did some catalogue work. But I stopped once I got married." She placed her hand on Sterling's thigh close to his crotch. "I just didn't feel the drive. All I wanted was to be Mrs. Sterling Hart."

Sterling brushed Harlow's hand off him.

Anger flooded Harlow's face at the obvious snub. Her diamond hard eyes glared at Sterling.

The waiter came back with Harlow's wine.

Constance asked him with twinkling eyes, "Do you have any popcorn in the back?" Then she uttered, "Ouch!" again and refused to look at Chapman.

Chapman picked up a cracker with an orange hued cheese on top of it. After devouring it he handed one to Constance. "This is pretty good. I suggest you fill your mouth with it."

Sterling tried to capture Justice's eyes with his, but she looked at everyone but him.

Harlow's anger built as she watched her husband. "Where are you from?" she asked Justice, her eyes narrowed. She sensed that something important was amiss.

"I live here in New York," Justice answered carefully.

"Obviously," she said. "But you have a strong accent. Are you from the south?" she asked in a disdainful voice.

"Yes," she said proudly. "I'm from Eastman, Georgia."

"Good Lord," Harlow said in a catty voice. "I never even heard of that country place. I hope that a yokel like you isn't finding it too difficult to get used to the big city ways of New York."

Justice's body became as stiff as a board. "Don't worry about me. I've managed to find a real fine man wanting to make me feel welcome," Justice drawled. "In fact," she said, "he is the spitting image of your husband."

Chapman sputtered and put his drink down on the table.

"I doubt that," Harlow sneered. "Why would…"

"Be quiet, Harlow," Sterling interrupted with a force that made Harlow blink. After a long silence he said to Justice, "You seem like the kind of woman who would really make a lifelong impression on a man. I think any man lucky enough to spend time in your company would never forget it and would find life almost intolerable not to be able to do it again."

Harlow stiffened and her jealousy nearly boiled over. But then she said, "Don't listen to my husband," she said in a deceptively mild voice. "He's always trying to make women feel beautiful and wanted." She took her hand and once again rubbed it lovingly across Sterling's stomach. "He said the same thing to me when I first time I met him."

"No, I didn't, Harlow." Sterling roughly pushed Harlow's hand off him, stood, and stormed out the room. As he stalked into the kitchen area he demanded, "Is there any liquor available in this place?"

The head maître d's right eyebrow lifted in a commiserating gesture, "Bored, huh? I have a stash in my office. How would you like a Long Island Iced Tea?"

"Can you make it a double?" Sterling asked in a grateful voice.

After Sterling quaffed his drink he sat on a bench outside the banquet room and waited. Justice, please come out. Please have to use the restroom or something.

Half an hour later Sterling saw the double doors open and Chapman was flanked by Harlow and Constance. "The ladies are ready to call it a night," Chapman offered as explanation.

Ignoring Harlow's look of fury Sterling and Chapman eyed each other.

"So am I," he said and headed towards the exit.

Once they got in the car and Sterling pulled into traffic, Harlow turned to him and screamed, "How could you embarrass me like that? In front of my friends!" With an accusatory look she yelled, "Why did you leave me sitting there all alone?"

"You weren't alone," Sterling said in a tight voice. "Chapman and Constance were there with you."

"And those women," she screeched. "One that you practically came on to right in front of me!"

"Lower your voice," he ordered harshly. "Maybe if you weren't being such a phony I wouldn't have abandoned you."

"What the hell is wrong with you?"

"Every time we get around others you pretend to be something that you're not, as well as pretend we have something that we don't," Sterling ground out through clenched teeth.

"We need to keep our problems private!"

"If you don't like my behavior, you know what to do about it."

With her lips pursed angrily, Harlow glumly stared out the window at the black sky.

CHAPTER 13

The next morning Sterling sat at his desk and nursed his hangover with a glass of orange juice.

Ada walked into his office with a steaming cup of hot coffee. "I thought that you might like this, Mr. Hart," she said with a concerned look. "Chapman called and said that he's going to stop by on his way to court."

"That's fine," Sterling said, gratefully taking the cup from her.

After Ada left, Sterling pulled out a piece of stationary. The pen in his hand bobbed up and down as he tried to figure out what to write. Finally he scribbled,

Dear Justice:

I know that...

His hand shook so much his writing was illegible. Sterling put the pen down. He turned to his keyboard and began pounding on the letters.

My dearest Justice:

I know that you probably hate me, but please let me explain. From the moment I met you on the plane my life hasn't been the same. I can't get you off my mind and barely sleep at night. I know that I appear to be a man who cheats on his wife, but my marriage to Harlow is a sham. Harlow and I were in the process of splitting up and divorcing when she found out that she was pregnant. I cannot abandon my child the way my father abandoned me. She and I are only together until the baby is born. I want him born in wedlock. I am working on a way to free myself. In the state of New York it's not easy to get a divorce. If you don't believe me please check out the facts for yourself.

I know that it was wrong for me to make love to you without telling you my situation. I lost my head and acted selfishly. But I would be a liar if I said that I totally regret it. The time that I spent with you is something that I will never forget. I would like to see you in person and apologize. Please, meet me at six o'clock Wednesday evening at Carbone's Italian Restaurant on West 38th street so I can apologize to you. If you don't come I'll understand and will not contact you again.

You have my heart,

Sterling, cell (513)927-1583

Sterling stared at the computer monitor. He read the words over and over again. A knock on his door interrupted his dour thoughts. Quickly he saved the letter and shut the monitor screen off. "Come in," he barked.

Chapman walked in. "I just thought that I'd stop by and check on you. That was some crucial shit last night, wasn't it?" he said, plopping down in the chair across from Sterling.

"It certainly wasn't my finest hour," Sterling acknowledged grimly.

"Man, I didn't know what to do. I wanted to get the hell out of there and follow you, but I didn't dare leave those chicks alone. Things might have gone from bad to Godawful."

"Did anything else happen after I left?"

"Harlow didn't say a damn thing. Your departure silenced her ass. But she was so pissed after she finished her nonalcoholic spritzer that she drank some real wine."

Sterling rolled his eyes in disgust.

"What did Harlow say to you on the way home?" Chapman asked with a raised brow.

"She yelled and screamed about me embarrassing her."

"What did you say to defend yourself?"

"I told her that if she didn't like my behavior she knew what to do," he said caustically.

"Has she figured out that you and Justice had an affair?"

"We didn't have an affair," Sterling snapped.

"Call it what you like, man."

"I made a mistake. And it has cost me dearly."

"Dude, you really took a chance leaving Harlow and Justice at the same table without you being there."

"I couldn't stand the thought of Harlow touching me. We have nothing, and I don't want Justice to think that we do."

"Well," Chapman said slowly, "Any person in the room could see that your marriage is on the rocks. Even if they don't know the whole story your body language and the look in your eyes when you look at Harlow makes you look like a caged animal."Chapman searched Sterling's face. "What's your next move? I know that you said that you weren't going to approach Justice until you were able to get your divorce, but after last night, if there's ever a possibility of the two of you having a future, you're going to have to do some damage control."

"I wrote Justice a letter," he said with a woeful expression.

"Another to follow your great escape note?" Chapman drawled. Sterling shot him a dark look.

Ignoring it Chapman said, "How are you going to get it to her?"

"I'm going to drop it off at her agency."

"What's in the letter?" Chapman asked.

"None of your business," Sterling answered in a strained voice.

"Damn man," he said. "It must've been good."

"Shut up, Chapman."

The bedroom was black from the drawn drapes. Justice stared vacantly into space. She heard three light taps on her bedroom door.

She didn't respond.

The door was opened and Scarlett came in. She sat down on the bed next to Justice. She took her hand and smoothed Justice's long hair. "Are you okay?" she asked softly.

"Yes," Justice answered in a monosyllable.

"It's three o'clock in the afternoon and you haven't come out of your room. You haven't showered or eaten in days."

"I'm tired."

"You're depressed," Scarlett gently corrected her.

"Yep." She listlessly threaded her hand through her hair. "I'm depressed."

"Justice," Scarlett said. "I know that it was hard to sit at a table with Sterling's pregnant wife, but I don't think that their relationship is what it should be."

"What do you mean?" Justice rolled onto her back and look at Scarlett.

"Sterling hauled ass and didn't come back in. He left his wife sitting at a table with his ex-lover."

"That's because he was afraid that I was going to out him to his wife," she said tearfully.

"I don't think so," Scarlett replied with a pensive expression. "If that was the case, he would have stayed there and run interference between the two of you if need be."

"Chapman was sitting there. He knew that he'd take care of things for him."

"But there's something else. Sterling looked really uncomfortable and he stiffened up whenever his wife touched him."

"That's because he knows that now he can't use me for sex anymore until his pregnant wife is willing to satisfy him," she said harshly.

Scarlett mused, "I think that there's something else going on there."

"His wife is having his baby," she choked out. "He's a family man." She rolled over and buried her face in her arm.

"The look Sterling had in his eyes when he looked at you... Harlow may have his name, but I really believe he cares for you."

"I wish that I could believe that." Justice's cell phone rang. "Hello, Ursula," Justice said in a dull voice.

"What's the matter with you? Are you sick or something?"

"No, I was just resting."

"Good, because tonight I need you to put in an appearance at a party."

"What kind of party?"

"It's a meet and greet. Some major magazine heads are putting it together. Also, designers will be there looking for talent. This is rare because they're usually in competition with each other but they're scouting models for the runway show in Paris next month. All you have to do is make an appearance."

"Can anyone come?" she pointed at Scarlett who was standing there.

"You can bring whoever you want. I'm going to send a courier over with two tickets. But I want you to be stunning because you represent Catwalk."

"I'll do my best," Justice promised.

"Good," she said. "By the way, someone left a letter for you with the secretary."

"What kind of letter?"

"I don't know," Ursula said. "I wasn't here when it was delivered."

"Okay," Justice said. "I'll come by and pick it up tomorrow." After she hung up she stared at Scarlett.

"I heard and the answer is no."

"Why not?" Justice wailed. "You might get some work out of it."

"I haven't gotten any work since I left Brabantio. I think that Cassius' wife has blacklisted me."

"Nina doesn't know everyone. You might run into someone The House of Brabantio doesn't influence."

Scarlett hesitated, looking almost fearful.

"At least you'll get some good food and wine out of it. These events always have the best caterers."

"Too bad the models only drink the champagne," Scarlett laughed. "I'll go only if you agree to do something."

"What is it?" Justice asked.

"Talk to designers about your sketches. Try to make contacts."

"I don't know about that."

"Why not? Your designs are great. This is the perfect opportunity to get someone to look at your stuff."

"I don't know if I'm ready."

"Even if you aren't ready, Justice, your designs are."

"Do you really think so?" Justice asked nervously.

"As a former model, I know so," Scarlett said emphatically.

###

Justice tightly gripped the large leather binder that represented years of hard work.

Scarlett looked at Justice's round butt. "That dress is fitting you like a second skin."

"I know," Justice said with a grimace. "I only bought it a couple of weeks ago, but I could barely squeeze in it."

"But you look great," Scarlett said admirably.

"I'm going on a diet tomorrow. If I don't I won't be walking down any runway."

The café was crowded with familiar faces from the industry. There was a clique of photographers she'd encountered while working on photo shoots. Justice recognized models from the covers of magazines. They were grouped together smiling broadly and laughing way too loudly. One particular one smiled brightly at Cassius, who wore a look of complete boredom. Then Justice spotted Raven.

She was leaning on the bar, posed while drinking a glass of champagne. The bone structure in Raven's face was so pronounced she resembled a skeleton. Her neck was long and emaciated as was the rest of her body.

"Scarlett," Justice whispered.

"I see her," Scarlett said in a sad voice. "I've also seen that look before. Raven needs to get some help before it's too late."

"She's not even 100 pounds wringing wet," Justice whispered in a concerned voice. "It's a shame."

Raven's vacuous stare around the room was replaced with one of interest when she saw Justice and Scarlett. Then she very deliberately strode over to a group of men. She tapped one on his back.

When he turned around, Justice realized that it was Miles. The look of irritation on his face at being interrupted was obvious. He stiffly bowed his head, listening to what she said. Then he turned his back to Raven and resumed his conversation with the others.

Annoyance flashed across Raven's face and she stomped back to the bar, leaned over to the bartender and said something. Even though Justice couldn't hear what was said, soon another glass of champagne was handed to her. Raven downed it and never turned back around towards Justice and Scarlett.

"I guess he's bored with her already," Scarlett said, shouting over the deejay's music.

"That's their drama," Justice shouted back, "and I don't want any part of it. Look," she said excitedly. "It's Caesar."

Scarlett hung back. "I'm not going over there."

"I don't want to abandon you," Justice said.

"You're not," Scarlett said. "Go and show him your sketches."

When Caesar saw her coming towards him, a huge smile spread across his face. He extended his hands.

Justice grabbed Caesar's hands and leaned over, kissing him on each check.

"Justice, how good it is to see you," Caesar said.

"It's nice to see you also, Caesar," she replied.

"I tried to sign you for the next show but you were already taken by an American house."

"Ursula didn't tell me." Justice pouted. "I would have rather modeled for you."

"It is not her fault. I was not sure that I was going to participate until the last moment. Then it was too late."

"I'm going to ask Ursula in the future to call you first to see if you're going to be a part of the show." She gave him a cheeky grin. "Maybe I'll try to stall signing my contract until you make up your mind."

"You have remained unsullied from this world you now live in." Caesar gave her an approving smile. "I've followed your successes. Congratulations on your contract with Nile Cosmetics."

"If it wasn't for you it wouldn't have happened."

"Are you happy, Justice?" He peered at her. "Did I do the right thing persuading you to come to New York?"

"Financially it was the best thing that could have happened to me," she answered.

"Financially? That is not enough for you?" Caesar now had an inquisitive look on his face.

"You know that my dream is to be a clothing designer."

"So modeling has not taken that desire from you?"

"No, not quite. I've applied to several design studios here in New York but I haven't heard yet. I don't even know what I would do if I were accepted. I need to be available for a modeling show when called."

"It is hard to be in two places at a time."

"I brought along my sketches, hoping to show them to a few designers." Justice shrugged her shoulders self-consciously. "I hoped that tonight someone might like my sketches and I could do some freelance work with them."

"Ahh," Caesar said admiringly. "You want to cut through the middle man."

"I know that's not exactly protocol at this kind of event."

"And designers are not usually willing to share the spotlight with others. It's an industry as competitive as modeling. If you like, I will take your sketches and show them to the right people." Caesar winked at her. "If I like what I see, I might even be willing to team up with you myself."

In an appreciative voice she said, "Thank you so much, Caesar."

"No," he said, reaching for her leather bound sketch book. "I'll probably end up thanking you."

After Justice finished conversing with Caesar, she went to the ladies' room. When she emerged she found Miles standing outside it. He had a drink in one hand.

"How are you doing, Justice?" he asked.

Not answering she went to pass him but he blocked her path. "I moved out from Raven," he said. "I found an apartment in Soho."

"Tell someone who cares," she replied and walked around him.

As Justice walked towards Scarlett, she saw her in conversation with Cassius.

Scarlett shifted nervously from one foot to the other.

Cassius moved in closer to Scarlett and she took a step back.

Justice quickened her pace over to them.

"The answer is no," Scarlett declared forcefully.

Cassius said derisively, "You don't mean that."

"I do mean it," she said. Scarlett turned to Justice. "I'm ready to go."

"So am I," Justice agreed.

Cassius gave Justice a venomous look. "You should stop giving advice, Justice," he growled before stomping off.

Justice held her hands out in confusion. "What the hell?"

"I'm sorry, Justice. Cassius thinks that I won't see him because I'm living with you."

"Oh good Lord," she said.

"I'm sorry for involving you, Justice," she said with a miserable expression on her face.

Justice watched Cassius rejoin Caesar and a chill ran up and down her spine. Yet she said, "Don't worry about it, Scarlett. I can take care of myself."

Harlow turned the lock to the safe at the office in The Inner Circle. She placed the receipts and paperwork from the wine testing benefit, then relocked it. She felt herself being watched and turned around.

Andrea leaned on the doorjamb. There was an undeniable smirk on her face that Harlow wanted to slap away.

"I thought that no one else would be here so I locked everything up," Harlow explained in a distant voice. "I'm going to miss the next meeting because I have to go out of town."

"Really?" Andrea drawled. "I'm surprised that you would leave New York at this time."

"This isn't the olden days, Andrea, when pregnant women were shut up in the house until they delivered. But not having any children, you wouldn't know anything about that," Harlow added with sarcasm.

Andrea's eyes narrowed angrily but she said in a smooth voice, "That's not what I meant. I just thought after last night, you'd stick around to watch Sterling."

"I don't need to 'watch Sterling' and whatever you have to say keep it to yourself," Harlow replied caustically. "I don't feel like hearing any of your dirt."

"I pity you, Harlow."

"I don't need your pity." Harlow added stridently, "Worry about your own damn self."

"You may not want it, but you have it. When I saw you sitting at the same table as your husband's mistress," Andrea shook her head sadly, "that must have been very uncomfortable for you."

A sudden feeling of bile rose in Harlow's throat but she tamped it down. "What the hell are you talking about?"

"That black woman that joined you at the table," Andrea offered triumphantly. "She's the one I saw Sterling kissing at Triomphe."

Harlow leaned on the desk for support. "I don't believe you," she said halfheartedly.

"It's true. She's some model. I've seen her in several magazines. Didn't you used to try to be a model?" Andrea asked in an innocent voice.

"How could you say something like that to me?" Harlow cried. "I know that we don't like each other but I'm pregnant."

"For years you've lorded it over me and all the other single women in our club that you're married," Andrea said. "We've had to sit by while you bragged about how great your life is." Andrea took a deep breath. "We have careers, Harlow, but you try to make us feel that our lives are incomplete because we don't have husbands. What you put up with so that you can boast about being married," she said scathingly, "I don't want any part of it."

After Andrea left, Harlow stared blankly into space.

When Sterling got to his office, he found Ada standing in front of his office door.

With a quizzical look he asked, "What's going on, Ada?"

"Your wife is here to see you."

Sterling thrust his hands in his trouser pockets. He said tersely, "Thank you, Ada."

Sterling slammed his office door shut. "What are you doing here?"

"Since you obviously don't want me around, I'm going to see my mother for a couple of days," she snapped.

"A phone call would have sufficed, Harlow. You didn't need to come here and tell me that."

"I need some money."

"I just deposited two thousand dollars in your checking account last week. What happened to that?"

"It's not enough."

With a skeptical look, Sterling opened his desk drawer and took out his checkbook. Quickly he scribbled out a check in the amount of a thousand dollars, signed it, and handed it to Harlow. "If you're squirreling away money for yourself after we divorce, just be honest and say so."

Harlow's eyes glittered angrily. She spat out, "What did I ever see in you!"

"A meal ticket," Sterling responded in a detached voice.

After Harlow left, Sterling cradled his head in his hands. His shoulders were slumped in utter misery.

Harlow shot Ada a haughty look as she stomped past her. She stood waiting for the elevator. The doors opened and she drew her breath in sharply.

Lyle stood on the threshold. He stepped out and they were almost touching.

Harlow looked at Lyle's boyish features with longing. She swallowed the lump in her throat. "Hey, Lyle."

"How are you doing, Harlow?"

"Don't you mean how are we doing?" she whispered.

Lyle's eyes narrowed sharply. "Don't start."

Harlow took his hand and placed it on her swollen belly. "It's a boy," she said.

"Congratulations to you and Sterling," he declared, drawing his hand away.

"You know that it's your baby, Lyle," she said softly.

"I don't know anything."

"Please," she said. "Can't we sit down and talk?"

"We've already done that," he replied in a curt tone. "And since this is the last time that I'll be seeing you I don't want to end it on a bad note."

Harlow fought back tears. "What do you mean, 'this is the last time?'"

"Today is my last day working at Lerner and Associates. My agent got me a part in a movie. I'm moving to L.A."

"Please don't go," she pleaded.

"Why not? I have nothing to keep me here."

As Lyle passed Ada on his way to his cubicle he missed the look of revulsion on her face.

Harlow bolted out of Lerner and Associates. Even though she was almost blinded by tears she spotted the black limousine parked in the holding lane. Harlow headed towards the open door held by Thomas. In her haste, she stumbled and her ankle turned over in her stilettos. Harlow catapulted face first into the gutter. Her head hit the cement so hard she almost lost consciousness. The ringing in her ears was her only evidence that she was still alive.

"Oh my God, Mrs. Hart," Thomas shouted in horror as he ran to her. "Are you okay?"

Harlow lay immobile.

Thomas peered down at her. "Let me help you up," he said in a fearful voice. Thomas dragged Harlow to her feet.

Her ankle throbbed from pain.

"Do you want me to go inside and tell your husband that you've had a fall?"

Harlow stared with a sort of confused look on her face. But she managed to eke out, "No, I'm fine. Please get me out of here as soon as possible. I need to make my plane."

Harlow leaned back against the leather of the vehicle. She ignored the anxious eyes of Thomas as he watched her through the glass. A throbbing headache pounded, making it difficult to keep her eyes open. All of a sudden a strange sensation began to unfold inside her stomach. Then a sharp, jolting pain rocked her body. Harlow clenched her thighs together in a futile hope to staunch the trickle that began to flow from inside her. The fluid began to wet the sumptuous leather seat. With immense horror she tapped on the partition. "Please take me to the nearest hospital," she said with despair. "I don't feel very well."

Thomas sped to the emergency room at Our Lady of Mercy Hospital. He slammed the gear shift into park and ran through the double glass doors. He returned in lightning speed with two nurses and a wheelchair.

Harlow covered her stomach protectively with the palms of her hands, hoping that would stop the movement inside her belly that jarred her to the core. As she was being wheeled inside, she attempted in vain to brace herself against the excruciating pain.

Thomas strode by her wheelchair and asked fretfully, "Now do you want me to call your husband and tell him what is happening?"

"There's no need. I already texted him from the limousine and he's on his way," she whispered.

Justice sat in a chair with a stupefied look on her face.

"Can they do that?" she asked.

"Unfortunately your designer hadn't signed the contract yet."

"How can I be too fat?" she exclaimed. "I wear a size four."

"Your designer saw you at the social and backed out. They want a size two model. And your butt and breasts make you look bigger than that."

"I can't help that," Justice declared hotly.

"But you've put on over ten pounds since I signed you." Ursula drew in a deep sigh of regret. "Maybe runway modeling isn't for you. But if you think it is, lose the weight and maybe I can get you signed for the next show."

"How about The House of Brabantio? Caesar discovered me. He might want to work with me until I lose the weight."

"Do you seriously not know?" Ursula asked in a stunned voice. "Caesar had a heart attack and died in Italy. He'd just gotten off the plane and said that he was feeling pain in his arm. They rushed him to the hospital but he died. It was on the news."

"Oh my God," Justice said stunned. "I've been so wrapped up in other things I didn't even know."

"At least he didn't suffer." Ursula patted her consolingly on her shoulders. "Even though Cassius is in charge The House of Brabantio has pulled out of the next show."

Justice wiped her tears with the back of her hand. "Cassius wouldn't sign me even if they were participating. He can't stand me."

"I know," Ursula said with a sober expression.

Justice was hastily walking towards the exit door when she heard her name being called.

Yes." She turned, but avoided the curious stare of Bethany.

"A letter was dropped off for you."

"I forgot about that." She took the letter from the secretary.

The outside envelope had the words scrawled: To Justice Fairchild from Sterling Hart.

Justice felt queasy.

"A very tall, dark, fine as wine man dropped that off for you," Bethany gushed. "At first glance I thought that he was a model but I know that he isn't because I would've seen him before."

Stuffing it into her oversized pocketbook, Justice said coldly, "If he wanted me to read it he shouldn't have put his name on the outside." She slammed the door as she stormed out of Catwalk Modeling Agency.

Sterling stared at the empty chair across from him at a table in Carbone's Italian Restaurant. With a heavy heart he listened to the heartbreaking voice of Al Green. After three hours, with laden steps he departed. Without Justice in my life, my heart will never be mended.

CHAPTER 14

Harlow lay in the hospital bed staring at the stark ceiling. She took her hand and smoothed it over her almost flat stomach. With unease, she picked up her cell phone.

Her mother answered after the fifth ring.

"Hello, Harlow," Cynthia said. "What happened? Why did you text me and tell me that you weren't coming?"

"I was on the way to the airport," Harlow blurted out, "and lost the baby."

There was a heavy silence.

"I'm very sorry to hear that, Harlow. What happened?"

Harlow could hear the sadness in her mother's voice.

"I fell," she replied in a dejected tone.

"How is Sterling taking it?"

"He doesn't know," Harlow said bleakly.

"How can he not know?" Cynthia exclaimed.

"I'm in the hospital and he thinks that I'm out of town visiting you."

"Why haven't you told him?

"He'll leave me when he finds out."

"I don't believe it. Sterling is a good man," Cynthia said with assurance. "If anything good is to come out of this it will be to make your marriage stronger."

"I don't think so, Mother," Harlow said with a hollow sound in her voice.

"What is going on that you haven't told me?"

"Sterling has only remained with me because of the baby."

"Your hormones are going haywire because of the trauma that you've been through."

"Sterling wants another woman. She's a young, beautiful, model. He wants out of our marriage so that he can be with her. And now he's free to go."

" 'Free to go,' " her mother echoed. "Do you know how hard it is to get a rich black man? And to find one that looks like Sterling, well, it's damn near impossible!"

"I have to let him go, Mother," Harlow whispered in a resigned voice. Lyle's face flashed before her eyes. "I have to let everything go."

There was another long silence. Then Cynthia said, "History

certainly has a way of repeating itself."

"What do you mean?"

"At one time, your father and I were on the verge of divorce. He also thought that he wanted another woman, but he got over that."

"How did he get over it?" Harlow asked.

"He came to his senses. We had a lot of things in common and a newspaper business to run. Once he had a chance to really think about it he realized she wasn't worth giving up everything that we'd built together. We got our marriage back on track and were together until the day he died," Cynthia ended with a triumphant lilt in her voice.

"But, Mother," Harlow whined, "Sterling and I have nothing in common. Now that the baby's gone…"

"Good grief, Harlow," Cynthia snapped. "You're thirty-five years old. Where on earth are you going to find another man like Sterling? He's handsome, wealthy, and straight. You'll find out that if you blow this you'll regret it."

"But I don't want a man who doesn't want me," she whimpered.

"So you're going to give him up?"

"What choice do I have?" she wailed.

"You can fight for your man and your marriage."

"I don't know how!"

"You have to be the one to figure that out. But I do know this. The pickins' are real slim nowadays for women getting a husband that's worth a damn."

Harlow brushed away the tears on her cheeks.

"After you're released from the hospital, are you then coming to Chicago?"

"I don't think so."

"Make him want you," Cynthia advised in a raised voice. "Go back to the person Sterling fell in love with."

The air between them was thick.

"Don't let this other woman take your man," Cynthia said in a stern voice. "Maybe you should still come out here and recuperate," Cynthia offered in a gentler tone.

"I think that I'll pass."

"I haven't hurt your feelings, have I?" Cynthia asked.

"No," Harlow lied. "But I think that I should stay in New York and work on my marriage."

"That's the daughter I raised," Cynthia said with a touch of smugness. "I know that I didn't raise a quitter."

###

"Mr. Richards, have you been able to find anything out about Justice Fairchild?"

"Yes," he answered without hesitation. "She's from a small town called Eastman, Georgia. She's an only child. She lived with her mother before coming to New York. Her father died when she was in elementary school."

"Is there anything else? Aren't there any skeletons in her closet?" Harlow asked in a waspish voice.

"Not that I can tell. I did pull banking information and it appears that before Miss Fairchild became a model she and her mother were on the verge of bankruptcy. There's no money there."

"I don't need her money. I need to know her Achilles heel." Harlow spat the words out.

"There's also an aunt who lives down the street from the mother and she's very heavy into the church. As a matter of fact, she and Justice's mother are missionaries in the church and held in very high esteem."

"Mmm," Harlow mused. "I want you to keep her file open. Everyone has some dirt they don't want made public."

"I need to meet with you regarding my payment for services rendered," Mr. Richards said.

"That's unnecessary. I already deposited your fee into your PayPal account," she said in a tight voice. "You'll get more when I know more."

"Will do," Mr. Richards agreed before hanging up.

In the Plaza Hotel, Harlow leaned back against the headboard on the bed and thumbed through the issue of Essence that she'd purchased from the hotel gift shop. Her attention was suddenly arrested by a picture of Justice in a makeup promotion touting Nile Cosmetics. Eyeing the pictures, Harlow felt a jealous rage course throughout her body. With all the strength she could muster, Harlow hurled the magazine across the room. It fell into the empty wastepaper basket.

The next day, Harlow took a cab to Yonkers. Looking at the GPS on her cell, she walked the short block to The Actors Prop Studio.

Once inside an elderly clerk beamed at her. "Hello," she said. "May I help you?"

"Yes," Harlow said. "I'm an actress and I need a prosthetic pregnancy device for a part that I'm playing at a local theatre."

"We have several in the storage room." She sized up Harlow. "You have a slender build. What month of pregnancy are you supposed to be?"

"The last trimester. Six to nine months would work."

"You'll need two then. One that will work for six to seven months and then you'll replace it with one from seven to nine months."

"Please let me see both."

Harlow stared warily at the items on the counter.

"They look harder to attach than they really are. The sides are lined with a latex suction that adheres to the skin. The material is sort of like pasties that strippers use. I have a small dressing room and adhesive tape. If you'd like, I'll show you how to fit them."

The next evening Harlow was sitting at the table. Her breathing became labored when she heard Sterling's key turn the lock of the front door. She slid as close as she could to the table. She felt Sterling's eyes bore into her back.

"So you're back."

Pasting a bright smile on her face, she looked at him, yet not completely turning around in her chair. "Yes, this afternoon."

"You should have called when you got to your mother's house," he said. "I called you several times while you were away. I couldn't get you on the phone and your mother didn't answer hers."

"I didn't think that you wanted to hear from me," she whispered in a forlorn voice.

"Don't start." Sterling bit off the words.

"I made a meal for us. It's spaghetti."

"You shouldn't have gone to the trouble, Harlow. I ate before I got home. As a matter of fact, I'm dead tired so I'm going to bed." Sterling opened his mouth to say something but then clamped it shut. "Good night, Harlow."

Once she was alone again, Harlow breathed a sigh of relief.

Sterling looked up from his computer monitor. "What is it, Ada?"

"You have a phone call," she said.

"I told you to hold all my calls, Ada. I'm on a deadline today."

"I know, Mr. Sterling, but he's called several times. I tried to fend him off but he said that he's very concerned about your wife."

"Who is it?"

"A Mr. Campbell."

"Who?" Sterling said.

Ada shrugged her shoulders. "He said that it was personal and wouldn't discuss it with me."

"Thank you, Ada."

Once he was alone again, Sterling picked up his receiver. "This is Sterling Hart. What is this about my wife?"

There was obvious hesitation from the man that reverberated through the phone line. "I'm Thomas Campbell. I was your wife's limo driver to the airport."

"And?"

"I'm very sorry about her fall, sir, and the loss of the baby."

Sterling almost dropped the phone. Wheels turned in his head. "Tell me more."

"Sir, when she fell outside of your building." Thomas continued in an apprehensive voice, "I wanted to go in right then and tell you but she stopped me."

"Go on," Sterling said in a chilly voice.

"I also offered to call you once we got to the hospital because I thought it was my responsibility but again she stopped me," he said nervously.

"She did?" Sterling ground out the words.

"Mr. Hart, I'm just so sorry," Thomas said sadly. "I hung around the emergency room and overheard the doctor saying that the baby didn't make it." Thomas stuttered, "I don't know why she fell the way she did. I was parked in the right place and all. I'm the sole owner of the car service and nothing like this has ever happened in my twenty years of owning it."

"Don't worry, Mr. Campbell. I'm not going to sue," Sterling responded slowly because his throat was so dry he could barely get the words out.

Relief was now reflected in Thomas's voice. "Please give your wife my good wishes, Mr. Hart."

Sterling stared into space for an hour before he called Ada back in. Looking at her with a closed expression he ordered, "Find a moving company that can move furniture tomorrow." Then he called home.

"Hello," Harlow said.

"I'll be home for dinner."

"What do you want me to cook?" Harlow asked in an animated voice.

"It doesn't matter," Sterling answered in a deceptively mild manner.

###

Harlow had dressed with care. Her makeup was flawless and she wore slippers with a small heel and fur across the toes. She wore a flowing peasant dress that stopped right above the knees.

Sterling stared at her with hooded eyes. "Would you like a glass of wine?" he asked.

"You know that I can't drink because of the baby."

"One drink won't hurt you," he said.

"If you think it's okay." She took the full glass of wine that Sterling poured for her.

"You haven't been sick since you got back from Chicago, have you?"

"I've only been back a day. But don't jinx me," she said nervously quaffing her wine. Harlow got up from the table and took her time crossing over to the stove. She lifted a lid off the pot and stirred its contents. "I've never made a pot roast before. I hope you like it." When she looked back at Sterling there was fierceness in his eyes that Harlow had never seen before. Then a shutter seemed to fall across them. "You sure are acting differently."

"Maybe I'm really seeing you for the first time, Harlow," Sterling said softly.

Harlow swallowed hard and stared at her husband.

Sterling emptied his wine glass and stood. He held his hand out to her. With an appraising look in his eyes he said, "Come here to me, Harlow."

A perturbed feeling filled her, but she obediently walked over to Sterling with a bowed head hiding her expression.

All of a sudden, Sterling spun her around, and his hands were like vises at her waist.

"What are you doing?" Harlow shrieked.

Sterling tugged at the top of her zipper.

"No," she shouted as she felt the zipper being pulled down. She tried to break loose and run, but his grip held her hostage.

Sterling yanked the dress off her shoulders, down her body, and let it fall to a heap around her feet.

"Oh my God!" Harlow yelped.

"You liar," Sterling spoke in a sinister voice. He stared at the beige prosthetic pregnancy device taped to her now flat stomach. "Where's my son?"

"I lost him," she cried.

"Were you ever really pregnant?" he demanded.

Her lips trembled. "Yes."

"How can I believe you? You are the most conniving woman," he said with loathing.

"It's your fault," she screamed. "You were so mean to me that day I was at your office it upset me and I tripped and fell."

"Don't blame this on me, Harlow," Sterling shouted.

"It's true," she wailed.

"You had the nerve to pretend that you were still pregnant. What did you think that would accomplish?"

"I don't know," she stammered now too afraid to lie. "I was just trying to buy myself some time. I couldn't deal with the loss of the child, much less tell you."

"Where is my son buried?" he asked

"I shipped the body to my mother," she whimpered. "She buried him in our family cemetery plot."

Sterling turned his back to her. "I can't stand to look at you."

His iciness terrified her and she wiped away tears of rejection with a trembling hand.

"I've already called a moving company and they'll be here in the morning. Take anything you want. Just get the hell out. I mean it, Harlow," he said with barely controlled violence. "No more games with my life." Then he stormed out.

"Get the fuck out of here!" Chapman exclaimed after Sterling finished telling what had transpired in the last hour.

Constance's mouth gaped open as she stared at the miserable countenance of her friend.

"And to think, I've been feeling guilty for wanting to divorce her while she was pregnant." Sterling shook his head in disbelief.

"I never liked her," Constance said, "but Harlow's behavior is way over the top."

"Can I spend the night here?"Sterling asked in a grave voice.

"Of course you can," Chapman and Sterling responded in unison.

"Good," he said.

The next evening, Sterling entered an empty apartment. He grabbed Harlow's keys from the kitchen counter and checked to make sure all were on the ring. Satisfied he slumped to the floor and cradled his head in his hands. Sadness overcame him and tears drenched his cheeks over the loss of his son.

CHAPTER 15

Scarlett sat at the kitchen table. "Justice, I need to talk to you about something."

"Okay? What is it?" Justice sat down.

"I've been able to transfer my classes to a school in my hometown. I want to leave New York. I wanted to leave earlier, but I've been waiting for these results."

"Results of what?" Justice said, looking at a paper in front of Scarlett.

"My AIDS test.

Justice gasped, horrified.

"It came back negative. I'm lucky. Rossi told me that he'd heard a rumor that Cassius was HIV positive." Scarlett stared at the speechless look on Justice's face. "I asked him not to say anything to you, and obviously Rossi kept my secret. I wanted to handle things my own way. I've had several tests and they're all negative."

"Is Rossi okay?"

"He's fine. Obviously if he is infected, Cassius got infected," she whispered, "after us."

Justice drew in a deep sigh of relief.

"It also appears that Nina has left him."

"Shut up!"

"When I called Rossi and told him my good news he told me Nina had taken the children and put in for a divorce."

"It's about damn time," Justice retorted. "I hope she and the baby are okay."

"Me too," Scarlett said. "Back home I can go to school full time and live with my sister. Frederic is already wiring my money to a local bank." She gave Justice a look of shame. "I'm sorry to spring this on you."

"It is all of a sudden," Justice admitted, not voicing her distress, which was compounded by the news she'd received earlier.

"I'm just done with modeling and New York and want to get far away from anything like it."

Justice groped for words but all she could manage was, "I understand."

"What did Ursula want so urgently with you today?"

Justice hesitated for a few seconds before saying, "Nothing

important."

Sudden wrath showed in Scarlett's eyes. "Can you believe that Cassius has tried to sleep with me since knowing that he's a danger?"

"He's a dog," Scarlett exhaled in an unforgiving voice.

"He damn sure is," Justice agreed.

It was her fourth casting call in a week. Justice mentally crossed her fingers that she would be signed. Her portfolio lay in her lap and her fingers nervously drummed it. Three other models had already been interviewed and left. She surreptitiously glanced at the clock on the wall. Three hours and still waiting.

The office door swung open and a tall, leggy brunette who had been calling in the other models announced, "Justice Fairchild."

Bounding to her feet she said, "Right here."

"They're ready to see you." The receptionist's eyes immediately traveled the length of Justice's body. With an unimpressed look she said, "Follow me."

Justice found herself seated in front of three people. Delores, an overweight casting director thumbed through Justice's look-book. The two men who'd never been introduced studied her. "You don't look like the photos that Catwalk sent over. You're fatter."

Justice said in an even tone, "I'm only a size four. I didn't know that you specified a size for your models."

"You look bigger than a size four." She pointed to a huge scale against the wall. "Strip and get on that scale."

Anticipating this, Justice had dressed in clothes that she could easily shed.

Delores manipulated the controls on the scale. "You weigh well over 130 pounds. It won't work out. In the photographs you'll throw off the balance of the other models." She held out Justice's portfolio. "Thank you for coming in."

Once Justice reached the street she burst into tears. After bawling for five minutes she noticed the pity in the eyes of people walking past giving her a wide berth. Resolutely she dried her eyes with the back on her hand and walked home.

A couple of weeks later, Sterling sat with his head bent over pages of files.

When his phone rang he grabbed it. "Sterling Hart here."

"Sterling, this is Roland Lerner."

"How are you doing, Roland?"

"I'm fine but I'd like you to stop by my office when you get a minute. I have something to discuss with you."

Sterling glanced at his wristwatch. "Actually I have time right now if you like."

"I'll be waiting," Roland said and disconnected.

Sterling walked down the hallway passing several clerks busy at their cubicles. He was unmoved by interested glances from several women. Once Sterling reached Roland's office, his secretary Julie smiled warmly at him. "How nice to see you, Mr. Hart."

"Nice to see you also, Julie. How's your husband doing since his operation?"

"He's all better and back at work. You know, ever since his surgery he seems to appreciate life more. He's taking me and the kids on a cruise this summer."

"That's great."

"I think it scared him. Marlon started thinking about all the things he said that he was going to do when he retired. But he now realizes that no day is promised to you."

Sterling rubbed his chin thoughtfully. He stared at Julie before saying, "Your husband is absolutely right."

When Sterling entered Roland's office, Roland got up and walked around the desk extending his hand. "How are you doing, Sterling?"

"I'm fine, Roland. What did you need to see me about?"

"Please sit, Sterling."

Once Sterling appeared comfortable, Roland cleared his throat. "Your numbers are way down and you haven't been bringing in your share of clients."

"The economy is too bad for me to feel comfortable putting clients in stock that I know isn't secure."

"It's really not your job to guess the stock market. Take some chances. Everyone is screwed the way the economy is right now."

"I know that I can't guess the stock market but there are certain investments that we know are going to topple and aren't worth the paper that the contract is printed on."

Roland glowered at him. "Things are better. Investors need to take more chances. They're playing it too safe."

"Older clients need to sit tight, not sell. I can't with a clear conscious suggest or give false information to people knowing that the likelihood is that they'll probably lose their savings."

"In the meantime, other larger stockbroker corporations are making a lot of money." Roland's eyes narrowed angrily. "Don't you want a Christmas bonus?"

"I don't need it. And I certainly don't want one if it means bankrupting someone who comes to me trusting me with their life savings."

"You're in the wrong business, Sterling."

"You're absolutely right, Roland," Sterling shot back.

"Then maybe you should look for a job elsewhere."

"Maybe you're right." Sterling stared at Roland long and hard. Then he said, "I'm giving you my two week's notice. You'll have my resignation on your desk in the morning."

A dull red flush of anger began at the top of Roland's head and disappeared under the collar of his Oxford shirt. "Let's not be hasty, Sterling."

"I've been thinking about making a change for some time, Roland," Sterling said in a diplomatic voice.

"What? Has some other firm offered you more money to go and work for them?" Roland asked resentfully.

"No," Sterling answered candidly. "I'm just tired of doing this job."

"Jobs aren't that easy to come by," Roland said curtly. "Think very carefully before walking out. A lot of men would love to be in your position."

Sterling placed his hands on the arms of his chair and hoisted himself up. "Then they can have it."

As Sterling made his way back to his office, he whistled.

Justice panted breathlessly from her five mile jog. Kicking off her sneakers, she ran up the stairs to the bathroom. She stepped onto the scale. Looking at the digital numbers she groaned. Dammit! I'm heavier than I was before I started working out. I haven't had any starches for weeks and I broil and bake everything. Feeling like a failure she went inside and called Ursula.

"Ursula Klein here."

"Hello, Ursula. This is Justice."

"Have you lost any weight?" Ursula asked in concerned voice.

"No," Justice said honestly. "And I can't figure it out. I cut out fast food and I don't know what it is to have a candy bar anymore."

"Maybe you should go to a doctor. See what's going on with your metabolism."

"I think that I'll do that. Can you recommend anyone?"

"Some of our other models have used Doctor Castle on Prince."

"I'll set up an appointment. I know that I'm too fat for the upcoming runway shows but is there anything else available?"

"No," Ursula said with regret. "I send your photos out for every campaign and the magazine representatives pick other models. I'm very sorry, Justice."

"Yeah," she said, "me too."

Sterling threw the rest of his belongings in an empty box.

"I sure hate to see you go," Ada sniffled.

"You'll be seeing me around," Sterling said and patted her gently on the shoulder. "After all, we're family."

"I don't know how long I'll last around here without you looking out for me."

"You'll be just fine, Ada. I may have gotten you the job, but you kept it."

She gave him a grateful smile.

Sterling felt ten years younger as he walked to the parking garage.

That same afternoon, Justice sat across from Doctor Castle. She had her hands clasped nervously together in her lap.

Doctor Castle's bushy eyebrows almost overpowered his eyes as he flipped through page after page of lab results. Finally he closed the file and looked up. He took his reading glasses of his face and focused on Justice. "I have good news and bad news for you. Which do you want to hear first?"

"The good news."

"Okay," he said. "There's absolutely nothing wrong with you. You're not fat, Justice," he said consolingly. "You're five feet ten and weigh between one hundred thirty and one hundred and thirty-five pounds. A lot of women would kill to be that."

"Not runway models." Justice shook her head, mirroring her confusion. "And I think that your test results are wrong. There has to be something wrong with me. It's just recently I've put on all of this weight."

"You're almost twenty-six years old. It happens. Metabolism changes and people put on weight as they get older. That's the bad news."

Justice threw herself face down on the bed and indulged in an unusual bout of self-pity. Then she walked over to the mirror in the bathroom. She stared at her image for a long time. Just before Justice opened her mouth and stuck her index finger down her throat as far as she could her mother's words came back to her. 'Promise me that you won't lose yourself up there in New York.' She willed the piece of baked chicken breast that she'd had for lunch to remain inside her. Then Justice shuffled back into the bedroom, picked up her cell phone, and called The House of Brabantio. "Hello, Cassius. This is Justice Fairchild."

"What do you want?"Cassius said coldly.

Justice barely controlled her anger. "I didn't want to bother you until things settled down. I'm very sorry about the loss of your father. He was such a good man and a mentor to me."

Cassius didn't respond.

"The last time he and I met I gave him a sketchbook with my designs in it. I wondered if you would mail it back to me."

Her request was met with a hostile silence.

Justice plodded on. "Of course, I'll pay for the postage."

"I don't know what you're talking about," Cassius answered curtly. "And I don't know anything about a sketchbook."

Justice tried to remain calm. "It's a huge, black leather binder. Inside there's over fifty designs that I created. My name is embossed in gold on the outside cover. It would have been in your father's possession when he had his heart attack."

"I never saw anything like that. And if you spread the rumor that The House of Brabantio has your designs, I'll sue you and take that apartment you purchased," Cassius stated bluntly.

"What?" Justice shrieked.

"Don't call me again."

Justice heard his phone slam down. After indulging herself with a night of fresh tears she called Ursula again. "Do you have anything for me?"

"No," she said. "I'm very sorry, Justice."

An all-encompassing hatred for Cassius enveloped her. Justice began to tremble. Eventually she said, "I'm very sorry too, Ursula."

Justice lay on the bed and stared blankly into space. With a determined look she pulled out a blank sheet of paper and began sketching an evening dress for a real size twelve model.

"So what now?" Chapman asked as they sat in the Starbucks where they'd run into Justice before.

"After not working for a month I'm bored to death. I've applied to several design schools and I'm waiting to hear."

"Did you apply to the New York Art Institute?'

"That was one of them. Why do you ask?"

"Justice is enrolled there."

"What!" Sterling sputtered. "How would you know that?"

"I was on my way to court and I saw her going in there. So later on, I went back and asked the secretary if she was a student." Chapman gave a sly smile. "It's amazing the kind of information a man can get if he asks real nice."

"Why didn't you tell me this before?" Sterling glared at his friend.

"You swore that you weren't going to try to be in her life until you could really be in her life. I didn't want to torture you so I decided to sort of keep tabs on Justice until you could do something about it."

"You're a good friend," Sterling said in a thankful voice.

"I try to be," Chapman grinned. "So now what are you going to do?"

A look of determination arose on Sterling's features. "I'm going to get that girl."

Justice kept her head bowed over her computer sketch book. She vaguely heard the door to the design studio open and shut. All at once a strange sensation flooded her. She smelled him before she saw him. Slowly she swiveled around on her stool and found herself staring into the enigmatic eyes of Sterling Hart. Justice almost toppled to the floor, saving herself from falling by gripping her worktable. Barely breathing, she grabbed her belongings and fled. Hours later, she lay in her darkened bed room with a towel on her forehead. When her phone rang she grabbed it.

"Justice, this is Mrs. Daley."

Justice could hear the concern in her teacher's voice.

"Are you ill? Why did you rush out of class the way you did?"

Justice did some quick thinking. "I got a sudden migraine and I thought that I was going to vomit."

"Are you feeling any better now?"

"I'll be okay," she mumbled.

"Good. You know we have a strict attendance policy at the school, but because you were in attendance for more than half the class I won't count this against you."

"Thank you, Mrs. Daley," Justice said gratefully.

"You left before you got your homework assignment. I need an evening wear sketch from you tomorrow."

"Yes, ma'am." Justice hesitated for a moment before asking, "Mrs. Daley, the new guy in class. When did he enroll?"

"Today," she said. "Why do you ask? Do you know him?"

"No, I don't know him. But I thought I did."

"Every female in the room fluttered around him at the end of class," Mrs. Daley chuckled. "I felt like I was teaching high school again."

"Did he flirt back?" Justice asked before she could help herself.

"No," she replied. "As a matter of fact, he was quite obviously disinterested to the point of almost being rude. I don't think they'll be bothering him again."

###

"She hates me."

Chapman stared at the dejected countenance of his friend. "She doesn't hate you."

"She can't stand the sight of me," Sterling corrected him. "And I deserve it."

"If she was unmoved by you she wouldn't have bolted. Just give it time."

"I feel like a stalker," Sterling said.

"That's because you are," Chapman chuckled.

Sterling glowered at him.

"Constance is planning a card party at the house and she said that you can bring Justice."

"Yeah," Sterling muttered sarcastically, "that's going to happen."

"It's not until September and that's a month away. You might be surprised at what can happen in that length of time."

Sterling gave Chapman an are-you- kidding look.

"You still have a chance. Justice is still single so that means that she's fair game."

"It might also mean that she's so turned off by men she doesn't want to be bothered with any of them."

"We can't let that happen. It would be a shame to let all that butt go to waste."

Sterling shot him another dark look.

Chapman put his hand over his mouth to hide his grin.

"I might have a job for you," Ursula said.

"With whom?" Justice asked excitedly.

Ursula leaned back in her chair. Her pencil dangled in her hand as she gave Justice an appraising look. "It's a clothing ad for a company out of London. They want to break into the American market."

"What size do they want their model to be?"

"They didn't specify. I sent your portfolio and they got back to me right away. So far, they want you."

"But I'm not the same size I was when I took those pictures," Justice said doubtfully. "I hate to get my hopes up and then have them back out."

"Your stomach is still flat as a board. You've really filled out in all the right places. Your face is just a little fuller."

Justice stood and crossed to Ursula. Bending down she gave her a big hug that was returned. "Thanks, Ursula. Now that I'm in school and not working, I can really use the money."

"Doesn't the money from your commercial pay your bills?"

"Usually," she breathed. "But now that I'm living alone, when I get my check I need all of it for my mortgage. Sometimes I have to call my broker to tide me over." *Thank God Scarlett hooked me up with her investment banker.*

"Do everyone a favor and drop ten pounds before they get here to finalize the campaign," Ursula suggested.

"I will," she promised.

Justice grimaced as she the fourth day in a row she finished the bowl of bouillon. *Damn! What wouldn't I do for a piece of skinless chicken breast with no seasoning?* Glancing at the lock she realized that it was time for her to go to school.

Exiting the subway, Justice lethargically climbed the stairs to the sidewalk. Once she reached the street, she almost collided with

Chapman.

He stood holding a briefcase. "How are you doing, Justice?" he asked in a serious voice.

She crossly tried to push past him.

He stepped in her path, blocking her.

"Do you want me to call the police and tell them that you're harassing me?"

"Go ahead," he said with a quirky smile. "I'm a lawyer so I'm used to being at the police station."

Justice scowled at him.

"I've been standing here for over an hour waiting for you."

"What the hell for?" she asked. Her eyes sparkled angrily. "Are you here to give me more advice on how to sleep with a married man?"

"You've been in class with Sterling for almost a month and you won't even acknowledge him," Chapman spoke chidingly.

"You think?" she spat sarcastically.

"You could at least be polite."

Her foot tapped impatiently. "Mind your own damn business."

Not at all put off Chapman said, "I'm going to do something that could cost me my bar card."

"What is that?" she quipped. "Be an honest lawyer?"

"That's a good one," he said unmoved by her hostility. He opened his briefcase, took out a large manila envelope and handed it to Justice.

Justice gave him a wary look. "What is that?"

"Open it," he said.

Justice did so and quickly skimmed the papers.

"They're the separation papers that Sterling is sending to Harlow. Look at the notary seal at the bottom. That should convince you that they're real."

"It doesn't matter," she said quietly and handed the papers back to him. "He lied to me."

"With all due respect," Chapman said, "I don't think that Sterling ever told you that he wasn't married."

"It was implied!" she shouted.

"Don't you understand how he feels about you? Sterling has loved you since he sat next to you on that plane. But he felt that he had to do right by his child."

"It's too much to deal with," she mumbled.

"Sterling has lost everything. But he still has hopes that one day you'll forgive him and let him back into your life. His divorce will be final next year. Is that so damn long?"

One lone tear escaped from the corner of her eye. "I've met his wife. She's not going to let him go."

"They have nothing," Chapman declared. "It's been like that for years."

"She'll punish him through his child. I can't be the person to separate him from his child. I know what it is to be raised without a father, and I can't be a part of that."

There was a profound silence and a solemn look on Chapman's face. "Harlow lost the baby."

"Good God! What happened?"

"She fell, but pretended that she was still pregnant."

"Good grief," Justice said aghast.

"When he found out it was quite a blow to him. But there is always a silver lining in every cloud. They now have no ties to each other."

A flicker of hope ignited in the pit of her stomach.

"Sterling is trying to make his way back to you, but in New York divorce is a long tedious process." He paused before adding, "He can't get over you, Justice."

"Why do you care so much?" she whispered.

"He's my best friend, and I want him to be happy." With an earnest expression Chapman said, "And I want you to be happy, too, Justice."

As Justice passed Sterling in class she said quietly, "Hello, Sterling."

Sterling grabbed the worktable to avoid falling.

That night, Justice lifted the edge of her mattress and withdrew the unopened letter addressed to her. With shaky fingers she read the letter five times before she went to her computer. She Googled New York City divorce laws and began reading. Once her research was finished, the ice around her heart had melted. 'It's better to have loved and lost than not to have loved at all.' Her mother's words reverberated in her mind. For the first time in a long time she slept a deep, untroubled sleep.

CHAPTER 16

When Justice got to class she found Sterling sitting at the table where she usually sat.

Her empty stomach fluttered nervously as she went to her seat.

She felt Sterling's eyes on her and looked at him out the corner of her eye. Then she acknowledged his presence with a brief nod.

A hopeful expression flooded his features.

Before she could respond in turn, Mrs. Daley walked into the room and smiled at her students. "Good evening, everyone."

"Good evening, Mrs. Daley," they chorused back to her.

"I have the grades for your sketches and I must say that I'm impressed. Not one student scored less than a B. Now I hope that you can transform your sketch into a finished project."

"So do we," one of the students shouted in a good natured voice.

Mrs. Daley looked at him. "I don't think that under usual circumstances you'll have to worry about that, Randy. But this assignment is going to be a little different from the others. I'm going to pair each of you up with someone not of your own choosing."

Groans were heard throughout the room.

Mrs. Daley held her hand up to silence them. "If you want to be a fashion designer you must learn to work with others. 'No man is an island.'"

"Not if we become famous and get our own labels," another student piped in.

"Even if you rise to that level you'll need helpers. Designers don't stitch each piece that they showcase." Mrs. Daley said in a very serious voice, "Your assignment is for you and your partner to come up with a garment to complement your partner's."

Justice raised her hand.

"Yes, Justice," Mrs. Daley smiled.

"Do you have suggestions about what kind of garments we should make?"

"No," she smiled. "This is your chance to let your creative juices flow. The only stipulation is that the garments can't be accessories. They must compliment what your partner already created but also be able to stand on its own. You will each get two grades. One for the ensemble and one for the individual piece. I will add up each grade and divide by two for your semester exam."

A hush fell over the room as the full enormity of how important the project was sank in.

"Now," Mrs. Daley dragged out the word as she pulled a hat from behind the podium, "names will be pulled out of this hat and that will decide who will be partnered up with whom."

Loud disgruntled groans reverberated throughout the room.

"After you're paired off, you need to meet with your partner and begin working on ideas. Mind you, there will be other assignments in the interim," Mrs. Daley said in a cautionary tone, "so don't wait until the last minute to work on your projects. If you don't complete your assignments, it will be very hard to earn a decent grade this term." Mrs. Daley shook the hat, making sure the names were thoroughly mixed. "I need a volunteer to draw names."

Mrs. Daley's students sat still their eyes transfixed on the object that would help determine their semester grades.

"Come on," Mrs. Daley said cajolingly, "don't be afraid. No one is going to blame you if they get paired up with someone they don't want to work with."

"Wanna bet?" Rose said teasingly. This was met with nervous laughter.

"I'll do it," Sterling offered in a clear voice.

"Pick me," Joyce shouted out in an eager voice.

Sterling merely smiled. He stood next to Mrs. Daley and dug into the hat. He pulled out two slips of paper. "Randy and Leslie are a team."

Immediately Justice sneaked a look over at Randy who wore a disagreeable expression.

"Abigail and Beatrice," Sterling said as he put the slips down on the desk. "Vince and Pedro will be working together. Also Rose and Brenda."

Is my name even in there? Justice she saw her choices dwindling.

Sterling dug his hand back in the hat and withdrew two names. "Justice and I will be working together," he said with a smug look.

"Check those papers, Mrs. Daley," Byron said.

Mrs. Daley looked at Byron in confusion, but still she obliged and took the papers from the palm of Sterling's hands. "Those are the names, Byron," she said in a reproachful voice.

Justice only vaguely paid attention to anything else as Sterling completed the task of pairing off the students.

Once Sterling took his seat next to her, they sized each other up.

Sterling wore a satisfied expression that he didn't attempt to hide. Though Justice didn't realize it her countenance was far from disgruntled. That could not be said for some of her other classmates as they looked at their partners.

"What did you do?" she whispered in a suspicious voice.

"Nothing," Sterling said sincerely.

Justice gave him a doubtful look.

"I just got real lucky." Sterling gave a heartfelt sigh. "And I must say it's about time." He took his sketchbook out. "Do you have any ideas about what you want your piece to be?"

"Not a one," she answered truthfully.

Mrs. Daley circulated the room giving the students their sketches.

"What did you make as your assignment?" Justice asked.

"I did a smoking jacket."

"A smoking jacket?" she said, surprised. "Isn't that a little outdated?"

He grinned. "I think with the rise in heating bills they might make a comeback. People are turning their thermostats down."

Justice's stomach made a grumbling sound.

Sterling smiled. "Someone's hungry."

"Someone's always hungry," she retorted only half jokingly.

Sterling gave her a look of inquiry.

"I'm on a diet," she explained.

Sterling's eyes settled on Justice's full breasts and his mouth became dry.

Under his stare, Justice's nipples hardened and were pronounced through her chiffon shirt.

"That's ridiculous," he murmured. "You're perfect the way you are."

Their eyes remained locked and Justice searched Sterling's. For what felt like an eternity, she devoured him with her eyes and as she did any residual anger she'd harbored seemed to dissipate, replaced by a feeling of expectancy that flooded through her, and a feeling she'd never experienced before.

Sterling's voice shook her out of her reverie.

"Justice, I want you to know something."

"I know," she interrupted him.

"What do you know?" Sterling asked and there was a slight tremor in his voice.

"Chapman told me everything." Justice said truthfully. "I'm sorry about the baby."

"It wasn't my time to be a father. I've accepted that," he said.

Mrs. Daley put their portfolios on the table and walked back to the front of the room. She addressed the class. "Because you and your partner will have to synchronize your schedules and do a lot of this project outside of class, you may leave for the night. But the workroom is going to remain open until nine so you may also stay. If you need anything I'll be in my office. If not, see you on Thursday."

The grating of chairs on the tile floor signaled that most of the students were more than ready to bolt out the door.

Sterling gave her a quizzical look. "Are you going or staying?"

"I'm going."

"May I escort you out?"

Justice hesitated only a second before agreeing. "I think that would be okay."

Justice and Sterling walked down the busy street. Although they didn't speak, but there was an aura of expectancy between them. He gave her a soulful look. "I'd like to sit down and talk to you."

Heat filled her lower extremities.

"There's a nice restaurant with a patio not far from here."

Justice stared at him, wishing that he'd picked a more secluded spot for them to talk.

"I don't want Chapman explaining or apologizing for me. That's my job."

"Okay," she acquiesced. Then the shrill ring of her cell phone shattered their peace. Looking at the call log she said, "Hello, Ursula."

"This is Jean Paul calling on behalf of Ursula."

"Hello Jean Paul, what's up?" she asked.

"I have unfortunate news for you," he said in a peremptory tone. "You've been released from Catwalk Modeling Agency."

"Why?" she asked in a weak voice.

"Your designer has officially dropped you from the show and we can't find anyone else to take you on. It's costing too many man hours to promote you, Justice."

"But Jean Paul, I thought that I had another week to lose the weight."

"Have you lost it?" he demanded.

"Not all of it," she admitted.

"Well, there you go. It's in your contract that you have to keep up your appearance, Justice. We're well within our rights to sever our ties with you."

"I've barely eaten in three weeks," she declared hotly. In a haze, she noticed the astonished look on Sterling's face. "I'm doing the best I can," she told Jean Paul.

There was a long silence.

"I'm sorry, Justice. But we don't have a choice."

"The least Ursula could have done was call me herself," she exclaimed emotionally.

"She's in Italy."

"Ursula is in Italy?" Justice repeated with dawning insight.

"Yes, Justice. She called me and instructed me what to do." There was another heavy silence and then Jean Paul said with a hint of sympathy, "Obviously you pissed off the wrong person, Justice. I'm sorry," Jean Paul said and hung up on her.

Suddenly Justice broke out in a sweat and gasped for breath. Her knees felt weak and her body trembled. Her cell phone slipped out of her hand and broke into pieces on the sidewalk. She felt herself falling, then grabbed, held tightly, lifted, and then carried. As she allowed herself to bathe in the safety of the strong embrace she heard someone ask anxiously, "Mr. is she okay?'

"She's going to be," Sterling replied in a terse voice.

Shortly thereafter she heard the sound of Sterling's Bentley alarm being disabled. Then she was gently placed inside. She opened her eyes.

Sterling peered at her. "I think that I should take you to the emergency room."

"There's nothing wrong with me that a good meal won't fix," she said quietly.

"What would you like to eat?"

Without hesitation she said, "I would like some grilled chicken from KFC."

"Done," he said.

As Justice watched, Sterling emerged from the restaurant with a huge bag in his hand an idea formed.

After he pulled out into traffic, Sterling said without a hint of shame, "No need to give me directions I know where you live."

"But I don't know where you live," she said in an unwavering tone. "And I'd like to."

"Done," he said and made a U-turn in the middle of Prince Street.

###

They sat on the floor eating grilled chicken, mashed potatoes, macaroni and cheese, and biscuits. After two chicken legs, Justice started putting the plastic lid back on her dinner.

"Finish your meal," Sterling instructed in a firm tone.

"All right," she said, picking up her last piece of chicken.

"I'm sorry that we have to sit on the floor," he said.

"I see that Harlow took everything except those plants on the shelf."

Sterling shrugged his shoulders dismissively. "I wanted her to have it. There are very few good memories that connect me to those furnishings. But I did purchase a refrigerator and bedroom set after she left. I can't live like a complete Neanderthal."

"So you don't miss her at all?" Justice asked and stared into his eyes, secretly wishing that she had some magical power enabling her to see into his very soul.

"It's hard to miss something that was never real. The person that I married never existed, and I would have never fallen in love with the real Harlow."

"How did she pretend to be pregnant?"

Sterling wiped his mouth with a napkin. "She purchased one of the prosthetic devices that actors use."

"Good grief," Justice exclaimed. "She must really want you to do something like that."

"It's not me she wants," he replied. "It's about winning the game. Justice, I need to apologize to you for not being honest about my marital status. If I had to do it all over again…"

"What would you do differently?" she asked.

"I'd like to think that I would have told you on the plane that I was married."

"Why didn't you?" she asked quietly.

"Because I thought that I was getting a divorce. Harlow asked me for one before I went away, but I wanted to try and make my marriage work. That is, until I met you."

"And then she told you that she was pregnant."

"Yes," he said. "I don't want to be my father."

"You aren't," she whispered.

"I feel guilty," he said with a mournful look.

"Why?"

"After the initial shock of learning that my child had died, I was sort of okay with it because it released me from being tied to Harlow. Even expressing that out loud makes me feel like a monster."

"Then I'm a monster, too, Sterling, because I don't want to share you. At the charity wine tasting I was consumed with jealousy of Harlow because she was married to you and pregnant with your child. She was living the life that I wanted. I hated her for that and I hated you too."

"I hated me. I sat right across from you and you wouldn't even look at me. I felt that if I'd been honest with you, maybe you would have understood. Or at least we could have been friends."

"That wouldn't have happened, Sterling. Had you told me that you were married I would have never let you into my life and we would have never been given a chance to know each other. It's been drummed into my head since I was child what a terrible sin it is to sleep with a married man. I still agree with that for the most part, but after I read about the New York divorce laws, I know that things aren't always black and white." She took her hand and gently touched his cheek. "I can truly say that I'm glad that you lied to me. I feel as if we've come full circle and we're back to the first night we were together."

"Thank you for letting me off the hook, Justice."

She searched his face. "Be honest, Sterling. Do you really wish that on the first night we were together that you'd told me that you were married and had a baby on the way?"

"No, Justice. It may sound trite but 'it's better to have loved and lost than not to have loved at all.'"

"Ditto," she murmured, sliding her hand in his.

He clasped it tightly and then raised her hand to his mouth, planting a kiss on her palm.

A thrill of pleasure ran up and down her spine.

Suddenly he demanded, "Tell me what that phone call was about."

A cloud shadowed her face. "Catwalk dropped me for good."

"They must be insane," he retorted angrily. "You're an excellent runway model."

"How would you know that?" she said with a self-conscious smile.

"Because I saw you," he admitted.

"When?" she exclaimed.

"I was in the audience at the Bryant Park show."

"You were!"

"Yes," he said. "I was so proud of you, Justice."

"Well, now I'm too fat for the shows and I've been blacklisted."

Sterling's eyebrows drew together in a frown. "Blacklisted? By whom?"

With tears in her eyes, Justice repeated everything that had gone on with her in the modeling world since she'd exited the plane at

LaGuardia.

Sterling sat with his back was against the wall and listened intently to every word she uttered. He gently brushed her tearstained cheeks. "I'm sorry to hear that these people made you doubt your beauty, Justice."

The vision of Raven's emaciated frame surfaced. Justice bowed her head ashamed that she'd bought into the almost unobtainable standards of beauty that were so prevalent in society.

"I think that we can do something about Cassius stealing your designs," he said musingly. "Chapman knows a lot of people. We'll sue Cassius."

"I thought about that," she said. "But as you can see, he has a lot of influence. I don't want to make any enemies in the designer world. That's my real dream."

"But he'll be showing your stuff as if they're his creations," Sterling protested.

"I've tossed and turned for nights, trying to come up with a solution. I'm in school learning the trade, and I've decided that if I have any real talent, I'll be able to create designs even better than the ones he stole. Sometimes being hungry for something can work to your advantage."

"Then the least you can do is let me put a hit out on Miles," he chuckled.

She grinned. "There's a recession on, and he's not worth the money." All of a sudden Justice's stomach lurched. She stammered, "Oh no, I think I'm going to be sick. Where's your bathroom?"

Sterling jumped to his feet, grabbed Justice's hand, and led her down the hallway to the bathroom.

Justice dropped to her knees and emptied her dinner into the toilet.

Sterling smoothed her hair.

He handed her a washcloth dampened with cool water.

Mortified, she cleaned her face. "I'm so sorry, Sterling."

Sterling helped her to her feet. "For what? Your body is reacting to not having food for so long." He said in a forceful tone, "I can't believe that you've been starving yourself."

"I needed to lose weight for the next runway show," she murmured.

"Well," he said firmly, "after we become famous designers, none of our models are going to be anorexic looking. Our clothes will be geared for regular people and stores won't even be able to keep them in stock."

"That's one of my goals as a designer."

"We think the same way about a lot of things, Justice. That's half the battle."

"That's more than half the battle," she corrected in a relieved tone. "I still feel kind of weak. Do you mind if I lie down? "

"Of course not," he said. "You can have the bedroom. I'll camp out in the den."

The sound of Sterling whistling in the shower lulled Justice to sleep as she lay in his bed.

Hours later, Justice woke. Cotton mouthed she stumbled to the adjoining bathroom. After turning on the light, she searched the vanity and found an unopened toothbrush and bottle of Listerine. Thankfully, she used both. Then she stared at her image in the mirror and grimaced. The makeup she hadn't cleansed before she'd fallen asleep had smudged and the black rings around her eyes made her look like a raccoon.

Then she saw the clean towels that Sterling had laid out for her. She grabbed the washcloth and after turning the shower dial as far left as she could she stood under the hot, stinging, spray. After she scrubbed herself thoroughly with the liquid soap she'd found, she dried and oiled her body. Now she was pleased with her reflection. Her soft skin glistened and was smooth to the touch. Wrapping a fluffy towel around her, she went to find Sterling.

The only light in the room came from the skylight. He lay on his back and his head was cushioned from the hardwood floor by a pillow. Sterling's arm was slung over his forehead hiding his eyes from her. His chest was bare and the silky hair on his chest disappeared down past his navel into the navy-blue shorts.

And that was where Justice's eyes remained transfixed. The silky material of his shorts was lifted by Sterling's penis. Her lips parted in anticipation.

"Do you need something?" Sterling murmured in his low sensual voice.

She ran her tongue around the fullness of her lips, wetting them. "You."

He moved his arm to get a clear look at his face. "Are you sure?" he said and his voice rumbled low.

"Now more than ever," she whispered.

"I don't want to take advantage of you," he said hoarsely.

"You aren't," she assured him.

"I can't stand the thought of something going wrong and you walking out of my life again."

"That won't happen," she promised.

"I wanted to take things slowly."

"It's too late for that," she said with a small smile.

"I wanted to romance you."

"You can still do that."

"I want to do right by you."

"That will come in time," she said in a soothing tone.

"I wanted to solidify our friendship and give our relationship a chance to grow."

"I want that too," she whispered, her heart soaring. "But tonight, I can't wait." Justice dropped her towel. "There's a fire burning inside of me that I need you to douse."

Sterling was thankful that he was lying down because he felt dizzy. But he quickly recovered and got to his knees. Like a lion stalking his prey, Sterling crawled the short distance to her, and palmed her left butt cheek. Once she was positioned over him, with his free hand he urged her legs open. Then he took his index finger and probed. Very slowly, Sterling slid his index finger up into her cavity as far as he could reach. Gently, he explored her. Soon he was rewarded with a wet squishing noise. Then never changing his position, he tasted her. Sterling licked away all of the liquid he'd aroused. He was rewarded with a cascade that spiraled into his mouth.

"Oh my God, Sterling," she screamed with pleasure. Had it not been for the control his tongue had over her she'd have fallen. She writhed and trembled at the same time. She cradled his head holding him steady and on course. She felt herself teetering on the edge of the cliff yet stilled herself from spilling into his mouth again, not wanting it to end.

Sterling stood. "Thank you, Justice. I have never tasted anything so sweet." Then for the second time that night he scooped her up into his arms.

"You're so strong, Sterling," she cooed.

"I hunger for you, Justice," he said quietly.

His words warmed her belly. "I hunger for you too, Sterling."

Sterling carried her down the long hallway to the master bedroom. Once inside he kicked the door shut before laying her gently on the bed.

In a sort of haze, she heard quick movements and then a naked Sterling joined her in the bed.

Eagerly, her hands clutched his penis and pulled it towards her. Then she moved her hand back in the opposite direction. She pumped him for an eternity. Then with the flat of her hand she propelled him onto his back. Justice positioned herself on one side next to him. Again, she maneuvered his body until he turned towards her. Sterling was so long, she had to scoot farther down toward the edge of the bed. The she traced the head of his penis with her finger careful not to scratch him. She took his head into her mouth.

Sterling moaned from pleasure.

One of her arms was slung around his waist, holding him in place. He arched towards her. With her tongue Justice licked the rim on his penis, while she lightly massaged his sack, pleasuring him the way he'd just pleasured her.

His body jerked. "Please, Justice, I can't wait any more."

Stilling him with her hand, she took him in her mouth and began to suck. Little by little she took him fully into her mouth until she could take no more. Very slowly she began to move her mouth up and down his rod.

He was at her mercy and she could do whatever she wanted to do with him. She teased, drank, and explored every piece of skin between his thighs. When Justice felt Sterling began to jerk inside her mouth, she lightly encouraged him with pleasure moans. His tempo began to quicken until he exploded.

He lay still for a minute before he flipped her on her back. He pressed his lips on her mouth and opened her lips. As Sterling's tongue caressed her mouth he entered her body in one smooth movement. He began to move and his endless strokes were long and hard.

At first, Justice didn't move, simply reveled in the sensation. Her thighs were open wide. Then she clamped her thighs next to his to increase the tension as she joined his long even strokes. After she was fully satiated, she screamed, "Sterling!" and let go.

Only then did he come.

Before dawn, Sterling rocked her world three more times.

The next morning when he woke, he felt Justice's breath fanning the area right between his shoulder blades. He raised his eyes to the heavens. "Thank you," he whispered.

Justice nudged him. "I thank him too," she whispered before they fell back to sleep.

The next time she woke, she lay on her side facing Sterling.

He devoured her with his eyes.

A shy smile enveloped her face.

Sterling took his hand and placed it over his heart. He lightly tapped the area over his chest two times and then three more.

She slowly moved her hand from under the covers and did the same.

"I don't have any cooking utensils so we'll have to go out to breakfast," Sterling said.

'I'd rather go to my place. I'll fix you a meal."

"That sounds like a plan," he agreed.

After breakfast they sat on Justice's couch. Sterling was reading the paper and she pretended to watch the news. They reality was that she was really watching Sterling and enjoying his presence in her home.

He lowered the paper. "Besides all the personal drama, how do you like New York?"

"I don't really know," she said honestly. "The only tourist thing that I've done since I got here was to go to Central Park with you. I'm still nervous about wandering around."

"I'd love to show you the city and all it has to offer."

"I'd love that." She grinned and leaned over and planted a kiss on his mouth.

"We have class on Mondays, Wednesdays, and Fridays. We can tour the city on the other days."

"How about your job?" she asked.

"My job is being a full time student."

"You quit?" she exclaimed.

"Yep," he said. "And I've never been happier. There's just one thing."

"What?"

Sterling wore a perturbed look on his face. "I want to put a ring on it, but I can't until next year."

Her heart thumped wildly. "Is that a proposal?"

"I think that I can do a better job of proposing than that. But it is a promise."

"And one that I'll make you keep," she quipped.

He gave her a disarming smile. "Before I bombarded back into your life, did you have any plans for today?"

"I was going to wash my hair."

"Your hair looks fine. I saw in the paper that there's an exhibition called 'The Golden Age of Haute Couture.' "

"I'm not really interested in looking at photographs of famous models."

"We're going to look at the clothes."

She grimaced. "It still feels like I'm returning to the scene of the crime since I turned out to be such a failure."

"You're not a failure, Justice," Sterling said in a serious voice. "You've had more success than some models have had their whole lives."

There was long silence. "From now on that's how I'm going to

215

look at it. Be thankful for what I had." She gave him a grateful look. "Thank you, Sterling."

"For what?" he asked with raised brows.

"For being you," she said and leaned on him.

Sterling put his arms around her and held so close she felt the beating of his heart. "You have my heart, Justice Fairchild."

CHAPTER 17

Justice's arm was tucked inside Sterling's as they strolled through The Metropolitan Museum of Art. Once they got to the special exhibit they took their time examining each black and white photograph that hung on the walls. "Look!" she said. "It's a photo of Beverly Johnson. Isn't she beautiful?" Justice exclaimed.

"Yes, she is beautiful, Justice. But so are you."

"You certainly know how to turn a girl's head, Mr. Sterling Hart."

"I aim to please," he said squeezing her hand.

"Look!" She pointed at another one. "It's a photograph of Audrey Hepburn coming down the stairs and Fred Astaire is taking the picture. And there's Naomi Campbell in Vogue. Oh my goodness, it's a photo of Twiggy. You know she still looked like that on America's Next Top Model."

"I thought you don't like reality shows."

"But I love Tyra. I admire the fact that she knew when to quit modeling and she channeled her drive into something else. That's what I want to do," she said wistfully.

"You'll realize your dream, Justice. I just know it."

Once they left the museum Sterling navigated the car in the opposite direction. "Where are we going?" she asked.

He slid her a sheepish look. "I texted Chapman and told him the good news. So he and Constance invited us over for a meal."

"I don't know about that, Sterling. I wasn't very nice to Chapman when he tried to talk to me about you."

"And he was quite amused."

"But aren't Constance and Harlow friends?"

"No," he said. "They can't stand each other. And even if they were friends it wouldn't matter to me. I'd make sure that she was nothing but nice to you. I make my decisions as to who I want to be with."

Less than thirty minutes later, Sterling pulled his Bentley into a parking space. "We're here," he said.

She swung her head around. "Where are we?"

"Brooklyn," he said.

Justice viewed the beautiful elm trees that flanked the long street. "This is a beautiful area."

"Brooklyn and Long Island are the places in New York to raise children," he said.

Her insides quivered with a sudden yearning.

The front door to the brownstone was flung open and Chapman stood on the threshold.

"Sit tight," Sterling said. He exited the car and walked over to her side. After opening her door, he extended his hand.

Justice placed her hand in his and together they climbed the stairs.

Once they reached the top, Chapman gave her a big, bear hug. "Thank you, Justice. You have saved Sterling's and my friendship."

"Why do you say that?"

"Before you two worked things out he was such a drag I thought that I'd have to drop him as a friend."

Justice chuckled. "I'll do the best that I can to keep a smile on his face."

Chapman stared at the contented look on Sterling's face. "I think that you have what it takes to do just that. Follow me. Constance has been cooking all afternoon."

Justice was impressed by the paintings on the walls. Their hall was lined with African American lithographs. "Is Constance a collector?" she asked in awe.

"No," Chapman grinned. "It's just an expensive hobby for her."

"I heard that," Constance grinned from the stove in the kitchen. "It's nice to see you again, Justice."

Justice relaxed when she saw the look of friendliness in Constance's eyes.

"Thank you," she murmured.

They feasted on chicken wings, macaroni and cheese, and potato salad. Justice sat next to Sterling at the mahogany dining room table and eyed the furnishings. "You certainly have wonderful taste, Constance."

"Hey!" Chapman said. "How do you know that I didn't decorate the house?"

"Did you?" Constance interjected.

"Naw," he said. "I just said whatever you think is best, dear."

"We started out trying to decorate the house together but it turned out to be a big problem," Constance explained. "I wanted him to be involved."

"She nagged me all of the time," Chapman cut in.

"Not nagged," Constance corrected him. "I asked."

Chapman looked at Sterling and Justice. He gave a small negative shake with his head.

"Our fighting got so bad I spent a couple of nights at my parents' house."

"I was scared to death," Chapman admitted.

"While I was there my mother told me to fight over things that mattered. My parents have been married for over forty years so I took their advice. I came back and decorated our house they way I wanted to without any input from Chapman."

"Thank God," he breathed.

"He and I still fight, but we get along better than when we dated. Our last big one was when I found Chapman staring at your picture in my magazine."

"What?" Justice exclaimed.

"And the minute I caught him he snitched on Sterling."

"Yeah." Chapman joked, "I gave him up."

"I knew all about you when we met at the wine tasting." She grinned. "Even though I didn't know if things were ever going to work out for Sterling that's the best time I ever had in Harlow's company."

A pained look flashed across Justice's face.

Sterling was so in tune with her he noticed right away. "What's wrong, honey?"

She looked down at the tablecloth. "I cried myself to sleep that night."

Sterling took her hand in his and gave her a look of apology. "I promise you that I won't be the source of any more sad tears. Only ones of happiness."

Justice drowned in his gaze.

The sound of the doorbell ringing broke their trance.

"I'll get it," Constance said.

A few minutes later they heard raucous laughter.

Chapman and Sterling looked at each other. They said, "Ada is here."

"Who is Ada?" Justice asked.

"My ex-secretary."

Ada followed Constance in the room. She had a huge cake plate in her hands.

"Don't tell that you brought your homemade pound cake," Sterling asked, rubbing his hands together hopefully.

"I sure did, Mr. Sterling," Ada beamed. "When I heard you were coming over here today I made it especially for you."

Sterling bounded to his feet and gave Ada a smacking kiss on her cheek. Then he grabbed the cake plate and put it on the table.

"I'll cut it for you, Sterling," Constance said.

"Make it large enough," he instructed.

"Mr. Sterling," Ada sniffed. "It's so nice to see you."

"Same here, Ada," he patted her shoulder. "I have someone that I want you to meet. Ada this is my girlfriend, Justice. Justice this is my second mother, Ada."

Justice allowed Ada to finish her thorough inspection of her before she spoke.

"It's very nice to meet you, Ada." Justice stuck her hand out.

Ada clasped her hand and held it a long time. "Sterling, she has a good heart. Keep this one."

"No doubt," he responded with feeling.

Hours later Justice sat in the car and watched Sterling as he and Chapman stood on the sidewalk conversing.

"I filed the official separation papers at the courthouse," Chapman said.

"How did Harlow react when you told her?"

"I haven't spoken to Harlow. Since she vacated the penthouse there was no need to. But I did send a copy of them to her mother's house. Is she still staying there?"

"I don't know," Sterling said. "But it's a good idea for you to send them there. Her mother will make sure she gets them. Harlow was in New York a couple of weeks ago."

"How do you know?" Chapman asked.

"I got my credit card statements." Sterling scowled. "She went shopping and blew fifteen thousand dollars on nonsense."

"And you have to pay for that because she's still you wife." He shook his head ruefully.

"We had separate savings accounts but a checking account with both our names on it has been depleted."

"Damn, man, she's really trying to break you."

Sterling said curtly, "Yesterday I canceled every card that we have together."

"That was smart. But she'll just open up others as Mrs. Sterling Hart."

"I signed up for credit card watch and tagged on my name with all the bureaus. I'll know what she's doing."

"That's a good idea. Keep all the receipts so when we go to court we have proof that she's done all of this since you two split. The judge will see how vindictive she is."

"Okay," Sterling said.

"Thank God you're finally happy."

"I'll be happier once I get rid of Harlow. Justice and I are getting married as soon as my divorce is final."

"And the rush is?" Chapman asked teasingly.

"It's not a rush since I feel like I've never really been married. And Justice isn't the kind of woman you just sleep with," Sterling explained. "She's the kind of woman you marry.

###

They sat at Justice's kitchen table. "Let's each write down every idea that we think would go with the other's outfit and then we'll go over it. Fresh eyes on our garments might be just what we need."

"That's a good idea," she said.

"Why did Byron tell Mrs. Daley to check our slips when you drew names?"

"He thought that I cheated because he knew that I wanted you so bad."

"How would he know that? We'd had no interaction because I was giving you the silent treatment."

"I paid him five hundred dollars to let me sit in his seat for the rest of the year."

Justice made a clucking sound with her teeth. "What!"

"He's a broke college kid. What did you expect?"

"So I'm only worth five hundred dollars?"

"It depends on who you ask. I think that you should multiply it by at least a million."

They worked in companionable silence. After an hour Justice said, "Would you like another cup of coffee?"

"I'd prefer water if you don't mind."

"Not at all." As she handed him a bottle of water her house phone rang. "Hello, Rossi," she said. "No. I hadn't heard. That's terrible news. Oh no, that's awful. He's going to suffer for everything that he's done. No jobs on the horizon, but that's okay." She shot Sterling a look of love. "But the other situation I told you about has turned out quite nicely." She giggled. "It's a long story so I'd rather tell you when I see you. You promise? Okay, love and kisses and tell Lucille I said hello."

"What's wrong?"

"Raven died from anorexia."

"That's terrible."

"They couldn't save her. The doctors tried everything."

"Is Rossi going to the funereal?"

"I doubt it. Raven was in St. Croix for a photo shoot and died while on location. And Rossi and Lucille are back in Italy for good."

"Why? I thought that they were helping to run things in the states."

"That was when Caesar was alive. Cassius fired both of them."

"What the hell is wrong with that guy?"

"Misery loves company," she said bitterly.

That night the ringing of the telephone roused Justice from a deep sleep. She looked over at Sterling to see if the telephone had wakened him.

He hadn't stirred.

Answering it she whispered, "Hello."

"Justice, this is Scarlett."

"Scarlett! It's twelve o'clock at night."

"I'm sorry," she said. "I forgot about the time change. Have you heard from Frederic?"

A sinking feeling filled the pit of her stomach. With the phone in her hand, she crept out of bed and closeted herself in the bathroom. "No," she said slowly. "I've called him three times and emailed him yet received no response. And I need to hear from him. As of yesterday my mortgage is past due."

"I can't find him," Scarlett said in a shrill voice. "It seems as if he's closed his business down and absconded with all his clients' money."

"I could kill you!" Justice ejaculated. "You told me Frederic was trustworthy."

"I never had a problem with him in the past. When he didn't reply I called the authorities and they said that all his clients are filing injunctions against his firm."

"Oh my God! That's all the money I had saved."

"I'm sorry, Justice," Scarlett whimpered.

"I'm sorry too," Justice whispered.

After she hung up she shuffled back into the room and weakly crawled back into bed.

Sterling's voice rang out in the darkness. "What's wrong?"

"Nothing," she mumbled and turned to him, burying her face in his chest.

Sterling stroked her hair until she drifted into a troubled sleep.

Sterling watched Justice only pick at her seafood and crab alfredo entrée. "You've been quiet for days. When are you going to tell me what's going on?"

"I'm going to look for a job as a salesgirl."

Sterling's eyes widened. "How are you going to do that and go to school full time?"

"People do it all the time," she said.

"I know. But we're in the accelerated program at school."

"I'm thinking about putting school on hiatus for a time."

"That's ridiculous. You have only another eighteen months."

"I need the money," she said bluntly.

"No, you don't."

"Oh, yes I do," she said, her bottom lip trembling. "I haven't seen my commercials being aired on television or received a residual check in awhile."

"I have more than enough money for both of us, Justice."

"I don't want your money, Sterling."

"That's an insulting thing for a woman to tell her man." He ground out the words, then threw his napkin on the table and signaled for the waiter. "Since you haven't really touched your meal we may as well go."

When Dominic appeared at their table, Sterling said, "We'll take our check and please box up her meal. She's going to eat it later."

They were quiet on the way home. Suddenly Sterling pulled over into a parking space in downtown Manhattan. He turned to her. "How much money do you need?"

Stonily she stared ahead staring out the window.

"Please let me help you, Justice."

Reluctantly she gave in. "If I can borrow this month's mortgage payment that will be enough."

"How much is that?"

"Eight thousand dollars," she whispered and hung her head.

Sterling got out the car and strode into the glass doors of Bank of America.

Less than ten minutes later he emerged from the bank. Getting back into the Bentley he handed her an envelope. "That's ten thousand dollars. Which bank holds your mortgage?"

"Chase Manhattan," she mumbled.

He pulled out into traffic. Less than two blocks and ten minutes later they were parked in front of her bank.

She sat still.

"Go on," Sterling instructed.

As he watched Justice stomp inside the bank he did some hard thinking.

Once they got back to Justice's house, Sterling warmed up her food in the microwave. "Eat," he said.

With far more appetite than she'd had at Sardis she ate her food. After she was done she said in a grateful voice, "Thank you, Sterling."

"For what?"

"For the money."

"I'd be a piss poor man if I couldn't look out for my woman," he growled.

"Looking out for your woman doesn't necessarily mean paying her mortgage."

"What's going on, Justice? Talk to me."

Grudgingly she told him about Scarlett's call, her attempts to find Frederic, and her job prospects.

Sterling rubbed his chin thoughtfully as he listened.

"I talked to the police and it seems as if Frederic has covered his tracks. All of the paperwork found at his office supports the fact that with the economy the way it is he went bankrupt because of bad investments. But the suspicious part is that he's disappeared. If he had any money he hid it." She drew in a resigned sigh. "I'm going to have to sell or find roommates. Even with two roommates, I'd have to charge them a lot to pay the whole mortgage. Then a job should take care of my other bills."

"I can pay the mortgage for you until we sort this out."

"Today I was in a bind because I was behind. But I don't want to take your money again."

Sterling looked at her. He voiced the feelings he'd had since he's watching her walk into the bank. "If you don't want my money, you can move in with me."

"What?"

"My penthouse is paid for so you can't feel guilty about the mortgage payment."

"I dunno," she said with a downcast look. "It was drummed into my head since I was a child that living together without being married is a sin."

"We're already living together. Ever since you let me back into your life we've spent every night together. It's a waste of time for us to keep two residences."

"My mother would kill me."

"Would you like me to call her and tell her that you're going to lose your home and be put out in the street?"

"You wouldn't dare!" she said horrified, at the thought.

"Of course I wouldn't. But I scared you. I also wouldn't let that happen. Let me help you, Justice."

She meditated for a while.

"I don't have any furniture. You could move all your things to my place. That would certainly help me out. I'm tired of my place being so barren."

"That's a feeble excuse, Sterling. You can afford to buy furniture."

"It doesn't even feel like a home." He gave a self-deprecating smile. "That's one of the reasons why I prefer to stay here. I'll cover your mortgage until we can rent this place out."

Justice started to protest.

Sterling's eyebrows met together into a fierce looking unibrow. "Do you know how upsetting it's for me that I can't give you my name yet?"

"That will come in time," she said, smoothing his frown.

Sterling said in a voice that brooked no argument. "This is the only way you won't lose the home you worked so hard to get." He took his finger and lifted her chin. "The money isn't important. We should fight about things that matter."

She felt her resolution giving way to his wants.

"Let me love you, Justice."

That did it for her. "When can you move my things?" she said with a small smile.

"Today is Wednesday. The movers will have it done by Friday."

"That sounds like a plan," she acquiesced.

Justice wandered around her new home with pleasure. All of her belongings fitted nicely in the spacious penthouse and made it feel cozy and warm. When she heard Sterling's key in the lock she went to greet him.

"Kiss me like you love me," Justice said with a sexy look.

Sterling held a large box that he placed on the tile foyer floor before he pulled her close.

As his mouth descended towards she closed her eyes in anticipation. Even though she was now familiar with his touch her insides still melted with molten hot pleasure as his hands leisurely explored her body. When they finally broke their kiss, she breathlessly leaned on him.

Sterling placed his head on top of hers and she cuddled even closer.

"Hey, lover," he whispered quietly.

"Hey back," she purred, burying her head in his chest, breathing in the scent of him.

"Don't you want to see what I brought you?" he teased.

"Not really," she said truthfully. "You're enough of a treat."

"Then I'll take it back to the store. But that's a shame," he said in a lamentably voice, "because it's sort of a gift that we'll both enjoy."

Now her interest was piqued. Justice dragged herself away from Sterling's embrace, picked up the box, after beckoning him with her eyes went into the den and sat on the loveseat.

Sterling sat close and watched her with an expectant look.

She slid off the, red, bow and then tore the flowered wrapping paper off. After she lifted the lid she gasped. Inside lay a sapphire bustier and matching panties. "Sterling they're beautiful." She planted a warm kiss on his lips. "Thank you."

He picked up the panties and held them out to her. "Look," he said gleefully, "they're crotchless."

"I've never had a pair of those," she said with an impish smile. "Wait here."Grabbing her present she bolted from the room.

When she reentered the den, Sterling sat on the couch with his arms folded in front of him. His eyes widened at the sight of her.

Justice posed in her new outfit. She'd fluffed her hair and donned six inch stilettos.

Sterling took his finger and made a motion.

She slowly turned around in a circle. Then she gave her best runway walk from one end of the room to the other. Planting herself in front of him in a voice full of desire she said, "Dinner is done. Are you ready to eat?"

Sterling stood and stripped naked. His shaft pointed at her. "I'm ready to eat, but not dinner."

Justice almost trod on Sterling's heels as she followed him to the bedroom.

Harlow sat across from Bartholomew Richards and read his report.

"Justice has been spending a lot of time with Constance Keen. They go shopping together and hang out."

"That bitch always did hate me," she said bitterly.

"They also do couple things."

"Trash hangs with thrash," Harlow said in a malevolent voice.

Bartholomew watched her with pity. "Justice has moved in with

Sterling."

That statement almost made her blackout. Once she'd gathered her wits she said with resolve, "I'm going to move her ass back out!"

He pointed at the printout he'd handed her at the beginning of the meeting. "Your husband purchased roundtrip airline tickets to Atlanta. They're obviously going to spend Christmas with her mother because he's also rented an Infiniti SUV. And he purchased a Blackberry in her name." Bartholomew handed her a slip. "This is the number."

Justice was in the bedroom when her cell phone rang. Thinking it was Sterling she ran over to it, almost tripping. "Hello," she said breathlessly.

The line went dead. She shrugged, threw it aside, and resumed her household duties.

A few minutes later she heard Sterling arrive home.

"Justice, where are you?" Sterling's booming voice reached her in the bedroom.

She shouted, "I'm in the bedroom folding our laundry."

The minute Sterling entered the room he gathered her in his arms and swung her around.

"What is it?" she gurgled.

"The realtor called me on my cell. Your house now has tenants."

"Thank God!" she said.

"And you're going to make some money off it. They're going to pay nine thousand a month to stay there."

"Who?"

"Some actresses with a recurring role on a reality show that's being filmed here."

"Thank God for reality shows and someone's fifteen minutes of fame. Now I can start paying you back the money that I owe you."

A pensive look immediately settled on Sterling's face. "What's for dinner?" he asked.

"I made country fried steak, mashed potatoes, and corn on the cob."

Sterling took his hand and slapped her on the ass. "That's all the repayment I need."

There was complete silence in the workroom as students

diligently worked on their latest assignment.

Justice was sketching dresses.

Mrs. Daley watched her as she erased, drew, erased, and then drew again. "I like the collar on that," she said musingly.

"Thank you," she said gratefully. "It reminds me of when I was a child. Puppy dog collars were all the craze."

"What age group are you gearing this outfit for?"

"I'm doing two different lengths. The mini skirt is for teenagers. But for women in their thirties I'll drop the hem to stop just above the knee. You'll still get the Lolita feel but they'll be more comfortable if the skirt hits just above the knees. Women in their thirties want to look sexy but not trashy. The lower hem line should make it suitable for happy hour on Friday nights."

"I agree," Mrs. Daley said with twinkling eyes. "Why are you doing mock pockets on some of the skirts?"

"I thought that would be appropriate for over thirty women. The smooth front will keep them from looking any wider. The young girls don't need that. I gave them side pockets because a lot of them don't like to carry a purse into a nightclub. It's such a hassle when you're asked to dance."

"That's a very good point," Mrs. Daley said, pleased. "At the close of class, I need you and Sterling to stay behind so I can talk to you."

Justice glanced at Sterling on the other side of the room. His brow was furrowed in concentration as he pinned material on a mannequin. "Yes, ma'am."

After class, Justice and Sterling sat in two chairs in front of her desk.

Mrs. Daley spoke in her forthright manner. "Some of the students have complained that the two of you are helping each other on your assignments."

"That's not true," Sterling said.

"The two of you have been seen together outside of class."

"You told us to meet with our partner to complete our semester exam," Justice exclaimed.

"I think that there's more to it than that. Of course it's none of my business but I have to make sure that it's your own work."

"Justice and I live together."

Justice and Mrs. Daley gasped.

"We knew each other before class," he said clearly, "but we weren't a couple. We are now."

"So I see," Mrs. Daley said.

"We aren't helping each other do our work," Justice said. Her face reflected her honesty.

"Justice is right. We have turned two of my bedrooms into workrooms. I don't go into hers and vice versa. I don't see Justice's sketch or garment until it's revealed in class. We have a healthy competition going."

Mrs. Daley watched them. "I believe you."

"There are only two weeks left before Christmas break," Sterling said. "Next semester we'll make sure we don't have the same teachers."

"That would be a good solution," Mrs. Daley said. "But I hate losing either one of you. I think both of you are geniuses in the making."

From the back seat Justice grabbed the bag of groceries. She locked the car and turned. Shocked, she dropped the bag and its contents scattered across the parking garage floor.

Harlow leaned on the post next to the elevator. She wore a black trench coat and knee high boots. Harlow strode towards Justice in a threatening manner. "What are you doing driving my husband's car?"

Justice mentally braced herself for an explosive confrontation. "I know that this may be hard for you to hear, Harlow, but Sterling and I are together," she replied with poise.

"You won't last," Harlow said cruelly.

Justice looked at her with some sympathy. "We will last. Try to understand that Sterling and I love each other very much."

"Sterling won't go through with the divorce. You're some country bumpkin! You're lower class."

"Your opinion of me doesn't matter," Justice retorted. Then she added with disgust, "And who are you to speak about class? At least I wouldn't pretend to be pregnant in order to hold on to a man."

A look of fury radiated across Harlow's face. "You're going to rue the day you ever met me!"

"I probably will," Justice retorted dismally. "I know that Sterling certainly does."

Harlow gave her an insolent look up and down her body. "I can't believe that my husband fucks you! You must be going down on him! Sterling can go a long time off that."

There was a long pause before Justice said in a measured tone, "I do that and more. Sterling makes love to me four of five times a week. And I don't have to beg him," she added with innuendo. "He told me that he never understood how you got pregnant since he rarely," she put her fingers up in the air in the quote unquote mannerism, 'fucked' you.'"

"I should beat your ass!" With a raised hand, Harlow took a menacing step towards Justice.

"Think very carefully about your next step, Harlow. I'm from Eastman, Georgia. We used to fight just because we were bored and didn't have anything else to do," Justice warned her. "And I never lost."

Harlow dropped her raised hand and took a step backwards. "Bitch! This isn't over." Storming off, she exited via the stairwell that descended to the street.

Feeling wobbly from the altercation, Justice picked up her scattered groceries and took the elevator to her home. "Sterling!" she shouted. "I have something to tell you."

She heard a feeble voice coming from the bedroom. "I'm in here."

Justice practically threw her wares on the counter and rushed to him.

Sterling was in bed and his bare chest was sopping wet his eyes a watery hue.

She took her hand and placed it on his forehead. "You have a fever," she said.

"And chills," he said. Then he was overcome with a paroxysm of coughing.

Going into the bathroom and returning with a thermometer she stuck it in his ear. "103. I think that I should take you to the doctor."

"No," he grumbled. "It's just the flu. All I need is some medicine and rest."

"I'll get medicine out of the cabinet."

After Justice doused Sterling with medicine, she sat on the edge of the bed and watched him grow drowsy.

"What did you have to tell me?" he whispered, groggy from the Nyquil.

"It can wait," she said quietly. "Get some sleep."

CHAPTER 18

Sterling sat propped up in bed with the breakfast tray Justice had prepared for him. He munched on a piece of toast.

"Thank goodness you've got your appetite back," she teased. "I was worried when you wouldn't eat."

"I was delirious from fever when I turned down your food."

"My mom is a better cook than I am. She'll fatten you up. You just wait and see."

"I can't wait." He grinned as he chomped on a strip of bacon.

"You were so sick I thought that I was going to have to call her and Aunt Minnie and tell them that we weren't going to make it."

"I would hate that. I'm really looking forward to meeting them instead of just talking to them on the telephone."

"Are you okay with what we decided?" Justice searched Sterling's face.

"It's your decision what you disclose to your family, Justice."

"We're not lying to them. We're just leaving out the fact that you're technically still married." Justice heaved a heavy sigh. "I don't feel like hearing Aunt Minnie's mouth."

Sterling said with some gratitude, "And I don't want your mom to think that I'm the kind of man who would take advantage of her daughter and string her along."

"Mom wouldn't think that. She's very discerning and sees the good in people. But I think that we'll have a better holiday with some things left unsaid."

"What excuse will you give your mother for living with me when you have your own place?"

She frowned. "I don't want her to know that Frederic swindled me. She would feel guilty about the money I gave her. I'll tell her that I want to be with you day and night." Justice leaned over and gave Sterling a kiss relishing the taste of bacon on his lips. "And that's the truth."

Sterling put the tray aside and pushed back the blankets.

"Where are you going?"

"Get dressed," he said. "We haven't been to the Empire State Building yet."

"It's freezing outside. I don't want you to get sick again."

"We'll be fine if we wrap up in those black wool coats you bought us."

"Why don't we wait until the spring? I think the Empire State Building will still be there."

A pout settled on his face. "Come on, Justice. I really want to go."

"Okay."

They stared out the window of the 102nd floor observatory. Twinkling Christmas lights illuminated the city and snow flurries were fast covering the ground.

Sterling drew her into the center of his arms and hummed the melody of 'New York State of Mind.' Then he whispered in her ear, "Look at the city, Justice. Together we can conquer it at work and at play. I know that it's not a macho thing to say, Justice, but you complete me." He reached into his pocket and handed her a box.

"What is it?"

"It's your Christmas present." His eyes glowed. "I wanted to give it to you while we were alone."

Justice tore the gold foil off the box and stuck it into the pocket of her coat. Then she opened the box. Inside was a large ring with three diamonds splayed across the center. "Oh my god!" she gasped. "It's beautiful."

"It's a promise ring," Sterling said. He took the ring and got down on one knee. As he placed it on the finger where an engagement ring would go, he said "I promise to always love, respect, and protect you."

"Oh, Sterling," she cooed.

Using the GPS Sterling navigated them through the heart of Eastman until he reached the outskirts. He made a sharp turn into the opulent housing development. "I can't believe that you haven't visited your mom in her new house."

"She understood what I was trying to accomplish. But this visit is long overdue."

Sterling pulled up into the paved driveway of the red brick colonial and shut the engine off. He stared at it admiringly. "You should feel proud that you were able to do this for her."

Justice beamed as she viewed the frozen yet carefully placed shrubbery. "Looking at it makes me finally find feel at peace with my modeling career."

"You're a good daughter, Justice." Sterling asked, "How many bedrooms?"

"There are three," she answered. "But it wouldn't matter if there were ten," she teased. "You'd still have to sleep on the couch."

"I hear what you're saying, but I'm going to die without you next to me," he moaned.

The front door was flung open and Evelyn hurried towards them.

"You walk like your mom," Sterling said before he exited the car.

Justice met her mother halfway and threw her arms around her neck. "Mom, I'm so glad to see you."

"I've been looking out the window all day." She hugged her back gripping her waist. Then she let go and held out her arms to Sterling. "Come on."

With a grin Sterling went and hugged her. After he released her he said, "It's so nice to finally meet you, Mrs. Fairchild."

"Call me, Mom," Evelyn requested in a shy voice.

"Then mom it is." Sterling felt a rush of pleasure course through him.

Suddenly Evelyn burst into tears.

"Mom," Justice said shocked. "Why are you crying?"

Evelyn wiped her tears with the back of her hand. "I know that I'm being silly," she said. "But when you look at Sterling, I can see it in your eyes that you've found the same love that I had for your father."

"I have, Mom."

"Dinner is almost ready," Evelyn said. "Come on you two."

From behind Justice linked her arm into Sterling's and said, "I told you."

"I can't wait," Sterling said with anticipation.

They were cleaning up the kitchen when Justice heard Minnie get home. Throwing down her dry towel, Justice ran towards her.

Minnie stared at Justice with love and allowed herself to be enveloped in her arms. She said gruffly, "I miss you, Justice."

"I miss you too, Aunt Minnie." Justice took her hands and pushed Minnie a bit away not releasing her. "You look good," Justice complimented her.

"Thanks to you," Minnie said.

"Why do you say that?"

"I'm not as worried as I used to be. Since I moved in with your mother I don't have to work as hard. With that new washing machine and dryer, I don't have to go to the Laundromat. And I don't have to run the shower for ten minutes to get some hot water. I even cut down my hours at work. I couldn't have done that if I was still living alone. You treat me like you're my daughter. I'm very grateful to you, Justice."

Justice leaned forward. She whispered in a conspiratorial voice, "I owe you too. I was getting worried about mother living alone and she refused to move to New York."

"We're both pretty set in our ways, Justice. And your mother and I enjoy living together because we know how to stay out of each other's way. Now," Minnie said, "where's this man of yours?"

"He's in the kitchen with Mom."

"Do you love him?"

"Yes. And he makes me happy. People in love aren't always happy but I am."

"That's good enough for me," Minnie replied.

The night closed in on them. The flames from the gas fireplace filled the room with warmth. Evelyn and Minnie were throwing the last bits of tinsel on the tree. Sterling and Justice sat together on the leather couch. His arm was around her shoulder and as instructed by her mother Justice was showing him page after page of childhood.

"Done!" Justice said thankfully closing the book.

"And not a moment too soon," Minnie said yawning with a smile. "I'm ready to go to bed, but I didn't want to leave. I was afraid I might miss something."

Evelyn darted a quick look at Minnie before she looked back at Justice and Sterling. "Sterling, it's okay if you stay in the room with Justice."

"But," Minnie protested, "they're not married."

There was a questioning silence that filled the air.

"That's okay, Mom," Sterling said in a smooth voice. "I think that I'd be more comfortable sleeping here on the couch. Maybe the next time Justice and I visit we'll be able to sleep in the same bedroom."

"What's the holdup?" Minnie asked. "The two of you aren't teenagers."

"Aunt Minnie!" Justice protested. "Don't scare Sterling away."

Unruffled Sterling said, "I have every intention of marrying Justice."

Justice held her hand out. She showed the ring. "What do you think this is?"

Minnie and Evelyn stared at it.

"Is it real? I thought that was cubic zirconium," Evelyn said.

"And that you bought it yourself," Minnie added.

Justice said proudly, "It's my Christmas present from Sterling. It's a promise ring."

"What is he promising?" Minnie asked suspiciously.

"He is promising that we'll always be together."

"And what did you give him?" Evelyn asked, still admiring the ring.

"We're going to the Poconos for New Year's. The trip is on me."

"Y'all flying around a lot without getting married," Minnie grumbled. "It only takes thirty minutes at the courthouse."

Evelyn searched Sterling's eyes and liked what she saw. "Be quiet, Minnie. They know what they're doing."

Dressed in black Harlow entered the penthouse. In the storage closet she found a stepladder. Climbing it, Harlow grabbed the small plant off the shelf and removed the device that was hidden from view. After she replaced the plant in the exact spot she went to the bedroom and repeated her actions. She stared at Justice's furniture and accent pieces with a ferocious scowl. She took her hand and angrily swept it across the nightstand, knocking the lamp to the floor. A small piece broke at the base. After she glued it back together she put it back in place and departed.

"Evelyn, aren't you ever going to take it off?" Minnie asked.

"Nope," Evelyn grinned.

"You're like that Mrs. Cleaver running around cleaning house in pearls."

Evelyn fingered her Christmas present from Justice and Sterling. "I absolutely love them. And who are you to talk? The only reason you took off the bracelet they gave you was because you had to wash dishes."

"You sho nuff right." Minnie laughed, knowing Evelyn only spoke the truth.

"My Justice looks beautiful in that red knit dress, too," Evelyn said.

"I now make all my clothes. I'm hoping that a designer will see me and will ask where I got my outfit from and then if I tell them that I made it, offer me a job," she chuckled.

That afternoon, from out the window, Evelyn watched Sterling as he shoveled the driveway, ridding it of the fresh snow that had fallen during the night. Then she looked at Justice who sat balancing her checkbook with a calculator. "I like your man, Justice."

"I like him too," Minnie agreed. "So he wants to be a clothes designer like you?"

"Yep," Justice said. "And he's good at it. To be honest, he's my only competition in design class. We both get the highest grades. After we graduate, we're going to design clothes together." With a smile, she handed her mother her wallet with a check tucked inside it.

"Just leave it on the table, honey," Evelyn said. "So you've given up modeling for good?"

"Yes," she said. "And I don't miss it." Justice looked at them. "I know that when I moved to New York the two of you were worried. You don't have to anymore."

"I didn't like you being alone up there." Evelyn added with a sheepish look, "That's some of the reason I sort of pushed you to go back to Miles. Have you run into him again?"

"Sterling and I were out to dinner at Charles in West Village. He was bussing tables. Miles acted like he didn't know me and vice versa."

As Minnie let the water out of the sink she made a loud snort of derision.

"I made a mistake encouraging you to give him a second chance." Evelyn sighed. "I guess it's true that a leopard doesn't change his spots." Evelyn finished.

"I'm sort of glad that I gave him another chance," Justice admitted. "It was a useful learning exercise. After Miles I was really able to judge whether a man is good or not. It's not what Sterling says, it's what he does. He goes out of his way to make life easier for me and I can count on him for things that matter."

"Is that why you moved in with him without being married?" Minnie asked.

"Sort of," Justice hedged. "Don't worry about that, Aunt Minnie. Sterling and I will get married and be together for always."

"It's only eight o'clock in the morning. Where are you going?' Naked, Justice rolled over and watched Sterling as he entered the room fully dressed.

"Chapman texted me. He wants me to look over the divorce papers that he's sending to Harlow."

"Okay. When you get back we should go shopping for things for our trip. We leave in a couple of days."

"Okay," After he kissed her on the lips he said, "I shouldn't be gone too long."

Justice was cleaning the bathroom when she heard the house phone ring. "Hello," she said, coughing from all the chemicals that had invaded her nostrils.

"Justice, this is Aunt Minnie."

Trepidation flooded her. "What's wrong?"

"Your mother had a mild heart attack."

"Oh my God!" she said. "What happened?"

"I don't know. She said that she was feeling tired. I thought that it was just all the excitement from the holidays. Then she said that her left arm was hurting her. I thought that it might be because we had more snow and she'd shoveled the driveway."

"Why was she shoveling snow? Where was that boy that I pay to do that?" Justice asked heatedly.

"He's still out of town." Minnie drew a sigh of resignation. "That night she got up and took some Bayer aspirin. The doctor thinks that saved her life."

"Good Lord," Justice said, placing her hand over her own heart.

"I heard her fall from the other room. They rushed her to the hospital."

"Is she going to be okay?"

"Yes. The doctor has already released her and we're back home."

"Doctor who? I need to talk to him."

"It's a Doctor Gilliard. I have his number. Your mother didn't want me to call you. I had to sneak in here while she took a nap."

"Why didn't she want me to know?"

"You know how she doesn't like to worry anyone. She's really fine, Justice. The doctor said that she needs to go on a diet and get some exercise. As soon as she feels better we're going to start walking with them other old people at the mall."

"I'm going to hop a plane and be there as soon as possible."

"You might want to talk to her first, Justice. She'll be upset her if she thinks that you miss your Poconos weekend because of her. The doctor said that she needs rest and mustn't get agitated."

"Call me when she wakes up," Justice said firmly. "Now what is this doctor's number?"

After she hung up she called Sterling. His cell went straight to voicemail. "Honey, call me."

Then she dialed the number that Minnie gave her.

"Doctor Gilliard here."

"This is Justice Fairchild," she said in a harried voice. "My mother is under your care. She's had a heart attack. What's going on with her?"

"Your mother has a heart arrhythmia."

"What's that?'

"She has an irregular heartbeat. I'm going to put her on medication and she should be fine."

"What is heart arrhythmia?"

"It simply means that she has heart palpitations. If she gets too tired or excited the muscles contract and she'll have an episode."

"Why am I just finding out about this?"

"She's never had an episode before. Now that she's older she needs to take it easy. And she needs to lose some weight and eat healthier."

"That's what I tell her but she doesn't listen," Justice said. "I think that I should fly down and consult with you."

"You're more than welcome," Doctor Gilliard said kindly, "but there's nothing that I would say then that I haven't already."

Sterling sat in Chapman's office. "The papers look in order. Why didn't you send them?"

"I did." He sighed. "They came back unsigned."

"I'll make her sign them. I'll embarrass the hell out of her in front of her mother."

"She might not care. I'm sure the apple doesn't fall far from the tree."

"I need to see Harlow anyhow." Sterling said angrily, "She approached Justice in the parking garage."

"No, she didn't," Chapman exclaimed.

"Yes the hell she did. Justice didn't tell me until we were out of town."

"What did Harlow say to her?"

"She insulted Justice and called her names." He said with a steely glint in his eyes, "No one messes with my girl."

"What are you going to do?"

"After New Year's I'll go to Chicago and take care of this once and for all."

###

Justice sat drumming her fingers on the arm of the sofa. When the phone rang she jumped. She grabbed it. "Hello."

"Hello, honey." Evelyn sounded tired. "Minnie told me that she called you."

"Thank goodness," she said crossly. "How dare you keep something this important away from me?"

"I was going to tell you as soon as I got the results. I just got off the phone with Doctor Gilliard. I'm going to be fine."

"I'm coming down."

"I don't want that. You deserve a vacation. I would never forgive myself if you missed your trip because of me."

"But, Mom," Justice protested. "The Poconos are always going to be there."

"And so am I," her mother said firmly. "And I want you to take lots of photos so I'll feel as if I went with you and Sterling. Do you understand me, Justice?"

"Yes, mother," she said tearfully.

"Good," Evelyn said firmly. "I just heard the garage door so Minnie's back with my medication. Call me tomorrow because I'm going to take another nap."

"Yes, Mother," Justice said dutifully.

When Sterling got home, Justice threw herself in his arms, almost knocking him off balance.

"What the hell!"

"My mother," she babbled. "Why didn't you answer the phone?"

"I'm sorry," he said, smoothing her hair. "I was distracted." Sterling scooped her into his arms and strode to the living room. Still holding her he sat down on the couch. "What's wrong?"

Almost incoherently, Justice explained everything, not leaving out one word that Aunt Minnie, her mother, or the doctor had uttered.

"If it'll set your mind at ease we'll go down there," Sterling said.

"We can't," Justice said. "It would make Mom feel guilty."

"Justice," he said cautiously, "it seems like everything is under control. We'll surprise her Valentine's Day weekend. She can't find fault with that."

"Okay," she said sniffling, as she lay her head on his chest.

###

"That's ready to go." Sterling slammed a suitcase shut. He took his hand and gently touched Justice's cheek. "Are you now okay about our trip?"

"I am," she responded. "I called home today and they were on their way to church. That's always a good sign."

"It is," he agreed. "What else needs to be done?"

"I need to gather my toiletries to put in my cosmetics bag."

Sterling snapped his fingers. "I forgot that I need shaving cream and razors. I'm going to run to Duane Reade and get some. While I'm out I'll gas up the car so we don't have to stop. It's getting kind of dark already."

"That sounds like a plan. I'll be ready by the time you get back."

Sterling took his hand and rubbed her backside. "Hmm," he said. "That feels good."

Justice playfully slapped his hand away. "Don't do that or we'll never make it to the Poconos."

"Oh, all right," he said in mock hurt.

Justice finished packing and took her bag to the foyer. Then she went to the kitchen and took a bottle of Diet Lipton Green Tea out of the refrigerator. As she gulped the liquid she turned to head into the living room.

Harlow leaned with her back against the closed door.

Justice sputtered, choking on her tea. It went down her windpipe and she began to cough. She tried to swallow, but a hard, burning sensation made it difficult for her to breathe.

With a look of satisfaction Harlow watched her.

I won't die in front of her. That would make her too happy.
Justice took the flat of her hand and began to pound her chest in the area right above her breast. Finally she felt some relief and straightened her body. She choked, "Get out of my house."

"This is Sterling's house, not yours," she said mockingly.

"But Sterling is mine," Justice retorted sharply. "So what belongs to him belongs to me."

"You think that I'll let you get away with stealing my husband?" Harlow demanded with a maniacal gleam in her eyes.

"You can't steal a person from someone, Harlow."

"I have something to show you." She brushed past Justice and practically glided into the living room. "I didn't know that you wanted to be an actress, Justice." She took a tape out of her pocket and popped it into the DVD player and turned on the television.

Justice remained where she was, too stunned to move.

Harlow beckoned her. "Come see this."

Slowly Justice walked over to her and stared at the television.

It was video of her and Sterling. They were both naked and she was on her knees pleasuring him. His hands were holding her head in place and his eyes were closed. A look of intense pleasure was on his face. Justice felt as if the wind had been knocked out of her, and placed her hand on her stomach to stop herself from heaving.

"I knew you were suckin' him," Harlow said condescendingly. She took the remote and advanced it to the next frame. "That goes on for some time so let's look at another." This time they were in bed. Justice was in the missionary position and there was another clear shot of her face. Their mutual gasps of pleasure were audible on the tape. In the next frame, Justice was on all fours and she and Sterling were making love doggy style.

Harlow glared at her. "Goodness, girl, did you have to do everything he asked of you? What a slut you are. I don't want to look at the rest of it again. You can have that copy and play it for Sterling since I have others at home." Harlow stared at Justice's now bent head. "Sterling needs to drop the divorce proceedings and you need to leave my husband alone." Harlow said derisively, "If you don't, I'm going to send a copy to your mother and that sanctified aunt that lives with her. I'm also going to put it on the Internet. We'll see if your mother can survive another heart attack after she sees what her daughter is doing with another woman's husband," she threatened before storming out and slamming the door behind her.

Justice sank to the floor in despair. Transfixed, she viewed the rest of the video as her world crashed around her.

She sat in the blackness.

Sterling walked into the den carrying a bag, and confusion was apparent on his face. "Why are you sitting in the dark like this?" He flicked the light switch and flooded the room with light.

With a trancelike expression Justice stood, walked over to the television, and turned it on. The video began to play. She stumbled back over to the couch and flung herself face down on it and sobbed uncontrollably.

"What is this?" Flabbergasted, Sterling stared at the television. "Where did this come from?"

"It's a gift from Harlow," she said, her voice muffled from the couch cushions.

"Harlow!" he shouted.

"Yes," she shouted back. "She let herself in with a key," Justice hissed, sitting up. "Evidently she had cameras in every room of the house. Why didn't you take her keys back?"

"She left them on the counter when she moved out," Sterling retorted heatedly.

"Obviously she had a copy made, Sterling." Justice stood, planted her hands on her hips and looked at him accusingly. "Didn't you think to change the locks?"

Mortification flooded his face. "I'm sorry about this, Justice. I'll take care of it."

"No you won't." Justice screamed, "I'm so tired of this shit, Sterling. She gets away with everything and you do nothing about it."

Sterling felt as if Justice had sliced his heart open. "That's not fair, Justice. You know that I have to follow legal procedure in order to get a divorce."

"I don't care," Justice said with a distraught look on her face. "Harlow said that she's going to put this on the Internet."

Appalled, he stammered, "That's what she said that she's going to do?"

"Yes! And send it to my mother." With a frazzled look she screamed, "I'll be a porn queen thanks to you not taking a firm stand with her."

There was a long silence as Sterling stared on in horror.

"I'm done," Justice uttered in a defeated voice. "I can't handle all of this."

"What!"

"Harlow will never give you a divorce and for the rest of our lives she'll make us miserable." She shrieked, "And I can't keep sleeping with a married man."

"I'll fix this," Sterling said with a tortured look.

She said bleakly, "You can't. And I can't sacrifice my mother's health for us."

Sterling took a step towards her, but she stepped back. "Don't touch me," she said, her face and voice full of dejection. "I think that you've already done enough of that." She sat weakly on the couch. "Will you go to the bathroom and bring me a cool washcloth to put on my forehead? I feel faint."

"Don't move," Sterling ordered in a grave voice.

After Sterling disappeared from sight Justice grabbed her purse and fled.

###

"What the fuck!" Chapman shouted.

"It's been hours. She's not answering her phone. She didn't take the car or I'd have Lojack track her down."

"She's probably gone somewhere to think." Constance added dryly, "I know I would."

"I think that I should kill Harlow," Sterling said grimly.

"What would that solve?" Chapman asked in a sober voice. "You'd go to jail for murder and Harlow would be crowing from her grave that she won."

Sterling jumped to his feet. With his hands stuffed in his pockets he paced the kitchen floor. "I'm going home. Maybe she'll turn up or eventually answer her phone."

"Have you called Harlow?" Chapman asked.

"Of course. She won't answer the phone," he said harshly. "But I called the airlines. She hauled ass back to Chicago."

"I know I would," Constance said.

"What exactly did she get you and Justice doing on tape?" Chapman asked.

"I looked at all of it after Justice took off." Embarrassment was obvious. "If it was in a video store, it'd be in the triple X section behind the wall."

"Damn!" Constance said scornfully, "That Harlow is one bitch and a half."

Sterling lay in the bed of the dark apartment. He heard a coughing sound and sat up. "Is that you, Justice?" he asked hope surging in his heart.

"It's Ada, Mr. Sterling. You really shouldn't leave your door unlocked. Someone could come in and kill you in your sleep."

"I'm not that lucky," Sterling said in a dour voice. "What are you doing here?"

"Constance told me what was going on and I came to talk to you." She turned on the lamp.

Pain was written all over Sterling's face.

With sympathy for him, Ada sat down on the bed. "I have something to tell you."

"What is it?"

"I don't think that was your baby Harlow was carrying."

"What?" Sterling bolted up into an upright position.

"Harlow was having an affair with Lyle Gardner."

"Are you sure?" Sterling said in a stunned voice.

"Well," she said, "I wasn't in the room with them while they did it, but Lyle bragged about it to a few friends at work. I also saw them together. The last time she came to the job, she was at the elevator begging him to talk to her. She took his hand and placed it on her pregnant stomach."

"Why didn't you tell me this before?" Sterling's eyes were narrowed in concentration.

"How do you tell a man that his wife is cheating on him?" Ada said with an uncomfortable look. "But I thought you should know that Harlow has a few skeletons in her closet. Maybe you can use it for leverage."

"Thank you, Ada," he said with heartfelt gratitude.

She leaned over and gave him a kiss on the cheek. "Handle your business, Mr. Sterling," she advised. Then she gave him a slip of paper from her pocket.

"What is this?"

"I sent Lyle's last check stub to him in California. I thought that you might want to speak with him."

"I think that's a good idea."

CHAPTER 19

A crimson moon cast a glow on the city. Sterling stood in the shadows and waited outside the rundown tenement. Finally, he spied his prey.

Carrying a lunch box in one hand and a hard hat in the other, Lyle was dressed in dirty jeans and a tee shirt splattered with cement. His gait was a tired shuffle. He put his key in the lock, jiggled it, and pushed it open.

Once the door was open, with mercurial speed Sterling was on top of him, slamming the door behind him.

"What the fuck is going on?" Lyle fearfully backed away from the dark form.

Instinctively, Sterling hit the light switch and illuminated the small room. Stone-faced Sterling watched him.

"What are you doing here, Sterling?"Lyle shouted.

"You were fucking my wife behind my back?" Sterling demanded in a menacing voice.

"You can't make me claim that baby," Lyle sputtered.

Sterling blinked only once.

"And I ain't taking no damn blood test."

"Why would Harlow want you to claim the baby?" With disdain, Sterling viewed the dingy walls and lack of furniture in the tiny apartment. "You have nothing."

With a pissed look on his face Lyle said, "I had enough for her. Besides, she pursued me. Not the other way around, man."

Sterling stared at Lyle's dirty work clothes. "I thought you were supposed to be an actor?"

"The part fell through," he said defensively, "but I'll get another job." Lyle pointed to a stack of tapes on top of the television. "Maybe I'll get a part in a movie starring your wife," he sneered. "She's not a good actress, but she tries real hard."

Sterling blinked one more time and then his hand whipped out and gripped Lyle's throat. He swung him around and slammed him against the wall. "Which one is it?" he said through clenched teeth. "Give me the video of you and Harlow."

Lyle gasped for air. "I'm not giving it to you for free," he eked out.

Sterling tightened his grip.

"I can't give it to you," Lyle gasped from pain. "I need the money."

Sterling let go and Lyle almost fell to the floor gasping for breath. "Get the tape," Sterling said in a deadly tone.

"I want twenty-five thousand dollars for it," Lyle said stubbornly as he rubbed his throat with his hand.

Sterling took his checkbook out of his inside jacket pocket.

Lyle went over to the television and grabbed a homemade DVD from the bottom of the stack and checked the label.

Sterling wrote a check for twenty-five thousand dollars and handed it to Lyle. "Is this your only copy?"

"Of course," Lyle said. "She's not good enough to make copies."

With a disgusted look on his face Sterling turned to leave but Lyle's words stopped him.

"You need to do a better job picking your woman," Lyle jeered.

"I have," Sterling answered and left.

Once he reached the street, Sterling took his cell phone and dialed his bank. "Member services, please," he said to the recording prompt.

"Yes, may I help you, Mr. Hart?" an account manager answered.

"I need a stop payment on a check. It's number 603 in the amount of twenty-five thousand dollars." After he hung up, Sterling muttered, "Harlow cost me too much already."

After the quick airplane ride from California to Chicago Sterling sat in a hotel suite and without emotion watched the video of his wife as she took it in the rear from Lyle Gardner.

In her room at The Marriott, Justice tossed and turned unable to sleep. She swept her hand across the empty side where Sterling usually slept. A fresh torrent of tears soaked her pillow.

Sterling let himself into his mother-in-law's house with his key. For the second time he watched the video of his wife on tape committing adultery. In the dark, he sat and waited.

When she came in, Harlow dropped a mountain of shopping bags onto the floor and walked to the kitchen. When she reentered the foyer, she found Sterling standing in the pathway between her and the door.

Fear made her drop her eyes and stare down at the floor.

With satisfaction, Sterling watched her grope for words. "I want the tape," he said through gritted teeth.

Harlow said in a sour voice, "I already gave your whore your copy."

"Be careful what you say about my fiancée," Sterling said with a menacing look. "It's all I can do not to strangle you and be done with it."

"Don't threaten me, Sterling. I'm not afraid of you." She screeched, "Now get out of here before I call the police."

"When I'm done you won't be calling the police or telling anyone about our conversation," Sterling snarled.

Harlow made an effort to appear unmoved but failed.

"I know about you and Lyle."

Now a wary look settled on her face as her eyes shifted away from his.

"I also know the baby wasn't mine," he said coldly. "If you don't give me all the copies of the tapes and sign the divorce papers for an uncontested divorce, all of your friends, including your mother, will know the kind of person that you are. You'll be the butt of a joke and probably be kicked out of The Inner Circle."

"I'll deny it," she said vehemently.

"Good luck with that."

Sterling strode over to the chair he'd vacated and grabbed a black leather briefcase. Positioning it on the coffee table he opened it. "Lyle sold you out," he said in a smooth voice. "This will go over the Internet if you bother me or Justice again. You know how you like to keep a spotless image. You'll never live this down."

Stupefied, Harlow stared at the tape.

Sterling placed it on the table. "That's your copy." Then he took out a stack of papers and a pen. "You went outside the marriage first, Harlow. If you contest it the divorce papers will state that you committed adultery and were pregnant by another man during our marriage. If you slander Justice or bring her name into this, I'll release the tape. Think of what people will say when they learn that you pretended to be pregnant after your miscarriage," he said in disgust. "Any judge would grant me a divorce."

"I hate you, Sterling," Harlow said, defeated.

"Funny," he said callously, "I have no feeling towards you at all."

###

Justice shouted nervously, "Sterling! Where are you?"

She cased the apartment for her iPhone. After a futile search, she picked up the house phone and called her mother.

Evelyn answered on the third ring.

"Mom," Justice said cautiously, "how are you doing?"

"I'm doing great," Evelyn said cheerfully. "But why does my caller I.D. give me your home number? You're supposed to be in the Poconos."

Justice sat on the bed. "We didn't go," she said disconsolately.

"Why on earth not?"

"It's a long story, Mom. What has the doctor said about your condition and you getting excited?"

"I'm feeling better than I did before I had my attack. But that's enough about me. Is anything wrong?"

Justice drew in a deep sigh filled with anxiety. "I kept something about Sterling from you and I don't know how you're going to take it."

There was a long, heavy silence.

"Is it that he's married?" Evelyn asked bluntly.

Justice almost dropped the phone. "How would you know that?" she stammered.

"His ring finger. Sterling is the color of smoke. The skin around his ring finger is lighter than the rest of him from his wedding band. Your father had the same marking."

Justice said in awe, "I can't believe you didn't let on that you knew."

"Why is he still married?" Evelyn demanded.

"Sterling has been trying to get a divorce pretty much since he met me." Justice took her time, explained the New York State divorce laws, and everything Sterling had done in order to free himself.

Evelyn never interrupted and listened intently to everything her daughter told her.

"That wife of his needs to go to church and fall down on the altar and ask for forgiveness," she said.

"She's mean and spiteful," Justice said. "And she has tapes."

"What kind of tapes?" Evelyn exclaimed.

Justice mumbled in embarrassment, "Sex tapes that she's going to release of me and Sterling if I don't leave him."

The only sound was the whirring of the ceiling fan in the background. Finally Evelyn asked disapprovingly, "So you're going to let her dictate your life?"

"I don't want you to be embarrassed that I'm your daughter."

"I won't be."

"Mom, you don't know what they look like," Justice whispered. "I make love to Sterling in ways as if he is already my husband."

"I don't want to hear anymore about this," Evelyn interrupted hastily. "I won't look at it, or let anyone discuss it with me."

Justice's heart soared and she felt liberated. "Are you sure it's okay for me to have Sterling, Mom?"

"Justice, when you were here I looked into that man's eyes. I felt as if I could see into his very soul. Sterling is an honest man who loves you to distraction." Evelyn said confidently, "He'll take care of this mess and work it out so that you can be together."

"What about Aunt Minnie?"

"Don't worry about her," Evelyn answered firmly. "I can take care of Minnie."

Awareness that she was being watched wakened her. She rolled over in the king sized bed and her eyes were drawn immediately to where Sterling sat in the occasional chair.

Twilight peeked through the Venetian blinds in the room, casting a shadow across Sterling's face. He looked exhausted. "Where did you go?" he asked in a strained voice.

"A hotel," she said. "I needed time to think."

"I called you so many times I lost count." He hung his head in despair.

"I can't find my iPhone. I must have lost it during the madness. I did try to call you today and couldn't get through."

"I was in the middle of trying to fix things, Justice." He said in a stressed voice, "I'm sorry about Harlow and the tape and everything."

"I shouldn't have lashed out at you the way I did," she said contritely. "It's not your fault."

Apology was written all over his face. "I'd said that I would protect you and I failed."

"You don't think like Harlow, Sterling." Justice shook her head in loathing. "It's hard to protect yourself against that kind of hatred." She got up from the bed and went to him. Naked, she crawled onto his lap. "I think that we love each other so much that we can weather this storm." She looped her arms around his neck and gave him a deep passionate kiss.

Sterling returned her kiss with all the love he had for her welling up in his body.

Breathless, she finally drew away. "I spoke to Mother and told her everything."

She felt Sterling's body stiffen in surprise.

"What did she say?"

"Mom wants me to be happy and if you're the person who can do that, she'll work with us."

He heaved a sigh of relief. "So you'll still marry me?"

"The minute I can," she promised.

"Get up," Sterling said and lightly patted her on the butt.

"No." She teased him by smuggling closer.

"You're going to miss a treat if you don't."

Justice scrambled to her feet. "I hope that the treat is you're going to get naked," she quipped.

Sterling stood and dropped to one knee.

Justice's jaw dropped.

"Harlow signed the divorce papers and we don't have to worry about the tape." Sterling reached into his pants pocket and took out a black box. Inside was a huge diamond princess cut solitaire. "I love you, Justice Fairchild. In one year, will you do me the honor of becoming my wife?"

Justice sank down onto the floor and held her hand out. "Yes, Sterling." Finally, tears of joy and relief cascaded down her face. "I will marry you."

EPILOGUE

They sat in a private section at LeCirque. Justice viewed the people who'd traveled far to support her and Sterling. "I feel so blessed that you're all here."

"I wouldn't have missed this for anything in the world," Evelyn gushed. "I'm so proud of you."

"I didn't think that it would be so much fun flying on a plane. When I heard the two of you were getting married, I thought that would be my first trip. But I like the fact that you chose Eastman. Then all our friends were there."

"I know," Evelyn said. "I'll never forget how surprised I was when they showed up for church. But they had it all arranged with Pastor that he'd do the ceremony in the chapel right after service."

"Once Sterling got his divorce we didn't want to wait any longer," Justice said lifting Sterling hand and kissing his wedding band.

Sterling smiled at Justice.

Justice drowned in his gaze.

Sterling tore his eyes away from his beautiful wife and cleared his throat. "And now all of our friends and family are together again. Justice and I would like to take this opportunity to thank all of the people that we love so much for being here and supporting us the last five years that brought us to this point."

Chapman spoke first. "Constance and I knew that you would get here. Didn't we, honey?" he asked, clasping his wife's hand.

"We sure did." She looked at Evelyn. "Justice made this dress for me. You have a very talented daughter."

"And son-in-law," Evelyn added.

"Your call was a gift from heaven. Lucille and I were tired of Europe," Rossi said. "We wanted to come back to New York and have a dirty dog from one of your street vendors."

Sterling's eyes opened wide with speculation. "Lucille, I thought that you were a vegetarian."

"I am," she retorted. "I don't think those hot dogs qualify as meat."

Everyone at the table laughed agreeably.

Scarlett raised her glass of champagne and even Minnie followed suit. "I predict that after your clothesline Fair Hart debuts tonight, you'll be famous."

"I hope that the critics love it," Justice said nervously.

"The teasers that we sent out for publicity got glowing praises," Lucille said.

"My wife has her hand on the pulse of fashion," Sterling bragged.

"You give a mention to Lotus Treatment Center." Scarlett said perusing the fashion show's program. "I've never heard of it."

"Don't you remember Lotus?" Justice queried. "She worked for Annabelle but now she has her own spa. I wouldn't trust anyone else to ready my girls for the show."

"How many models do you have?" Scarlett asked, placing the program in her oversized pocketbook.

"Twenty-five," Justice said.

Scarlett said, "They usually don't allow new designers to show so many pieces."

"We're only showing five outfits," Justice said. "But the same outfit is being worn by five different models. They range from size four to sixteen."

"That's what's going to make them famous," Rossi said to Evelyn. "Women are tired of dieting. If you're naturally thin you're blessed. But the normal size of American women is a size sixteen and they're tired of being measured by those almost unattainable standards."

Sterling said assertively, "As the Fair Hart models walk the runway one right after the other; everyone will see how beautiful our clothes are for women of all sizes. The only thing different about the garments is the selection of colors. They range from soft, hues to jet black for night life."

"That's genius!" Scarlett exclaimed. "But you've never explained how you got so far so fast. That's almost unheard of in the fashion industry."

"I was sitting in the subway station waiting for my train," Justice explained. "I had on a dress that Sterling made for me and this young guy came up to me and asked the label. His name is Ricky and he works for Michael Kors. Ricky gave our card to Michael and here we are."

"Michael is a mentor for people," Sterling said. "He's so successful he doesn't need to be cutthroat."

"Justice, speaking of cutthroat, what do you think of the House of Brabantio being a part of the show tonight?" Lucille asked.

Justice shrugged her shoulders. "Cassius can't hurt me anymore."

Rossi said, "It's the first time since Caesar's death that he's participated in a runway show. He's even having a hard time getting his clothes stocked in department stores. Participating is his effort to get the Brabantio name back in good standing."

"Let him bring it on," Sterling said and placed his arm around Justice's shoulders protectively.

Justice lovingly rubbed her husband's thigh.

Evelyn and Minnie beamed as they watched them.

###

The strobe lights at Bryant Park only enhanced the beauty of the Fair Hart models as they catwalked the runway. Each model strutted her stuff as she strode with an alluring confidence. As one model passed another they gave each other a congratulatory hand slap.

Journalists scribbled furiously and photographers almost blinded the models with flash bulbs, anxious to get a shot of each garment that debuted. Ringing applause and a standing ovation was given after the models final walk.

Sterling stood and extended his hand to his wife.

Justice allowed Sterling to help her to her feet and didn't let go as they ascended the stairs to take their bow.

They'd practiced it. Sterling bowed and then faced Justice and clapped. She gave a dainty curtsy. It was only after the applause ended that she allowed herself to bask in the adulation of the patrons of New York Fashion Week. As she clutched Sterling's hand tightly, her eyes met those of Cassius Brabantio.

The bitter expression on his face left her unflustered.

There was a grave hush in the room as the skeletal bodies of the House of Brabantio models graced the runway. Disapproval was evident as the critics murmured behind their programs. The emaciated bodies of the models galvanized photographers to take many shots, disapprovingly shaking their heads with every photo.

Justice sat and stared in stony silence as she recognized her designs float down the runway.

Minnie leaned in from behind and said loudly, "Ain't that one of them sketches I seen in your book when you was in Eastman?"

"It is," Justice replied in a wintry tone.

"I don't recognize those clothes, Justice," Evelyn whispered in a confused voice.

"Cassius altered them. But the designs are mine," she said.

At the close of his line a frail Cassius took his bow. There was a small scattering of applause that grew thunderous when a portrait of Caesar was flashed onto the huge television screen behind him. Beaming with false pride Cassius resumed his seat.

Justice and Sterling looked at each other.

The next morning Sterling opened the door of the master suite gently, not wanting to wake his wife.

Justice's head popped up. "I'm awake, honey."

"Good," Sterling said. He climbed back into bed and rubbed the small bulge of her stomach. "Good morning, son," she said.

Justice chuckled. "We don't know yet if it's a boy."

"It's a boy," Sterling said, laying his head on the skin he'd just massaged. "When are you going to tell everyone that you're pregnant?"

"Today," she said. "I waited until after the show so that Mom and Aunt Minnie didn't nag me about doing things."

"Good thinking. They're out there right now pestering Scarlett because she won't eat grits." He beamed. "I read the morning papers. Every critic gave us rave reviews."

"When I went to sleep last night I knew." Justice glowed with an inner peace. "I just sort of had a feeling."

"Cassius sure got hazed. There were scathing remarks about his models, presentation, and accessories."

Justice said dryly. "It's just so sad that Cassius has ruined the name of The House of Brabantio. From the grave Cassius' mother got her way. Cassius has tainted Caesar's legacy."

"The critics said the designs were beautiful, but the wrong colors and fabric were used. It's poetic justice. That's a lesson to be careful what you steal. But at least now there's also an earnest discussion about weight. The papers said that the industry is going to start looking into the design houses that promote these malnourished models. Photographers even complained about the models makeup and hair. They said one model looked like a drag queen and another needed to pull a comb through her hair," Sterling said, chuckling.

"Shush," she said. "We're not going to laugh at Cassius or anyone else. We have a baby on the way and I don't want to bring our child bad luck by enjoying others misfortunes."

Sterling immediately sobered. He resumed his previous position with his head on her stomach.

Justice felt the baby kick. "Ouch!" she laughed. "The baby agrees with me!"

"You're both right, Justice," he said as he rubbed her belly soothingly. "That's only one of the many reasons why I love you.

You're so forgiving."

Justice took her hand and stroked Sterling's head. "I can afford to be generous," she said. "I have everything I've ever wanted. I love you with all my heart and soul, Sterling Hart."

"Ditto, Justice Hart," Sterling said. His voice trembled with love as he cuddled even closer to his wife and his son.

Available on Nook, Amazon.com, and Createspace
Website: http://michelecameronauthor.com
Facebook: aggieauthor@cfl.rr.com
Twitter: michele.cameron16@gmail
Instagram: michelecameron_16

Other Books Available by Michele Cameron

November 2014

Eyes That Lie released September 2013

ABOUT THE AUTHOR

Michele Cameron, a native of Bridgeport, Connecticut, is a graduate of North Carolina A & T State University in Greensboro with a B.S. degree in professional Writing and English Education. Ms. Cameron currently teaches high school English in Orlando, Florida.

Cameron's first novel Never Say Never (Genesis-Press, Inc., January, 2008) was given a four star rating. Romance in Color named her the New Face among African-American writers.

Her highly anticipated second novel, Moments of Clarity. (Genesis-Press, Inc. October 2008) received a five star rating from Affaire de Coeur.

Cameron has been a featured guest on numerous notable BAN radio stations including, Mr. Media Interviews, Conversations Live with Cyrus Webb, Black Author's Network, I Just Finished, Coffee With an Author, EDC Creations, the morning show, "Who You Calling Old?", The Write Vision with Celeste Kelley, Circle of -Seven with Austin Camacho, and The Literary Diva.

She has written numerous articles on the internet including the websites, APOO Book Club, Affaire de Coeur, Black Author's network, Sormag, and The Book Place.

Cameron's third novel, When Lightning Strikes! (Genesis-Press, Inc., August, 2009 followed by Unclear and Present Danger, (February 2010). These latest novels received 4.5 and 5 stars respectively.

----

www.ingramcontent.com/pod-product-compliance
Lightning Source LLC
Chambersburg PA
CBHW070909180626
46817CB00003B/984